BLOOD QUEEN

Ariel Rae is R. A. Desilets's adult pen name.

Consider checking out her young adult work:

Carter Ortese is Trouble
Break Free
Start Small
Girl Nevermore
In a Blue Moon (Blue Moon #1)
Hipstopia (The Uprising #1)
The Collapse (The Uprising #2)
My Summer Vacation by Terrance Wade
The End Diary

BLOOD QUEEN

ARIEL RAE

SPACE FOX
BOOKS LLC

This book is a work of fiction.

Cover design by Rachel A. Desilets

ISBN-13: 979-8-9888483-6-3

Space Fox Books, LLC
First Edition
Paperback Edition: 2024
spacefoxbooks.com

To the little fox inside all of us.
If you are not sly enough, death becomes the victor.

This book may contain circumstances not suitable for younger readers and is recommended for adult audiences.

If you'd like to read about the content in this book, please visit the publisher's website spacefoxbooks.com for additional descriptions for any sensitive topics.

This series has a 2.5 novel called Mister Nightmare. It is not required to read this book prior to Blood Queen, but there are events within Blood Queen that will spoil parts of Mister Nightmare. The suggested reading order is:

Blood Hunted
Blood Trail
Mister Nightmare
Blood Queen

SCARLET

A frown marred his face. "You haven't touched your food." His voice carved canyons across my body, trailing over my skin like smoky ash. Hearing it, sitting here, and being in this room hollowed out my insides. He sat at the other end of the massive dining table inside an over-sized ballroom. The ceilings were so high, the slightest movement echoed in the space.

This grandiose display of wealth mirrored his late father. It was ostentatious. While I hadn't been inside Leveret's court for long, with every passing minute, I craved to set the thing ablaze. I itched for the dagger I no longer had.

I stared at the male across from me, the Fae who ordered me to sit down at the other end of the table, as if we were going to have a cordial meal. He hadn't commanded me to eat—yet—but as more and more of the meal disappeared from his plate, his gaze grew distraught as he considered me.

His dark eyes, carved cheeks, and blond hair mirrored another.

1

One I didn't dare think about. Not here. Not in this place.

Not when I had no power.

Not when *he* had never told me he had a *twin*.

"I see no reason to eat when I don't have good company," I spat.

His lips pressed into a thin line. Leveret's dark eyes roamed over my body. I suppressed a shudder. "I could force you to eat."

"You could." My eyes narrowed.

"But I won't." The not yet hung unsaid inside his words. "If you opt to kill yourself, that's your choice. All I demand is that you sit with me."

"You demand too much."

His jaw worked. "It's too much for you to *sit* with me? Trust me, little rabbit, I could do a lot worse."

"I'm sure." I reached for the fork and knife, considering both objects.

"Don't get—"

Leveret didn't finish his sentence, because I sent the knife sailing at him. It tipped end over end. As he moved out of the way of my first projectile, I flung the fork. The prongs sank into the skin of his shoulder. His nostrils flared as he tore it out and tossed it to the ground. Beads of his blood skittered along the utensil's path, and red bubbled up on his white tunic.

Guards moved toward me, but he held up his hand. "No, leave her. I think it's time I teach her something about manners while she is a guest in my court."

"A guest who cannot rise from this chair." I leaned forward because I at least had that much power over my body. "Such a guest isn't a guest, but a prisoner."

Leveret's lips curled. "Out," he snapped at his guards.

The other Fae exchanged glances but took their leave as he gave them another rough glare. As soon as the door closed behind them—the sound echoing in the cavernous dining hall—he crossed the length of the table and grabbed hold of my chin.

I tried to stab him with the spoon, but he snatched it out of my hand and threw it across the room.

"So disobedient."

"There's no one worth obeying. You have no power over me, not really." I swung at him, but he caught my fist in his hand.

"Don't I?" His eyes flared to life with liquid fire. He smelled different from Voss too, with a burnt orange edge to the fiery ginger scent. His fingers dug into my chin as he forced me to gaze up at him. "I could make you do anything." His words choked me. "But I won't. And ask yourself, why not? I could make you *enjoy* my company. I could make you fall in love with me. But I don't. Ask the right questions, little rabbit."

"I don't care for your answers or your lies." My jaw ached under his grip.

He huffed out a breath. "My *lies*. Let me guess, my brother poisoned you against me? My brother told you everything you need to know, and because you heard it fall from his lips, you believe him?" Leveret dropped my chin but did nothing to open the space between us. "The truth about him will come out, as I promised you as much, but unfortunately, I cannot have you starve in my court. *Eat.*"

His magic swept over my body.

"You said you didn't care if I died." My mind fought against his command, but it was no use. It wrapped around my nerves and every single muscle inside me. The only finger I seemed to be able to move was my pinkie, which held no benefit. Since I had no utensils left, my fingers scooped up a melange of vegetables. I chewed without permission. The flavors were good, but I would still kill this male.

I envisioned his blood leaking over the tiles. And this time? It would just be payback.

Leveret hopped onto the edge of the table, watching me eat with intensity. His scrutiny made my skin crawl. His head tilted to the side as if he were considering a riddle and not another living being. "Despite what you may believe, it serves no purpose to have you starve. Though, I doubt you would actually go hungry since my brother will be here in two days' time. I don't need him to believe I tortured you."

"This *is* torture," I said in between mouthfuls. "Being forced to do things against your will is—"

"*Don't.*" The command rippled over my skin, and I frowned while swallowing what I was going to say. "Fine. You want to be released from all of this? You can do whatever you want except try to kill me and you cannot run away from this court." His irises swirled.

The new command rushed over my skin. His mistake.

I punched him in the balls.

As he wheezed, I shoved the plate in his face, smashing his nose into a bloodied mess. He grabbed hold of my wrists and slammed me back against the wall, twenty feet away. My breath left my lungs, and my body ached from the impact. He hovered over me, pinning me underneath his weight. Oil dripped from his face as he snarled.

"You are an ungrateful bitch."

"And you're an asshole, so we're even." My lungs hurt, but I squeezed the words out.

"*What did my brother tell you about me?*" His magic pulsed over me again, and I wasn't sure he was consciously doing it. Leveret's nature was to use magic indiscriminately, much like I had been with my killing prior to meeting Voss.

"That you want to be like your father. You want power for the wrong reasons. And the humans would come to harm under your rule."

His nose wrinkled. "No wonder why you hate me." His breath rolled over my skin. "I will admit I am quick to anger, but Voss is, too. He would sooner rip someone's heart out of their chest than have a confrontation. He is no saint, and I am not all sinner. I am going to let you go, but if you hit my balls one more time, I will force you to tie yourself to my bed. Understand?"

I spat in his face.

"I see you take my words literally. Perfect."

"Don't Fae do the same?"

"Voss has a tendency to. We are *not* the same."

"Clearly. He never made me do anything against my will."

Leveret let go of my hands and took a wide step back from me. A cloth napkin from the table drifted over, and he wiped his face off with it. He continued his consideration of me. Every sweep of his eyes felt like an invasion. "I have made you come with me, sit down, and eat food. That's all I have done."

"*Made* is the key word."

"Okay, arguably, I can understand how taking away that choice would be frustrating, but I thought we could *talk* over dinner."

"You cannot possibly try to sound like a reasonable being after everything you put me through."

"You harpooned me with a fork, hit me in the balls, made my nose bleed by shoving my food back in my face, and spat on me."

"Yup."

"And you are grinning."

"Yup."

"You have no shame."

"None."

"I see why he likes you—you are independent and challenging."

Rubbing my wrists, I didn't dare go after him again. I felt like we were on the precipice of something, and I wanted to see what he would say without my interference. Though, I continued to assess exit plans, as well as any weapons I might have access to.

"I, however, find that tiresome. I would rather have obedience."

"That's never going to happen," I said with a shrug.

"I can see that. Alas, I still need to try to… How should I say this?"

"I won't change my mind, so you can save your breath."

"If you do not have the full scope of information, you will never change your mind. Perhaps it's best if we start with something small, something simple. But, seeing as how we are both covered in food, I propose we clean up. Then, I will show you why you should not trust my twin."

"And trust you instead? Unlikely."

He held up his hands, a smile quirking on his lips. It wasn't the overconfident smirk Voss wore, but a wary expression. "Time will tell. It will take him a couple of days to get here. Now, I ask you, do you want to come with me and get clean without my forcing you, or do I have to make you shower?"

Oil covered the front of my shirt, and I smelled horrible after riding with the other two Fae. While I did not trust Leveret, the more I led him to believe I was compliant, the more likely I would get an opportunity to end his life or escape. If I acted the part, it would bide time for Voss to reach me. Leveret was right. He could make me do anything, but thus far, he hadn't made me do anything horrible or against my morals.

Though he still had *made* me. Voss had given me a safe word, a way out, a way to tell him to stop or say no. I always felt in control when I was with him because I *trusted* him. With Leveret, there was none of that. This was a threat. Either I complied or he would take away my choice, which really was no choice at all.

I didn't want to feel his magic crawling along my skin or flowing into my body again. It was horrible. While I had seen more Fae during my travels and I knew not all of them were like this, I was still shocked that humans willingly became Fae followers. To plenty of Fae, we were nothing but insects, and now that I knew how compulsion felt, I believed Voss's vision of the future was impossible. How could he feasibly change the other Fae when manipulation came so easily to them? If the human wasn't protected through marriage to a Fae or on Faerie wine—which came with its own downsides—how could we live cohesively? It was too easy for the Fae to manipulate people.

"I will bathe if I have my own room." I held my nose up high. "And a change of clothes that I approve of afterward. I will not have you dressing me up like some kind of doll."

Leveret's eyes lit up as magic swirled around me. He smirked. "Deal."

I blinked. "That was not…" The tug of his magic pulled me with him through the room. "I was not making a deal," I growled, trying to stomp on his heel as he headed toward the elevator.

He danced away from me. "You need to be more careful with what you say if you don't want me to misinterpret, especially if *you* are going to take *my* words literally."

"That is very manipulative of you."

As he pressed the button to the penthouse and the elevator doors shut, he leaned against the wall, considering me. "How so?"

"Blaming me for *your* use of magic."

He shrugged. "If you stopped fighting me, I wouldn't have to control you."

I glared at him and took another swing at him, this time aiming for his jugular.

He grabbed my fist with his hand, threatening to crush my fingers under his strength. "Tell me that Voss never once manipulated you, and I will release all my magic. I will let you walk out into the wilds by yourself, but only if you can say he never manipulated you one single time. *Be honest*." His magic swirled around my skin, choking any lies from coming out of my throat.

"He never intentionally compelled me," I said.

The fire died out of Leveret's eyes as he released my hand. He placed his on my shoulders and forced me to take a step back from him. "Never compelled you, sure, but you cannot say he never manipulated you, can you?"

I swallowed, glaring.

Leveret nodded. "I understand. I was once under my brother's spell. Once, I thought the world of him. We used to be inseparable, like Corvin and Bram. But as we grew up, the distance between us became vaster as he felt he knew more about the world than me. He called me stupid, all for following my dream. If anyone disagrees with him, he will do whatever he needs to get his way. Don't you see it?"

Clenching my fists at my sides, I backed up against the other wall of the elevator. His hands dropped away from my body but stayed stiff. "Your words mean nothing if your actions show no trust."

"Trust goes both ways," Leveret said.

The hair on my arms rose, because this conversation felt very similar to when I had first met Voss, before I knew him and his mission, before I helped him kill the king. Before...

The elevator dinged, and Leveret gestured for me to go first. After walking down a hallway, we stepped into a modern, bright apartment with windows lining every wall. The tall ceilings made our footsteps echo. There were sparse bits of furniture, all very angular and impractical looking pieces.

"Your suite will be on the left. I don't have clothes for you, but

I will send for multiple styles of outfits so you can choose your own once you are clean."

"What happens if I don't shower now that you forced me into a deal?"

Leveret's lips twitched. "Let's just say you don't want that to happen. See you in a bit, Scarlet." Leveret turned toward his suite and shut the door behind him.

As soon as he was gone, I stepped back onto the elevator. The moment I clicked the button for the lobby, this bubble of horrific pain welled inside my chest. I felt like I couldn't breathe, as if the air inside me was being expelled out. No matter how much oxygen I took into myself, I didn't feel it. By the time I hit the tenth floor, I slammed my fist into the emergency button, stopping the elevator in its tracks. The weight on my chest eased, but it still pressed against my ribs. As my fingers hovered over the lobby button, the ache increased, and my vision turned hazy.

Fuck.

I pressed the button for the penthouse and headed back up. When the doors opened, Leveret stood shirtless, leaning against the threshold of his bedroom. His arms were crossed over his chest as he assessed me. The scar on his cheek seemed deeper underneath the light in here. He was as fit as Voss, and it made me want to carve into his flesh all the more.

"How far did you get?"

"Tenth floor." I hated how much he looked like Voss. It was a deception on its own, no magic needed.

He nodded. "Well, the water is nice and warm. I'll see you soon."

As the door shut for another time, I stared after him. There were knives in the kitchen, but all of those he could heal from. I needed the toxin of sparrowbone, and I only had the necklace to use against him. I needed him to let his guard down so I could get close enough to kill him. A vague plan formed in my head, and I wasn't sure I liked it.

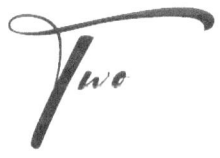

VOSS

We didn't stop until the horses tired. After that, we looked for the closest court to exchange them. It hurt me to know the mare Max was so fond of was now traded to someone who wouldn't nearly care as much as she had, but I would worry about getting our horses back once this journey was over and my brother was no longer among the living.

With every passing second, I cursed myself for my foolishness and idiocy. I should have seen this coming. I prided myself on being steps ahead of my siblings and thinking about every angle. Somehow, Leveret knew this would happen when she had arrived at his court. He had gained knowledge I never had, and the only thing I could think of was my wretched father.

The late king had likely told Leveret about this, perhaps as a contingency plan. He had been determined to make one of us follow in his footsteps, and when I never groveled at his feet, he likely turned to Leveret. My siblings believed I was the favorite son, but it

11

was only because my father admired my bullheadedness.

Leveret, however, had unyielding loyalty. I think my father knew, deep down, that I would try to kill him someday. Which meant he intentionally left me weak in the face of my twin, never letting me learn what it would mean to take the throne while my brother still lived and breathed.

Even after his death, he pulled the strings. He had been treating us like puppets our whole lives, and here I was again, falling victim to his manipulations.

"Voss!" Elspeth's voice penetrated through my thoughts as night crept upon us. We were making good time, but not nearly good enough. "We need to make camp for the night. If we die on the way there, we'll be of no use to her."

I pulled on the reins and slowed the horse, waiting for the other two to catch up. The fear coursing through my body was not something I was used to, and the sooner I could remove the ailment, the better. "I can immolate anything that stands in our way."

Elspeth huffed out a breath. She combed her fingers absently through her tangled hair. "Look, we want to get her back, but it's clear Leveret is using her as a lure. He's hoping you'll tire yourself on the journey and not be able to fight once you arrive. Think about the long-term effect of this."

"I am," I growled. The horse danced under the aggression edging my voice. The impact was more than just the future of the combined kingdoms, but *her* future. What would remain of the woman I fell for after my brother was done with her? What would I have to do to ensure her safe return to me, mentally, physically, and emotionally?

And what would I be capable of if she were cut from this world?

Elspeth breathed out, eyes softening. "Okay, think about the arrangements, then. You need to be prepared for confrontation. Leveret has stolen half of the royal power. If you show up unrested, you'll weaken yourself further. If we die instead of rescuing her, then—"

I waved my hand, understanding where she was going with this. It was hard to tamp down the mix of emotions swelling within me. Harder still to focus on the fact that she was right. Elspeth had a point. If Leveret won during our encounter, Max would be stuck with him forever.

I couldn't let that happen.

"We will sleep for five hours, give the horses a rest, and continue on before daybreak—as soon as we reach the next court." My companions nodded in agreement, and we carried on into the dark night.

It took us less than an hour to arrive at the next court, and less time to find accommodations. While Leveret had stolen half of my power and technically shared the royal crown, none of the Fae citizens seemed to be aware of that. They still shrunk under my gaze, awaiting any command I deemed fit to give them.

The meal we had at the tavern was tasteless on my tongue, and the bed I forced myself into felt like rocks underneath my aching body. The absence of her invaded my senses, dulling the comforts of the world until they were nothing more than grievances.

It was about an hour into my sleeplessness that a knock sounded on the door.

"Come in, Penn."

The hinges creaked as he opened it and slipped inside. I had my hands folded behind my head as I stared up at the ceiling.

He paused near the door. "I came to check on you."

"Consider myself checked."

He stayed silent for a moment. "It doesn't have to be this way."

"And why is that?" I sat up, staring at him. He made no move toward me. His eyes surveyed me, as if he didn't recognize me. My jaw clenched. "I would tear the world apart to get you back, same as her."

"And your anger will get us all killed."

"It hasn't so far."

Penn held up his hands and dared to take a step toward me. "You told me to remind you of your humanity, should you ever reach a point where you were losing yourself."

I narrowed my eyes. My magic swirled around me, threatening to burn the inn down with me and Penn trapped inside.

"I think that time has come, Voss. In the end, all kings succumbed to the same thing—greed. Power goes to their head, makes them become something else. You need to find an anchor, something to keep you steady in the storm. Because right now? You're out to sea."

A feral snarl escaped my lips. We stared at each other for a few moments as Penn's power swelled around me. Water pooled along my skin, cooling the fire raging inside me.

"I don't care if you end up using Scarlet as your anchor. You just need one."

I swallowed. "I think that's the problem. She is mine and having her cut off is like…" Shaking my head, I didn't know how to put the emptiness into words. My brother would die as soon as I got within reach, and I would repair every vicious feeling I had inside me by making sure Max knew who was in charge—of her *and* the world.

"Well, if you need another, I'm here."

"I can't ask that of you."

"You didn't ask, but I am offering just the same. We've been through a lot together, and I have no intention of letting you set adrift without me."

"Even if I drag you with me into the abyss?"

Penn's eyes flashed. "Call me a masochist if you like, because even then." He turned back to the door, opening it. "I miss her too."

"I thought you hated her."

"I hate how she will be the death of you someday, either by your emotions, her ambitions, or both." He glanced over his shoulder, his turquoise eyes showing the sorrow behind his words. "But if you can somehow avoid that? I've never seen you happier." He stepped into the hallway and shut the door between us.

Three

SCARLET

The shower did little to clear my head, but it did intensify my resolve. I would find a way out of this, like I had everything else. Perhaps if I were more agreeable, Leveret would use less magic on me. I could try to be pleasant, at least until I had an opening to stab my necklace through his eyeball.

His magic, however, I could not stand. I hated how it snaked along my skin and dipped into my veins with icy venom. Even now, with the heat of the water dripping off me, I could still feel the tingling sensation of his control.

Towel drying my cropped hair took a few moments, and I opened the bathroom door to find an array of clothes that had been brought in for me. I wasn't sure how Leveret had garnered so much in such little time, but he shared the throne of the kingdom. I ran my fingers along the fabrics. There was a bit of every style out there, but I wanted practicality. I settled on a pair of fitted but stretchable jeans and a loose t-shirt. My boots had been cleaned, likely by magic. I dressed quickly. I still felt empty without my sparrowbone dagger pressed against my side.

Voss had given mine back to me, after I had stabbed him.

Trust goes both ways.

There would be no such mercies here. Leveret's gaze held none of the lightheartedness of Voss's. While Voss found my violence amusing, Leveret had made his thoughts known. I would likely never see the dagger until I escaped, or Voss rescued me.

The fact that someone had to *rescue* me was just as frustrating. Whenever this was over, I was going to be sure to stab Voss. He deserved it. I wouldn't have needed rescuing had I known what I was getting myself into

Again.

I let out my breath and twisted the knob.

Leveret perched on the edge of his couch, eyes snapping up the moment the door opened. Darkness churned in his irises with a hint of the fire magic burning inside him. "I figured."

"Not to your liking?" I fought back the urge to roll my eyes. I wouldn't win any favoritism by acting like a brat. While Voss liked that side of me, his brother obviously felt differently.

"I bet you would look stunning in a dress."

"A bit gender normative, don't you think?"

He shrugged and tapped his fingers on the glass he held in his hands. It contained amber liquid. "Some traditions exist for a reason." I ignored how much my blood boiled as he held the glass up. "Do you want some? It's fifty-year-old brandy."

I narrowed my gaze, because most Fae drank wine—the human kind and Faerie wine—and occasionally beer. It immediately made me suspicious that he had something else in the penthouse.

"I like the bite. Here." He poured out a slosh of liquid from the decanter into another glass. His fingers pulled out a vial from his coat pocket. "Faerie wine," he said as he uncorked it and poured a single drop into the glass. Leveret crossed the room and held the drink out to me. "I know you won't trust me without a drop, and I would like to have a civilized conversation with you about the possibility of a future together."

I gritted my teeth, chewing his words. A future. With him. The only future I wanted was one that ended in his blood. "And I am supposed to believe it's not poison?"

He rolled his eyes and took a sip from the glass himself, never taking his dark gaze off me. "You are a cautious little rabbit." The drink hovered between us.

I took it. Our fingers ghosted against each other's. "How do you know I won't escape once your magic is out of my system?"

"I have plenty of guards outside, and if you try anything further, I will bind you against the wall." The way his eyes blazed at his words told me he wouldn't mind being tempted. I swallowed back my disgust. "Drink."

It wasn't a command, but magic swelled around me like a threat. I took a sip. "It's hard for you not to use your magic."

Leveret frowned, clearly annoyed that I picked up this knowledge so easily. "My father taught us to use everything to our advantage. Letting that go doesn't come easily, especially when one is trapped in a room with another predator."

"Who will come out on top, I wonder?"

The brandy had a caramel taste and barely any burn to it, which meant it was likely expensive. On that level, Leveret did not differ from the extravagance of his father. He desired nice things, so he acquired them—no questions asked.

"I wondered that myself. While I want to be civil with you, I feel like I should disclose something. I fully plan on using you to my advantage."

I snorted. "As most Fae would." Most, but not all. I knew that now.

Crossing the room to stand in front of the large windows, I could see the expanse of his court and the wilds from up here. The view was impressive, but it made the desolation of our landscape much more prevalent. The deserted plains and sand dunes stretched on for miles, with small outcroppings of trees near the old riverbeds and waterways. When I was younger, this state was lush and green, only baking to yellow hues in the hottest heat of the August sun. We were in the waning part of summer, where night storms should be rolling in and waking the vast landscape.

Instead, there were only the dusty remains of what the invasive species left behind.

"I am trying for honesty," Leveret said as he joined me at the window.

"Don't hold your breath for my applause." I could feel his scowl.

"Truly, why did my brother marry you?"

"Because I am charming." I tossed him a grin.

"No, you're not." Leveret took a sip from his glass. "You are difficult, a puzzle. You are not someone who caves easily to the whims of others, and you present a challenge. I would like to say it is because of the prophecy, though I doubt it."

"Prophecy?"

"He never told you?"

I narrowed my gaze as Leveret's eyes roamed over me again. Forcing myself to still despite his scrutiny, I took a seat on the couch. "I think I want to be sitting down for this, otherwise I might try to stab you with a spoon again."

"Not the best choice for a weapon, if we're being honest."

"I worked with what I had."

"You should have thrown the spoon first and kept the knife."

"Next time."

His gaze turned into liquid fire as he took a seat on the other couch. Leveret slung one of his arms over the back of the cushions like he didn't have a care in the world. I supposed with his power and having me temporarily trapped under his roof, he didn't. At least until Voss arrived.

"Parts of the prophecy were lost to time, as it was foretold long ago—before our kingdoms were locked away from each other and before I was born."

"And how long ago was that?" I asked sweetly.

Leveret did not answer but plunged onward with his story. "To be honest, my siblings and I never put stock into the words, but my father did. He felt it reflected his inevitable demise, losing his rule. For that reason, he made sure to never fulfill his end of the prophecy."

"Which is?"

"*Whereas she was the reflection of the full moon, he glowed like the midday sun.* If he never fell in love with someone who looked like the moon, nothing would come between him and his rule."

"That doesn't give us much to go on."

"Ah, but the rest that we know does. *Together, they would become the next rulers of the world, the likes of which had never been seen before.*" Leveret downed the rest of his drink, considered the glass, and waved his hand at the decanter. It floated toward him, refilled the glass, and drifted back to the counter.

"But if he joined with someone who had that description, he would become that ruler. So, I don't understand why he would avoid it?"

"It also contains the words *inevitable end.* The context is unknown, but to my father, that might as well have been a death sentence."

I frowned, thinking about the prophecy and everything that

wasn't mentioned in it. I had a hard time believing in divinations, but I knew magic existed. "That's it? It could mean *anything*. It could mean the end of our worlds being separate for all he knew. There's really nothing else?" My heart pounded in my chest, but I pushed the feeling down, unwilling to give into the new fear rising inside me.

What if Voss's end was inevitable? What if I were the cause? Heat rushed through my limbs. As much as I wanted to stab him, as much as I wanted to watch him grovel at my feet, I didn't want him to *die*.

"My father was extremely paranoid, especially toward the end. As soon as he learned that part of the prophecy, he caved in on himself. He searched for ways to make our family invincible. If we couldn't be killed, the prophecy wouldn't apply to him." Leveret swirled the liquid in his glass and gave me an icy stare. "Honestly, I was surprised he allowed you inside his court, but his ego was bigger than his paranoia, it seems."

"Maybe he became his own undoing because he wouldn't allow one of you to rise to power in his stead." I shook my head, taking another long drink. I nearly spit it out as I remembered something else. "Wait. You said you thought the prophecy might have meant *you* to Voss. That's what both of you think? I'm the reflection of the full moon?"

Voss had said it when we had first met. At the time, I paid little attention to it. I hadn't paid attention to a lot of things.

"When taken literally, yes, you resemble the moon in comparison to our sun. We have fire magic, after all. There's not much to misinterpret there." Leveret's tongue flicked out, catching a drop of liquid from his lower lip as he stared at the glass. "Like I said, you are a complicated puzzle."

I rolled my eyes. "You're saying Voss only fell for me because I intrigue him."

"You are intriguing." Leveret shrugged.

"Because of my physical appearance."

"I never said that. You do have a rather… cumbersome and unique personality."

"If you think this is the way to get me to turn against your brother—"

"Isn't a part of you annoyed right now? Frustrated by how he never explained this to you?"

"He said those words once, when I first met him." I ran my fingers along the rim of my now empty glass. Leveret's magic pulled it out of my hands and placed it on the end table. "But no, he never explained what they meant."

"And don't you feel that since you are married, he should be open and honest with you? I believe you should have no barriers with the partner you are supposed to rule with." Quicker than I could track, Leveret had placed his glass on the table and crossed the room. His hand wrapped around my throat, not applying pressure, but his thumb pressed against my pulse. His breath rolled over my lips as he held me inches away from him. "Don't you want someone who will be brutally honest with you, never shying away from the wicked and hard truth of what you are?"

"And what am I, Leveret?"

"A murderer. A vile thing with a black heart and anger coiling through her. But deep down, you are *scared*."

I swallowed. His thumb caressed my skin, and I ached to tear his eyeballs out.

"You are terrified more than anything of that darkness inside you because you fear what will happen when you allow yourself to fully submit to it and embrace who you are." Leveret's words drifted over my skin, causing me to shiver. "But I'll tell you a secret, little rabbit. My brother isn't the only one attracted to such things. The difference is… I would let you be everything you need and more. He will always

22

keep you locked in a cage."

"Locked in a cage like you did to me earlier?" I narrowed my gaze at him. "As if I can trust you after that." The words came before I could suck them back in. So much for faking compliance.

"Devoss ultimately wants subservience. He might make you feel otherwise, but he will always want to be in charge and will want to rule. If you want to be on top, I'd let it be so." He released his hand and took a step away from me, opening his arms wide in an invitation. For what? The moment didn't last long, because he backed into his chair and sat down with a flourish, snatching up his drink once more. "So, what do you need to know to make your decision?"

"What decision?"

"Who you will become Blood Queen with. Because it's me or him."

My mind went blank, because what Morna and Cumina had told me was that becoming Blood Queen would kill the male I drank from. "I thought…" I lowered my brows. "Wouldn't that kill you?"

A smile tugged at his lips. It was a deep, treacherous knowing that came from years of perfecting one's arrogance. "Is that what you believe? Would you want it to kill Devoss, I wonder?" He tapped his fingers on his glass with one hand and pushed his hair back with his other. I hated how much light it reflected, how he seemed to glow in the same ethereal way as Voss.

Except… I didn't hate it. I *missed* it on Voss, and that made my anger well inside me.

"That's what I was told would happen." I lifted my chin, refusing to answer him.

"Well, if Devoss never corrected you, I am sure he had his reasons. But no, while you do drain the blood from the king, the royal power would bring the king back to life, assuming you care enough to do so."

"And you think I would care about you?"

Leveret's smile stayed on his lips. "I don't think you care enough yet, but I also have no intention of letting you get your hands on anything sharper than a butter knife."

"I could still use it to scoop out your eyeballs."

"I'm sure. Would you care for another drink?"

My head was swimming from the information and the first glass of brandy, but with the sun setting and my rescuers nowhere in sight, I figured why the heck not? "Sure."

The grin spread across his features with a look that made me feel like I had lost this battle. "Excellent choice. We have much to talk about, you and I."

"Then talk," I said as the glass filled up with a bigger serving than last time.

Leveret wanted something from me—something other than luring his brother in, and if I could figure it out, then perhaps I could make it work in my favor. My plan to act amicably seemed to be working—perhaps not quite as smoothly as I wanted with my missteps, but he was willing to talk.

Leveret refilled his glass and considered me with hooded lids before waving the decanter back to the counter. "You are interested?"

"As interested as I can be with you, since I am forced to be here."

He chuckled, and it rolled over me like soot, making my skin feel gritty. "Fair enough. My father raised his children as assassins, fighters, and warriors—blood hunters. The more we could do to benefit his rule, the better. The difference between my twin and I happened when we visited an old shop on the outskirts of town. Now, as Devoss believes, it was our father who destroyed Faerie."

"Wasn't it?"

Leveret shook his head. "Faerie was already dying by the time my father put the Fae door curse in place. To be honest, I am not sure why Faerie started to die, but I have theories."

"Which are?"

"Maybe another day for those." Leveret took a sip and gestured to my drink.

I stared at the glass, glancing at his steady eyes.

No magic swelled off him now. He was as relaxed as he could be. If I played this right, I might get an opportunity to reach out to Voss. Leveret nullified his magic the moment he offered me Faerie wine. All I had to do was wait it out. Once the wine was out of my system, I could contact Voss again, warn him about Leveret.

For now, I needed to play nice and not give the twin any reason to be suspicious of me.

I drank a large gulp, letting the liquid dance along my tongue before swallowing.

He nodded, looking satisfied. "We visited an artist. Devoss became enamored with the images of what used to be, but my father wanted none of it—no reminders of what Faerie resembled before. If there was proof, then someone might use the prophecy against him. He asked the painter to stop creating, offered to pay him coin to paint a hopeful look into the future of Faerie, show a united front." Leveret let out a breath. "When that conversation didn't go as planned, my father ordered him to be killed. Not by the boy who was staring at the paintings with rapture, but me."

A snarl curled on his lips. "That was the day I started hating Devoss. My father had walked out of the room, hands already stained with blood. He took one glance at us. I made the mistake of standing at attention, too scared to move from the door, whereas my brother had wandered off into the shop. My father grabbed the back of my neck and threw me into the room with the painter, who already lay in a pool of his blood, half-burned. The smell alone was enough to make my skin crawl." Leveret slugged down the rest of his drink and put it on the end table, staring at the empty glass.

"What happened after that?"

"He asked me to finish it. Said it was to prove I had what it took to be the next leader of our world. The asshole never meant it, of course. He never wanted anyone to take over. That was the whole point of the curse. If no one could kill him, he didn't have to worry about the prophecy."

"Then why bother leaving Faerie?"

Leveret shrugged. "You opened the door. You tell me. What do you remember?"

"Not much. The color of the sky. The smell—"

"Like something stale and rotten?"

I swallowed and nodded. I had been ten when I opened the door, but that smell I remembered. My parents hadn't listened to me when I told them the fun things about the door and the world behind it, so I thought telling them about the awful part would have made them believe me less—a child's nightmare.

They had told me monsters didn't exist.

"It was uninhabitable. By the time you opened the door, mobs had formed. Everyone was ready to leave the moment we had the ability to. We had become restless. We had fought endlessly, healing too quickly to die and not quick enough to avoid the madness setting in. Do you know where Devoss was during this?"

I shook my head.

"While I was in the field, trying to make the Fae see reason, trying to prevent our brethren from turning against one another, he turned his back on us," Leveret's voice spat from behind his clenched teeth. "He, Penn, and Elspeth wrapped themselves up in the Central Gallery."

"Which was… what, exactly?"

"Art. Our people were riled and angry, and he went to a fucking art gallery."

That didn't sound like Voss, unless he was looking for answers. He was constantly thinking about how to make the world a better place.

"You look like you don't believe me."

"I'm having a hard time—"

Leveret waved his hand. "Seeing the male who was so set on taking the throne as anything other than a *hero*?" The word came out of his mouth with such vehemence, I flinched. He continued, "He was planning while there, of course. He was arranging to usurp control the moment he stepped onto earth. While I was fighting for our people, he was preparing for a future where he could be king."

"But without the door being opened, what could you really do?"

"Nothing." Leveret snarled. "But I still *tried*. You understand? I tried to stop the madness. I tried to cut through the chaos and fix Faerie. He did *nothing* until he came here, until the opportunity presented itself." He gestured to me. "You."

"Me."

"A girl capable of killing the king. A girl who hated the Fae so much she would do anything to get revenge. A girl who was vulnerable."

I slammed my glass on the table. The remaining brandy sloshed out of it but paused midair. The liquid spun back into the glass. I clenched my fists. "I was *not* vulnerable."

"Weren't you?" Leveret crossed the room in another flash. He grabbed my glass and drank the rest of it himself. "You wanted someone to accept you for who you are. You wanted someone to see you and save you."

I slapped him. The sound echoed throughout the room. This had not been a part of my plan, but he was getting too close, too up in my face, too comfortable confronting me. I didn't want to be psychoanalyzed while I was here. I would have plenty of time to do that for the rest of my life.

"I never asked to be saved."

Except now. Now, I hoped for it. And it would be the first step on Voss's long list of amends to make.

"No, but that's what he does. He believes he can save everyone, but that's the problem. Sometimes, we save things through sacrifice."

"And you're able to give the world what it needs?"

"Not just me. Me with someone who I allow to become their own person. I would never ask you to stand in my shadow."

I narrowed my eyes. I wasn't standing in Voss's shadow… Was I? When he ran me out of the court after we killed the king, I remembered the Fae's eyes on me. So many Fae watched me with anger and venom, but there were a few who held pity in their gazes— pity for me, the Fae Slayer. The one who had been responsible for sending them to their early graves. The monster. The killer.

"Stop," I whispered.

"Why? Because the truth is too hard?" He ran a finger down my cheek. "I will tell you a secret—the truth never gets easier, no matter how many times it hits you in the face. I realize this was too much for you all at once, so we can take a break for the night." Standing straight, he offered me his hand. I knocked it away. "You truly are a challenge, aren't you?"

"And you're telling me that does *nothing* for you?"

"Oh, it intrigues me greatly. What doesn't interest me is having my brother's seconds while you are still hung up on him. I can wait. If we are going to rule together, I can have all the patience in the world."

"What are you going to do once he gets here?"

Leveret took a step back, allowing me space to stand on my own. "The better question is, what are *you* going to do?"

I arched an eyebrow.

"My brother may have been using you as a means to an end. You are part of his plan for ruling over both of our societies. Even if you succeed in stepping out of his shadow, the alliance to the Fae Slayer is the only way to appeal to the humans. So, what are you going to do when you see him next? If I get my eyes scooped out by a spoon, what does your betrayer get?"

I worked my jaw and took a few steps toward the bedroom I had gotten changed in. Leveret captured my wrist and whirled me around.

"I'm afraid not," he said.

"I can't sleep in my room?"

"I would never trust you with such a thing, no. Not while you are on Faerie wine."

I rolled my eyes. "I would rather wait for it to wear off—"

Leveret scooped me up and threw me over his shoulder. I slammed my fist into his spine. "Fuck, stop. That hurts." His voice dripped with mocking. He took no time bringing us into his room.

"Asshole!" I yelled as he flung me onto his bed. I bounced once before scrambling to the other side. "I am not sleeping in here."

"Then stay awake all night. I don't care." His magic whipped around us and slammed the door shut. A tether slid around my ankle.

"If you think this is the way to make me fall in love with you, you're an idiot."

"I'm not trying to make you fall in love with me. I have plenty of time for that. I'm trying to make you see the dark side of him." Leveret ran a hand through his hair. "You can take that side of the bed or not. I will sleep, and if you do anything... Well, I don't suggest it, unless you want to be underneath me without hope of escape."

Leveret didn't seem to mind my intense stare or the way I seethed every time he moved. I plopped down on the floor with my back pressed against the bed, refusing to climb into the thing with him. It took a while for his breathing to even out, and longer still for the Faerie wine to wear off. By the time both happened, I was ready to lose consciousness, but instead, I fell into the darkness of Voss.

VOSS

Nothing but darkness for hours, until she stood in front of me like the reflection of the moon. Her mouth opened as if she were surprised to find herself here. I rushed to her, crushing my lips against hers, not letting her say a single thing until I had my fill of her. One hand cupped the nape of her neck, savoring the warmth of her skin. Her breath came rapidly, but she met me with the same ferocity as always.

I wanted to pull her into me and never let her go.

But my hold on her faltered as Max punched me in the face. "When were you going to tell me that becoming Blood Queen wouldn't kill you?" She opened the space between us, cutting me a delightful glare that made me want her all the more. "What the hell, Voss?"

I blinked, rubbed my jaw, and smirked. It would have been more fun if she had stabbed me. "Did you want it to?"

"Maybe I do now!"

"Like I told you, I will enjoy the day you try."

She scowled, and it was like the sun shining straight on my face. "Sometimes, I don't know if I hate you or really…" Pressing her eyes closed, she shook her head.

"If it makes you feel better, I only just learned it myself."

Max's eyes curled at the edges as she considered my words. "I'm not here to yell at you. Not yet, anyway. I need to tell you something."

As her voice turned serious, I realized how dire of a situation she was in. I was so relieved to see her I forgot myself—forgot my twin held her captive. My jaw clenched, and I spoke through gritted teeth, "Are you okay?" I ran my hands along her cheeks, cupped her chin, and tipped her head up so she would meet my gaze.

Her blue eyes stared at me, searching mine. "For now. Your brother's been… obnoxious."

"Obnoxious," I repeated.

"He hasn't tried anything. And I don't think he will. He claims he wants to… *earn* it." She spat the words out of her mouth as if they were poisoned.

I snorted. "Like that would ever happen."

"I need to tell you something important, Voss. It's about my plan to—" She bit her lower lip, and I wanted nothing more than to capture it between my teeth. "I'm not sure how to explain this to you."

"Then don't. I trust you."

"You shouldn't trust me. I *was* going to kill you to become Blood Queen. I'm not sure I trust me."

"I know."

She wrinkled her nose and glared at me. It was adorable. "How can you take this so calmly? I wanted to *murder* you." Her face grew red.

"Yes."

"And you are okay with that?!"

"I may have a masochistic kink with you." I brushed my thumb against her jaw, tracing my fingers along her cheek, around to the back of her neck. My hand tightened around her. "Plus, I enjoy punishing you when you try."

"I am a fucked up person, Voss."

"As am I."

"I think we might be too self-destructive together."

"I don't care."

"Maybe I do."

"You realize you can't leave me even if you wanted to, right?"

"Oh? Are you commanding me?"

I clenched my jaw, because even if my brother had, I would never take her choice away from her. Only when she wanted me to, and even then, she'd have a word to get out. My hand captured her wrist, the one where she wore the red jasper bracelet. It was our wedding band, and for as long as I was alive, a part of her would always be mine. I planned on being hers, once I murdered my brother and bathed us both in his blood.

"I wouldn't dream of it, not with magic anyway." A smirk tugged at the corner of my lips.

"You are insatiable."

"But you like it."

"Okay, so if I became Blood Queen, you would have… what? Pretended to be dead to teach me a valuable lesson about losing you?"

His lips quirked. "An interesting suggestion I hadn't thought about, but no. And there is still a chance you could kill me. If you don't care enough to bring me back, it doesn't work."

"Care enough as in…"

"You have to love me." I leaned forward, pulling her by the nape of her neck until our lips crashed together. She tasted so much like darkness that I groaned. I had missed her. Spending any time away from her was madness, something I cared not to repeat.

"And you think I do?" she muttered against me.

"I know you do."

"Cocky. Egotist. Arrogant. Asshole." Each word came out clipped as I stole the air from her lips. "I will enjoy stabbing you and drinking you dry."

"I'm sure you will, and I will have deserved it. I will gladly give you every last drop if it makes amends for my wrongdoings."

"You do deserve it." She took a step away from me, shaking off my grasp. "I will enjoy killing you *and* your brother."

Magic churned around me as I gazed into her thoughts. There was conflict in there, internal confusion I couldn't put my fingers on. Max was building walls around herself, so well I couldn't see through them anymore. It annoyed me, and it wouldn't do. Once I got her back in my life, I would lock the door and keep the rest of the world out for as many days as it took to break her of this rebellious attitude.

"You want to rule over the Fae by yourself?" I challenged.

She put her hands on her hips. "Maybe I do. Morna and Cumina seemed certain a woman would do better than the men have."

I placed a hand on my chest, sucking in a breath. "You called me a man."

"Males. I meant males." She clenched her fists at her sides, face turning gloriously flushed as she scowled at me.

"You aren't fooling anyone, little fox. I will take back what is mine as soon as I find you and save you from him."

"That's the thing, Voss, I'm right where I need to be for now." Her jaw worked in thought. "But I need to—"

Whatever she was going to say died on her lips. The fire inside her eyes sputtered out. Her gaze went blank. Another voice came out of her mouth, one I wished I would never hear again.

"I should have known you couldn't leave well enough alone."

"Get out of her head."

"I'm not in her head, brother. I am simply using her to send you a message. My guards will shoot to kill. You *and* her. The only thing keeping her alive is your absence from her life. You try to save her, and I would sooner sacrifice her than myself. You understand?" Her lips curled in disgust. "Imagine how it would look with these eyes staring vacantly into the void."

"The prophecy—"

"Says the *end* of something. That's all we know. Why not the end of her? Why not the end of the world? Why not the end of the Fae or humans? It could mean the end of anything, Devoss. Make no mistake. Stay away, or she dies." She disappeared from my dream.

I bolted upright as energy crackled around me. The sheets burst into flames. Everything inside me ignited. Alarms in the tavern flared to life, adding to the cacophony of angry noise running through my veins. Penn rushed in, turquoise eyes swirling as he used his magic to douse the fire.

There I sat, the Fae king, in a smoky, ashen mess, blinking slowly. A part of me had unfurled, ready to unsheathe chaos. I would end the world if it meant getting her back. I gazed at my oldest friend. "I need to kill him."

"I know."

"He used her to speak to me."

"She broke through his compulsion?"

I shook my head. "Faerie wine that wore off. I'm not sure why he gave her wine, but if she wasn't being compelled… Why is he still alive?"

"Perhaps a lack of sparrowbone… What exactly did she say to

you?"

"She said she's right where she needs to be." My jaw worked, trying to edge through what I had felt from her. There was something more she wasn't saying, I was sure of it. There had been a strange uncertainty deep inside her. "And he said if we attempted a rescue, he would kill her."

Penn frowned. "Would your brother sacrifice the prophecy to destroy everything you hold dear?"

"It's Leveret." I stared at Penn, because that was enough. He was my twin, and our lives had taken a divergent path long ago. I went to the side of wanting to fix what was broken in Faerie—what had been broken for a long time—whereas he wanted to keep the Fae happy and weather the storm. We both thought we were right. Keeping the status quo would annihilate us. I had learned as much from my time studying the old texts and art my father hadn't destroyed.

While my twin and I had different thoughts about the world, he was still my twin. We were both capable of doing anything if it meant getting what we wanted.

I would do anything to save Max. He would do anything to become the sole king. One of us would die, and I wouldn't allow it to be me.

Elspeth yawned in the doorway. Dark circles had formed under her eyes. "You sure know how to ruin my beauty sleep. Let's see it." With brisk steps, she sank down next to me and cast her magic over my skin. The burns cleared rapidly, my scorched limbs cooling as they healed. I hadn't felt the pain when it happened. "Can we be more careful in the future?" She stood up, let out another yawn, and chuckled to herself. "Sorry, I forgot who I was talking to."

"Leveret threatened to kill Scarlet if Voss attempts to rescue her," Penn offered.

She let out a sigh. "I can't say I'm surprised. He's always had a strange way of looking at the world. And what of the prophecy?"

"He doesn't seem to care." I rolled my shoulders and tossed off the ashen remains of the covers. "I can't sleep anymore. Do either of you care to ride soon?"

"I don't think the cook is awake, and I want to eat." Penn took a long look at my expression before letting out a breath. "I'll get the horses ready."

"Good boy."

"You know what? Maybe I should let Scarlet kill you and become Blood Queen, because I want to kick you in the teeth."

I smirked.

Penn shook his head and left the room with a sigh.

"You need to be nicer to him."

"I am plenty nice."

"Voss."

"Elspeth."

She glared at me for a few seconds, her birchwood irises churning. "He would do anything for you, including self-sacrifice. That kind of friendship shouldn't be taken for granted."

"I do not take him for granted."

"Does he know that?" Crossing her arms, she arched an eyebrow. "Because I'm not sure he realizes how much you care."

"I care plenty." I stepped into the bathroom, grabbed a towel, and used it to dry my drenched hair. My body was covered in soot. We would have to stop again tonight so I could clean, but the anger pulsing through me insisted on leaving immediately. The ash could wait.

Besides, I had done this to myself.

Elspeth rolled her eyes. "You don't have to be such a martyr." With a wave of her hands, the soot, ash, and water disappeared.

"And you could have done that yourself."

"I don't want to waste the royal magic on trivial things. At least, not while I am sharing it with Leveret." I clenched my jaw. "I'll see if there is anything I can do to hurry Penn along."

"I'll pack our food." But the nod Elspeth gave me spoke volumes about her disapproval.

As I marched to the stables, I tried to rid the thoughts from my head. Penn knew how much I cared about him. He understood what Scarlet meant to me, so he knew why I was becoming increasingly… I stopped moving. Irrational. I was becoming irrational.

I scowled and continued walking.

This unyielding malice I felt toward my brother and clawing need to get her back… none of it would do. Even though I knew these feelings were worthless, my mind refused to part with the *worry*. Max consumed me. For better or worse.

Five

SCARLET

"Stay away or she dies?" I whirled on Leveret. The tether tightened around my ankle, a reminder of my status here. He had yanked me out of the meeting with Voss, and it was just as well. The more time I spent around Voss, the more my resolve weakened. Every time I spoke with him, I wanted to kill him less and less.

But I needed to, right? To fix the world?

Except now there was another possibility to contend with. I could become his Blood Queen, *and* I could keep him. After I stabbed him for not rescuing me faster and not having the foresight to know that his twin could control me.

However, I didn't have time to reflect on this new knowledge. Leveret's arms had fixed around my middle, still wrapped there, as if he had physically plucked me from the darkness and dragged me out of Voss's head. I pulled against him, but his hold was firm, merciless. The fact that he *touched* me, along with his words of warning against

Voss, bubbled along my skin. Rage curdled inside me. He had used me to speak to his brother, and he had shut the connection down.

"You won't kill me," I hedged. My fingernails dug into his skin, scraping downward to rip him open. I maneuvered to get enough space for a well-placed kick, but Leveret wasn't having any of it.

Leveret hissed but didn't loosen his hold. "And how do you know that, little rabbit?"

"There is no point. What good would it do for you or your new kingdom? Especially when you know I could get the humans onto my side."

"While technically you could get the humans to follow you again, it serves me little to have them as a united front. And from what I am hearing, the movement has grown to be bigger than you and the underground group you were working with." He pushed me away from him, and I scrambled to the far side of the bed, putting as much space between us as possible.

My eyebrows arched. Had Quinn done it? Of course, I had wanted my friends to succeed, but I heard nothing during my travels. I had no way of knowing what they accomplished.

"You didn't hear? Well, of course you wouldn't have. You were too busy drenching yourself with the blood of my family." Leveret let out a breath and ran his hands through his blond hair, leaning back onto his pillows. The move opened more space between us, giving me air to breathe. He continued, "The group you were traveling with made quite a breakthrough on the old servers."

"Quinn succeeded? All those people finally pulled through?"

Leveret nodded solemnly. "So, you understand why the Fae need a ruler sooner than later. If we are not united under one king, I fear what will happen to my people. Devoss has us on the brink of civil war, and one with the humans brews right around the corner."

Hearing this was music to my ears. I had finally done it—created enough chaos to make the revolution possible.

"You act as if the Fae are helpless," I scoffed.

"And what will happen to your humans, I wonder, if the Fae are at war with each other? How much blood must be shed to push through to a new, united future?" He narrowed his gaze at me. "How many people are you willing to lose for your idea of freedom?"

"There is no freedom so long as we can be ruled by the Fae's compulsion."

"You act as if the Fae control everything." He used my earlier language against me. "Raskos's club is an example, and I know you spent time there. Some humans there make money by giving Fae consensual pleasure—playing into kinks others are not so comfortable with. It's a middle ground, where both sides can meet without the use of compulsion."

"And what about courts like Namir's? For every place like Raskos's or Alpin's, there are three more that are horrific and corrupt."

"But you admit there are some worth saving." A slow smile crept up his lips as I let out a low growl. I wished I had something more powerful to stab him with. His voice crackled along my skin when he spoke. "I believe if you had your way, you'd destroy all Fae to start over, despite knowing that some courts are harmonious."

I glared at him. "You're not on my list of successful courts."

A chuckle escaped him as his brows lowered. "Why? Because I controlled you, little rabbit? I am one Fae in my court, but you would condemn everyone because of my actions? Tell me, how does that make *you* better than us?"

I clenched my fists at my sides, disliking how he was mincing my words. The Fae were not the victims here. Except, I could have killed more selectively. Leveret would *not* be an exception. He would not sway me onto his side, because he had proved he would do whatever it took to become the next ruler—including controlling me.

"I never claimed to be better," I spat the words out from in between my teeth.

"An eye for an eye makes the whole world—"

"Then stop taking the eyes of humans." I crossed my arms over my chest. "One side must stop first. One side must decide when it will be enough. And if the Fae won't unite under one leader, then the humans will take advantage of that." I tilted my head to the side. "So, I ask you, Leveret, how many Fae are you willing to lose in the war with Voss? How many are you willing to sacrifice? How many are you willing to condemn?"

"It seems we're at an impasse."

"I wouldn't call it something so quaint. We're on opposite sides of the war."

"A war that hasn't started. There's still time to turn it around."

"And what do you plan to do with the humans once you have ultimate control? Will you tell the other Lords and Ladies to treat them equally? Give them food and water? Or will you let them continue to rule however they want?"

Leveret's eyes narrowed, and that was the only warning I had before he moved. He crossed the king-sized bed in a flash and thrust his hand out. It wrapped around my neck, pulling me close to him. The movement was so fast, I didn't register it until my breath choked in my throat.

"Maybe I haven't made this clear to you yet, but Devoss does not have the interests of the humans in mind. He will always do what *he* believes is best, even when it is not what is best for the people."

"And what will you do?" I coughed out the words from under his grip, wrapping my fingers around his and tearing them from my skin. I rasped in a breath.

Leveret sighed. His dark eyes glowed like hot, smoldering

embers.

"Refusing to answer the question is very telling, Leveret."

"I need more time to think."

"This isn't something you should have to *think* about. It's—"

"Go to sleep." His command washed over my skin, weighing down my limbs and eyelids.

"Fuck… you." I fell backwards into darkness.

❧ ✄ ❧

Pain shot through my head as I merged back into consciousness. It took me several moments to orient myself. I huffed out a breath as memories of last night flooded in. I glared at my ankle, as if that would unleash the chain from me.

At least the asshole wasn't here, but I had to use the bathroom. I gritted my teeth. If he didn't walk through that door soon, he'd figure out how feral I could be.

I tested the bounds of the tether, seeing how far I could walk. The circumference reached his side of the bed, but not his nightstand. Tracing the boundary, I only had a few feet on the other side. There was more leeway toward the foot of the bed.

The tether itself seemed to be linked to the bedpost.

Narrowing my gaze at the post, I decided fuck it. If Leveret was going to chain me to his fucking bed, he couldn't get upset when I broke the frame.

My boots were still on, as I hadn't undressed last night. I licked my lips and aimed a well-placed kick where the post met the base of the frame. Nothing happened, but that was fine. This was wood. Wood broke with enough force.

Unless he had magically reinforced it.

Naw, he didn't know how dangerous I could be. He thought I was a rabbit, not a fucking fox.

43

I never thought I would miss Voss's nickname for me.

Kicking again and again, I made myself continue, even as the heel of my foot ached. I wanted to scream, put a full-throttle wail behind each one of my attacks, but I didn't dare alert him. Besides, I was making enough noise with the sound of my foot slamming against the wood. On the ninth try, something snapped inside the pole.

"Yes!"

I thrust my boot down again, and the post came toppling over in splinters. The tether was still attached to the pole, and as it fell, the magic pulled me with it. "Fuck!" I yelped as I landed hard on my hands. Growling, I snatched up the post. It was ridiculously tall, but not as heavy as it appeared. At least I had a weapon that couldn't be separated from my body now. I had dealt with worse.

Racing toward the door, I peeked outside and glanced around the penthouse. Vacant. I had no idea where Leveret had disappeared to, but I thanked the universe for small mercies. I walked out the entrance door and into the narrow hallway that led to the elevator.

There were guards at the end of the hall. They were talking to each other and hadn't noticed me yet.

I couldn't go through them, but my eyes slid to the stairway and the emergency exit. Was he watching every exit or just the entrances? I flung the door open and started down the stairs, not caring how many flights I had to descend for my chance at freedom. It was awkward, carrying a wickedly long pole, but it would make a great bludgeon if it came down to a battle.

The sound of my boots on the stairs echoed throughout the space. My heart pounded as I rushed downward. I imagined what would happen once I burst out the doors. I imagined hitting Leveret across the temple while screaming, getting my rage out in that one hit.

I didn't care how his daddy dearest corrupted him or treated each twin differently. This was a family feud; they needed to work it out in therapy or a battle to the death. I didn't have to be in the middle of it.

Regardless, I wouldn't let Leveret command me anymore. Not if I could help it. But, as I ran, I thought about a back-up plan. If I got caught again, what would my next steps be? Leveret would know my complacency was a farce. He wouldn't believe the facade twice. Which meant... as I got to the ground floor, I pushed all thoughts from my head. Next steps didn't matter right now.

Escaping mattered. Continuing the revolution mattered. Especially now that I knew they had succeeded. I could find them. We could win this.

I pressed down on the emergency escape handle and cringed as an alarm sounded throughout the building. It took two steps for me to be surrounded by Fae. None of them were Leveret.

At least there was that.

"Oh, hi, boys. How's it going?"

One of them pulled out a sword. "You should go back upstairs, Fae Slayer."

"You see, that's a *really* long walk, and well, I just don't want to." I rushed forward, using the pole like a bat and cracking him across the skull. Blood poured out of his temple and ear. Down he went.

My feet became leaden, and I looked down to see thick dirt layers covering them like cement. Stupid Fae magic. "No fair. I'm at a disadvantage here," I pouted.

"Stand down, Fae Slayer," another guard growled.

They *never* learned. "Make me." My voice became sing-song, the kind I did before a kill. To hear it come out of me again made my skin crawl. Voss had shown me that there was so much more to the world than I had seen, but in a war, I would use whatever I could to my advantage.

The guard rushed forward. I grabbed the sword from the fallen soldier and thrust it into the new one's gut. As he collapsed, someone wrenched one of my arms backward.

"Stop this." His magic coiled along my skin, tasting like poison as it seeped into my muscles.

"Instructions unclear. Did you mean for me to stop breathing?" I gasped out.

"Cute, Scarlet, but the magic and you know exactly what I mean."

My fingers released the sword, except for my pinkie. The handle dangled from the singular finger for a long moment before the weight took it back down to earth.

It landed straight in the neck of one of the fallen Fae.

"Oops," I said.

Leveret's nose wrinkled as if he smelled something rotten. "You are such a worthless—"

"Human?" I smiled sweetly.

He pressed his eyes shut and pinched the bridge of his nose. "I was not in the bedroom because I was making your *food*. Actually *making* it myself, as a peace offering. And then I get word you are murdering my guards."

"To be fair, you left me alone tied to a bed. And I really had to pee."

"You could have used my bathroom."

"You never showed me where it was."

"Unbelievable." He let out a breath. "So long as you are staying in my court, you will not hurt another one of my Fae." The compulsion settled over me, and it made my mouth taste like ash. He waved his hand over the earth magic, and it shattered around my boots, leaving them covered in dust. "You! Get the healers and see if there is anything you can do with this mess since it's not sparrowbone." He gestured to the twitching guard, who had the sword lodged in his neck. "Don't take that out until the healer gets here."

Leveret spun me around. "And you—" His eyes swirled a dangerous red. "—follow me, bring the pole, and do not use it as a weapon." He whirled. The tether around my ankle snapped out of place. I trailed after Leveret with the pole still in hand.

Inside the lobby of the building, there was a tray covered with a silver lid. He pulled it off the table and marched toward the elevator. Once we were inside, he stabbed the button for the penthouse.

He turned to me, seething. "Do you have absolutely no shame? Those Fae have spouses!"

"You tied me to a fucking bed and left me there."

"To get you food! When I left, you were sleeping. Peacefully."

"Nothing I do is peaceful." Except, it had been until I woke up. Leveret forced me into a dreamless sleep, and even though I woke up like I had a hangover from hell, I had slept. No nightmares, no dreams, no distractions.

No Voss.

I curled my fists around the pole.

"I'll say." Leveret stepped off the elevator and held the door to his main living space open. "Now, we're going to eat. And I'm going to ignore everything that happened this morning, because I am fairly certain everything is fixable."

"Except your bed."

He pressed his lips into a thin line. A snarl escaped his mouth. "Everything is fixable."

"You sound like Voss."

Leveret slammed the tray down on the counter and grabbed hold of my neck, twisting me around so my back pressed into the bar. "I am nothing like him." My breath lodged under his hand, but I stared at him with disgust. He claimed to be the better person, but he had done nothing to prove such. As his fingers dug into my skin, his eyes widened. He dropped his hand quickly and stepped back from me. "Eat your food." It wasn't a command, just a resigned request.

I blinked, rubbing my neck. "Would it be so bad? To be like him?" I wasn't sure where the words came from, but they were out there.

Leveret narrowed his dark gaze, looking over my body as if searching for a trap. He gestured to the stools and leaned against the kitchen island. "Why don't you eat something, and I will explain."

On an exhale, I took a seat, uncovering the food. It was a steaming pile of eggs—though I wasn't sure where he had gotten them, as most chickens had been eaten by the hoswisp swarms. There was also some kind of meat and wilted leafy vegetables. It smelled decent enough, and it surprised me he had made it, if he hadn't been lying.

"What is there to explain? You two hate each other."

"Yes, we do. To be honest, I find Devoss to be rather... innocent."

I snorted.

His glare hit me like a ton of bricks. "He's an idealist, perhaps is a better way of putting it. He believes he can fix things if enough Fae see his viewpoint. Like now, for instance, he sent missives out to employ the humans, to stop using compulsion, and has created punishments and fines for those who do not comply. But in your experience, has implementing a law ever changed anything?"

I shrugged, because I had been too young when the Fae came over to remember much of human politics. I am sure it wasn't so simple—nor would it be now.

"You can't say things are different and magically make them different. Change needs action, and sometimes, change needs war."

"You still haven't told me what your changes would be. What do you bring to the table?"

Leveret shrugged. "I didn't say I was proposing change, because I am not an idealist. I know the Fae won't change, so why bother trying?"

"A fatalist then. But how is that better? Rolling over and accepting it because what? You are too lazy to—"

He thrust his arm toward me again, but stopped himself, staring at his fingers. His body had been ready to pounce. Leveret pressed his eyes shut and dropped his arm. When he opened his eyes again, they were swirling with fire. "I am not *lazy*, and I am not *scared* of change."

"But you plan on keeping the status quo."

"Because the status quo can help us get to where we need to be. Right now, we need to beat back the hoswisp swarms. We need to stop the spread of flames and destruction from the fire pauldrins. So long as monsters exist, the Fae and human squabbles can wait."

"Squabbles. How quaint," I scoffed, disgusted. I didn't feel like eating anymore, and I pushed the tray away.

Leveret glared down at the food but didn't force me to eat it. "You cannot ask the Fae to put their lives on the line to tame the wilds while simultaneously taking away their lifestyle."

"Even when their *lifestyle* destroys someone else's?"

"It's one or the other at the moment. Devoss is trying to do both. He's trying to do too much, and it will end up getting more Fae and humans killed in the long run. Think about it—if you sacrifice a few people now to save millions, is that not worth it? I am not saying change can never occur, but it must happen steadily, gradually."

"You're only going to make violence inevitable. We need change now. At least Voss is trying to address this from every angle."

"And spreading himself too thin." Leveret crossed his arms over his chest. His jaw ticked and gaze narrowed. "No Fae will trust him;

no human will, either."

That's where he was wrong. If Voss and I united, then we could have some of the Fae and the humans on our side. We would have a fighting chance. I believed there could be a better world. I had to have hope for a future.

Especially seeing as how I was a part of it.

"We will never see eye to eye, will we?"

"No, we won't." I stared at the fork that came with the tray. There was no point in trying to escape, not when I wouldn't get very far, but if this asshole tied me to the bed again, I was going to stab him in the eyeball. I only needed to survive one more day, and it looked like he wouldn't kill me.

A mistake I would capitalize on.

"It's a pity that he met you first, because if he hadn't brainwashed you, perhaps you would understand the need for caution. The Fae don't like change, and they won't follow someone who presents it so rapidly."

I leaned forward. "And you represent all the Fae? You know they would follow you without a shadow of a doubt? What about Alpin? Would he be on your side?"

Leveret frowned. "You pose interesting questions, little rabbit. I do, however, wonder if you are asking the correct ones. Now, eat your food before I make you."

"I'm not hungry."

"Don't test me."

"Because it's a test you'll fail?" I yanked the plate back to my side of the bar, muttering curses as I picked up the utensils and forced myself to eat. Everything tasted like plastic.

"I have things I need to accomplish today, and since you cannot be trusted with an inkling of wiggle room, you will not leave this apartment." His magic washed over me, and I shuddered. I threw my fork at him as he turned to walk away, but it clinked off whatever magic cascaded around him.

I growled as I was left alone.

My hands curled into fists. He might have trapped me here, but there were *plenty* of things I could do to this apartment to make him regret his word choices. I smiled, finally feeling my appetite coming back as another plan slipped into place.

VOSS

We rode for the rest of the night, not encountering any roving hoswisps. I was grateful. As much as I itched to kill something, it would have held us up. Being cut off from Max festered inside me. Despite my aching body, I longed to reach her. The separation was creating its own kind of madness, and I only had myself to blame.

However, this was not the first time my twin used a weakness against me. If I had anything to say about it, it would be his last.

Regret hit me hard again at letting her go by herself.

Max needed me. She had said she was where she needed to be, but I felt her panic. It licked at my mind like a toxin. I needed her— no, I *wanted* her. She kept me grounded, and the link I had with her fueled my powers, while my own flesh and blood had been siphoning them from me.

As the sun rose, so did my need for vengeance. All along, the plan had been to kill my brother, but knowing he had Max created an empty chasm inside me. The blazing heat brought some comfort, because as the sun baked us, it was a reminder of how close we were to the end. We'd have to trade horses soon and attempt to rest again before the confrontation with the last of my kin.

But the idea of sleeping while she was trapped with him fractured my soul in half.

"Voss," Elspeth pulled her mount next to mine. "I have to ask, what will be the plan once we reach Leveret's court?"

I sighed, slowing my horse down a fraction so we could have this conversation. We had been riding hard for the last hour. I had pushed us, stretching our limits. While I knew it wasn't good for the horses or us, I couldn't fight the baser instinct inside me that screamed to protect her.

"We need to find a way in, whether by brute force or—"

"It won't be from brute force." Penn's horse trotted up next to ours, falling in line. We walked in a row, and the clamber of hooves surrounded us. "You know as well as I do, Leveret has a massive number of guards and likely an army. You, however, are arriving with the two of us." Scowling, Penn ran a hand through his gnarled black hair. It stood up at odd angles, the usual loose curls pulling wildly in mats away from his face.

We were worn from this journey.

"And you know as well as I do that the three of us are better than any army he could ever come up with. We've fought bigger battles than anything Leveret has faced. If we brought anyone else with us, we'd risk turncoats. I can't have that on my side. I trust you with my life and hers." My gaze fixed on Penn. Maybe some of what Elspeth said was getting through, because Penn needed to understand how much I needed all of them.

It had been the three of us. My friends, companions, confidants. Adding Max felt like perfection. But that version of perfect included them.

"You're risking turncoats with those you left behind," Elspeth pointed out.

"That's not my problem today."

She huffed, but her eyes crinkled with knowing. "We need a plan to overtake your brother. The three of us will not charge in there with nothing but our wits. I refuse to sacrifice myself for the prophecy."

The prophecy none of us knew in completion. I wondered if my brother did, if that's why Max was seemingly unharmed. I wondered how long his knowledge would keep her safe, or if she would wear him down until he was nothing more than his backwards thoughts. If Max brought Leveret to the brink, which she very well may, my little fox would be in trouble. My brother hated being teased and tormented, which she would do relentlessly.

"You're right. If we reach her unprepared, we're of no help at all. What do you think is best?"

Elspeth laughed, leaning her head back to catch the sun. "I'm going to bask in the first part of your sentence for a moment."

I glowered at her.

"We have a few options. We could wait for a shipment and sneak in with the supplies."

"That could take weeks. What else?"

"We could make a diversion. If we stay out of sight while we force the guards to deal with something else, we might be able to sneak over the walls."

I snorted. "Climbing fifteen or twenty feet?" I paused, mulling it over. "Actually, if I use the royal magic to provide a lift from the wind, then I could get us over."

"You'd be using too much power," Penn cautioned.

I shook my head. "I haven't used any magic since we left."

Patience was something I had in spades. Going without magic while I was tied to my twin and wife was a small price to pay in order to be at full strength to save her. "If that's the only magic I tap into, I should be fine to battle my brother."

Plus, if my little fox made my twin's life miserable, I should have that in my favor once we arrived. While he might need her physically alive, she would do everything in her power to break his spirit. That was worth something.

At least, I had to hope that was her plan. She hadn't exactly been forthcoming.

Elspeth let out a breath. "This idea is better than charging in with nothing, but I like it less than sneaking in with the supplies. There are plenty of things that can go wrong with us scaling the walls."

"Yes, but any plan brings risks. The longer we wait, the more we risk my wife." Which I refused to do. "Sneaking over the wall is safer than attacking head on. Hopefully, we can confront my brother without his guards, if the diversion is big enough."

"But they will come running the moment he summons them, once they realize what we've done," Penn said.

I smirked. "They won't if they can't join him."

"What kind of diversion are you thinking, Voss?" Penn swallowed, deep lines forming around his mouth. "And why do I get the feeling it's going to be something entirely reckless and stupid?"

"Because it is." I grinned in full, because it *was* reckless, but also brilliant. "We track the closest colony of hoswisps, and we lead them straight to the walls. The guards will have to hold them back while we sneak inside and confront my brother. If luck is on our side, it will take the guards plenty of time to get the swarm under control, and we'll end my brother's life. Once he's gone, I can use compulsion to make the guards surrender."

"And if we get stung in the process?"

"Penn, have you no faith? I can heal now."

"Hoswisp venom requires the royal magic to heal, Voss. You would weaken yourself if you had to heal one of us." An edge of worry crept into Elspeth's voice.

"Then no one gets stung, agreed? I am open to other suggestions, if you have one. We need something big enough to distract the guards, but not so big that we risk dying when we leave the court."

"It is fire pauldrin pup season…" Elspeth stated.

"No, no. Absolutely not. I like that idea worse than Voss's." Penn glared at us. "I am going nowhere near a fire pauldrin mother during pup season."

"But they are so cute," Elspeth whined.

Penn's turquoise eyes swirled as he sent water flying into Elspeth's face.

She screamed as it struck her, drenching her hair. Her locks stuck to the sides of her face. Her eyes swirled with birchwood as she readied a strike back.

I held up my hands. "Elspeth, you can dry yourself off. Penn, that was uncalled for."

"Fire pauldrin pups, Voss!" He threw up his hands. "It's like she wants us to die."

"Wants us to die?!" Elspeth's hair wrung itself out and began drying as her magic swept over her features. "I want us to survive. Throwing a few cute pups at them and waiting for the mothers to immolate the guards would be an *excellent* distraction."

"As long as we don't get set on fire in the interim. No, I will take the band of hoswisps, but we need fresh horses. Our mounts need to outrun the herd."

"Same thoughts, Penn."

Elspeth scoffed. "Fine, but if I get stung by a hoswisp and die, I'm coming back to haunt both your asses."

"I won't let you die." My statement came out firm and confident, but inside, I wavered. Maybe I should have brought an army. Ever since I met Max, I had doubts creep in. Prior to falling for her, I never second-guessed myself, something I couldn't afford to do with her life on the line. She was my weakness, but as soon as I ascended her, she would become a strength.

I needed Max. She was my compass. As Penn had put it, she had become my anchor, someone to ground me. I desired her sass. I loved her complexity. And the challenges she created for me? Perfection. Her ideals of the future mirrored my own. She would fight with an unyielding fierceness to get it.

She needed to be fighting beside me. As it should have been all along.

Gaining the crown had been a curse. Sending her away, the first mistake of my rule. I had fought hard to gain the throne, but now the power seemed like a hazard more than anything. And with her absence? It was a weight dragging me down into the deep.

If she heard my thoughts, Max would likely stab me in the shoulder and tell me to suck it up. Or she'd defend my vision of the world with such ferocity, she would burn all who opposed it. I craved the bite of her violence, the gouge of her into my skin. No matter what, I had to make her mine again.

Soon, little fox, soon.

SCARLET

By the time Leveret entered the apartment again, the sun had begun to set. I had done an ample amount of redecorating around his penthouse. Once I had discovered his kitchen knives, I had carved long decorations into his wall—ranging from obscene, crude graffiti to threats. Every single garment he owned was in tatters. The breakables were scattered throughout the textiles. His apartment looked worse than the outskirts of Raskos's court, which made me smile widely as he opened his entrance door.

I lounged in the middle of the couch—which now had springs sticking out of it. A mild discomfort for maximum chaos. I sipped his expensive brandy, deciding it would be better to be drunk on it than let it slip idly through the floorboards.

That shit was too tasty to smash.

Though, now that he was back, I felt like chucking the last glass at his head.

"Welcome home, darling," I said, draping my arms over the back of the couch and dangling the glass haphazardly between my fingers. "I would ask how your day was, but I don't give a fuck."

"I thought I removed the sharp objects." Leveret cast a long gaze around the space, stepping a few feet into the room. "Do you still have them on you?"

His magic washed over me, forcing an honest answer. I spat the words from my mouth. "No, but I figured you'd force me to give them up. They are the new decorations in your mattress."

Rolling his eyes, Leveret crossed the space and went into his bedroom. His sigh could be heard from the living room. He reached the threshold again, and his dark eyes landed on me. "Are you happy?"

"Not happy. That's not the right word, but perhaps... pleased?"

Leveret nodded once, as if he understood something about me, and waved his hand across the space, eyes spinning with liquid red hues as his magic worked across the penthouse. Every broken object mended, every stitch of furniture went back into place, including the spring that had been poking me, and every piece of furniture righted itself.

As if my last three creative hours had amounted to nothing.

Except...

"You have a little something." I gestured to Leveret's nose.

He crossed to the mirror hanging above the mantel and cursed as he pulled out a handkerchief. As he dabbed at the dribble of blood from his nose, I smirked. The same rules applied to him as they did Voss, which meant he was equally at risk of using too much of the royal line's magic, which he did carelessly.

Leveret seemed to have a higher threshold than Voss, as Voss had me to feed from whenever he used too much magic. Perhaps it was from the combined bond with his twin and my marriage? But when we were together, Voss had a way to refuel the magic—me. If

Leveret got any ideas about blood bonding with me, I would kick him in the balls until he puked.

Or at least, I'd try to.

"Is your tantrum over?"

I sat up and clasped my hands around the brandy. "Must you make it sound so childish?"

"Was there anything mature about what you did?" He turned toward me, arching an eyebrow.

I was getting under his skin. Good. "I was thinking, Leveret. You want the crown, as does Voss, but the crown has an unfortunate side effect."

"And what's that?" He shifted his stance and crossed his arms over his chest, leaning back on the pillar of the fireplace.

"Me."

He barked out a laugh. "Okay, this is rich. Continue."

"Well, the prophecy has to do with the rulers, right? Which includes you and me. So, whoever ascends to the full power of the throne, you or Voss, will be stuck with me for... well, however long I live."

"I fail to see the issue."

"There's no issue unless you want me throwing these *tantrums* every night to prove a point. I don't like you or your morals, and I hate how you've used compulsion on me. I also don't trust you."

He sighed. "I thought we were making such good progress, too. When I asked you to think about if Voss manipulated you, you—"

"I thought about it but realized that even if he had told me the truth, I would have done everything the same."

Leveret blinked. His eyelids flattened; gaze glazed over. "Is that so?"

"Yes, because we're like magnets. Violent magnets, but magnets, nonetheless. And I was so blinded by my anger to get revenge on the king, I likely would have listened to *anyone* who gave me that offer, no matter what the strings were."

"And if his plan blows up in his face, which it will, you'd rather go down with him?"

I shrugged. "I've been planning my entire life to die."

"That's…" A frown pulled at his lips. "Commitment."

"Anyway, you could, you know, walk away? Give up your claim to the throne? You won't win, but perhaps you don't have to die." Even though I planned to kill him the first chance I got.

Leveret snorted. "You think you or Devoss will stop me? With what, his two sidekicks? I don't think you understand, little rabbit. No one has control over me. No one."

"Fine, but mark my words, if you so much as hurt a single hair on his head, this will be your hell for the rest of your life." I chucked the glass at his face.

He caught it easily, but his magic swirled around him again. Another trickle of blood formed as he placed the liquid back into the tumbler.

"Come on, Leveret. You don't want this."

"You know the only way to give up my claim to the throne is through my demise, right?"

"I fail to see the issue," I echoed his earlier words.

Leveret stared at the amber liquid, swirling it in the glass before taking a sip.

"That was mine," I growled.

"I seem to remember you passing it to me," Leveret scoffed. The sound trailed along my skin like ash. "If I am hearing you correctly, you want me to die so you can have your happily ever after with my brother."

"Haven't you lived long enough? Centuries or the like?"

"I haven't lived long enough to accomplish what I want, which was a *united* Faerie. It will never be such under Devoss's rule, so no, I will not roll over and *die* for your husband. Now, if you are done with this half-baked argument, I have prepared dinner in the dining room."

"And if I say no?"

"I think we know how this goes."

"Do I have to wear a dress?"

He held up his hands. "I do not wish to be stabbed in the middle of the night, so no. You can wear whatever—" His voice cut off, and he cleared his throat. "You can wear something appropriate for dinner, and if you don't, then I will put you into a dress."

"Nice catch."

"I am capable of learning."

"Are you? Tell me, Leveret, how will you treat humans underneath your rule?" I leaned over the edge of the couch and blinked at him.

"As I said, they are secondary to fixing the wilds."

"Humans could *help* with the wilds, if you made us feel safe enough to do so."

"Do you speak for every human?"

My mouth dropped open, annoyed by hearing my words once again turned on me. I couldn't speak for everyone, as he couldn't speak for all Fae. Sure, not every human would join the armed ranks to help the Fae rid the wilds of the creatures in it, but several would, especially if there was pay for doing so.

"Come. Dinner is waiting."

I slammed my jaw shut and held my tongue for any further objections. Voss would be here soon. I had to hope he would come prepared for a battle and wouldn't push himself too hard beforehand.

If he pushed himself too hard and failed to rescue me now...

well, I'd have to do something equally as reckless.

And in the meantime, I would wear Leveret out. I would do everything I could to push the upcoming fight in Voss's favor. If Leveret had a harder time calling magic, that would be ideal. Though, I feared what would happen if I pushed too far, remembering how his magic clung to my skin like spiderwebs.

I shuddered at the thought.

I changed into something *appropriate* for dinner, which was a loose fitted top, tight pants that stretched enough to allow me to kick him in the face should the opportunity arise, and my boots. Always my boots. The leather had worn down to perfection, and they had molded to my soles. There was no way I would give those up, so long as I had a choice in the matter.

When I exited the guest room, Leveret gave me an assessing gaze and nodded. He offered his elbow, but I ignored it and instead breezed by him and into the elevator.

We rode in silence, and by the time we reached the dining room, a cacophony of noise rose from the space. Tons of Fae milled around the giant table. Goblets and glasses sloshed, all filled to the brim with alcohol. Their faces were flushed red, eyes dancing and full of light.

In contrast, human servants with large purple bags under their eyes held up hors d'oeuvres on silver platters. Their cheeks were sunken, and they resembled the humans who had been in the king's court—lifeless and without hope. Whenever they leaned over to offer a Fae something, they flinched at any wide motion and winced whenever voices grew too loud. They might not be undergoing tortuous death rings, but this was only a guise of civility.

Leveret might claim that *someday* the humans could have a better life, but the state of them right now spoke louder than his words. If they were treated this way now, he could never be the king. There was nothing he could say to convince me otherwise.

He pulled out a chair on his right side, no doubt a power move to show that the Fae Slayer was being cordial in his court. "Remember, you aren't allowed to hurt any Fae in this room, hurt any of my staff, or do anything to embarrass me." His voice was a low whisper.

The magic swept along my body like smoke, but I refused to flinch this time. As I sat with my hands folded in my lap, I considered his words. Embarrass was such a specific one and would be likely where I found the most amount of wiggle room. And still, my smallest and weakest finger seemed to be unaffected by his magic. I could curl my pinky around the steak knife with malice and murderous intent. Whenever I grabbed it in my hand, the feeling dropped from my body like a sack of bricks.

Maybe I could use this to exploit something once Voss arrived. If I could break through the barrier of his compulsion, I could seek revenge.

I tapped my foot a few times. It was strange how Leveret's magic seemed to settle everywhere, except for my last finger.

"Whatever line of thinking you are doing right now, stop it." Leveret gazed at me, irises pooling with liquid fire.

I wanted to gouge his eyes out with a spoon as he turned his attention to the Fae.

"As you can see, we have a very special guest in our presence tonight. The Fae Slayer has decided to visit us. At first, it was to kill me, but I think over time she will become amiable to our court. The likes of you should forgive her for her past transgressions, as she did not know better. We all know how humans can get with their silly, idealistic thoughts." He smiled, and a few Fae chuckled.

I curled my hands into fists. My mouth opened, and I found the words I was looking for. "Yes, it was *very* idealistic to think I could change the world on my own. I now realize I would need the help of a Fae to bring about a new future, one both Fae and humans could be proud of." My smile curled on my lips. "And Leveret has positioned himself well for such an event." I reached over and placed my hand on his, not betraying the disgust I felt inside for touching him.

"What are you doing?" he hissed.

"You said embarrass. I can't embarrass you if I am propping you up. I can, however, make you angry." I gave him a bright smile.

He raised his voice, speaking over the few Fae who started to gossip in hushed tones. "I assure you, the future we seek is one where the Fae are in a better place. It will be like Faerie never ceased." In a lower voice, he said, "Now, sit there, look pretty, and shut the fuck up for the rest of the meal. Only answer when spoken to, and only say positive things about *my* ideas. If you don't know how I stand on something, say you will defer to me."

The magic crawled down my throat, choking me from the inside out. I huffed, but I had known it was coming. I couldn't keep pushing Leveret's buttons without consequences. Smiling pleasantly at him, I gave him a wink, doing my best to make it seem like I had something else planned.

I didn't, but it unsettled him enough to make him trip over his next few words.

"I—I invited you here tonight as a celebration of sorts. My brother should arrive in our court early tomorrow, and we shall have the final say in the matter of who will be your rightful king and leader. I ask for you to stand with me during that time so we can ensure our victory. We will become the new royal court."

Several cheers echoed throughout the table, and my stomach soured. If everyone was on the lookout for Voss, then it would be harder for him to reach me. I hoped he had a plan, because charging into the court without thinking would get him killed.

As the first course was served, my insides felt hollowed out. Dread coiled around my stomach. My abdomen cramped up as I picked up the spoon, fully intending not to make a scene with the magic spurring me onward. But my body revolted. Everything inside me screamed, and I felt like I was falling apart. The ache in my gut didn't subside, even with the first few sips of the soup I forced down.

Leveret's gaze solidified on me after making endless small talk with the Fae to his left—another Lady from a different court. I couldn't keep track. Pain jolted through me.

"I have to go to the bathroom," I said in a low whisper to him.

"You had time when we were in the apartment to—"

"No," I growled, because he wasn't understanding. I kept my voice low, as the magic pulled on me. "I have my fucking period, asshole."

He stared at me like I had said something foreign. What had Elspeth said? The Fae *planned* theirs? Must be nice being full of magic. But both twins said their siblings were Blood Hunters, so I tried a different method.

"What do you smell?" I said through gritted teeth.

He rolled his eyes over me. His gaze narrowed before his lips quirked into a smile. "I wonder, can Devoss smell you wherever he is? And how insane is he right now if he thinks I am *hurting* you?"

I paled.

"Oh, this is perfect. Absolutely perfect. I could kiss you."

"If you do—"

He chuckled. "I know. I will get another fork to the chest or something less original than that. Go clean yourself up and be back in ten minutes or less. Do whatever… you humans need to do." The command swept over my skin, but for once, I didn't fight it. Getting out of his presence for now was needed.

I rushed to the bathroom in the lobby and cleaned everything up the best I could. My underwear were a lost cause, but I had to keep them to prevent myself from bleeding everywhere, and it wasn't like these bathrooms had feminine products.

Sighing, I sat down on the toilet and contemplated what Voss must be going through. I worried about him, because this would likely make him try harder to get here. Tears stung my eyes, but I blinked them away, refusing to cry now. I felt helpless to stop Leveret, helpless to inform Voss of the truth, and hopeless to change things. I could feel it coming—the end of me. Leveret had let me get away with too much, but I needed him to be as weak as possible when he fought with Voss.

Tonight, I was going to stab Leveret with my tiny necklace with the one finger that refused to listen to his commands. After that... well, I likely wouldn't remember any of this. Not a single thing.

I was risking myself, but only because Voss was coming for me. If he didn't win, well... I likely wouldn't remember losing him anyway. Leveret would make sure of that as payback.

Leveret said he wanted me to come around on my own, but his anger would get the better of him. I had seen it happen already. There was a thin line between his tolerance and his rage, and I had crossed it more than once.

With a sigh, I finished my business, made the best substitute I could, and walked back into the dining hall with my head held high. When Leveret looked at me, his expression was elated with a broad smile. He looked younger like that, almost like I could see the boy he once was, before his father shaped him into the rotten male he had become.

In another life, perhaps he and Voss could have ruled together. We, however, did not live in a land of optimism, so I had no hope of reconciliation.

Leveret stood and pulled the chair out for me.

I thanked him, plastering on my best smile.

"Whatever you are planning, stop it."

I buried the thought in my body, digging a hole so deep only I could reach it. "Stop what?" Blinking innocently, I grabbed up my fork and knife. "I was only planning to eat. Can I eat?"

"You can eat." His magic loosened as he sank into his seat. His gaze swept over me with suspicion. "Whatever you are up to—"

"I wouldn't dream about anything right now, not when I am so weak and vulnerable." I batted my lashes. "And in pain." I gestured to my stomach, pouting my lower lip.

"Sarcasm doesn't look good on you."

"I don't know what you mean."

Leveret leaned back as a servant took away the first bowl and replaced it with another dish. This one was a steaming pile of roasted vegetables and some kind of meat. He shifted forward, gesturing for me to do the same. "You and I are going to have a long talk tonight. It so happens that having your period has put me in a good mood, and it's the only reason I am not going to punish you. But if I don't like your answers later, there will be consequences. Got it?"

I plastered on my brightest and widest smile. "Understood, sir."

Leveret snarled as he took up his own utensils.

Eight

VOSS

Shortly after sunset, we stopped at a smaller court—one neighboring Namir's. We were so close now, and in a few more riding hours, I could confront my brother. I was ready. My body thrummed with eagerness for his blood.

As soon as we were settled at the inn, however, we received a scytheseer from the Lady of the court. These courts bordering my siblings' lands were the ones most likely to revolt. There was growing unrest among the Fae—worse now that I had temporarily left my post in the royal court. Hostility seemed to spark among those we passed, but I had no other choice. I didn't trust anyone else to get Max out alive.

My royal guards were likely to use her against me instead of keeping her safe—and Lylle, while he had proved trustworthy among them, wasn't the strongest Fae. If luck were on my side, Alpin and Lylle would hold it together for three more days—to give me enough time to bring the Fae Slayer home.

Leaving Penn and Elspeth to get some much needed rest, I ignored their judging stares as I went to meet Lady Mayte. Her court was hospitable enough, despite the undercurrent of tension. Besides, if I had to shove my hand into someone's chest and disintegrate their heart, I would.

Mayte's court was small. The protective walls stretched wide enough to fit about two hundred Fae, and even fewer humans. The intensity here seemed less strained than previous courts, but several Fae stole quiet glances and contemplative looks as I strolled to the capitol building. With such a small court, everyone would be talking before the end of the night, but there was also less of a possibility of a revolt. No one could fight the royal magic—and none of these Fae knew how encumbered my magic had become. I planned to keep it that way.

As I opened the door to her building, Lady Mayte waited in a large, worn leather chair in the middle of the lobby. The walls, floor, and furniture were the same brown, with every wooden surface gleaming with polished perfection. Their town had been built around a small suburban center, which seemed to fit her fine.

She stood up. Unlike Lady Burke, Mayte dressed in more practical clothing, wearing a flowing mid-length skirt and tighter shirt. Her eyes were like the Earth's sun, bright yellow and fiery without magic. "King Balgair."

I stiffened, still despising the formal title. If Penn were here, he would have asked me what I had expected to happen once I took the throne.

Forcing a nod, I said, "Lady Mayte."

"I am grateful to see you today. What brings you to stop by our court?" Her eyes flashed as her head tilted to the side. Her brows furrowed.

"I am on my way to visit my twin. Seeing as how we are the only remaining members of the royal line, it is prudent that we come to some kind of truce."

She clasped her hands behind her back and rocked on her heels. "I heard about your siblings. I am sorry for your loss."

"Not much of a loss."

A sliver of a smile pulled at her lips. "Then the rumors may have merit? Did you send the Fae Slayer to kill your remaining relatives?"

"I did not trust them for a variety of reasons." I needed to tread lightly with my next words. She could stand on either side of the brewing conflict, and if I was persuasive enough, perhaps it would be mine. "You understand how the last king coveted power, and sadly, he passed that trait to most of my siblings. I believe, however, there can be truces made and peace created among the courts."

"Between you and Lord Leveret?"

I nodded sharply, although I desired no truce from him. "How are your feelings about my brother? You live close enough to his court."

She shrugged. "I have traded with him some. He seems agreeable to most Fae."

The hidden language was there—he was, unlike me. My brother would rather stand on the bloodied backs of humans than make Fae seek peace. Perhaps meeting with Mayte was a mistake. Anything I said could add fuel to the movement against the royal missives. I cast my senses out, using a modicum of magic to brush her thoughts. I sensed no malice, but there was underlying distress. Pushing any harder would draw attention and increase the risk during the battle against my brother—which would put my little fox in more danger. So that small amount of emotion I gleaned from her would have to be enough.

"Yes, I suppose he is. I do hope to implement some of his ideas. Perhaps I moved too quickly for the Fae to adjust adequately to the new system? There have been some positives to the missives." I left the last part not as a question, but as a statement. Exuding confidence while still welcoming a response.

Catering to the Fae was tiring. It would have been easier to split their throats open like Max wanted to do.

The Lady gazed at me as her lips pressed into a thin line. "For the humans, perhaps. For my Fae..." Mayte's eyes shifted to something behind me.

I turned, but there was nothing there. Forcing my gaze back on her, I found myself unnerved by her detached manner of speaking.

"Forgive me," she offered. "We are a small court in comparison to some, but I think how the Fae are treated by their own brethren warrants a discussion, perhaps? Often, we were overlooked by the late king, but surely, you will be different."

The words felt like a thinly veiled threat. "I would prefer for all courts to prosper under the new rule. My first steps were to clean up the hoswisp nests near the capital, but once that is complete, we will expand the army and spread outward. If we unite the humans in our efforts to tame the wilds, we'll all have much easier lives."

"It's a clever story, King Balgair. One I am sure helps you sleep at night." Her eyes flashed to rich gold. "Perhaps one of these days you will remember where you came from."

I scowled. "You should speak candidly, Lady Mayte, as that is the only way things will change. I do not care for riddles or half-truths."

She ran her hands through her thick black hair. "I will be honest then, my King. I think you are walking a dangerous line, and you forget how the Fae, myself included, hate being neglected."

"And you feel as though I am neglecting the Fae?"

"You forget you are the *Fae* King. The humans never agreed to have you in charge."

"That is what I am fighting for—for one people, united."

"The humans will never unite under a kingdom, because they never *were* united. Their history is full of war and viciousness. Moving forward with them is a mistake—one Earth will pay for."

I let out a breath. "Frankly, Mayte, they were here first. We have to find a way to live in peace, otherwise we will know none."

"So be it. I believe you are creating your own grave."

"A threat?"

She shook her head and held up her hands. "I am not powerful enough to threaten the line of the king, nor would I dream to, but once Leveret and you *decide* where to go next, you should watch your standing. There are plenty of Fae talking about what comes next, and if Leveret is gone, I do not believe they will have reason to wait. There was already upheaval at Raskos's court."

"With Lady Burke, correct?"

Mayte nodded. So, the rumors I had heard whispers of were true. It hadn't been that long since I had left her court behind, or Raskos's, but in that time frame, a battle had broken out between the two.

"And if Burke is willing to go to war, who knows who else will follow," she added. It wasn't a threat, because a settlement had occurred between the two courts, but the underlying meaning was there. This much chaos would only beget more.

I swallowed, watching the shifts in her tones and her eyes. Mayte didn't have control over her court—they would join the other side of the war, and not because she believed in it, but because her people did. "Thank you for your honesty."

"Am I going to have my heart burned out now?"

I rolled my eyes. "That was one time to make a point. As long as you do not personally come after me, Mayte, we will have no issues."

A smile slowly curled her lips. "We will see, Devoss Balgair. Thank you for coming to my court. I hope you enjoy your accommodations this evening." She turned and walked through an oak threshold, out of the lobby.

My fists curled at my sides. It would be easier to kill every Fae who stood in my way, but withholding violence was for the good of the kingdom. In my soul, I wanted nothing more than to ignite everyone and be done with it. But burning the world down wouldn't unite the Fae under my rule. Not yet, anyway. Patience would be the way out here.

But I had no desire to be patient while my wife was still out there—with *him*.

I hastened back to the inn. After checking in with Penn and Elspeth, I learned they had traded for fresh horses. As soon as we were rested, we could start a new journey into the night. A few hours would be enough for us to get our strength back.

As we sat down for a meal in the dining room, I found it impossible to focus. A sense of wrongness stretched across my skin. The food became no better than ash on my tongue. My mind spun, and I pressed my eyes closed to rid the dread from my body, but it was no use. It invaded my senses, flooding everything. Deep and unbidden in my chest, a wave of terror washed over me. A hole had been torn straight through my soul. My vision blotched out.

"Voss?" Penn's voice, but he sounded miles away.

Everything flooded white. "Fuck," I barely could breathe out the word.

"Penn, use your water. Voss, what's happening?" Elspeth exclaimed.

My magic flared around me, because I *knew* that smell. It was her blood. My little fox was trapped in Leveret's court, and now she was bleeding. If he had touched a single hair on her head—

"Fuck, that's the ceiling."

"Penn, focus. Put it out."

"He's fucking on fire, Elspeth. How am I supposed to put him out?"

"Voss?!"

Someone slapped me, but I was unreachable. I tore at the walls, trying to break through to see if Max was okay. Somehow, my little fox had made it to me before. Maybe we could do it again. She was bleeding. She could be dying.

And if I lost her—

"Voss!"

Darkness consumed me. It took over, instinct pulling me out of the inn. I marched past the gate, into the wilds. Drawn to her. I needed to get to her. I would do *anything*.

"Fuck, Elspeth, what do we do?"

"I've only seen him like this once before—"

"After his father gave his court to Leveret. I remember. Fuck."

"Penn, I think one of us has to go in."

"It isn't going to be you. He'll rip your head off."

My eyes focused on the horizon. Their babble mattered not. The only thing that mattered was finding Max. I needed to reconnect with her. Needed to feel her around me, under me. I needed to heal her. Fix her. Be with her. Tangy blood hit my tongue—not hers. It didn't matter whose it was.

Pain exploded across my right arm.

Then darkness.

❧ ✄ ❧

I whirled around in the emptiness detached from my body. Growling, I spun until my eyes landed on the dark-haired, light-eyed Fae who had brought me here.

"You fucking blood bonded with me, Penn?" I bellowed. My voice echoed in the darkened space. Magic swelled around me, but I fought against the urge to set him on fire. The wicked desire licked at my skin, begging me to shove my anger at someone—anyone.

But not Penn.

"You weren't responding." He outstretched his hands in front of him in a placating gesture. Eyes wide. A frown formed on his lips.

I narrowed my gaze. "What do you mean, I wasn't responding? Max is bleeding. Out there in the real world. She's at the mercy of my fucking twin brother, and I need to save her. That's all that matters."

Penn crossed the space between us, his eyes swirling to keep his presence firmly in my mind. "Voss. *Think*. He might have given her a paper cut to drive you to the edge. It could be anything. Did it smell like enough blood for her to bleed out?"

I crossed my arms. "This still doesn't explain how I wasn't responding."

"It was like you went into a trance." He scratched the back of his head, shoulder rising.

"A trance?"

"Like when your father stripped you of your court."

My shoulders sagged, and I ran my hands over my face, collapsing into a chair that I summoned out of nothing. Exhaustion weighed on my shoulders as I realized the severity of his words. "That bad?"

"You practically lit the inn on fire."

"Mayte said some cheeky things before I left, like she knew something was going to happen."

Penn sat across from me, leaning forward on his knees. He was close enough to touch me, but he didn't. "We shouldn't come up with conspiracy theories, Voss. There's no proof she's involved in this, nor does she understand your connection to the Fae Slayer. I don't think anyone truly understands it. Even your brother. Besides, if Leveret killed her now, he would have nothing to hold over you once we reach his court. You do realize he's going to use her against you, right?"

"He already has," I snarled. "The only reason we're crossing the kingdom is because of him. We're losing ground, giving space for the distraught Fae to rise against me, and it's all due to him."

"It's because of her, not him. You cannot be separated from her. Whatever happened when the two of you got married and blood bonded… it's something we've never seen before. It has to be from the prophecy."

"The prophecy my father destroyed." I gritted my teeth together.

Penn pressed his eyes shut. When he opened them again, his blue eyes held endless sorrow. Elspeth was right. I didn't deserve a friend like him. Not with everything we had been through. Penn was the good I sought in the world.

"Elspeth told me it also might be that… period thing she mentioned." Penn wrinkled his nose. "She said she was due for one, right? Or… at some point? How often do you think those happen, anyway? Once a year?"

I snorted. "I believe it's once a month."

"Once a month?!" His eyes widened in horror. "You know what? I don't want to know what you two are going to do with the—" He stopped talking.

"You tapped into my mind, didn't you?" I gave him a smug smirk.

"What the fuck, Voss. Like, honestly, what the hell is wrong with both of you?"

"A lot of things. It's why we work. It's why there's no one else for me." I gave him a knowing look.

Penn shook his head and had the audacity to laugh. It filled the space around us with lightheartedness and pierced straight through my vicious emotions, lodging itself into my veins and calming me down. "Yes, obviously. I understand Scarlet is your hope for the future, how she's the one and only for you. I *get* it, Voss." His eyes gazed into mine. "But in order to assure her safe return, we can't run in there literally on fire and hope for the best."

"Have I told you that your logic bothers the fuck out of me?"

Grinning, he said, "That's what I am here for, right? Keep you in check? Also, you wasted a lot of magic just now by practically setting the inn ablaze."

I sighed, pushing us out of the darkness and into the wilds. Penn and Elspeth stared at me.

"You good?" she asked, kneeling to check the damage on my arm. They had cut deeply.

"I don't know. You tell me, Penn." I caught my friend's eyes.

He nodded firmly. "He's good."

I frowned, pushing Penn to the corner of my mind. He was easier to keep out than most, because we had done this before. Still, his thoughts and whirling emotions of panic, sorrow, and fear filled that corner. His affection for me ran deep, and I hoped someday he'd find the right male to return that loyalty without a shadow looming over it.

Elspeth stitched my arm together and crouched on her heels. I was on my ass, likely dropped by one of them during whatever chaos I had created. "Was I right? Is it likely her... time?"

I shrugged. "I have no idea, but the logic makes sense. It serves no point to kill Max now. My brother likely fancies her for the prophecy so he can be the ruler who takes over the world." Running my tongue along my teeth, I took another moment before admitting my fears. "What if she's not the same when I find her?"

"What do you mean?"

I stared at Elspeth. "She can be controlled by him because I married her. I put her in this position. What if... whatever he's

78

doing…" My teeth gritted, not willing to continue that line of thought. My brother was a miserable Fae, and he would do whatever he could to break me, including break her. Max was my biggest weakness, and he would exploit my feelings for her. My father had taught him, after all.

"Everything can be healed with time," Penn said. He shifted on his feet, scowling. Lines formed across his forehead. "Even emotional scars. If you still intend to ascend her, you'll have plenty of time to figure it out."

"Besides," Elspeth said, standing up, "she's strong. And we'll help her get through it. You'll help her." She offered me her hand.

With a sigh, I took it, allowing her to hoist me up. "Okay. We need sleep, and I need to offer some coin for repairs to the innkeeper."

"Thankfully, Penn put most of the flames out before they could cause more than burn scars."

"Still." I let out a breath, gazing at the horizon. She was there, alive. Her scent was strong, which meant my brother hadn't bled her dry. It would have already soured with the passing of time if he had killed her. My friends were right, and I had to let logic win. "Four hours work for both of you?"

They nodded, and we headed back to the inn. It pained me to walk in the opposite direction of her, but this was the best plan. We needed sleep. While barging in and setting everything on fire was tempting, the less death I could leave in my wake, the easier it would be for me to gain a foothold in the aftermath.

Nine

SCARLET

Leveret slammed the door shut behind us, making me jump. I kept my eyes on him, not wanting him to catch me unaware for a second. He prowled toward me, and I glanced around for anything I could chuck at his head.

"Sit down." The command crashed over me, so forcefully I couldn't make it to a chair. I curled up on the floor, glaring at him. His gaze narrowed. "How are you finding ways around my magic?"

"You should be more specific."

"You're a brat."

I rolled my eyes. "Says the prison guard."

"You weren't supposed to be a prisoner here," he snarled. He wiped his hand down his face in a gesture that was so much like his brother, it made my heart ache. "I wanted you to get to know me and what I intend for the world."

"And still, you have not told me your full intentions. Not that I would believe them at this point. I saw your servants. They were practically skeletons." I leaned back on my hands, faking nonchalance despite my pounding heart. "You've told me what you intend for the Fae, but nothing of the humans. You've told me what you intend for me, but nothing about what happens if I *never* consent. Which I won't."

"Okay, fine. What of the humans? Who cares?" He threw up his hands. "Right now, the humans wouldn't survive a single hoswisp attack if it weren't for our intervention."

Thinking about Anya's eyes, cold and vacant as the toxin took over her system, turned my insides to ash. Leveret deserved whatever was coming next for being so calloused.

He continued, "So no, they are not a priority. What happens after the wilds are conquered? I'm not sure. Nor do I care, because the hoswisps are a massive problem right now. And you know what's not a problem? The status quo—the humans being human, and the Fae being Fae."

"I'm human." My lips curled. "I'm human, and you are thinking about, what, keeping me as your *pet*? Only taking me out to play whenever *you* feel like it?" My fingernails dug into the wooden floor. "As much as you might not want to hear this, Leveret, what you do to humans matters to *me*."

"You are intended for so much more than humanity, and the fact that you keep hanging onto these notions is weighing us down."

"There is no us," I spat.

He ignored me, pacing the length of the living room. I was still sitting in the middle of the space. "Perhaps I need to consult someone else on this matter. It seems whatever I say to you is falling short of hitting the mark."

"There is no mark to hit when you don't care about people."

His eyes turned fiery as he stared at me. "I will be back later. You will be dressed appropriately for bed, and you will be curled up on your side of the bed. I don't care if you are sleeping or awake. You will not find a creative work around for my command this time." Leveret left the room, slamming the door with such force it shook the walls.

My feet stood as my body became rigid. It moved under his command, checking off the list of tasks he set for me. But as my body did so, I focused on my hand, on the one finger that never seemed up for obeying him. What if it could spread? Down my arms, into my limbs…

I changed clothes into something appropriate for sleep, as he had asked. The necklace pressed on my chest.

The magic was a current, and everything inside me was pulled along with it. My legs weighed, my arms leaden, forced to do whatever he said. My pinky, however, swam against it.

I had created royal magic from nothing. I had conjured myself into another plane of existence. *The likes of which had never been seen before.* The stupid prophecy spoke of rulers, plural. Voss, Penn, and Elspeth acknowledged I could do things they had never seen anyone do—human or Fae.

As I passed by the threshold of the doorway into Leveret's room, my arm thrust out, catching the side of the frame. My legs stopped. Frozen. My fingers dug into the wood, curling so hard my nails threatened to break. I had stopped the command, but my body ached against it. Pain and tightness coiled in my gut, at war with what the Fae had told me to do.

So, I could fight his compulsion. Maybe I couldn't break through, but I could *fight*.

Releasing the doorway, I allowed the magic to pull me along, no longer wanting the mental and physical war to be waged inside my body. It was knowledge I needed, and it gave me a glimmer of hope. If I held out for the right time, I could make him pay.

I curled up on the side of the bed he was referring to, but never would I call it *my* side. I didn't belong here with him. If anything, my necklace belonged lodged in his eye. I toyed with the pendant, the tiny sliver of sparrowbone that was more an afterthought than anything. Tonight, I would stab him. The little sword wasn't strong enough to pierce through the flesh in his neck, and it wouldn't do much damage anywhere on his body.

But his eye. It would be harder for him to fight.

A smile curled on my lips as I pressed my eyes shut, forcing myself to steady my breathing. If I had any hope of Leveret letting his guard down, I would need to be as close to sleep as possible by the time he got back. Now, it was a waiting game.

☙ ✄ ❧

The mattress depressed as he shifted under the sheets. Leveret's smell surrounded me, burnt oranges and ash. The taste and fragrance of him threatened to choke me, but I stayed still and kept my breathing even.

"I know you aren't asleep, little rabbit."

I kept my eyes closed, refusing to acknowledge him. His fingers trailed along my hair, and I suppressed a shudder.

"There's a lot about humankind I don't know, I admit. And perhaps that's the first step to a better path with you. Once we're ruling together, I would need you to help me guide... human relations, even though you are so much *more* than them. But, perhaps, if I cannot change your mind, I can use you to better the way we interact." He let out a breath. "I'm not sure what good it will do, to be honest. Most Fae are set in the way they see the world, and a simple *missive* won't change that. Don't you see?"

I wanted to argue, tell him it would never hurt to try, but I also no longer wanted to engage. Leveret said these things to open a path between us, form a connection that never would exist. He looked like Voss, but the way he acted didn't hold a candle to his twin. Besides, this all was likely for show. Leveret needed me, but he didn't want me.

Voss, however, did. And he understood me. That deeper connection couldn't be forced.

Leveret sighed and rolled away. I listened as his breathing evened out, and I waited. Endless minutes passed. Time no longer held meaning in the dark. It was in this quiet that I poked at the veil between Voss and me. I had fought against the compulsion earlier, and I wondered if I could break through whatever wall Leveret had built between us.

I wanted to tell Voss everything that was about to happen. I wanted to threaten him, tell him he better rescue me or else. Why was my future dependent on someone else?

But instead of breaking through, I needed to save my strength to fight Leveret's compulsion physically.

Once his breathing had remained the same for a while, I wrapped my hand around the necklace. The small sparrowbone sword was cool under my touch. With a slow breath, I unclasped the latch and pulled it out in front of me. I tested my fingers, sensing the edge of resolve in my muscles.

I had pulled apart the world to save Voss before, and I could do it again if it meant helping him once he arrived. He'd better be grateful for this.

Rolling toward the middle of the bed, I could barely see the outline of Leveret's body. He was sprawled on his back, chest rising and falling, with no shirt on. Heat emanated from him in waves. His face was serene, and save for the scar, the relaxed look made him resemble his twin so much more.

Biting my lower lip, I raised the sparrowbone above his face. I tested a few times, feeling the resistance of the magic that swirled in my bones under his command. He had told me not to hurt him. I could feel the edge of that command, the precipice. The magic was finite, the compulsion not real. If my body wasn't magic, then the magic couldn't be inside my body.

After a few adjustments, I gritted my teeth together. Now or never. I slammed my fist down, bringing the small pointy necklace with it. The compulsion tore at my skin, ripped through me, screamed at me to stop. But I fought it, because this was how I *won*. I vowed to fight until there was nothing left in me to do so. I was a hunter. The barrier threatened to push me back, but I smashed through it.

My tiny sword plunged straight into Leveret's eye.

He woke up screaming, casting magic at me. The concussive wave hit my chest, and I hurdled across the room, landing hard on the floor. The wind left my lungs. My ass ached. Leveret snarled, ripped the necklace out of his eye, and threw it across the room. His gaze hardened, but his eye was a bloodied, messy shell.

Magical binds wrapped around me.

"If my healers can't fix this—"

"I hope they can't," I spat through a wheeze.

His hold tightened, squeezed my lungs, and made it impossible to breathe. His one good eye was an explosion of fiery colors. "You're staying right there until I get back." He stalked out of the room, leaving a blood trail behind him.

My heart thudded in my chest, threatening to escape without me. Every breath I attempted ripped in and out of my lungs. What he used now wasn't compulsion, but actual magic pressing against my body. It felt alive, writhing against my skin and coiling around me. I coughed on my next inhale and couldn't stop once I started. It hurt. Everything hurt.

But if Leveret was blind in one eye, it would be worth it. It would make the battle with Voss harder for him. Anything to give Voss the upper hand. Anything to save him.

Because if he didn't win now, I would kick his ass.

No matter what happened next, it had been worth it, especially if the healers couldn't fix Leveret. Sparrowbone slowed the Fae's natural healing ability, which was why it had been my choice of weapon. While it was possible for them to heal after an attack, performing major repairs on an eyeball differed from stitching skin back together.

Besides, Leveret isolated himself in his penthouse, away from any Fae who could help him. By the time he reached anyone, it might be too late.

I hoped.

Focusing on my breathing, I forced myself to calm down. My throat was raw from coughing, and it took a long time for my pulse to slow. I lay there, wrapped in his magic. It wasn't until the front door opened that my muscles tensed again.

It had been worth it, I told myself.

I hoped.

The light flicked on as soon as he entered the room, causing me to wince from the sudden brightness. Leveret stood in the threshold and glared at me with his good eye. His other was covered with a thick layer of gauze. "It will heal but will likely take *weeks*." The words rumbled out of his mouth in a growl. "But that was the plan, wasn't it? Make it easier for Voss to fight me once he arrives? You don't need to answer that. It's rhetorical."

He crossed the room and sat on the edge of the bed, staring down at me. "You wanted me to be damaged for the fight, but here's the thing, little rabbit, I always get my way. And while you're smugly sitting there, believing you've given Voss the upper hand, I am about to take that back. Tenfold."

My eyes narrowed.

"Ah, yes. You blood bonded with him. You wanted to do anything for him, right? You wouldn't even consider the possibility that maybe, just maybe, he brainwashed you into thinking you need him."

"He—"

"Shut up!" he roared, the command so crystal clear it seeped into my bones. "You think you can resist my compulsion now, but what if we blood bonded? What then? I would be *everywhere* inside you."

My body stilled. My mind raced. Panic coiled around my gut and my nerves.

No. He wouldn't.

"I will." Leveret reached into his pocket and pulled out a small blade. He grabbed my hand, pulling my arm out of his magical coils. The rest of my body was stuck, but I thrust my fist out, trying to get his face. He dodged to the side, grabbed my wrist, and dragged the knife along my knuckles.

I held back the scream at the sharp pain, but watched in horror as he brought my hand up to his mouth and sucked. Fuck it, I was already in a lot of trouble. Why not more? I jammed my fist into his mouth.

He wrenched back, tightening the bindings once again. "You fucking bitch."

Everything inside me ached as my breath wheezed out of me.

Clenching his jaw, he brought the blade to his skin, cut open his wrist, and held it above my face. His blood dripped onto my chin. It was warm and smelled as burnt as the rest of him. "*Open and swallow.*"

I fought against the command. My body shook. Sweat beaded along my brow. Leveret clenched his fists, tightening the magic so much I gasped for breath, and his blood trickled onto my tongue. It was ashen and rotten, tasting of ruin. He clamped my jaw shut, and I felt the moment it rolled to the back of my throat. I sputtered against him, fought hard to keep it out, but ultimately, I swallowed.

Fuck you, you fucking piece of shit. You're—

That's enough of that, isn't it, darling? Aren't you tired of fighting? Aren't you tired of seeing the world collapse around you while you still fight for it?

His thoughts invaded my mind. But no, this couldn't be it. I needed to stop him. I needed to do something before—

Wouldn't you rather give up?

As he pushed his thoughts into my head, I latched onto my memories. The ones I never wanted him to see. And I buried them down. Under my rebellion, under my cells, I made them so small that even I forgot them. They melted away under the weight of his command, becoming nothing. A phrase to make it stop. A nickname that would never be his. I had no idea if this would work.

Voss...

I buried it all. Digging deeper and deeper. Pushing layer upon layer on top of it. Until it—

He continued, *Cave into the solace of knowing you tried your best, and ultimately, that's all that matters. Wouldn't you rather feel love and peace than all that hatred in your heart?*

—disappeared.

My body relaxed as every thought in my head melted away. I *had* tried my best, hadn't I? I had done everything I could do. And giving up? That sounded... nice. Relaxing. Perfect.

"I'm going to let you go now."

I nodded. My limbs were lighter—my body felt... safe. Warm. I stood up, giving Leveret a sheepish smile. "I don't know what came over me. I am so sorry."

Leveret's eyes glittered, looking so much less angry now. I was glad to see him happy. He traced his fingers along my jaw. I swayed into his touch. "How are you feeling?"

"Better." I smiled. "And you?" I gazed at his eye as tears pricked my own. I don't know what I had been thinking earlier. This Fae had been my everything. I lived and breathed for his male, and I was horrified that a nightmare would have overcome me so much that I would *hurt* him. My past had made me lash out. It was an accident. A horrible accident that I was worried may happen again. "Are you going to be okay? Truly? They can fix it?" My fingers traced along the side of his cheek.

He pulled me into an embrace. His scent was of burnt oranges and… ash.

His smell felt wrong

It's not wrong. It's perfect. You're safe. The voice inside my head calmed me. This was right where I needed to be.

I sighed against him. "I feel strange. It's almost as if I missed you while you were still here." I ran my hands along his shoulders. His warmth filled the space between us.

Leveret grasped my wrists. "We should go to sleep, little rabbit. It's going to be a long day in the morning."

Gazing at him, I wondered why we hadn't taken things further yet. He was everything to me, wasn't he? And if he was, then why hadn't I given myself to him? I had been with so many other Fae, and none of the emotions I felt before were more powerful than this pull toward him. It was all-consuming. My thoughts were nothing without the male standing next to me.

"I think we should—"

He pressed a finger gently on my lips. "I know what you think. I can feel it, but darling, I don't want there to be any confusion. When I finally push myself inside you and make you come, I want the only thing to be my name running through your mind."

I cocked my head to the side, because of course his name was the only one I thought of. He was my world. I had given up my notion of vengeance and settled down with him. My partner. We were going to rule the world together, and he was going to make the decisions for us. It was nice not to worry about what happened next. So nice.

But if he wanted to wait, I would wait. I would do anything he asked. "Okay." I shifted onto my tiptoes and placed a kiss on his cheek, tracing my fingers along his jaw. "Whatever you think is best."

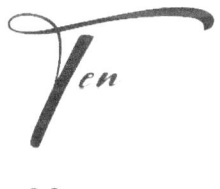

VOSS

Fatigue settled deep into my bones. Sleep had eluded me most of the night, but I forced myself to recuperate best I could. Knowing my little fox was still at the mercy of my brother became impossible to ignore. Our horses were fresh, and I had bathed, but the aches in my muscles had spread throughout my body. Weariness unfurled in our group, and none of us could break its hold.

Traveling the last few hours felt like days. We had left a wide berth around several courts instead of stopping. Any more visits, and I could be pulled into more unnecessary political conversations. Any further delay would result in some Fae's untimely demise. Most courts in this vicinity had experienced a backlash as my siblings had fallen. In the wake of their deaths, there was plenty to figure out— something I had no intention of assisting with, at least not now. Rumors about the unrest across the other courts grew from the little I heard when passing other travelers. Lady Burke became a constant mention, the port city seemingly at the hub of discussion.

When we finally caught sight of Leveret's spires, my heart flooded with relief. Either way, it would be over soon, ideally with my twin's blood seeping into the floorboards. Under the shadow of his skyward buildings, we made a wide perimeter, looking for the closest hoswisp nest. Our horses had experienced a leisurely pace during this stretch, as we needed them rested. After an agonizing thirty minutes, we found an occupied nest. My brother had maintained the wilds around his court. Curious, considering how he never seemed to care about anyone except himself.

Though, I supposed hoswisp venom was equally toxic to him as it was to another Fae.

But finally, we had our plan. My magic thrummed with the need to be unleashed, but I kept it tamped down.

We pulled to a stop a few meters away from the nest. Penn placed a hand on my shoulder, sensing my emotions through our new bond. I shook him off and rebuilt the wall between us. Having his concern reside in my head was difficult enough without him touching me.

"I want to see if I can give you some of my power." He held out his hand this time, reaching across the space between our horses.

With a sigh, I placed my hand in his. Warmth pulsed through my arm, but died quickly. It wasn't like with the Fae Slayer.

"Did that work?"

I flexed my hand, considering the feeling. "I don't think so."

Penn shrugged, letting out a breath. He had deep bags under his eyes, and his cheeks were sunken, holding none of his normal buoyancy. It was my doing. I had run them ragged.

I opened my mouth to say as much, but he cut me off.

"It was worth a shot to try it." He glanced at Elspeth, his gaze solidified with determination. His brows lowered. "Are you ready?"

She arched her neck from side to side and rolled her shoulders.

"I would be better if I had more time to stretch before we started the next leg, but I know Voss. We won't get a moment's rest now that we're so close." Her voice edged with amusement, despite the weight we all carried.

I grinned. "Glad to know someone's been paying attention."

"How do you want to do this one, Voss?" Penn shifted his eyes to the nest. It was quiet inside, with all the creatures asleep for the day.

"Well, one of us has to wake them up and charge straight into the guards while the other two sneak in from the side."

Penn narrowed his eyes. "And since I have better magic to cover myself from sights, let me guess… I am the sacrificial pauldrin?"

"As it were, yes. Though, to be clear, I do not want you to die."

"How touching."

You know I love you, Penn.

Do I?

I winked at him, and he rolled his eyes.

"Oh good. I had almost forgotten how *annoying* you two are when blood bonded. Though this will come in handy for communication." Elspeth clapped her hands together, tossing her auburn hair behind her shoulders. "Okay, here's the plan. Penn riles up the colony, rushes toward the main gate. When he gets close enough, he'll cloak himself and maneuver the horse—and himself—out of the line of fire. The guards will lure the hoswisps in the rest of the way once they use magic on them. Voss and I will wait at the north side wall, as that side has the least amount of guard towers. If you don't make it in fifteen minutes, we'll go in without you."

Penn's brows came down. "You do realize if I am late, it probably means I have died?"

"Nonsense. I'll know if something happens to you, because you can tell me." I pointed to my head. "He won't be late, and we're not splitting up now." I narrowed my gaze at Elspeth. "Why would you even suggest something like that?"

She shrugged. "To motivate Penn. He hates being left behind." Elspeth's eyes sparkled with mischief.

I ignored her and focused back on my dark-haired friend. "Are you ready?"

Penn's nervous energy bounced off him in waves. His jaw worked as he looked at the spires of the colony. "You're sure you can cure me if I get stung?"

"Get to the north side before your lungs blacken, and yes, I can. I've done it before." I sat up straighter in my saddle and rolled my shoulders. There was so much anxiety in his mind, I knew there was only one way to get him to refocus. I lowered my voice to one of a haughty royal. "Are you questioning my abilities, Penn?"

"Yes! Of course, I am. Up until a few days ago, you hadn't been able to heal a paper cut properly."

"Fair, but as far as I'm concerned, I'm better than Elspeth now." She snorted.

I nodded at Penn. "We'll see you in fifteen minutes or less."

Penn grumbled to himself. He pulled his horse around as we backed ours up, and he cast a giant wave at the colony. Screams erupted from the nest as he sighed through our bond. It would wear off, but I wondered what Max would do once she discovered she wasn't the only one residing in my head? She had a bit of a jealous streak, after all.

"You're not helping, Voss!" Penn yelled as the horses danced away from the chaotic mess. He maneuvered his mount toward the entrance of my brother's court.

If Leveret were anything like me, my twin would be paranoid enough to realize this was a ploy. As soon as his guards were distracted by the front gate, he would know we were on our way. I had no confidence that this would work to our full advantage, but any edge we gained over my brother would be a win for us.

As Elspeth and I readied our positions, nearing the wall, the swarm of hoswisps chased Penn, following him with bleating howls, raging mewls, and a rampage of feet. This colony seemed particularly angry, which boded well for us. The more time the guards spent engaged with the vermin, the less back up Leveret would have.

How are you doing, Penn?

I am beginning to see why Scarlet tells you to fuck off so much.

Oh, really?

This is not the time, Voss. His frustration dripped off him, seeping into my brain. Penn's focus was on himself and the horse. His magic cloaked him into the surroundings, diverting the guards' attention away from him. The closer his horse raced to the tower, the more his magic pulled against him.

Peel off now, I ordered him, careful not to overstep. The last thing I needed was to send a wave of compulsion toward him.

Except instead of listening to me, Penn pulled up short. The herd was practically nipping at his heels, but he jumped off his mount.

Penn, this wasn't a suicide mission. My heart slammed against my chest.

Same thoughts, Voss. He bent over, grabbed something off the ground, and clambered back onto the horse. The beast panicked and danced, threatening to rear back. Penn snatched hold of the reins and got the horse under control. His mount tore toward us. Fear lit the animal's eyes.

It's nice to know you care, Voss. Penn moved quickly; the horse spurred on by the eminent danger. A few hoswisps followed him, but most stayed the course toward the gate as several guards yelled for back up and shot arrows into the midst. Penn narrowly avoided getting impaled by an arrow, and once he was well out of range, I breathed easier.

The three incoming hoswisps would be the only remaining problem.

"Ditch?" Elspeth asked.

"Seems like the most logical solution. If we bury them alive, there isn't much evidence to show we were here."

Elspeth let out a shudder. "I don't care how mindless and murderous these creatures are. Being buried alive is one of my nightmares."

"Would you prefer we let them inform my brother of our arrival or sting us?"

Penn's horse kept galloping, and he lost his riding form. He hadn't been much for riding when we first came over, and he was hardly any better now. But watching him flop around on top of the mare was ridiculous.

As soon as he was close, I gathered the royal magic around me, ignoring the strain in my neck and the ache in my head that it brought. Elspeth raised her hands. Together, we created a crater behind Penn's horse. The three hoswisps tumbled into the abyss. Elspeth collapsed the sand on top of them. She let out a breath and hopped off her horse. I did the same. Penn's ride pulled up short and bucked him off.

He landed hard on the dirt and glared at the beast, which took off running into the wilds.

"What did you stop for?" My voice came out in a harsh whisper, because I didn't dare scream at him like I wanted to. He had come so close to ending his life, and for what?

He stood up, dusted off his pants, and pulled out a dagger. Not just any dagger—Max's sparrowbone. I swallowed, taking it from him. "This was on the trail?"

Penn nodded, face solemn. "No blood, if that helps any."

I curled my hand around the grip, tightening my fingers so much my knuckles bleached.

"For the record, I hated this plan," Penn added, rubbing his ass. "But we'll save her, Voss." He clapped my shoulder, and his resolve snapped between us.

Pressing my eyes shut, I forced myself steady and slipped her dagger into my belt. She would need it back sooner than later, and I would make sure it reached its rightful owner.

"You're right. We will. And besides, this is the best part of the plan." I pushed air magic around us, lifting the three of us. Penn groaned, still rubbing himself as the earth fell away. I guided us onto the top of the wall, and we jumped down to the other side. It was eerily quiet the moment our feet hit the ground. We listened, but as soon as we were sure no rush of guards was coming, we headed toward my brother's buildings.

The streets here mirrored my father's court, and we cut through them knowing the shortcuts by heart. My brother had fancied himself the rightful heir to the throne. It didn't help that my father gave him full control of our court. The late king had given my twin his knowledge and his toxicity, but the small semblance of hope my father had left, he had given to me.

He intended for me to rule from our birth. It was in our names, after all. Devoss Balgair, the youngest of the family, but given the name worthy of leading. There had been meaning behind our names—Leveret was aware of it and wouldn't let me forget.

Neither would my siblings, which was why they hated me from my birth.

But as the years wore on, my namesake became less important to my father. He was fed up with my inability to become as vicious as he was. He hated my unwillingness to follow his orders. I didn't want to be in charge—I wanted to bring us back to the Faerie of yesteryear. While my siblings bickered over power, I searched for hope. Earth had been a blessing from the Mother, a chance to start over.

And what did we do? We fucked it up.

While Max had assumed it was because of the Fae in general, that's where she had been wrong. No, our rulers put us into this situation. Once we removed my father and siblings, we could turn everyone else around. The higher Fae would take longer, but I knew the Fae—I believed in them. Once they saw how beautiful the possibility was, we could start anew with something true. We could meld forces and create a world we were always supposed to have with beautiful valleys, blissful sunsets, and tranquility.

"You have a lot of work to get to that point, Voss."

I cut a glare at Penn.

"You're practically oozing your thoughts. You okay?"

We leaned around a corner, checking for guards. So far, the streets had been clear. We had crossed through the city, not encountering a single member of my brother's army. The hair on my neck rose from the quiet. Distant shouts and battle cries from the hoswisp fight told me the diversion was still happening. We had time, but likely not much.

"Yes, there's plenty to be done." Starting with saving Max from Leveret. She deserved happiness after everything she had been through—after everything I had put her through. "And I'm fine."

"Sure."

I gritted my jaw and shoved a larger barrier between us.

We ran through a courtyard. Penn and I used magic to cloak us, and we rushed up the stairs into my brother's building. As soon as we opened the doors to the lobby and stepped through the threshold, I froze. Elspeth and Penn came up short next to me.

My eyes landed on my brother, standing tall and regal on the top of the staircase. He wore a pressed tunic and crisp black trousers. His hair, his eyes, everything about him reflected mine, save for the scar running along his face.

I set my jaw and stood up straight. Her scent was *everywhere* in the lobby, but Max was nowhere to be seen. "Where is my wife?" I growled the words and took a step closer.

"Oh, she'll be right down." Leveret's eyes roamed over us. His lips curled in disgust. "You look… terrible."

"Should I have showered before our battle to the death?" I spat the words out.

"There's nothing wrong with being presentable. That was always your problem, Devoss. A whole lot of talk and nothing to back it up."

This again.

"Seeing as how there isn't a single guard here to help you, I could say the same for your level of *defense*." I clenched my fists, keeping my magic tucked away for now. I needed to see Max before I murdered him.

"Clever distraction you made." Leveret let out a tired breath. "But you see, I still have a one up on you, as always."

The elevator next to him dinged. The doors slid open.

And my eyes landed on Max. She stepped out of the elevator and looked at me with widening eyes. Fear slid across her features as she traversed the mezzanine to Leveret. Her hand curled around his chest. Leveret tucked his arm around her, fingers squeezing her waist.

She wore a dress.

My heart broke. This wasn't her. Nothing about her stance said she chose this. But the fear that coated her features, the pain in her eyes, it hollowed out my insides. I had never seen that look on her face. That fear was genuine.

"Are these the people you told me about?" Her voice dropped into a breathy, wavering whisper.

People. My body chilled as I stared at her. She didn't call Fae people. Cold, icy hatred toward my brother tore through my veins, threatening to consume me from the inside out. If I had the ability to make his death last a thousand days, I would.

"What did you do?" My voice shot out. I took a step closer to the stairs. My gaze shifted to my brother.

Max shrunk behind Leveret.

A smile curled his lips. It accentuated the scar covering his cheek. "What you never had the guts to do." His hand cupped her cheek, forcing her to look at him. She put on a pleasant smile. But it never reached her eyes. Her soul wasn't into this. She was clinging to him but dying inside.

My hands curled into fists. Whatever was left of Max's personality was probably screaming, begging to be let out.

"She's better this way. Compliant, easy. I understood why you liked her how she was before—defiant and complicated. She's your type. I never understood the appeal. Perhaps that's the art admirer in you." Leveret's fingers trailed along her skin, and I fought the urge to light him on fire. While our infernos could burn against each other, both of us had royal magic. I needed to play this right. "But I never liked them as mouthy as her, nor did I appreciate how she murdered my furniture. Repeatedly."

I smirked, allowing my nonchalance to surface despite the terror warring in my stomach. I couldn't think about what had happened to her. Instead, I contemplated how to break every single one of the fingers that dared to touch what was mine.

"Just murdered your furniture? You got off easy."

Leveret dropped his hand, curling his fingers into a fist. Only now he turned to look at me in full. His eye was stained red, completely bloodshot and almost black.

"Except maybe not. That makes the dagger to my chest seem tame."

He narrowed his eyes.

Good, I wanted him riled.

Max must have done the damage to his eye before he controlled her. The sparrowbone necklace she kept around hadn't just been for show, except now it was nowhere to be seen. My brother likely hadn't taken kindly to his eye being skewered, but inside, I simmered with pride.

I am cursing the Mother that I have to experience these emotions with you right now. Penn's voice grumbled in my head.

"She and I had a disagreement. Seems she still wanted you alive. But it's fine. She'll learn to love me once you are out of the picture." Leveret's smile did nothing to offset the coldness of his gaze. "Isn't that right, dear?" As soon as his eyes flickered to hers, she nodded enthusiastically. My nails dug into my palms.

"Any love she has toward you would be a facade, much like how you tricked Fae into following you."

"Tricked them? I seem to remember our court willingly leaving you behind."

I snarled. "Because of false pretenses. Nothing you said was ever the truth. What did you promise this time? To become the new royal court? That's not how this works. The *royal court* is the only one."

My brother shook his head. "Promises don't need to be kept." He ran his fingers along her jaw. She swayed toward him. "Besides, it's settled. She wants me now. All I have to do is deal with you. Oh, but first." He smiled at her. "Why don't you allow Devoss a little peek inside your head? It looks like he still thinks there's something he can save."

Max's thoughts flooded my brain in an instant.

Who are these people? Are they going to kill us? I am so scared. Devoss is the evil twin. He looks scary. Why is he looking at me like that? He doesn't know who I am. There's so much hatred in his eyes. I can see why Leveret warned me about him. Leveret needs to be in charge. He's so nice and admirable. He's going to take our kingdom into a new world. Oh, but I hope there isn't too much blood.

Voss. Penn's voice calmed me amid the storm of her emotions. *This isn't her. Block her out. Shut it down.*

I loved hearing her voice, but Penn was right. These weren't *her* thoughts. They were Leveret's—poisonous and stinging. It was a ploy. He wanted to give me a disadvantage, like she had given to him with the attack on his eye. I knew that, because in the whirlwind of her thoughts was the memory of the attack. Max *apologized* to him afterward for hurting him.

Little fox, come back to me, I pressed the plea into her head, but cut off our connection so I wouldn't have to hear any more.

"What do you want, Leveret?"

"I want a fair fight. It was clever, making my guards deal with the hoswisp swarm, I admit. But it's not fair to have three against one. Command the two of them to stay back and not get involved in the fight, and the two of us will battle it out once and for all."

Max clutched her hands into the fabric of his shirt. "But darling, so soon after the accident?"

"I'll be fine. Why don't you wait for me on the sidelines? I won't be long."

I glanced at Penn. *Do you see a way out of this?*

If you don't do it, he'll compel us to. At least this way you can add your own underlying commands to the magic.

I looked toward Elspeth. Her lips were pressed into a thin line. She looked me over and nodded. "End this."

"Your guards and allies cannot interfere, and neither can Elspeth nor Penn. We battle until one of us concedes or dies. Are these terms agreeable?"

"Deal," Leveret said as the magic of the deal coiled around us. It pulsed throughout the lobby, weaving into the court.

Max sank onto one stair as Leveret marched down the flight. Her cool blue eyes were on me. The disdain etched across her face made me think of our first meeting in the alley.

I longed for the days where she threatened to put a knife into my chest.

"When this is over, little fox, we're going to talk about your aim. You couldn't have taken out both?"

Her head tilted to the side. The skin around her eyes crinkled with an indistinguishable emotion. Red colored her cheeks. Embarrassment. From Max.

"Yes, I'll be sure to talk to her about that." Leveret's magic coiled up his arm, ready for the fight. "Tell them to back up."

"Give us the floor," I commanded. Penn knew the underlying meaning. If there was a chance to get Max free, he would take it. He could stay out of the fight, but by removing the Fae Slayer from my brother's court, we would at least prevent one part of the prophecy. I had to hope whatever we did next would work.

Leveret's lip curled in a predatory smile as he slammed his fist down. His magic opened a chasm in the floor underneath me.

SCARLET

ittle fox. The words bounced around my head with an echo. His twin's voice shattered something within me. The sound of him etched into my soul, creating a sense of longing and loneliness which threatened to collapse me from the inside out. Desire and promises of things that used to be edged his words.

But none of those thoughts could be right. I didn't remember anything about this Fae. Once I had separated from the revolutionaries, my rage and blood lust had overtaken me. I succumbed to my ideas of vengeance until there was barely anything recognizable about me left. Something about the story didn't sit right. I hadn't killed without reason, had I?

"Deal," Leveret said. The searing sting of magic coiled around the lobby, pressing against the walls and reverberating off every surface. It tasted like ash.

Why did everything with him taste like ash?

I sank onto the top steps as Leveret walked down the remaining stairs to meet his twin. I hadn't been paying attention. It felt like a fog had overwhelmed my body. What had they agreed to?

"When this is over, little fox, we're going to talk about your aim. You couldn't have taken out both?" Devoss's eyes glittered, dark amber pools searing straight into me. There was teasing behind his words, and his voice coiled around my skin like liquid fire. It felt warm; it felt like home.

If I had never met him before, why was he so familiar?

This must be a trick. Leveret told me Devoss liked to trick people, make people believe he had their best intentions at heart. Once he convinced them he was good-natured, he would pull the rug out from under them, change everything about himself and his morals. He relied on complacency.

I stiffened as Leveret's feet landed on the lobby floor. His magic wrapped around him and again, the taste of ash coated my tongue as he launched his first attack. His fist thrust into the ground, and the bottom floor thundered. The lobby split apart at the seams, creating a chasm Devoss had to leap across to keep his footing. Leveret sent another wave of magic whipping toward his brother. This time, the room crackled with lightning.

Devoss tossed a hand up, redirecting the bolt. It pierced a pillar. Without waiting a breath, Leveret growled and tossed another wave at Devoss. The water hit him dead in the chest but turned to steam that shot back toward Leveret.

Leveret screamed as the heat curled around his flesh, melting him. He smelled like burnt oranges, and I wrinkled my nose. He would be fine. From the stories he had told me last night, I knew Leveret had put up with worse from his younger twin. He had always survived.

But if I was so in love with Leveret, why was I not more worried?

Surely, I should be worried. Surely, I should care more about being his little rabbit?

I had never felt like a rabbit.

I had always felt like a predator.

I felt like a fox.

Little fox, come back to me.

Leveret snarled, causing another quake. The ceiling split. A large slab of concrete came down, but Devoss used his magic to splinter it apart. Shrapnel went everywhere, hurdling straight toward me.

Before I could suck in a gasp of surprise, Penn pulled me backward and across the landing, giving us plenty of space between the battle below.

I let out a yelp, but neither of the two fighting men heard me.

"Scarlet, we need to talk." His hand clamped around my mouth. He smelled like the ocean and tasted like salt spray. There was something familiar about that, too. "You need to break through whatever hold Leveret put on you. I'm going to let go of your mouth, but if you scream, I will have to silence you. I don't want to. Understand?"

He said the words, but they held none of the venom I expected from the three horrible people Leveret claimed would come to our court. The woman—Elspeth—watched everything with wide, watery eyes as worry etched her brow.

Evilness didn't feel fear, so why did she?

I had seen true evil. Hadn't I?

Penn dropped his hand from my mouth. He whirled me so I was facing him. Leveret's and Devoss's fire magic met in the middle of the space. Heat washed over us. The last thing I saw was a rising pillar of flames before I set my eyes on the deepest turquoise eyes I had ever seen.

"Why do I feel like… I've seen you before?" I asked.

Little fox echoed through my head.

"Because you have. I know what's happening right now is confusing, but Leveret used compulsion on you."

I scrambled to open the space between us, steadying myself on my feet as one man below screamed. I didn't know who was hurt, but I wasn't about to tear my eyes away from this Fae.

"And why should I believe you?" Crossing my arms over my chest, I narrowed my gaze. "I don't *know* you."

Penn sighed. "You are still the same, even when you're not." He searched my eyes. "What do you feel toward Leveret? If he wins, what's there?"

Little rabbit. An ache stabbed me in the gut. I would always be his, right? His helpless little rabbit. His to do whatever he wanted to, because he held my heart.

"Scarlet?"

I frowned. "It's just Maxine now."

He shook his head, lips parting downward. "It's not, though. It's Max. You've never been called Maxine, not by those who know you." Penn took a step closer to me. "But to most of us, you are still Scarlet the Fae Slayer. You blame yourself for your family's death, even though it happened because of the royal family. They did this to you. They put you here. Leveret is part of that."

Pressing my hands to my ears, I fought against the well of nausea creeping up my throat. "Leveret didn't kill my brother…"

He hadn't been there that day. After my family died, my brain got messed up. I went on a revenge plot with the revolutionaries and ended up killing a lot of Fae. It must have been insanpheria or something, because Leveret *saved* me from myself. I had left my thoughts of revenge behind because of him. But…

Little fox.

Come back to me.

I could say no to Leveret, right? He was the one who gave me the space to find myself. He knew what was best for me. Leveret had healed my emotional scars. He had shown me there was more to life than killing. As the rightful heir, Leveret would lead us into a new era.

I had to trust him.

But I couldn't say no.

I wasn't allowed to. But I could say no before. With a word... with... *switch*.

Because...

Little fox.

Come back to me.

Switch.

I clutched the sides of my hair, pulling the strands away from my scalp. It felt as if my insides were exploding. My memories and thoughts swirled together in a hellish whirlwind. There was heat, anger, and pain. It shook throughout my core.

"Penn," a soothing feminine voice called. I glanced up to see Elspeth next to him. She had curled her hand over his shoulder. Her gorgeous red-tinted hair cascaded in waves around her shoulders. Despite how beautiful she was, I didn't feel any jealousy toward her. That was strange. Didn't I envy most Fae for how effortlessly stunning they were? "Don't push her right now."

"But she can stop this. The deal is that *we* cannot get involved, and neither can his guards. She can do whatever she wants."

I could stop this?

My eyes roamed over the destruction in the lobby. Shattered glass and concrete littered the floor. Tiles were smashed. Wood smoldered from the heat of their magic. A hazy smoke filled the air, covering my skin just like Leveret's magic. The two of them grappled together, both bleeding. It was easy to tell them apart because they moved so differently.

Leveret was all-commanding, never bending and unwilling to let Devoss get the better of him. Devoss was angles and fluid motion. He was hard edges and glorious plains.

I narrowed my gaze, because that was weird. I was *admiring* this Fae. This male who came in here and threatened to destroy everything Leveret had worked for. My gaze raked over his body. His jaw was set, pulsing as blood dripped from his nose. Fire blazed in his eyes as his blond hair wafted in their magic's updraft.

These two were in a fight. While I should be worried about Leveret and my heart should be looking to him, I sought his twin. I blinked, staring at the two of them in battle.

Devoss's eyes left his brother for a second. Just a moment, and our gazes locked. A void opened inside me and wrenched me back from the abyss. Words I could never forget because they were placed alongside my soul, deeper and more commanding than anything else.

You will come back to me. Now and always.

I rose, feeling dark ice roll through my veins.

"Scarlet?"

I shoved down every emotion I had. Because only one of them could walk out of this, and I had decided which one I wanted. There was only one way to end this, and the path became clear before me. It always had been. We would rule together. I would be his queen, as I was always meant to be.

Leveret screamed as Voss cracked one of his fingers backward.

"Stop!" I yelled, rushing toward them. I raced through the debris, hiking up my skirts.

Yanking Leveret out of Voss's grasp, I stared at the Fae. "I understand why you are so angry, Devoss. I understand the sibling rivalry. I understand you believe you have some entitlement or right to me, but Leveret showed me a softer side of myself. I need him now. And I don't want you to hold it against us that your little fox switched sides."

Voss stared at me. He blinked and licked his lips. A sigh escaped him. "It looks like you won." His gaze flickered to his brother. "There's no point in fighting if I cannot get her back." He pulled out a sparrowbone dagger and handed it to me, handle first. "I will let you do the honors, as I'd rather my life be taken by someone who once knew all of me than someone who never knew me at all."

His dark eyes stayed glued to mine as I took the dagger from his hand. My fingers shook around the hilt.

"Thank you for understanding," my voice was barely more than a whisper.

Leveret chuckled. "This will be fun to watch."

"I couldn't agree more."

Twelve

VOSS

"Stop!" Max's voice rang out over the space as I cracked one of Leveret's fingers all the way back. She rushed for us, dress pulled up around her thighs as she trampled down the stairs. Yanking Leveret out of my grasp, she took a defensive stance between us. Defending *him* from me.

She snarled as she looked at me. "I understand why you are so angry, Devoss. I understand the sibling rivalry. I understand you believe you have some entitlement or right to me, but Leveret showed me a softer side of myself. I need him now. And I don't want you to hold it against us that your *little fox switched* sides."

I blinked, staring at her for a moment. The block was still up between us. I couldn't discern what was true anymore, but I decided it no longer mattered as I licked my lips. I sighed. "It looks like you won." I shifted my gaze to my brother. "There's no point in fighting if I cannot get her back." I unsheathed Max's sparrowbone dagger and offered it to her. "I will let you do the honors, as I'd rather my life be taken by someone who once knew all of me than someone who never knew me at all."

My eyes shifted back to her and stayed there, hoping I hadn't made a mistake as both Penn and Elspeth sucked in a breath.

"Thank you for understanding," she said as she wrapped her fingers around the handle. There was a tremor in her hand that would haunt me for the rest of my days.

Leveret chuckled. "This will be fun to watch."

"I couldn't agree more," Max smirked. She whirled around and plunged the dagger into my brother's neck, screaming as she brought it down over and over again. Tears spilled from her eyes as red splattered her body. My brother was dead before he hit the ground, and her thoughts cascaded back into my head.

All at once, she recognized who she was, Leveret's compulsion gone with his death. But it was jumbled, mixed together, and she hated it. She hated herself. The tears didn't stop, and she was gasping for breath even as she continued stabbing him. Anger filled her veins—frustration at not being able to stop him sooner, rage at me for not reaching her before it got this far.

And I deserved it.

I coiled my arms around her. "Little fox."

She dropped the dagger. It clanged to the floor, echoing hollowly in the smoldering destruction around us. Her nails dug into my arms. "Voss."

"You're okay. I have you." I ran my fingers through her hair, turning her gently toward me. Blood freckled her skin.

"I'm not okay." She looked at me, and the depth of her blue eyes showed absolute horror. Watery film covered them. "I will never be okay. What happened… What he…"

I searched her memories. Relief at knowing she was physically okay was brief, because her mental side tormented her. Her mind was cluttered, with every thought begging to be felt at the same time. I searched her eyes with mine. "I would like to compel you this one time. Just this once, so you can get some rest while we get out of here and clean up. Is that okay?"

She blinked at me. Fat tears ran down her cheeks, and I brushed them off with my thumb. She nodded, choking on her next words. "I trust you." Despite her anger and frustration, those words were true. I wasn't sure I deserved them.

I hadn't seen her cry before. If my brother hadn't already been dead at her feet, this would have been a motive for me to turn him inside out. I pressed a kiss to her forehead. She leaned into me. Her breath came in harsh, angry spurts.

"*Sleep, little fox. I'll wake you up soon.*" With my arms firmly around her, she collapsed into them, blood splattered clothes and all. I let out a shaking breath, running my hand across her forehead and pushing her hair behind her ears. She looked more peaceful like this, and I hoped it would bring some small comfort to know she was safe. I pressed my nose into the curve of her neck. She was alive.

We'd be okay.

"I thought she was going to kill you," Penn said, coming down the steps now that the deal had been dissolved.

Clutching her to my chest, I rose, whirling toward the guards. They had shown up, but not on time.

"Back!" I shouted, pushing coercion into my magic. They had been attempting to breach the lobby. "You will let us leave with no negative recourse. And you—" I looked at one of the female guards. "We have two horses in the wilds—three, if you can find the last one. Fetch them, give them a good home here, but take our items and saddle three fresh horses so we can leave."

The Fae nodded and scrambled to comply.

Elspeth placed her hands on Max's body. Her eyes swirled as she searched for injury. "There's nothing I can heal, it's all… inside her mind."

I nodded, lips pressed taut.

"That was tough."

"You felt it too?" I glanced at Penn, fighting my welling rage.

"It was intense. It was like she flooded your mind on overdrive. She… remembered herself all in one go."

"What I don't understand is how she did it." Elspeth looked at us.

The guards shuffled outside, talking to one another, but I ignored them. They could wait endlessly for all I cared. My magic felt fuller now that my brother's corpse cooled on the floor. Max curled farther into me, and I held her close.

It was a relief. With my family dead, no one could rapidly replace me with a rise to power. If I died, it would be a gamble who became the next in charge, and most Fae wouldn't risk it. It made me breathe easier about leaving the royal court unattended. I had few friends there—Lylle and several other guards—but now that I was alive had had better access to the royal magic, I could face whatever happened next.

"Max buried herself behind two words. I felt it when the dam ripped open. *Little fox.* A nickname Leveret knew nothing about. She tied everything to that."

She tied everything to me. One of the reasons she felt so angry was because she had needed me—needed my voice to guide her back from the abyss. She had never depended on someone else like that, not since she was a child. That helplessness she felt fueled the burning frustration inside her.

"And when she heard you say little fox, it cracked the dam," Elspeth hummed.

I nodded. "It was the catalyst. Something Leveret would never call her, but *I* would."

"That kind of magic should not be possible."

"I'm beginning to think it's not magic… it is simply her. She's part of the prophecy for a reason." I pressed my lips against her forehead again, savoring having her in my arms. There was a lot to sort out between us, plenty I was sorry for—which was a new feeling for me. I had regrets, and most stemmed from letting her out of my sight. A mistake I wouldn't make again.

My little fox had proved herself capable, even when faced with the impossible. I was in awe of her, and I hoped she would get the time she needed to heal.

As soon as I could, I would provide whatever she wanted. If she never wanted to see the royal court again, done. I would give her my heart, my love, my endless devotion. If she needed me to grovel at her feet, I would do so. There would be cracks that needed time to heal, but as long as I had her back in my life, it would be enough. I would accept whatever happened, and whoever she became now because of it.

"The horses are ready, sir."

"That was fast."

"Seems someone had found the horses and brought them in, so it was a matter of securing your saddlebags and placing them on new mounts." The female guard gave me a wide smile. "I hope you have safe travels back to the royal court, Your Highness."

"Are you well liked in this court?"

"Sir?" She blinked at me.

"Seems I am in need of someone to watch over things while I am gone. You understand the missives?"

"And the consequences, sir." She nodded so rapidly her blond hair brushed the dust from the wilds off her shoulders.

"Excellent. Make a team of Fae guards you trust. You are in

charge until I can return with a better plan. You are to remain neutral in any upcoming altercations unless I call on you. Understood?"

She swallowed. "Whatever you need, sir. It's good to have you back in court." Taking a step toward me, she lowered her voice. "Plenty of us were sick of Leveret being in charge and hated it when your father stripped you of your title. It's good to see you back."

I breathed out. "Thank you."

My magic prodded her mind and felt nothing but sincerity. She was loyal to me, but she had wished I had fought harder to take leadership back from my brother. Ah, well, there was no going against my father until it was absolutely necessary. I had needed to play along as the subservient assassin until the timing was right.

"Everyone else, move back. Give us space," I thrust my magic at them as a command.

The guards collectively took a step backward, opening a wide corridor for us to pass through.

"Anyone else think this is eerie?" Penn whispered.

"Of course it is, but we have other things to worry about right now," Elspeth snapped at Penn.

She's testy.

She hates not being able to heal things, I told him.

"I hate you *thinking* about me like I am not here." She tossed up her hands and marched to the nearest horse, pulling herself on top of it in a swift motion. Her eyes cut through the Fae around us, and they looked sheepishly away.

Without discussing it, I handed Max to Penn. He held her as I got comfortable in my saddle, and he passed her up to me. "Yes, Penn, I know she's adorable when she sleeps. But she's a vicious little fox, and you shouldn't forget it."

He held his hands up. "Not my type, Voss. But yes, she looks… peaceful."

Good. I had placed a feeling of serenity into my magic, and I was glad it had worked. As much as I wanted to wake her up right now, to prove to myself she was still here, I allowed her this. Her dreams blanketed her mind like an early morning fog, covering the earth with the promise of a new dawn. I couldn't ruin what she felt right now.

We started back the way we had come, heading straight toward Alpin's court for a pit stop for rest before going back to the royal court. Once we arrived at the royal court, there would be much to accomplish. Whatever the consequences were for my departure, it would be worth it.

I finally had her back in my arms.

Nothing else mattered.

SCARLET

The darkness was warm and comforting. It was quiet. I nestled in the delicate space, savoring how none of the ash-riddled magic was in my system any longer. It took me a while to blink away, and longer to figure out where I was. The ceiling was arched, and the bed was gloriously cushy. I sat upright, glancing around the bedroom. It was the third-floor suite with the tub where Voss and I...

We were inside Alpin's court.

And I had been asleep for the trip here.

I glanced down at my clothes. Not a dress, but airy pants and a flowing shirt. Narrowing my gaze, I shifted my hand to investigate my underwear. A wadded-up rag was balled against me.

Well, that was fucking embarrassing. It was also kind of adorable that the Fae I was traveling with had no idea how to handle this kind of thing, because the sheer amount of material between my thighs was enough to dry out a waterfall.

Letting out a long sigh, I pressed my eyelids shut and recalled a few things from the past… how long had it been? Voss's lips had been on my cheek as he murmured, *"Wake up whenever you are ready."* I had no idea how much time had passed, but my stomach growled.

The room was now empty, and it was nice to have a moment alone with my whirling thoughts. It was overwhelming to parse through what had been real and what hadn't been. When I knew Leveret was going to take over my mind, I had buried everything Voss meant to me behind his nickname for me. It had felt like ripping a part of my soul off and stuffing it into a blender, but somehow, it had worked.

When he called me *little fox*, the memories had opened, flooding my head with nonsense that had been impossible to sort through. Which had been for the best, because if Leveret could have sensed anything from my thoughts *after* I had realized how much I wanted to kill him, my plan would have been ruined.

And after that…

Voss. He looked so much like *him;* it had terrified part of me. He had asked for my permission to remove the fear, the frustration, the anger, even if just for a moment. I had been desperate for an escape, so I allowed him to. A part of me wished I had been stronger, and I hated how I wasn't able to emotionally overcome Leveret's compulsion on my own.

I swallowed, not wanting to face this new reality. I felt hollow. The vengeance that had fueled me through the whole damn apocalypse was gone. Missing. Left behind was a hollow echo of anger directed at myself. As much as I wanted to blame Voss for what happened after we were separated, I had gotten myself into this mess. My need for revenge was so great, I ignored everything else. And now? Now, the thought of killing more Fae made my stomach roil. The world wasn't black and white. There were shades of grey.

And I had chosen Voss.

Leveret was horrific once I drove him to have no other options. He hadn't treated his humans very well, but he was no Namir. Maybe he could have been saved. But I had made my choice, and I realized I would always choose Voss. Over everyone else.

The certainty of that settled into my bones, along with a deep-seated anger at him for letting me go in the first place. I didn't want to kill him anymore. Maybe stab him in the chest for all the shit I went through, but I didn't want Voss dead.

Voss chuckled inside my head. *I knew one of these days it would come to pass.*

Voss.

Hello, little fox.

Where are you?

I could sense your unease about seeing my face. Which I understand, as what my brother did… it is unforgivable. I promise to help you work through it, if you'll let me. But for now, I am sending Penn up with a tray of food. Does that sound good?

You don't need to tiptoe around me.

Gruff silence met me on the other end for a moment. I had to prod at him to make sure he was still there. *I promise to work on myself, if you promise to work on you,* he said.

I swallowed, not sure what that looked like yet. There were too many things jumbled up inside my head, so many feelings. I wanted to be near him, to touch him, to taste him. But seeing him… the face I wished so desperately to forget. It was… hard.

I'm sorry.

Did you just… apologize? That was strange. I hadn't even needed to stab him for it.

Yes. Voss's hesitation struck straight into my soul. *I never wanted you to feel this way, and I hate it. I feel powerless to fix this, and that is not a normal feeling for me.*

I clenched my fists together, because this *sucked*. We should be celebrating being united, not shying away from it, but Leveret's face was plastered across my memories. I grit my teeth together. *I'm not giving up on us. I refuse.* Tears stung my eyes, but I didn't allow them to fall.

The door opened at the bottom of the stairs.

Me neither, little fox. But you need time to heal, and I will give you whatever you need. Go easy on Penn. I can't stand the thought of you being alone right now.

"Please tell me she dressed you in something appropriate?" Penn's voice arched up the stairwell.

Rolling my eyes, I pulled the blankets up higher, not wanting to admit how *safe* I felt hearing his voice. This was real. It had happened. They *saved* me. I hated how I needed saving.

"You're good, Penn," I called out. My voice was hoarse, as if I had spent the night screaming.

Penn let out an audible sigh as he crested the stairs. His turquoise eyes roamed over me as a frown tilted down his lips. "I was going to say some quip about how I won't play babysitter all the time, but you really aren't doing well."

"No shit." I ran my hand through my hair and glared at the Fae. "Why is Voss sticking us together?"

He shrugged as he placed the tray of food down on my knees. My mouth watered from the smells. I leaned over it, ready to grab the utensils as he snatched the knife off the plate.

I arched an eyebrow at him. "You know, I might threaten dismembering, but I don't actually mean it."

"Well, we'll see how you feel when you realize I had to blood bond with your husband when you were indisposed."

Heat clawed up my spine.

Penn held out his hands. "He smelled your blood. He thought Leveret had been killing you, but... turns out humans are just gross."

I snorted and leaned back. "This is a perfectly natural bodily function." It didn't leave my notice what he said. Voss had been worried about me.

Of course, I was. His voice rumbled deep inside me.

"Fae control that with their magic, but you... you just like... every month? Like that?"

"Penn?"

"Yeah?"

"I'm going to need you to shut the fuck up and focus on the important part of this conversation. You *blood bonded* with Voss?"

Penn rubbed the back of his head, making his dark locks stick out at odd angles. The bags under his eyes told me more than he ever could. "When he thought you were bleeding because of Leveret, he lost his mind. Almost burned down an inn, which we still have to pay for repairs on."

"Penn," I growled, trying to make him concentrate.

He let out a sigh. "I had to go inside his head to break him out. I think he's worried that if you hear me inside his mind, you'll want to shank me. Also, he believes you don't want to see his face, what with... you know."

"And he doesn't think I'll shank you anyway?" I glanced around.

"Your sparrowbone is in the nightstand, and I'm only telling you that because you just promised *not* to stab me."

"I made no such promise," I huffed.

"How was it then? You don't actually want to dismember me?" Penn sank onto a chair and eyed me warily. "How are you feeling?"

I let out a breath. "Honestly?"

Penn nodded.

"I feel like shanking you will make me feel better." I wrestled the tray of food into my lap and took in the array. There was meat, vegetables, flat bread, and… Sucking in a breath, I glanced up at Penn. "Is this butter?" I didn't let him answer before slathering the bread in it. I had to use the fork to do so, since he stole my knife, but I didn't care. It was heaven melting on my tongue as I inhaled the flavors.

"Scarlet," Penn pressed.

I hummed, because *nothing* was going to destroy the flavor of the butter I was eating. Real butter. I didn't know how someone kept a cow alive, and frankly, I didn't care.

"How are you feeling, really?"

"Like shit. Happy?" I sucked the last bit off my fingers and stared at him. "Is that what you want to hear? I feel like garbage. Someone got the better of me. I hate how hard it was to push him out of my head—to *feel* like myself again. I hated being turned into someone I wasn't. It felt like being trapped. It was—" Like being stuck inside the pantry again.

My list of shortcomings flooded my brain. I regretted not being able to save Anya. I should have been able to kill Leveret at the beginning. His eyeball would have looked better if I had scooped it out of his head. But now the necklace—the last piece of my friends I had with me—was gone. Destroyed by the male who forced me to obey him. And when I thought about Voss's face…

No, I growled at myself. Because I was not letting that male destroy the best thing in my life.

"Penn, be honest. Why is Voss not talking to me in here?" I pointed to my head. I could feel him, but he was staying quiet, which was unusual for him.

"He wanted to give you time. In case…"

"They didn't sound alike." I picked up the fork and stabbed it into a piece of meat. It smelled gamy and rich. "And their smells were vastly different. I wouldn't confuse that."

Penn wrinkled his nose. "What do you mean, their *smells*?"

"Fae have… a smell to them," I shrugged, because their scents had been one of the ways I had identified Fae during my life. They smelled, sounded, and tasted distinct.

"Like all Fae have a smell in general?" Penn leaned forward, as if I were saying something mind blowing.

"No. You smell like the ocean—salty air, specifically. Voss is like candied ginger. His brother was like… It was like standing in a smokehouse full of burnt oranges."

"That's… not normal." Penn frowned. The lines under his eyes grew more pronounced as he looked inward. "Voss agrees, but everything we're learning about you makes us think there was more to the prophecy than any of us ever realized."

Wow, it was annoying watching two people have a conversation when you weren't a part of it. I filed that information away for the future.

"Leveret thought that too. I can't remember exactly what he said, but it was like we were supposed to change the world together?" I shook my head and pressed my eyes shut. Whenever I tried to latch onto my memories from that time, a pulse pounded through my mind. Voss's evil twin had done wonders to my brain.

"Don't push yourself too hard. It's okay."

"Is it?" I opened my eyes and stared at him.

Penn cleared his throat. "It's hard to explain, but I can feel a lot of what you are experiencing right now. It's filtered through Voss, but yes, I can say it will be okay. You're stronger than you realize, Scarlet. You'll get through this."

Tears brimmed in my eyes. "I don't want to get through it." I shoved the meat into my mouth and hefted the tray onto the bedside table. Barely chewing, I continued, "I don't want to be strong. It was awful, and I don't want to remember it."

"He could make you forget, if you wanted. But none of that would be real, Scarlet. Forgetting doesn't make the emotional side disappear." Penn placed his hand on top of mine. I stared at his fingers. He continued, "You broke through Leveret's compulsion because you didn't bury yourself when you suppressed your memories."

"What if I want to bury all of it?" I took my hand back and pulled my knees to my chest. All this fighting had brought me here—to a place where I needed to *recover*. A pang welled up in my heart, because I hated how I had gotten here. I hated how I couldn't look at the face of the male that I—

I cut the words off.

Little fox, were you about to say you love me?

I was not about to say anything, Voss.

Oh, there are plenty of things you're saying inside your mind. Actually, it's more like your thoughts are screaming. What can I do to help?

You'll give me anything?

Anything. Voss paused.

During the pause, Penn's face sank, and a frown marred the dark-haired Fae's lips.

Voss sighed, but I could feel the smile curling on his lips. *We are not stabbing Penn.*

"Why does it always turn toward violence against me?" Penn glared at me.

"I like how you can hear us." A giggle escaped me.

"I hate it. Personally, I want out."

"Why did you do it, then? Why not Elspeth?"

Penn let out a breath. He squinted. "Maybe you're not yet aware of this, but Voss and I have a history. It would have never worked in the long run, because Voss is... well, I'm not interested in the chaos that comes with being with him, and frankly, I am too boring to entertain him. You, however, are his perfect match. Volatile, reckless, impulsive, angry, brash—"

"Is this supposed to make me feel better?"

"—while also having endless amounts of patience and hope." Penn chuckled. "You've made him the happiest I've seen in decades."

How was it possible to hear this and still need more reassurance? My hope had died the moment Marcy turned away from me and toward a Fae for comfort. I destroyed every bridge I had ever created. How could Voss be any different?

"Wait, what happened to Cumina and Morna?"

Penn shrugged. "We're not sure. We didn't run into them during our travels, but that means nothing."

"Leveret sent them away from his court under compulsion. You don't think they are still—"

"Wandering the wilds endlessly? No, it wears off on Fae without reinforcement. The royal magic only goes so far. Plus, Leveret was at half-strength."

"Which means Voss is at full strength now?"

"Not… exactly." Penn let out a breath. He scooted his chair closer to the bed. Using his fingers, he plucked a piece of meat and popped it into his mouth.

I glared at him and took the tray back, finally eating again. It was a rotten trick, taking something away from me only to make me want it, but he looked satisfied as he sat back and eyed me. No doubt that had been Voss's idea.

"Because of the prophecy, your marriage, and the blood bond, we think he won't be at full power until you become Blood Queen."

"Which I can do without killing him?"

Penn's expression turned serious; his lips pressed into a thin line.

"You can bring him back, yes, but you have to want it. For the record, I think it's a bad idea."

It's a great idea.

"No, it's a *terrible* idea," Penn answered.

"How long are you going to be blood bonded to him?"

"Probably a few days."

"It's going to get real awkward once my period is over then, huh?"

Oh, we don't have to wait for that, little fox. Just say the word.

Penn ignored both of us. "When your body is flooded with the royal power, there's still a chance you'll turn against Voss. It wouldn't be your fault, because magic runs on instincts. Yours have told you to hate us your entire life. And while you've gotten to know us, and Voss believes you've changed, you could still… well, fail at bringing him back."

"How? Leveret made it seem like a for sure thing."

"Bringing someone back from the brick of death… it's hard, nearly impossible. If you truly love Voss, your magic will want to bind with him and bring him back, but if you don't, then…" Penn waved his hands, but the look on his brow told me there was plenty he wasn't saying. "Anyway, I'm hoping that from your travels and seeing Alpin's court—"

I sucked in a breath, remembering that my friends should be inside this court. With any luck, I could find them, assuming they made it. "Sorry, continue."

Penn shook his head. "My point is, we're not monsters—not all of us. We will make this better."

"But it doesn't have to just be us fighting for change, right? We could… recruit others?"

"So you become Blood Queen, and instead of ruling with Voss, you—what?"

I shrugged. I didn't know what came after that, but why did it have to be the king and queen in charge? Why not someone else? Maybe the humans, or maybe a group of people. I could become Blood Queen, and we could both give up the throne. Move on.

"I don't know if I want to become Blood Queen. If Voss's missives don't work and the Fae don't change—" Plenty of them hadn't already. I had seen enough of the royal courts to know most were not falling in line. "—then drastic measures need to be taken."

"The revolution."

My stomach roiled at the thought of another bloody battle, another war. I shook my head. Leveret had messed me up. I needed time to get over what happened, but the thought of losing more people—the thought of losing Voss—made my world tilt sideways. Having the Fae be in charge might not be the solution we needed, but... maybe it was the only way to keep Voss.

"The revolution." I nodded, eating a few vegetables. They soured in my stomach. How many more people had to die? I slammed my eyes shut.

Little fox. Let those thoughts go. They aren't yours.

It's gotten so messy in here.

Complicated is okay. Messy is fine. We'll sort through it. You need to give it time.

Time we don't have. Voss... what happens when the civil war starts? It will start. It's only a matter of time.

I will see what I can do to prevent such things, but you need time to repair yourself. You can't fix a broken kingdom when you're still mending a broken heart.

And what are you going to do while I mend?

Help you, if you'll let me. There was a sly hint behind his words, a nervous energy behind them that let me know more than he was telling me.

"Penn?"

"Sorry, I was trying not to… gag."

"You said Voss lost his mind for a bit, when he thought Leveret might have made me bleed. What did he feel when he saw me in the court lobby?"

Penn's eyes swirled. "The depth of his soul had never experienced that kind of hell."

Sounds like you need to heal too, Voss.

The world needs it more than I do.

You can't fix a broken kingdom—

Little fox. If you use my words against me, I will stuff my cock so far down your throat—

Don't threaten me with a good time, Voss.

I hate both of you so much right now. Penn's voice.

I blinked, rearing back. "How did you—"

Penn arched an eyebrow. "You both went too far into his mind, which is where I am." He let out a breath. "Are you feeling better?"

"A bit, yeah."

"Good. I have other things I need to do, and I truly cannot be part of this conversation anymore. Do you want Elspeth to keep you company, or should I send Voss in?"

I chewed on my lower lip. I had to get over Voss's resemblance to Leveret. Like he said, we had to fix ourselves. If we had any hope of changing the world, it needed to start with us.

Plus, I missed him.

Maybe if I stabbed him, I would get out my unresolved feelings. It would certainly help calm the anger I had inside me.

"Yeah, send him in." I didn't get to finish the words before the door below the staircase opened. Voss hadn't gone far after all.

He climbed the stairs, and when his dark eyes met mine, a bolt of lightning shot through me. "Are you sure, little fox?" The sorrowful depth in his gaze was enough to make my eyes brim with tears.

"I'm going to drown myself in beer, so I don't have to bear witness to whatever is going to happen next."

"Build up your walls, Penn." Voss moved to the side so his friend could slip down the stairs. His eyes stayed on me. "Hi."

"Hi."

I had missed him so much, and yet, looking at him was shattering my soul into a million pieces. I clenched my jaw, raised my chin, and refused to glance away, because we *would* fix this.

VOSS

Her stare turned into a glare of defiance and determination, despite the heartbreak swelling inside her chest. The pain tearing through her was almost too much for me to endure, but I would. I had to. For her.

The door below closed as Penn headed into the hallway. His thoughts whirled as well, but I was glad none of them involved jealousy. We were truly friends—the best of—and he wanted nothing more than my happiness. And hers, which was strange considering how often she threatened to stab him.

I let out a breath as I watched her. She plucked at the food in front of her, but her eyes continued to sweep over me. Despite the way she was approaching this, I felt how unsettled her mind was. She was safe; she knew that, but my face… Max needed time to heal, and I wasn't sure how much we had.

"I have an idea."

"Does it involve your blood?" Max pressed her eyes shut and

131

shook her head, eyes drifting to her food now. The words escaped her lips on instinct, a defense against the rest of the world. If she placed herself at a distance from everyone else, she couldn't get hurt.

But she had been hurt, anyway.

I wanted to bring my brother back so I could kill him myself, but I was glad she ended him. Perhaps it would provide her closure over time.

"Only if you want it to," I offered.

As she stabbed through a few vegetables and shoved them into her mouth, she sighed. I waited as she ate. She picked at her plate more than anything.

"I wanted to kill you for a long time," she finally broke our silence.

"I know."

"And I wanted to become Blood Queen so you would die—so the royal line would be dead." Her brows furrowed, but her blue eyes stayed on the tray. Her fingers curled into fists.

"I know."

"And your sisters—"

"I know all of it, Max. And it's okay."

She glared at me, a little spark of the fire before the fear welled inside her. And then frustration that she had to carry this new myriad of emotions.

Using her name unsettled her, proved she belonged to me. A part of her was frustrated that such a statement was true. But there was another part that was grateful for it. I would never give up on this, because she would heal.

I ran my tongue over my teeth, debating my next words. "I don't care that you plotted to kill me, as I certainly gave you enough reason to. You are subject to your emotions and feelings without anyone interfering with them, and I'm sorry for what my brother did."

Her jaw worked as she shoved a piece of meat into her mouth. Anger flashed through her eyes as they glossed over. She went back to that place, into the darkness where his words and nothing else surrounded her.

Fuck, it felt like losing her all over again.

You aren't losing me. Her blue eyes flickered to mine, surprise coloring her expression. A flush rose to her cheeks. "I refuse to let him get the better of me, especially now that he's dead."

"Did you just listen to my thoughts?" I arched a brow.

"Yeah. It was like… you were broadcasting it." She swallowed and took a swig of water to clear her throat. "What is happening to me, Voss?"

"We're not sure. Perhaps the blood bonding, perhaps the marriage, perhaps the royal magic, or perhaps the prophecy."

"Or option e, all of the above?" Max moved her fork through her food. "What happens now?"

"Now, we get you help."

"We don't have time for that."

"We have to make time for it. If we're going to fix this kingdom, you need time to settle. You can't look at me without unease running through your body. I know you're fighting it, and I appreciate that, but these things take time."

"I hate it. I want to look at you, but… I see him. You don't sound like him or talk like him. Your scent is different, but your face—"

"Come on. I look nothing like him."

Max snorted, a ghost of a smile cresting her lips. It made my heart melt. She let out a breath. "I think I need to change."

I arched an eyebrow but stayed silent and waited for her to continue.

With a sigh, she placed her tray aside and ran her fingers through her hair. Her eyes fixed on me, still holding that air of defiance. "My life has been about revenge, making the Fae pay for what was done to my family, but everyone responsible is dead, and I don't feel any better. The king died, and it didn't fix anything. And what happened? I got myself kidnapped by a—"

Her thoughts spiraled around us, going to a dark place. I couldn't have that. She wanted me to stop her, and she hated how she needed me, but it was still there. Despite her anger and frustration at needing someone else, she had trusted me enough to hide everything about herself behind *my* nickname for her.

She trusted me.

I wouldn't take that for granted. "Close your eyes for me, little fox."

Her eyes fluttered shut.

"No sassing me?" I crossed the room, approaching the bed.

She shook her head. "Not that you deserve my compliance." Her nose scrunched at the end.

"I always deserve it."

She let out a breath, then admitted, "But you did save me." The crux of the matter. Her anger that she wasn't able to save herself.

"You've saved me plenty. I was repaying a debt."

Her lips twitched. "You also told me a lot of truths recently."

My jaw set. There was more to unpack between us, including the intricacies of becoming Blood Queen. Originally, I had planned to keep her ascension secret. I had planned to have her make ill-informed decisions again. But seeing how everything had changed her—how I had inadvertently led her to this pain—I wouldn't make the same mistake again. I refused to be responsible for any further anguish. While I intended to make her Fae because I wanted a lifetime with her—not just her mortal life—she would need to know the full story. I wanted her all in with this—with *me*.

I would explain everything before we headed back to the royal court. For now, I needed to repair what was broken between us. While I loved her defiance, I didn't need it to be because of *him*.

"Keep your eyes closed." I climbed onto the bed next to her and wrapped my arms around her waist, pulling her into me. Her warmth surrounded me as I pulled the covers over us.

"Voss…" My name was music in her voice.

"Keep your eyes closed, okay? We're going to do something new. And remember, we can stop at any time. Whenever you want, you say the word."

Her chin wobbled, and I pressed my lips to her cheek.

He never gave me a way out.

I know.

I needed it. I didn't realize how much I needed it.

My fingers traced under the hem of her shirt, settling on her hip as I positioned us. Turning her away from me, I pulled our bodies together so she wouldn't have to look at me. I nuzzled the back of her neck, inhaling her with every breath.

Last night, before we put her to bed, Elspeth had been the one to clean her up. After the trauma Max had experienced at the hands of my brother, it felt right to trust Elspeth to care for her. Also, having her close for me was intoxicating. I hadn't trusted myself not to push her too far before she was ready. I would *always* listen to her, but underneath that was a well of desire to claim her again.

I splayed my hand out over her stomach, running my thumb in circular motions along her skin. I gently brushed the scar I had created when I saved her once before. She hummed and relaxed into me.

"So, what's the plan?"

"This is the plan." I could feel her confusion, and I chuckled. "Intimacy, little fox."

"Intimacy," her voice deadpanned. She opened her eyes and her lashes lowered as she looked at my hand on her stomach. Her fingers traced over mine as she snuggled closer to me.

"Yeah, a thing people do when they like each other."

A snort escaped her. "And you think I like you?"

I pressed my lips to the shell of her ear. "I know you do. But I can wait for you to admit it whenever you're ready. I, however, am not afraid of what it means. I love you, little fox. When I thought I had lost you, I was prepared to destroy the world if it meant getting you back. I tried to tell you before he cut us off, and I can't wait any longer, because I can't stand to live in a world where you don't know how much I care about you."

She sucked in a breath. "Love."

"Yes."

"How do you know?"

I pulled our bodies flush together. "Close your eyes."

She did so immediately.

"Feel."

Several moments went by in our calm space. There was a thread between us, pulsing with every beat of our hearts. It stretched through the blood bond tying us together, but it was more than that. It was solid and would be completely consuming if I let it.

"Do you understand now?"

SCARLET

I swallowed as the thrum stretched between us. Voss said it. He wasn't afraid of what it meant. He *loved* me. His feelings stretched through every fiber of my being, straight down into my core. They filled all the empty spaces inside me and threatened to burst out of my skin. My marrow turned molten in my bones.

It shouldn't have changed anything between us.

But it changed everything.

"I understand." My voice was barely a whisper between us. His body was warm, pressed against mine. His scent of sweet, tangy ginger surrounded me. Everything about him screamed Voss, but seeing his face still made something coil inside me.

Voss's arms tightened around me, his fingers pressing into my skin. The weight of him felt heavier with the confession between us. Everything was almost electric. It felt like something alive passed between us, but was this love?

Prior to today, my life had consisted of little outside of rage and revenge. Every day, I had a mission, one where I plotted someone's demise. But now? Now, it was about creating something new—fixing and saving our world. And whatever Voss and I had formed throughout our time together felt delicate, like the last petal on a wilting flower.

I wanted it to blossom.

I ran my fingers along his arm, savoring the warmth underneath my touch. Pressing my eyes closed, I realized how much I had missed this—missed *him*. "Why did you let me go?" The words edged past my teeth, squeezing out through a high-pitched need inside my soul. The admission of weakness made me want to shed blood.

It had seemed so easy for him. But now he said he loved me.

Voss breathed into my hair, his breath mingling along my skin and threading deep into my soul. The long exhale held pain and so much more. "It wasn't easy. It was never easy." He opened himself up to me, putting his memories on display.

I sucked in a breath as smoldering ash and paper spread around him. As the fire burned so hot, it dipped into his bones. The deep, aching hollow he felt from the moment he forced me to flee his court.

His sorrow at knowing how wrong he had been.

His frustration at making the mistake.

His joy when he finally held me back in his arms.

But what hit me harder than any of that was how he gazed at me as I lay asleep, and how deeply he wished he could change everything I had been through.

Voss pressed his lips against the side of my neck. It sent shivers along my skin and made my body fill with a gentle heat. "If I could go back and give you the innocence you deserve, I would, but I am afraid you would not be the same woman I fell in love with. But it is my regret that I could not change your present."

I wrapped my fingers around his arm, holding him close. "I regret not blinding him." The joke fell flat, even to my ears. Shaking my head, I pressed my fingernails into Voss's skin. "I regret not listening more. Maybe if I had heard what you said, then perhaps—"

He growled.

I tensed.

"Sorry. I dislike hearing you speak negatively about yourself." His fingers moved in circles against my skin. "I hate anyone speaking negatively about you."

"I saw what you did to Emille."

He chuckled. The low, throaty sound danced along my skin, creating a brightness I hadn't felt in days.

Had it only been days?

"I would do it again in a heartbeat. If anyone dares to touch you, they will meet the same fate."

"What if I want them to touch me?" I teased.

The possessiveness coursing through Voss hit me like a wave. The anger he felt was all powerful and consuming. "Like I said, they will meet the same fate." His fingers tightened against my skin. Our bodies were so close, and heat radiated off him.

The next exhale I took relaxed me into his hold. "What are we doing next?"

"We are going to stay here until you feel well enough to face the chaos we've created."

"What chaos?"

"Are you telling me that you went on a killing spree of the royal family without thinking about the shattered world it would create in its wake?"

I snorted. "When you put it that way…"

Revenge had been thick through my bones. It had taken up permanent residence in my veins and had blinded me to the consequences. The shambles I left behind seemed minor compared to the destitution the royals had created over the years. That much power residing in one corrupt family should never have been possible.

That much, you and I agree on.

I sighed, fighting back an eye roll. "You're here with me. You don't need to poke around my brain."

"Oh, but it's so fun to poke you."

I narrowed my eyes, glancing down at his arms. His skin was sun-kissed. Pressing my lids shut, I tuned out the reminder of the other twin. I tried to tamp down those memories into nothingness, but the careless way he compelled me...

"Little fox."

"Mm?"

Voss's breath danced along my skin. "Stay with me, right here. We don't have to think about the future or the past. This moment— me and you—this is all that matters."

"We have to think about the future." I frowned, mulling over what he said earlier. "You said we created chaos. What's happening?"

"Between my missives and your blood trail, the Fae grew angry. There is a revolt afoot, more than just the revolution with your humans. A part of me is concerned about the two fronts attacking simultaneously. We do not have enough Fae on our side to fight two wars."

My jaw worked as I ground my teeth together. "Are you really scared of the humans?" The revolution had been a pipe dream. I knew Quinn would be able to rally people, but I wasn't sure of the end result. I had envisioned a future where humans didn't have to fear compulsion, but what did that truly look like? Would there be space for all of us to coexist when it was so hard for the Fae to contain their magic?

"I'm not scared of the revolutionaries, no. I fear the ugly side of war. If the Fae choose to attack the royal court and try to end my reign as king, plenty of innocents will get caught in the crossfire."

I swallowed. I had been fighting to save as many people as possible my whole life. War was stark, and destruction would be imminent. "So, what's the plan? Prevent the two fronts from fighting each other?"

"I have some ideas about how we could appear as a more united front. Perhaps we could convince the humans to aid the side of the Fae who want to live side by side with them as equals? Regardless, none of that is our concern today."

"It should be."

"I disagree." Voss ran his hand up my arm, over the shoulder, up to my neck. His fingers trailed along my jaw, raising goosebumps along my skin. "What matters right now is making sure you are okay to continue."

"I'm—"

"Little fox, if you claim that you are fine when you can barely look at me without anger, I will wrap my fingers around your mouth to shut you up."

"Then I'd bite your fingers off."

"An appropriate response."

"Well, yeah."

He chuckled, and it warmed my skin. "I missed your violent side."

"If you give me a minute with my dagger, we could have some fun together."

His fingers stilled in their steady tracing of my skin. "I saw what you did to my twin. While I admit it was warranted, I would like to feel more confident that I do not end up like him."

"Afraid I'm going to kill you?"

"More terrified than I will ever admit."

"But you just—"

"Shh…" His hand on my stomach pulled me close, and the other settled on my neck, holding me firmly, but not applying any pressure. "If anything will be the end of me, it will be you, Max. And I will happily die by your hand if it means fixing the world. But is it selfish to hope that we could find the light at the end of the tunnel together? That we could make it out of this alive?"

I sucked in an unsteady breath. Wasn't this the same hope that blossomed inside me? I wished for a future of more than death and destruction.

"Voss, if you are saying this to appease me, I swear—"

"No swearing needed. I understand your dagger will be through the muscles of my throat before I had time to laugh. There are no tricks here. If it is possible, I'd like to keep you. It is something I wish for, but I know you will not be settled until we change the world. But perhaps we should hope for it. You've been searching for revenge, and now it's time to search for something better—an ending where *you* can be happy."

Happiness felt fleeting, but with Voss's arms around me, with the liquid fire of his voice brushing against my neck and the smell of ginger invading my scenes, it *was* possible.

Because I dared to feel a hint of it now.

I dared to hope.

It was such a small spark, but if it were ever to be ignited, a Fae who specialized in fire seemed like just the thing.

"I specialize in more than fire now."

"Oh, yeah?" I bit my lower lip, allowing myself to get lost in this heady feeling of being near him. I had missed this, missed him, missed feeling wanted. Arching my back, I pressed my ass against him, testing his resilience.

"Do you want me to show you?" His tongue grazed my neck, threatening to make me come undone in an instant.

"Yes," I said, feeling breathless already. I needed to approach Voss like I did everything else. In my life, I had never shied away from a challenge, nor did I run from my fears. No, I stood up to them. And if my body was going to fear Voss instinctively after what happened with Leveret, then I needed to face that like I did everything else: head on and recklessly. "Show me what I've been missing out on."

I could feel his feral grin through our bond, with a self-satisfied elation running through him.

Oh.

That's right, little fox. I'm going to take what's mine.

"Voss," his name came out of my lips breathlessly, because everything he wanted to do expanded between us. And I was going to give it to him.

VOSS

My name was music in her voice. The excitement she felt snapped between us like a lightning bolt. Energy ruminated off her, which only added to the fuel inside me. The *need*.

"I'm going to remind you how much you mean to me, and while I will take this part of you, remember we stop any time you say so." I pressed my lips against her neck again, brushing my fingers down her chest and trailing underneath her breasts. "You have the control here, little fox, even if you let me borrow it for a while."

I stilled in my exploration of her and asked, *Let me take care of you?*

Do your best. The smile grew across her face, because I could sense it without seeing it. She wanted this—had been waiting and hoping for it. For me to force her into the present by not allowing her to think about anything else but her body.

I ran my hand down her stomach, tracing the barest of skin underneath the hem of her shirt. She sucked in a breath as my fingers dipped into her pants.

"Voss, I have my—"

"I don't care. Besides, we both know where this is going."

She swallowed. Her hesitation made me pause, because she was still not feeling as confident as she used to.

"Little fox?"

Max shook her head, and I felt the moment she threw her hesitation out of her mind. She wanted this—wanted me. Determination flooded her instead. "You better take care of me." A threat and demand all at once, which I loved hearing her say.

As my lips traced the skin on her neck, I reveled in her taste. Her body was so warm, and her flavor was like divinity on my tongue. "I can think of a few ways to make you relax."

Last night, I had asked Elspeth to help put her to bed. My companion had cleaned her up. Just in case she had woken early, I wanted someone gentler handling her. I hadn't wanted her to panic at the sight of me. Healing came with time. This was a first step, one she was willing to take, and one I would provide as long as she would let me.

Hooking my fingers under her shirt, I caressed the skin on her stomach, slowly trailing up her ribs.

"Voss."

"Yeah?"

"Would I be on my period in our mind?"

"No, you wouldn't, but don't mess with my plans, little fox." I licked the shell of her ear. "And none of them involve having you in an imaginary world when I can have you here."

"And if I say no?"

My heart stuttered, because of course I would stop. I would rather throw myself off a cliff into a swarm of hoswisps than do anything to make her uncomfortable. But this question of hers was probing. The fear edged into her mind, even if she tried to will it out of existence. I would take my time with her, and I would give her the space to process as needed.

"You know the word." Tracing the side of her neck with my tongue, I whispered, "But I think you'll like it." Pride swelled in me as I watched those little bumps cascade along her sensitive skin.

"But what if I need you to fuck me? What if I need to forget—"

"Have I ever left you wanting?" My fingers trailed over her ribs, up to the underside of her breasts. Her skin was soft as I cupped her, feeling satisfied as her nipples hardened under my touch. "I'll take care of you. Promise." My thumb brushed over the peak, and she bucked her ass against me. With my other hand, I pulled her hips into me, dipping my fingers into her pants. "Are you okay?"

"Yes." The word escaped her lips in a breathy whisper.

Hearing the word was magical. She had spent so much time fighting the connection between us, but she was here with me once again. Despite everything that happened, she wasn't running from her feelings anymore. She wanted this without trepidation.

I found her clit and made lazy, slow, circular motions against her. She sucked in a breath and moaned. My other hand trailed to her other breast, finding her pebbled nipple and twisting it between two fingers.

"Fuck, Voss. I missed you."

Chuckling, I kissed her cheek. "I never thought you'd admit as much, little fox." Massaging her breast, I continued to toy with her, easing her into this. She groaned as I quickened my pace on her nerves, keeping my movements steady. Her hips were grinding against my hand, seeking me out.

"Voss, please."

"Please, what, little fox?"

"I want you to fuck me."

"What happened to your hesitation?" I pressed down on her nerves, slowing my movements to nothing more than a pulse of my fingertips.

She sucked in a breath. "Gone the moment you started touching me. Voss, take me. Take *all* of me."

I stilled. I had told her I was going to but hearing her say it— offer it—fueled something deep and primal inside me. I wasn't sure if she fully understood the amount of power her words held. "Max."

She swallowed, and her body tensed. "Voss," she whispered my name as she turned in my arms. I allowed her the space, letting my fingers drift across her skin as she moved. Her eyes were closed, but she opened one pale blue eye and peeked at me.

My heart threatened to stop.

Her other eye popped open. Her hands reached for me, tracing my face with her fingers. My jaw ignited underneath her touch. I swallowed as she watched me. "Voss." My name was nothing more than a whisper, and I had to tamp down every part of me that longed to claim her.

"I—" She pressed her eyes shut for a moment, blinking for a long time before meeting my gaze again. "I care about you, but I might still hate you. A little bit."

I smirked. "That's fair."

"Is it? After everything we've been through? Is it really fair for me to still have this… venom inside me?"

"I betrayed your trust by not telling you the whole plan, and I won't make that mistake twice." I clenched my jaw. We would have a talk before she ascended, and I hoped she would still elect to become Blood Queen after she knew the truth. Brushing my fingers along her skin, I added, "I love you, Max. I intend to earn that from you this time. I fucked up by letting you out of my sight once, and I don't intend to do that again."

"Voss, shut up and fuck me."

I chuckled. "I'm not going to fuck you." Wrapping my hand possessively over her ass, I brought her flush against my length. She let out a gasp. "But I am going to take what's mine."

She bit her lower lip.

"Shy again, little fox?"

"I've never—"

"I know."

"But with you—"

"You want to, because you want me to fill you. You want to offer me something you've never given to anyone else."

She nodded. "I still think about what you did to me in that dungeon."

I smirked, feeling a pulse straight into my groin. "Get on your stomach. We're going to start nice and slow." She listened to me instantly, rolling over. I had to bite back my internal satisfaction of her obeying me without question.

More than that, I wanted her to know that this trust was earned.

I inched her pants down, showing her smooth skin of her ass. No matter what, I would make sure she enjoyed this as much as I did.

Or maybe slightly less than I was about to.

A crack rang out as I spanked her.

Max jolted and cried out my name as her fingers dug into the sheets. I could get used to hearing that noise on her lips more often. Running my tongue over my teeth, I did it again. The resounding slap against her ass made my cock impossibly hard, especially as her body clenched underneath me.

The best part was the wanton desire rolling through her thoughts. She had missed me, and she desperately wanted me to use her like this.

"Still so fucking responsive." I kneaded her skin, already turning red from just two smacks. "I missed you, little fox."

She turned her head, pouting her lower lip out. Her eyes scanned me, lingering on where my brother's scar was. "I want to remember this—remember you being you. You're not him."

"I'm not." I ran my fingers underneath her shirt, and she lifted herself up to help me get the material off her. Pity, as I could have set the thing on fire instead. I tossed it to the ground as I trailed lazily along her soft flesh, feeling each notch in her spine.

Max exhaled, and her breath edged with pleasure. "You always gave me a choice. I could stop this at any point." Her blue gaze was pointed, searching.

I nodded solemnly. "Always." A sharp pain ran through me, knowing full well how my brother had snatched her choices away from her. She would *always* be safe with me.

"But I want you to do one thing for me," she said.

I lay next to her. My fingers reached the back of her neck and curled around her nape. I brought her lips to mine, sinking my teeth into her lower lip. She gasped in a breath, opening for my tongue to taste her. She was perfect. There was endless promise behind the way we connected, and I was never going to let that go.

"What do you want, Max?" I whispered the words against her swollen lips.

She shuddered as the magic behind her name skittered across her skin. Goosebumps rose to the surface, and I couldn't help but smirk. "If I need to relax during it, tell me to. Use your magic to make it easier for me to take you." Max nibbled her lip as I pulled back. I searched her gaze. Other than allowing her the respite to sleep, I had avoided compulsion with her.

"I mean it, Voss." Her brows lowered as her gaze turned into a glare. "I don't want it to hurt."

"I won't let it hurt."

Her glare turned deadly.

"If it makes you feel better, then I will promise you this. I will use my magic only to make you relax for me, but I will be careful with that command. The word *relax* could mean more than just your muscles. It could apply to your morals or inhibitions." I ran my tongue along her cheek, tracing a line to her ear. "When you hear me say *relax* tonight, I mean your muscles and only your muscles, nothing else. Not your mind, not your mental state. Got it?" Tossing a small command behind my words, I let the weight of them settle on her skin. She needed to know exactly what I meant. Max would always be in control. If she needed a way out, she would have it. "If you need to say switch, you say it."

She nodded, eyes wide and pupils blown as she licked her lips. "Does magic always feel that way when it's—"

"Done by someone you trust?" I cupped her jaw and forced her to look at me. "Yes. Now, I distinctly remember you offering something that I was already planning on taking. But it's good that you want it as much as I do." I spanked her again, and her body clenched. She was about to cry out as my hand smacked her another time, but I captured the sound with my mouth. Instead, she moaned against me.

I sat up, letting her rest languidly on the pillows, and stared at the red outlines of my hands that formed across her skin. There was something so desperate about the way I wanted to invade her. I sought control, and Max made me feel anything but. She was a challenge, a perfect complement to me.

"I can't believe no Fae ever thought to take you this way."

"They were too busy trying to prove me wrong."

I hummed to myself, running my fingers in between her cheeks. She wiggled her ass. I slapped her again, so she'd know exactly who was in charge right now. "I can't imagine why anyone would ever try to put the mouthy Fae Slayer in her place." Chuckling, I tested her puckered hole.

"Voss, what about lube—" Her breath cut off as she realized exactly what I was doing. "Are you magically creating lube?!" Her voice hitched at the end as she narrowed her eyes at me. "You're a fucking show off."

I smirked as I pushed my finger inside her, prodding her entrance. She bucked against the bed. With magic, I placed bindings around her hands and legs, forcing her still for me.

"Voss—" She gasped my name as I worked up to my second knuckle. Her muscles tightened, but I wasn't ready to use magic yet. I wanted this to be pleasurable for her, and I would make it. We just had to go slow.

Some things—no matter how painful the restraint—were worth the wait.

With my other hand, I trailed to the front of her, found her nerves, and ran two of my fingers around her clit in slow circles. Her hips sought more pressure as I pushed farther still, sinking to the last knuckle.

"You're so tight, Max."

She moaned under me.

"But you're going to take me like a good girl, aren't you?" I stroked her clit, watching as she tried to move against me. Slowly, I eased my finger in and out of her, growing a steady rhythm. I needed her to get used to the feeling of being filled. It took a few moments before her muscles loosened.

She panted against the bed; her breaths muffled from where she stuffed her face against the mattress. "Voss, I need—"

"Remember to tell me if you want me to stop," I said, because I knew how self-conscious she was about herself right now. But as I told her, I didn't care. I would have her and make this feel good for her. Using my other hand, I dipped one of my fingers into her pussy, and she clenched around me.

"Fuck," she breathed.

I worked a second finger into her ass, stretching her slowly as I pushed in. Her fingers fisted the sheets as she trembled underneath me. She wasn't able to get much movement from where I bound her, but I felt her rising pleasure through our bond.

She was exactly where she needed to be.

Slowly, I stretched my fingers apart. She let out a cry.

With my other hand, I distracted her by hooking my finger inside her slick walls. She bucked against me as I found the spot that made her fall to pieces. Max gasped for breath as she fought me, but I watched the small shifts in her body as she crested the edge.

I needed her to break so she could come back together stronger than before.

When I started to push in my third finger, she screamed into the mattress. I stopped, letting her catch her breath. "Max."

She whimpered into the sheets as I stroked her nerves. Her body writhed.

"Max…"

Her muscles loosened as her hips started moving, seeking her pleasure. "Need." One word, the only coherent thing she managed.

Kissing her shoulder, I used my magic to coat her with more lube and slowly pushed my third finger inside, working my fingers back and forth as her orgasm built. I could feel it welling up from the invasion of me. Her body shivered as pleasure ripped through her. Gloriously, she came apart.

I pulled out of her, licking the side of her neck. "I think it's time I take what's mine."

"Mm…" Her lids were half-closed as she looked at me.

"Remember what I said," I told her.

She nodded.

I had hiked her pants down earlier, just enough to give me access, but now I ripped them off her. I enjoyed how relaxed her body was now. Tossing my clothes off, I climbed between her legs, using my magic to pull them apart in their bindings. I grabbed a pillow and tucked it under her hips.

Dropping to my knees behind her was my idea of worship.

I ran my fingers against her tight hole again, pressing on it as I used magic to conjure more lube. While I had her permission to make her relax, that was a last resort.

"Voss…" she whined.

"Such a needy little fox." I ran the head of my erection against her, making sure I got myself soaked. She groaned as I pushed the head of my cock into her. Working in and out, I let her get used to the size. She turned back to the mattress, panting into the sheets. I thrust farther inside her, pulling out each time and adding more lube to make her nice and wet. She opened, relaxing into me. My fingers curled into her hips for more leverage.

She let out a gasp. "How—" Words escaped her, but I could still hear her whirling thoughts.

"About a third of the way."

"You feel so fucking big." She shuddered as I pulled all the way out again. She wiggled back toward me, seeking me out. While Max had never done this before, her body was ready to give me what I wanted.

"You're so tight." I pushed in, halfway now, getting farther and farther inside her. Her body started clenching against me. "Max," I said, slapping her ass. Every muscle tightened but released after that. "Better?"

"Fuck," she gasped.

I thrust in farther.

While I had been with my fair share of Fae in the past, anal wasn't something I often did. But knowing I was her first? First ever take this part of her? It was enough to make me want to come right then and there.

She was giving this to me willingly. And while she might not be ready to say the words, I knew what it meant. She trusted me, and I would make sure I would be deserving of that.

Max pushed back against me as her walls clenched. I reached around and pinched her nerves. She rode my hand, but her muscles stayed tight.

"Relax, Max." I cautiously sent the command into her, directing it at her muscles.

Her mind swirled, panic welling inside her, but even in the temporary haze of emotions, her muscles unclenched. I pushed the rest of the way inside her as her emotions settled into a wave of pleasure.

She breathed out a sigh. *Sorry, I was worried your magic was going to—*
I know.

I never want to feel that way again. She didn't have to explain, because I felt it. As soon as she realized my magic hadn't touched her emotions, her mind had relaxed too. It worked as promised.

Running my hands along her hips, I pressed my fingertips into her skin. *How do you feel?*

She moved forward and sank backwards onto me with the small amount of space she was able to get. I inhaled, forcing myself to relax too. Her breath came out as a heady whisper. "Full."

I smirked. "Not quite yet. But soon."

SCARLET

His words coiled around me, holding all kinds of promise within their wickedness. I could barely breathe as he slowly pumped in and out of me. This side of Voss was the one I needed. He challenged me to take all I could, and he reminded me I had a choice while thoroughly taking advantage of me. I chose this—chose him.

As he pressed into me, my nerve endings ignited. I had never felt anything like it—so *claimed*. Every part of my body felt electrified, and there was just enough pain to short circuit my system. His slow strokes, his care and attentiveness, were destroying me in the best way possible.

Magic welled up inside the room, and somehow, Voss rubbed it against my clit while keeping his grip steady. I shook from the effect, and I felt his pride at watching me fall apart through our bond.

"You're so fucking beautiful, Max." His hands moved up my sides, over my back, so light but still holding possession. The tender

155

touches compared to the sure movements of his thrusts made my body ache with need.

Voss would catch me whenever I fell.

"Come for me, little fox." He snapped his hips forward, which pushed my head further into the bed. I gasped for breath. He felt so big like this, pushing on parts of me I never knew existed. Everything ignited from the inside out. My body sang with need.

One of his hands settled on my hips, while the other wrapped around my shoulder. He got leverage and worked to a faster rhythm. I panted as he fucked me.

His magic swirled around my nerves. I moaned into the mattress. It was too much. The build was unreal. My body clenched as I came, falling into oblivion as he continued to take what was his. My nails dug into the sheets as everything inside me threatened to burn out. It was too much—too many sensations, and my nerves felt fried. It was all so intense.

But I didn't want it to stop. I wanted to remain on the cusp of pleasure and torture.

"One more," he demanded, leaning over me and licking the shell of my ear with his wicked tongue. I wasn't sure I would survive another orgasm, not with my body already on the precipice of extinction. His magic danced along my skin, and that combined with the snap of his hips, he coaxed another one out. I fell apart for the last time, my body clenching around him as I tumbled toward oblivion. Voss chased my release with his as he came inside me.

Filling me in a way no one had before.

His fingers coiled through my hair. My body was so languid and spent, I was no better than a puppet for him to use however he wanted. He lifted my head up and kissed me, long and slow. There was a claim behind it, a tender possession that hadn't existed before.

He owned me.

And I was glad to be his.

Pulling out, he gave my ass a playful tap. Everything was so sensitive that I yelped from the impact. I turned my head to glare at him. The amused smirk I knew so well spread up his lips, and damn it. I wanted to crush myself against him and take his breath away.

"Come here," I murmured.

"Let me clean you." He stepped up to the tub—the stupid tub that took up half the bedroom—and ran a washcloth underneath the warm stream of water. Voss made quick work of cleaning himself, and then gently ran the towel over me. He had loosened the magical hold on me, but moving was an impossibility.

With every swipe of the cloth, my body threatened to skyrocket into space. Tossing the towel away, he kneaded my ass with his fingers. His lips pressed a chaste kiss on the reddened skin. "How do you feel?"

"Come here," I said as I lazily rolled off the pillow that had been keeping my hips aloft. I gestured in an invitation.

Voss laid next to me, bringing me into him. His eyes traced every line on my face, every curve of my body. His arms tightened around me as I nuzzled into his warm chest.

"I missed you," he said.

"With the blood bond, we were hardly apart." I chanced a glance up at him.

He stared at me with fiery eyes, acting like I hadn't said a single thing.

"Fine. I missed you too," I admitted.

That smirk was back, only it was no longer infuriating. It did things to my stomach I wasn't proud of. I had planned to kill him, but now... I couldn't imagine leaving this behind. We'd survive whatever came next. We had to. If he had the audacity to hope for a future, maybe I should too.

"Here," Voss said, offering his neck to me. "I need you to be at full strength."

I climbed on top of him as his fingers cupped my ass. Heat seared through me for a second, but the ache was gone in an instant. I narrowed my gaze at him. "Did you just... heal me?"

His eyes glittered.

"Show off."

"Little fox." Voss's eyes darted down the length of my body. "Please?" His blond hair was tousled away from his face. His lips were swollen. Desire burned between us, despite everything we had already done.

The hope he felt made my body tighten. It was so rare to hear a plea fall from Voss's lips, but when it did... I gave him a coy smile, feeling more like myself than I had in days. There would be healing to do still, plenty I had to deal with, but for right now, I was safe with him. I placed my teeth against his neck.

"Is this what you want?" I asked, keeping my voice low.

"Yes." He tightened his grip. His magic coiled around us as I slid my teeth into his skin.

I languished in his taste. The blood bond solidified between us, becoming a tangible thing. At the edge, I also felt Penn. He was drinking at the bar, had consumed three ales already from the look of it, and tried to wedge us out of his mind.

"He'll be out of my head soon."

"I can't believe you blood bonded with him. Show me what happened?" I licked the already healing wound on Voss's neck.

"I don't know if that's a good idea."

As I pulled back from him, I searched his face. Voss closed off. He had opened to me earlier, showing me everything he had done in my absence, except the part with Penn. I narrowed my gaze, but there was no hint that I should be jealous.

Although, the possessive part of me was.

"Voss."

"Max."

"Are you… blushing?" I asked as red rose to his face.

He grabbed the nape of my neck, lowering his voice into a growl. "I don't know what you are talking about."

"Then show me."

He pressed his eyes shut and images spun through my mind. As soon as the smell of my blood hit the air, he had lost it—truly and purely lost his sanity to terror. His emotions had become all-consuming, not allowing him to plan like he usually did. Shame colored the memory. He had wanted to hold it together, to be strong for me. He felt like he had failed.

His eyes opened, bright fiery red. "I would like you to share with me when you are ready."

"Oh, I can show you this at least." I pressed the image of Leveret's destroyed apartment into his head and the moment of pure satisfaction I had when I slammed the tiny necklace into his eye.

Instead of seeing the smirk cross his features, Voss's lips pressed into a thin line. He pulled me against his chest, his fingers trembling on the bare skin of my back.

"Voss…"

"I came so close to losing you. It was the worst feeling in the world, and it stemmed from my poor decision to let you go. We're stronger together, little fox, and I will never make that mistake again." His hands trailed up my back, tangling in my hair. The second time he made me this promise. "I'm sorry."

I wanted to say something comforting, but I had no comfort to give. So instead, I offered him this, "I want us to make it out of this alive too."

Hope felt elusive, but there it was, blossoming in my chest

without my permission. Whatever we faced on the horizon, at least it would be together.

᪥ ✿ ᪥

We dressed and headed downstairs to meet with Elspeth and Penn in the tavern. Penn swayed in his chair, drunk off his ass. They were seated at the same table as during our first venture together. Being in Alpin's court made me feel safer. This was a great distance away from Leveret's court, and I realized how far they must have traveled while I was out to get me somewhere secure.

Unfortunately, that meant I had lost a day. My stomach growled despite the meager amount of food I ate earlier. Whatever loomed on the horizon was much closer than before, and I would need my strength to be ready for it.

There was plenty to discuss, but from the look of it, Penn wouldn't be in any shape for planning what comes next. First, if my friends had made it here, maybe I could find them. Did they have any ideas? Had they attacked the Fae? Had the revolution started while I was trapped inside Leveret's court? I wondered what we would find once we made it back to the king's court.

"Penn, you need to slow down," Voss's voice rang out over the table. His hand was on the small of my back, possessive with his leading. I could feel him vibrating with an uncertainty, like if he let me go for even a second, I would disappear.

We both had things we needed to heal from.

"I stopped drinking when you stopped..." He made a lewd gesture with his hands.

I giggled. Voss arched an eyebrow in my direction, and his hand squeezed my skin. "You think this is funny, little fox?"

"Drunk Penn? Yes. Yes, I do." I shifted my gaze to the turquoise-eyed Fae. "I am sorry."

160

"You're not." He waved his hand. "But do you both have to be so… violent? It's like… you'd rather consume each other than have sex."

"That's not normal?"

"No." Penn frowned, staring at me. "Sit down, all of you." His gaze shifted and refocused. He blinked. "It's like there are… seven of you."

Voss pulled out a seat, but when I lowered myself into it, he scooped me up instead and settled me in his lap. "I'm not letting you go yet." He nuzzled into my shoulder.

I huffed out a breath but decided to enjoy his warmth.

Elspeth motioned over a server, and she ordered for the table. She requested a pitcher of water with her eyes resting on Penn. "I, for one, am glad to have you back, Scarlet, but I am not happy to have that back." She flicked her fingers to where Voss's lips trailed along my neck. His fingers tightened on my hips.

"Would you rather he be angry and setting this place on fire?" I asked, placing my hand on Voss's chest and leaning into him. "Because I quite like it here."

Elspeth ignored me. "We also need to plan for our arrival back at King's Court. Everything was dropped, which likely means—"

I screeched as a small, round, fuzzy creature appeared in the middle of the table. It had massive eyes, the tiniest clawed hands, and short little feet. Its ears shifted, as if testing the surrounding air. Its giant golden eyes landed on Voss and held out its hand.

Voss grabbed the piece of parchment from the creature's claws. "You have to wait a few moments for our food," he told it.

I blinked, staring at the creature that had appeared out of nowhere. No one seemed surprised except me. The round ball bobbed up and down, which I took to mean it agreed. Its gaze shifted to me, and it blinked slowly. Its fur was gray, which offset the golden, glowing eyes. The pink clawed paws clenched and unclenched as he watched me. The creature wasn't much bigger than a teacup, and the letter it had passed along was almost the same size as it. It was... adorable, save for the two sharp fangs poking out of its fluff.

Voss had read the missive while I continued gazing at the creature. "It's from Lord Alpin. He requests we visit him at his quarters in another hour, once we've eaten..." Voss crumbled the parchment and tossed it onto the table. The creature watched it with a cross look on its face. "I will join him, of course. Don't you worry."

The creature bobbed again.

Once the food arrived, Voss tossed one of his vegetables to it. It snatched the food out of the air, opened a maw that practically took up its body length, and inhaled the piece in a second. It popped out of existence again. How it had a mouth that big hidden underneath its fur, I had no idea.

"What the fuck," I said.

"Scytheseer. They can bend space to their will, making them the perfect messengers."

"Why have I never seen one before?"

"Why would you have? The humans have their computer networks, we have scytheseers."

I blinked, staring at him. "You have a creature that can bend space to its will."

"Yes."

"And why have they not taken over?"

Elspeth laughed, her voice rich. "You saw the creature, right? It is the equivalent of your pets. They like us because we feed them, but they aren't overly intelligent—just enough to get their next meal."

"They can *bend space* and you are telling me there is no intelligence there?"

She shrugged.

"Sometimes I think the Fae don't deserve magic because you don't realize how *magical* it is."

Voss offered me a piece of bread, and my cheeks warmed as I remembered the last time he fed me—on the back of his horse. I took it and kissed him on the nose.

Penn spoke with his mouth full. "This version of her is too... agreeable. I don't like it. She's definitely going to kill you."

I crossed my arms over my chest. "I don't intend to kill him."

"You say that now, but I know you. You're... fickle." He dipped his bread into the broth. "More importantly, I know him. And he will piss you off again."

Frowning, I snatched a fork from the table and stabbed a few of the vegetables on the plate. "Shut up, Penn. You're drunk."

Penn shrugged.

"He's right. I probably will piss you off." Voss's hand snaked along the hem of my trousers, teasing my skin. He pressed me back into his lap, along his hardening cock.

Insatiable.

You love it, he teased. "But I think we'll be able to work it out."

I rolled my eyes.

He used his free hand to eat. "There are some things we should discuss, but perhaps once we are back at King's Court." Voss played with me, brushing his fingers lightly along my skin and dipping lower. Impossibly, my body wanted him again. "Much like you don't intend to kill me, I don't intend to make you upset with me again."

I trust you.

His lips pressed against my neck. *And time will prove that the trust is deserved. Thank you, little fox.*

"What do you think Alpin wants?" I asked.

Voss shrugged. "Likely to discuss what made me abandon the royal court so quickly or to give me an update. Whatever it is, I expect bad news." *If Alpin needed to interrupt my breakfast to demand an audience, even if it was a polite request, there was a reason for it.*

"Whoa," I said, shifting so I could look at Voss. "I think… I heard all of that." Blinking, I focused back on the present, getting out of Voss's head. He narrowed his gaze at me, curious. He hadn't been projecting his thoughts, but I had gleaned them all the same.

I cleared my throat, hoping we could ignore the oddities of whatever bond was between Voss and me. We had other things to worry about. "Well, if there is something wrong, we'll tackle it together. After all, there's no competing party for the royal magic now." A smile slid up my face. "Which means you and I can kill whoever gets in our way."

"We don't need to kill everyone," Elspeth said, rolling her eyes.

"Try telling them that." Penn snorted. "If one of them killed me, I'm betting she'd beg him to fuck her over my dead body, and he'd be more than happy to oblige."

"I'd only kill you if you asked nicely, Penn," I said, arching my voice.

And I'd only fuck you if you were really wet. Though, Voss's pain at thinking about the death of his friend came through loud and clear.

"See! That's the problem. The ale isn't helping. I need fucking Faerie wine."

"Oh. Did you find my bag while you were out there? I had a flask."

Voss shook his head.

I sighed. At least they had recovered my dagger. There were a lot of items I had left behind at Leveret's—too many in a place where I had already abandoned so much. I made a solemn vow to search for Quinn's necklace someday.

Penn stared at me. "When you showed Voss images earlier, did you really do all that to his apartment?"

I smirked. "Of course. But the asshole cleaned it in less time than it took me to destroy it."

The black-haired Fae frowned. "Strange. The Balgair line isn't known for *fixing* things." He gulped down some water. "I am very grateful you stabbed him in the eye. He deserved much worse."

"Worse, like getting stabbed so many times I'm fairly certain his mother wouldn't recognize him?" Elspeth asked.

"Much worse," Penn glowered, and I wondered about the history there.

How is it that the thought of you stabbing someone makes me want to fuck you?

Because you're as fucked up as I am.

Voss rolled my hips over him. *Maybe I'm worse.*

"Stop it, already." Penn reached for another tankard of ale, but Elspeth slapped him. He huffed out a breath and slumped onto the table.

"So, Lord Alpin?" I coughed, trying to refocus on the subject at hand out of pity.

Voss nodded. "As soon as we're ready, we'll go. Elspeth, I want you to look for our horses."

"What is Penn going to do?" Elspeth asked.

"Sleep it off," Voss said. "I'll ask Alpin if he has any Faerie wine to get us through the next week or so."

"Could you… compel him not to care about the blood bond? Or not pay attention to it?" I asked.

Voss's brows lowered over his eyes as the three of them stared at me. I shifted uncomfortably.

"Your whole thing is about people having free will, and at the first taste of power, you are asking Voss to use his magic to get rid of Penn's free will?" Elspeth gaped.

"I don't enjoy seeing him miserable."

"Who are you and what have you done with Scarlet? Voss, that's not Scarlet. It must be a changeling." Penn placed his head down on the table, clearly too drunk for this conversation.

"There are no such things as changelings." Voss rolled his eyes.

"How do you know?" Penn slurred. His cheek was smashed against the dark wooden table.

"Penn is going to sleep it off. Elspeth will find our horses and trade whatever we must to get them back—all of them. And I will meet Alpin with my wife." Voss stared at me. "And after that, you and I have some things to discuss." His heated gaze seared straight into me.

Eighteen

Voss

Alpin's home was a converted farmhouse. I appreciated many things about the male and his court. He never felt the need to present an ostentatious front to his court just because he could. He held power without a heavy-hand or demand for complacency. And his court was a stunning combination of old and new. No facades like the other Lords and Ladies created.

He was respected, and it was one reason I trusted him.

Tucking Max against my side, we walked up the couple of stairs to the wooden wraparound porch and knocked on the weathered door. Max shifted on her feet next to me, already looking more like herself than when we found her. Confidence trickled back into her, perhaps from the fantastic orgasms and food or perhaps from being free of the rest of the royal line.

We had figured out a future—now we had to defend it from whoever challenged us. Alpin would be an excellent ally in whatever approach we took next, assuming I could convince him to fight.

The door opened, and the long-haired Fae himself answered. He took a step back and gestured for us to come inside. "Devoss Balgair and the menace of our society." Alpin clicked the door closed. I was about to lecture him for his word choice, but his orange eyes were delighted with mirth, skin crinkling around the edges of his lids. "Come. I had a friend brew some tea for us. There's much to discuss."

He walked into the living room. Max glanced around the space; her blue eyes wide as she took it in. Alpin lived modestly, and I'm sure she had expected something bigger—most Fae did indulge, but he was the pinnacle of what I wanted our society to become. Alpin signaled how it was possible.

The Lord offered us the love seat as he sat on the couch across the coffee table. Pouring three cups of tea from the same pot, he sipped his own. "I find most business meetings are better to be discussed over a hot beverage."

"Even in the late summer?"

"Early fall, depending on who you are asking." Alpin's lips twitched, looking at Max.

Her knee was touching mine. The small amount of contact did more to calm my nerves than she realized. Whatever we were walking into by going back to the royal court, we were doing it together.

"If I can speak frankly, Voss?"

I nodded, picking up a cup.

"I am not one to judge, and I sense how you two are... connected. But leaving your court while it was in turmoil was a dangerous move for the crown." His eyes glittered as a frown parted his lips. "I mean no disrespect, of course. I would have done the same for a loved one, but I question the timing. The kingdom is in jeopardy."

This was the expected outcome, of course. Leaving at such a time was bound to create the opportunity for someone to attempt a coup. While I had wanted to leave Elspeth or Penn behind, that also would have been risky. Without me there to heal either of them, it may have been a death sentence.

"It was a risk I was willing to take. I suppose you invited us not to talk about risks, but likely what occurred while I was gone?"

Alpin sipped his tea. "Indeed. While you were out, some of your hoswisp patrols have started what they are calling a revolution."

I snorted. "Let me guess—Iobhar?"

"He'd been trouble already, I take it?"

Blowing on the surface of the tea, I took a small sip. It was earthy in flavor, mixed with a hint of citrus with a semi-bitter aftertaste. Max copied my movements, staying oddly quiet during this interaction. She watched Alpin with deep scrutiny.

You okay?

She scowled. *Will you ever stop checking in on me?*

Sending my satisfaction that I riled her, I refocused on Alpin. "He had been rather vocal about his distaste, so it does not surprise me to hear he's started something. And the other courts? The ones previously run by my siblings?"

"Livid—except Averett's. Honestly, I believe they are happy to be done with him, since he left the court in shambles. I've had a few others reach out with scytheseers, asking for guidance. Most have accepted my assurances that things will settle shortly. Some have not and have decided to follow your brothers' court into the uprising."

"Namir's?"

"Corvin and Bram. Seems they had contingency plans set with their advisers if they failed to kill you at Lady Burke's."

"Figures." I placed the teacup down, because I wanted to throw it. The other set of twins had always been close and had searched for the Fae Slayer as long as I had. If they had found her first…

Max's hand rested on my knee. *They didn't. You did.*

I placed my hand on top of hers. *Thank the Mother for that.* "So what, they started a coup? Who received the power of the court?"

"Did you know Emille had a cousin, Eero? I was unaware until he rose to power. Seems that the whole family was a bunch of rotting apples. I am not sorry for what you did to her, but I am sorry you've made an enemy of so many courts."

Letting out a breath, I steeled my nerves. I had been prepared for an uprising from my late siblings' courts. It was a surprise that it came from the twins and not from Namir. With my brother's violence and influence, I had believed they'd be the first to ride into battle. Regardless, the Fae who lived in the royal courts tended to take after their leaders. Max would have had quite a spree in any of their courts. But with Eero rising to power, it made sense why he would be quick to join the "revolution." With his other family members dead, he would seek revenge.

"So, Eero and Iobhar joined forces?"

Alpin nodded.

"Quaint," I bit out.

"And it seems several Fae were distraught when you freed the Fae Slayer. Those who were joined them." His eyes darted to Max. "What say you in this matter?"

She shrugged. "I accept it will be a challenge, but I don't think it is as dire as you believe. If we can get one half of the Fae to follow Voss and the humans to follow me, then we'll have no trouble squashing the opposition and setting everything in motion."

Alpin nodded, folding his hands in front of him. "The humans who were in my court planning a coup against the crown?" He let out a breath and shook his head. "I could not allow them to stay while acting against the crown, of course, but I had a feeling they were part of your original band of misfits. I assisted them with finding safe lodgings outside of my court. It is my assumption they are alive and well."

Max's mouth gaped open. Her eyes flitted to mine, ever the question, but I did not know the answer. If her friends were amassing an army against the royal court, then we would meet them eventually. I hoped she could bring them to our side.

Alpin continued, "I admire your optimism, but I don't think it is warranted. Humans have never been able to defeat the Fae, so it will be a civil war. Many will die on both sides, and it will be a tragedy for both our kinds."

"Perhaps, but those who survive would remember it being a gruesome part of our history. One that will serve as a warning to never allow us to cross that path again."

I set my jaw, but I wanted to gape at her. She spoke like a Fae, like a queen who had already decided how the future would unfold simply because she would will it into being.

My queen.

Alpin narrowed his gaze on her, orange eyes igniting with a hint of magic. "Ah, you are assuming your side will win in this scenario. If the other side wins, they will view it as glorious, as the time they defeated the Balgair reign." His eyes shifted to me. "Let's hope you do not allow them such power, Voss."

"I have no intention of letting them walk away unscathed." I placed the empty teacup down. "So, Eero, Iobhar, and I am to assume some other Fae rose to power in my siblings' courts who feel similarly?"

"Again, not Averett's. As I said, I believe they are happy to move forward and put the past behind them. When he left, he took the power with him. They've been without a true Lord or Lady for a long time, which left them in a disheveled mess."

"Why do Fae courts only have one ruling family?" Max leaned forward, putting her teacup down. She glanced at us. "All courts have a single leader, but why not a committee or multiple people? Centralized power seems like a curse instead of a blessing."

"Leveret and I shared a court, as did Bram and Corvin."

"Wait, you had a court?" A little frown pursed her lips. "Leveret's court was yours?!"

"Still is, I suppose. At least, it is now that Leveret's dead."

Her mouth dropped open. "I thought you didn't have a court."

Alpin laughed. It was a full-bodied belly laugh that filled the space around us as I stared in shock at my little fox. That she would say something so customarily insulting in front of another Fae...

I fell farther in love with her at that moment. It was like stabbing me in the chest all over again. This knife cut deeper, and it made me want to take her over the back of this forsaken couch. I ran my hand along her leg, squeezing the inside of her thigh possessively.

"Not having a court for a Lord," Alpin wheezed.

"You never mentioned it," Max said.

"My father stripped me of my title, but there was no way to do it formally without killing me. So, I agreed to leave the court to my brother. He cared more about power than me, anyway."

"Says the king who hunted down a weapon to use against his father in order to stage a coup and claim the royal throne?"

Alpin chuckled. "She has a point, Devoss."

"What I meant was... I never cared for *frivolous* power. Running a court was time consuming and unnecessary, especially when there was something else I could be doing." Like chasing little foxes across the wilds. "Plus, the goal was always to claim the throne. I couldn't do that if I sat in my court daydreaming about the day my father would be dead. And you met my brother. Ruling with him would have been as entertaining as watching a hoswisp build a nest.

Tiresome and grueling."

"How do they build nests?"

"They use dung." Alpin placed his teacup down and sighed. "Well, it's been most entertaining, but I, unlike some Fae I know, must watch over my court. Lady Burke has been much more willing to consider favorable deals lately, and I feel I should take advantage of that prior to her changing her mind. Lord Raskos also wanted to establish trade. I'm not sure what occurred between their courts, but a strange civility seems to be happening between them."

"Lord Raskos and I need to exchange some words when this is over."

"Indeed, I heard." Alpin looked at Max. "Do not mistake my next words for pity, but I understand what you have experienced, and I do not wish that upon my worst enemy. Nightmare and I have an understanding when it comes to my court. I do not allow him to feed on my subjects, but instead on me."

Max sucked in a breath. "You do that to protect your humans?"

He chuckled. "My humans, like I own them. My dear, I fear you've been in the clutches of the Fae for far too long. Perhaps we will all benefit from the reminder that we do not own anyone else, but instead need to live in harmony. I admire what you are trying to do, though I do wonder if you will survive to see the end result." His gaze swept back to me. "Best of luck, Devoss Balgair. I put a word into the market for everyone to sell you wares at cost, and I will give them additional compensation should you need anything. I will also spare some guards for you when the time comes. And…" He reached into a pocket on the side of his couch and pulled out a small vial. "I heard Penn was getting intoxicated at the tavern. I take it he's trying to stay well enough away from your mind."

I closed the gap between us, grabbing the Faerie wine. Alpin was observant, almost too much so, but at least he was on our side. "I appreciate it, Alpin. Truly."

With a final nod, we stood and saw ourselves out. Max threaded her fingers through mine as soon as the door closed behind us.

"When were you going to tell me about your court?"

"Not really mine if I am not there to rule." I cast a glance over at her and pressed my lips to her forehead. "I never considered it mine, as Leveret made it into what he desired. Once my father stripped me of my position, it made it impossible to fight for. Plus, there was more at stake."

"That's fair."

"But maybe one of these days we'll go back and transform it into what it should have been all along. I would love to invite artists in and compensate them for their creativity."

Max grinned. "Such big dreams, Voss. We'll have to live up to your expectations."

With her by my side, I had no doubts. I was excited to see what she could do when—I swallowed, cutting the thought short. That was part of the longer conversation we needed to have. "Why don't we collect some items for the road?"

She nodded, a wild look on her face. We strolled to the market and checked out the shops. I delighted in watching her pick out new riding pants, new tops, and another set of boots. Max and I collected supplies, making sure the four of us would eat well. It was only another day's ride to get back to the royal court, but we might have to camp outside King's Court while we came up with a plan to rescue the hostages—assuming there were any. I wasn't leaving anything to chance.

When we were finished, I pulled her through the alley, pausing under the shadows of the buildings. Dropping our bags, I lowered hers as well, freeing her hands.

"Do you know why I brought you back here?"

"This is where you married me." She shrank back against the wall and let out a breath. "I always imagined something different. I mean, I wasn't one of those girls who planned it all out, you know? I had some friends who did, but I was only ten. Then, after the portal opened, it seemed fruitless. But I always thought it would be… bigger."

"Bigger?"

She rolled her eyes. "Not your cock, Voss."

"I didn't explain what was happening then, but I want to now." I stepped up to her, placing my fingers around her wrist, the one that held our marriage band. "I want you to become Blood Queen."

"Voss—"

I kissed her lips, not letting her interrupt this. "Let me finish. If you become Blood Queen, you'll have the chance to bring me back, but it will bond us together. My life force and yours. What happens to you happens to me." Curling my fingers around her hand, I pressed her palm against my chest. My heart beat wildly between us. "And you'll ascend. You'll become Fae. You'll have magic. You'll be—"

"Everything I've fought against my entire life." Max pressed her eyes closed, and I could feel her shutting down through our bond. She didn't want to become Fae as a part of her still wanted to destroy us and our society, but she was beginning to see the possibility of something else, something more.

She opened her eyes. "So, you are allowing me the choice?"

"As I should have done when I married you."

Max shook her head. "There are so many things stacked against us now. We have the Fae who are planning a coup, we have the Fae who have fallen into line, and we have the human revolution on the horizon. That's two war fronts, Voss, unless we can get the humans on our side. I'm not sure if I can do that while being Fae."

"But…" I prompted, because the way she worried her lower lip told me there was more. I could fish it out of her head, but I enjoyed how she opened up to me, allowing me inside without having to rummage around myself.

"But it would be easier to fight if I ascended. And you said we'd share power, meaning we'd be stronger together." She let out a breath. "As much as I want to say it's a bad idea or it repulses me, it… doesn't. Maybe it would have when we started this journey, but it feels like a lifetime has gone by in a short amount of time."

"You can take time to think about it."

Her lips pressed into a thin line. Resolve settled across her mind, thick and pointed. "If what Lord Alpin said earlier is true, then we may have a fight on our hands sooner than we thought. We need to be at our strongest for it."

"You think we need to do it before we leave here?"

She nodded. "I mean, I don't know. That seems the most logical. We're safe here, for now. And if we're going to temporarily make ourselves vulnerable, it should be here. Right?"

"Right."

"Plus, I hear magic allows you to control your period, and I'm all about not having this anymore."

I wrinkled my nose. "Not sure if that's a good enough reason to make a life altering decision, little fox."

She wrapped her arms around my neck. "It's a great reason. You've obviously never had cramps before."

I hiked her legs up, and she wrapped them around my waist as I settled my hard cock against her core. "Want to show me?"

Chuckling, she pressed a kiss to my cheek and opened her mind to me. *What in the Mother.* It felt like her insides had gone through a blender and were slowly seeping out of her.

"And you deal with this… monthly?"

"Yup."

"Fuck that. Let's go make you my queen."

She laughed as I carried her, awkwardly walking out of the alley with her still wrapped around me. Her laugh was music to my soul, and I didn't care what happened to the rest of the world, so long as I got to hear that more often.

Using my magic, I forced our bags to follow behind us back to the inn.

Penn. I pushed the thought out into my companion's head.

What, Voss?

It's time.

Nineteen

SCARLET

His joy came across our bond without an ounce of trepidation. The strength of his positivity was enough to knock away my fears. With my legs wrapped around him and our purchases magically floating behind us, I savored the feeling of his arms around me. His warmth flooded me. The beating of his heart pounded firmly against me.

"What can I do to make you feel better about this?" His breath glided over my ear, sending chills down my body. There it was. Through our link, he could sense everything he needed to about me in a few moments. My fears threatened to consume me, and Voss sensed them. He always did.

"What if I hurt you?"

"You mean accidentally?" His arms tightened around me. "Because just a few days ago, you were considering how best to display my detached head on a mantle." His breath teased my neck as he spoke.

I laughed. I wasn't sure I was worthy of his trust, not when there was still hesitation inside me. What if I failed to bring him back? I couldn't imagine myself living in a world without him. And we'd be linked. Our lives. Forever.

If we had any hope of uniting the humans and the Fae, it might be from a union like this. If the Fae Slayer and a Fae could bond and be happy together, then perhaps others would believe in the missives Voss sent out as king.

But Alpin's words prickled at the edge of my mind. Perhaps it was too hopeful and optimistic, so I settled on something smaller. If I became Blood Queen, it would solidify my relationship with Voss forever. It would put us on the same level. We would be equals.

We already are.

No, you understand magic way more than I do. And you could tie me down with nothing more than it.

He chuckled, pressing his lips to my cheek and hiking me up to get a better hold on my ass. "You'll need training. You won't learn everything overnight."

I leaned back to get a good look at him. His eyebrow arched. I ran my fingers through his hair, enjoying the feel of the silky locks. "I murdered tons of Fae, and you doubt my ability to learn a little magic?"

"Never doubt, no. Worry you might light me on fire? Perhaps."

I nuzzled his shoulder. "You know, a part of me is still worried about why your step-siblings wanted me to become Blood Queen so badly." There had to be a reason why Morna and Cumina craved it. What weren't we seeing?

"They are not privy to the information we have now. They believed you would end my life and become the sole conveyor of power. But we know you can bring me back by using the transfer of magic. While I am on the brink, you should be able to imbue our souls together."

You will come back to me. Now and always.

I was certain that had already happened more than once already. I wondered about when Voss healed me; if he had traced those words onto my essence, making us more entwined than either of us could imagine.

Would it be so bad? His voice purred inside my head.

"It will be if they can use it against us." I huffed out a breath, still mulling over how this would benefit his step-siblings.

Voss shook his head as he walked up the stairs to the inn. He stopped just shy of the threshold, freezing at something I couldn't see. The happiness I had felt earlier seeped straight out of his body. He swallowed. It was the closest to worry I had ever felt from him.

"Before you two do this, we need to talk." Elspeth's voice.

I unwrapped myself from Voss, and he placed me gently on my feet. His hold didn't cease but slid up to my waist instead. Turning, I faced Elspeth and Penn. They took up the threshold of the doorway, not allowing either of us inside.

Penn looked less inebriated, though not by much. While his eyes were bright, red rimmed each. Dark half-moons undercut the lightness of his skin. I felt awful.

Voss pushed the vial into his palm, which Penn took with complete relief across his features. It wasn't enough liquid to last forever, but it would be a reprieve. Penn put a single drop on his tongue and breathed out.

Elspeth eyed the exchange, but continued, "Because this changes everything. The dynamic of the kingdom, the royal line, the royal magic—*everything*, Voss. And we fought too long and too hard for you to do something like this without talking it over first."

"What's there to talk about?" Voss straightened.

Elspeth let out a breath. "How about we have lunch, and if you two still feel the same afterward, I will give you my blessing as long as Penn oversees."

"Why Penn? Wouldn't that be…" I shifted my gaze to him. Based on how miserable he was being in Voss's head, I couldn't imagine being in the room with us would be any better. At least right now, he looked peaceful.

"Because he can sense Voss and could give you fair warning if you aren't bringing him back soon enough. We can have lunch while the Faerie wine is in his system and talk before you make this life-altering choice." Elspeth's brows furrowed low.

Penn let out a sigh and ran his fingers through his hair. "And no, it will not be fun for me. I'm not a voyeur, and the Mother knows Voss doesn't like to share."

Voss's fingers pressed into my skin.

Penn's attention turned to Voss. "Please, Voss. We're asking for a conversation beforehand as your advisers to quantify the risks involved."

"What about the risks if we do nothing?" Voss tilted his head to the side. "You both know as well as I do this needs to happen."

Elspeth let out a breath. "I'm going to be brutally honest. I don't trust her right now."

Voss let out a low guttural sound from his throat.

"Any hesitation could lead to her accidentally killing you, Voss."

I flinched as Penn said those words. He was right, of course, but the mistrust in his voice was plain to hear. I no longer wanted to hurt Voss, but the opposite. I planned for a lifetime with him, and any risk to that, including myself, I would gladly remove from the equation. Hearing my fears reflected in Penn's voice was too much to bear, especially since he had likely felt those coming from me too. My darkest fears shoved right back in my face.

Anger welled inside me. "Please, Penn, tell me how I am going to fuck this up? Why don't you enlighten me?" My voice dipped into a growl. Part of this was a defense. I hated where he was coming from, because I *could* ruin everything. Still, I couldn't fight the tight feeling inside me.

Voss pulled me into him, whether in a protective gesture for me or his friend, I wasn't sure.

Elspeth held out her hands, her eyes softening around the edges. The open expression was so unlike her, it made me pause. "We're asking for a conversation, nothing more. This is more for us—to be certain this is the right move. Sometimes, it's not about you."

Voss let out a breath, and I winced. They were right. While Voss might have been king, power could corrupt. They were here to keep us in check, and since I joined the group, Voss had done things the other two disapproved of. It was fair to talk it out, especially if I were to become their queen.

It was a strange thought.

Perhaps I would become the change the Fae needed to see. Or maybe I would burn them from the inside out. Penn's fears were valid.

He huffed out a breath. The depths of his turquoise eyes reflected the ocean. "We don't want to lose either of you."

Elspeth slid a glance between us.

"Fine," I said, conceding. From his time connected to me, Penn should know I needed Voss as much as I needed the air inside my lungs, but they were owed a conversation. This decision could change everything. "Discussing over food sounds great."

Voss's hand found the small of my back, pulling me into him possessively. "I appreciate your doing this, but we don't have to." His voice was low, the barest whisper in my ear. His concern for me blanketed my veins. While he respected his friends, he didn't want this to hurt me. He sensed my unease.

But this was bigger than us—it always had been.

My gaze met Penn's. His turquoise irises held more fear than my victims'. He was terrified of losing Voss. I felt the same about Quinn and Marcy. The best I could do was to be honest with him and show a willingness to listen. After all, wasn't that the whole point of this? To be a better leader than the previous reign?

If we were going to fix what was broken, it had to begin with our group.

"We do," I said, pulling his lips to mine. *Even if it doesn't change our mind, maybe we need to change theirs.* My lips rested against him. Chaste, not distracting from our current situation.

Relief relaxed Penn and Elspeth's expressions as we moved to a table in the converted office space. They closed the doors between us and the rest of the tavern. We could have a more private conversation here, and after hearing the pain etched in his friends' voices, we needed it.

Once again, instead of sitting in my own seat, Voss pulled me on top of him. I rolled my eyes but settled onto his lap. He was comforting, and he needed the same himself. After almost losing me, he didn't want to let me go, even for a second.

"Okay, we're listening." Voss turned his attention toward his friends, resting his hand on my leg. His thumb worked up my inner thigh, causing me to shudder against him.

I was a little sore from earlier, but the closeness I felt to him now… It was something new. Bigger than the last time I was with him. It felt stretched taut, like a bowstring ready to fire. I was unsure of what lay in the crosshairs.

"First, we're worried you will die," Penn said. The way his lips pulled taut and the glassy look in his eyes spoke volumes. "Even if she wants to keep you alive, there's the chance she won't be able to bring you back."

Fear shot through me. "What does he mean?" I tilted my head to look at Voss. "There's a chance I could fail?"

His face remained annoyingly stoic, and Voss shrugged. "There's always a chance. It takes a lot of power to bring someone back from the brink. I called to you when the venom almost dragged you under, and you'd do the same for me now. I'm not worried about it, because I've seen what you can do." His fingers pressed into my thigh, holding me tightly. His voice lowered. "And what you can do is fantastical—too intense for words."

"But I could kill him?" I turned to Penn, who was the reasonable one in this scenario. "Accidentally, I mean."

"Technically, it would be more like you didn't revive him, but yes, you could be the reason for his death." Elspeth picked at something under her fingernail as the door swung open.

Servers came in with water, some kind of ale, and plates of vegetables and cured meat. They put the food down and fled the room. No one spoke as they set everything up, but I wouldn't have been able to, anyway.

The thought of Voss dead, unmoving and cold. Not his brother, but him. It would leave me alone in this world, isolated. My thoughts darkened. They whirled with terror, creating a tornado in my heart.

Penn let out a breath. His gaze intensified on me, maybe from sensing the same unease blossoming in my chest. Letting out a breath, he pushed the ale away from him, grabbing the water instead.

Voss's previous thoughts had made me feel like it would be easy. He remained steadfast in his belief in me, but now that Penn and Elspeth were expressing their fears, it became a very realistic weight on my shoulders.

"What if you're wrong, Voss?" I whispered.

"Nonsense." He brought one plate closer and loaded it up with food, reaching around me. His body pressed against mine. "I have full confidence in you, little fox. You've already immolated a Fae with your mind. I am surprised you two are as worried as you are."

"I'd be an idiot not to be concerned," Penn grumbled, downing his glass of water in a few gulps. "The only thing you didn't rush into was killing your father, and that's because you needed to find the weapon first. Ever since then, it's been chaos, and you know it."

"Yes, but perfectly organized chaos."

I could feel him smiling against my shoulder as he pressed a kiss on top of my clothes. The heat seared through my shirt, making my skin combustible.

"Voss, what if they are right?" I turned so I could face him. Frigidness iced over my veins. "If I fail—"

"You won't." His brows lowered as he searched my gaze.

If I failed, it would be the three of us remaining, trying to unite a kingdom that refused help. I couldn't do this without him. I wasn't sure I could breathe without him. He had become my buoy in the open ocean. He kept me from drowning.

I had already felt it once, when Leveret pulled me under.

"Little fox," Voss paused, wrapping his arms around me and pressing me close to him. "You won't fail, but your fear… it won't do." His lips brushed my neck, soft and gentle. His touch was enough to flay me open. "We can wait. When you are ready, when you are confident." His resolve was intense and heady through our connection. He knew I could do this, but he wouldn't push me until I understood the same thing. Voss snaked one hand up my neck, cupping my jaw. He turned me toward him. His dark eyes were liquid fire, bordered with amusement. "You won't kill me."

"But—"

"But we will wait until you believe the same." He pressed his lips to mine, nipping my lower lip with his teeth. When he pulled back, he smiled. "And when we're ready, Penn will supervise. If you do not trust yourself, perhaps you can trust him?"

Penn and I locked eyes. His brows lowered, and he nodded at me. Understanding snapped between us, and I didn't need any bond to explain it to me. Penn understood my fears because he held the same ones. Voss's life mattered to both of us.

There was no doubt that someday I would become his queen, because I wanted to have all of Voss like he had all of me. I focused back on my plate of food as a blush crept up my cheeks.

And I enjoyed it. Thoroughly. His chuckle resonated into my very soul. I gasped as he sent me an image of myself, naked and strewn before him. Every inch of my skin bathed in his blood. *Don't you want it, just a little?*

I jammed my elbow into him as heat flooded my body. How was it possible to be this turned on by him?

Penn groaned. "Even with the Faerie wine, I can still… *sense* how disturbing you are being. Elspeth, what did I do to myself?" He hit his forehead against the table and pressed his eyes shut.

She sipped her ale and stared at the three of us. "Honestly, Penn, what did you think would happen?"

"I don't know."

If we're relying on him to be the one to save you if something goes wrong, I think we need to give him a break.

Voss hummed against my skin. *Funny, Elspeth told me earlier to be nicer to him.*

Maybe you can listen to the women in your life?

He went quiet. His thumb trailed along my lower lip as he gazed at me, watching every flicker of my expression as if I were art. His other hand rested possessively on my waist.

I will be nicer, but remember that you're the one who threatens to stab him.

Only when I am bored.

You get bored quite often, little fox.

What can I say? I need entertainment.

Penn grimaced, taking out the vial again. "I cannot believe this is wearing off so quickly." Sweat beaded along his brow.

"Are you… okay?" I tilted my head to the side as Voss's grip fell away from me.

Penn's eyes focused on me, and he let another drop fall onto his tongue. His irises were churning ocean currents. "No, Scarlet. I'm not okay. I am terrified of a great many things, including losing the reckless asshole sitting behind you."

"Penn," Voss's voice warned.

"No, I need to say this. You are both insatiable. You both act like you want to consume each other. That's fine, because it's your journey, but I desperately want to be out of your head, Voss." He swallowed and added, "I don't want to lose either of you."

Taking in a breath, I forced my racing heart to relax. Tension unfurled inside me. I leveled my gaze at Penn. "We are going to make it out of this alive. One way or another, we're standing together at the end of this. And if I need to change or do something differently to keep him, I will. I refuse to lose anyone else. Okay?"

I had already lost too much.

Easy, little fox. Voss's fingers pressed into my skin. I had been tapping into his power without realizing it.

"It's going to be war, Scarlet. You cannot keep that kind of promise, as not everyone makes it out alive."

Elspeth let out a breath. "There is a logic behind ascending her. Having two Fae with the use of royal magic—sharing instead of siphoning it—would strengthen our side. It would allow us to potentially win with ease, and perhaps, less death."

That's all I wanted. I slumped into Voss's hold, allowing his power to drain out of me like a tub being unplugged.

"And we're going to save the world. Together. Isn't that the whole point of the prophecy?" I asked, looking around the table.

The words *inevitable end* echoed in my head, but I refused to believe that part of it. It could mean anything. It could be the end of my human existence for all we knew. If we fixed the world, saved my friends, and made the Fae and humans live together harmoniously, wouldn't we be deserving of a happily ever after? There was no preordained bullshit that was going to stop me from trying.

"We'll do it when I'm ready," I said, echoing Voss's earlier words. My nerves felt fried. The more we examined what could go wrong, the more my anxiety flared to life.

Voss's hands curled against my hips. "I know it's wrong of me, but watching you two argue…" His voice was low in my ear and only meant for me.

I could feel his length hardening.

"So inappropriate, Voss."

He cleared his throat. "We'll be as safe as possible with Penn overseeing, and Elspeth ready to heal, just in case. Since we're not doing it tonight, let's focus on more pressing issues. How are we going to take back the royal court?"

"Take back?" Elspeth asked.

"Seems Iobhar had some ideas in my absence." Voss stabbed at his mound of potatoes and offered one to me. I glanced at him, and he shifted his hold on the fork. "You don't have to eat if you don't want to."

I swallowed, knowing Voss had seen into the parts of my memories that I longed to bury. My fingers curled around the metal, and I slid the bite in between my lips.

He let out a low sound, almost like a purr. "I like feeding you, and if he ruined that for us, I will go down to the depths and tear his soul straight from the Mother to punish him all over again."

I paused, mouth gaping as I stared at him. The words coursed through me, penetrating my heart. "I refused to have it be ruined forever." But the chalky taste in my mouth told me how much work I had to do.

"We'll get there." He brushed his lips against the shell of my ear. "If I pushed you too hard today to accept the position as my queen—"

"You didn't."

Maybe something like this got easier to talk about over time, but in the inn's tavern over dinner was not the moment. Voss had withheld the truth, but I would have still killed the king had I known his plan. I had needed revenge more than anything. And even now, he never pushed me farther than I wanted to be pushed. He always gave me an out—sometimes to the point of infuriating me.

But if I were being honest, I loved how he gave me control. The respect he held even as he defiled me woke a primal part of my brain. I wanted to claim him, conquer him, and becoming his queen? That was part of it.

However, I felt too out of control right now. My thoughts bounced between being absolutely sure and terrified. Deciding now would be a mistake, one that could lead us down a dangerous path.

"Pardon me for interrupting whatever is happening right now," Elspeth said, using her fork to point at us. Her eyes landed on Voss and stayed there. "What do you mean, Iobhar had some ideas?"

"It seems there was an uprising in our absence." Voss frowned, but I could feel the tendrils of worry creep into him. "And I should have killed Iobhar when I had the chance."

"You do have a habit of making things harder for yourself." Elspeth let out a sigh and stabbed at something on her plate that broke into two pieces. Part of it skittered across the table. She glared at it, as if it had committed a capital offense. "Well, we have plenty of planning to do prior to getting back to the king's court."

VOSS

My eyes were pinned on her as she flitted around the room, stuffing things from our dismantled pack together in a way that I would have to reorganize before we left. If Max needed more time to decide, I would give it to her. If I could pause time without it destroying me in the process, I would.

Bitter disappointment tried to well inside me. I imagined my magic flowing through her veins, bringing us together for the rest of our lives. I longed to have my blood feeding her. A joining on a level more powerful than blood bonding and our marriage.

I wanted to consume her.

"What?" she asked, straightening as she stuffed another shirt into the pack.

I cringed, but pushed off the wall and crossed the room. Gently, I wrapped my fingers around hers. "Let me?"

Her eyes met mine, and she let out a breath. "I don't know what's wrong with me. I've never felt so…"

Curling my arms around her, she leaned into my chest. Her ear rested over my heart. Fingers pressed into my shoulders as she kept a tight hold. Max didn't need to explain it to me. I felt it. The ebb and flow of every tumultuous moment I longed to flush out of her and set on fire. Every memory she didn't dare forget, but wished she could pack away until it no longer hurt her.

If I could end the feeling of helplessness, I would, if only to stop her suffering. I would give her emotions a body, so we could carve it into pieces, until she realized how much power and control she truly had. At least, she had power over me.

My jaw ticked. "I know," I told her. Bringing my hand to the nape of her neck, I grabbed hold and pulled her so she faced me. "If you want me to do anything, you can ask."

"Even stabbing you?" Her mouth quirked for a flash, but quickly settled back into the frustrated pout she had been wearing.

"Especially stabbing me." I brushed my lips against her forehead. "Give me your anger and anguish. Destroy me from the inside out. Just don't destroy yourself."

She swallowed but nodded in acquiescence.

I frowned, not enjoying how agreeable she had become, but we had our battles, and perhaps fighting with me was too much. Though, I hoped she would get her sass back someday, because I missed the taste of her bitterness.

"Can I finish packing for us, so you stop destroying our clothes?"

"Says the man who lights plenty of mine on fire."

I chuckled and stepped away from her. She sank onto the bed and watched as I pulled the pack back together.

"You're so particular."

I glanced at her.

"So, why is it that you love—"

"Getting you completely messy?" I arched a brow and placed the last items in the pack. Bending down, I picked up her boots and brought them to her. She had been wearing slippers for our stay in Alpin's court, but for the next part of our journey, she needed to be better outfitted. "I enjoy seeing you unkempt."

"Why?" Her cheeks flushed.

Because watching Max become unhinged was akin to letting part of my soul run free. She was a piece of art when she was at her worst, and I wanted to explore every moment she existed.

"It turns me on."

She snorted.

"And I think it turns you on, too."

Her gaze heated as she looked at me. "How can you be so sure?"

Because I can feel the liquid threatening to pool between your thighs.

Max scowled as I knelt in front of her and placed her foot inside the boot. "You're a show off, you know that?"

"Obviously."

Her jaw pulsed as I slipped her other foot into her boot and laced them both. "Do you think we're making the right choice?"

"Going back to the royal court?"

"No, by not… ascending me now?"

I shrugged. "You aren't ready, so of course we're making the right choice. Would I like you to be at your strongest when we head into enemy territory? Of course. But you've been resourceful for your entire life, little fox. Nothing will stop that now. Magic or no, you'll find a way to survive."

She swallowed, and I heard the protests before she spoke.

I shook my head, silencing her. "You are a fighter. Say it." Cinching the boots tighter, I challenged her with nothing more than a look. I dared her to disobey me.

Her breath came out in a short huff. Her face reddened. "Fuck you, Voss."

I smirked. "That was the correct answer, little fox." Pulling hard on the strings, I tied the final knot and stood up, keeping my gaze on her. She shivered, and I felt the flutter of her desire through our bond. Not like it was before, when she wanted to surrender. No, this was an inkling of her. The warrior, the assassin, the being of vengeance wrought on a world that didn't deserve her.

"Shall we?" I offered her my hand. Her fingers curled into my palm, and I hoisted her up, pulling her close. "Let's go kill some Fae."

"I thought you would never ask."

❧ ✄ ❧

When we reached the stables, I passed our pack along to Penn. He took it with a solemn nod.

The Faerie wine had worn off, and he decided to keep the rest of it for when he absolutely needed a break from us. His eyes met mine. *I'm glad you chose to wait.*

I didn't. She did. You should thank her.

His turquoise gaze shifted to where my fingers interlocked with hers. The Fae Slayer and Fae King, off to destroy whatever coup Iobhar tried to hold in my stead.

Maybe if she stops threatening to kill me, I will.

Tell Penn that I will threaten him whenever—

"If all three of you continue talking inside your heads, I will find the first hoswisp nest on the road, give you all a sleeping draught, and leave you for the monsters to pick clean." Elspeth breezed by us, knocking into my shoulder on the way with her head held high.

"She was—"

"I don't care what she said, Penn!" Elspeth whirled around. Her eyes churned with flecks of gold. "I will not be the fourth wheel on whatever fucked up journey this is."

Max laughed. "As if Voss would allow anyone to come within five feet of me."

"He's going to have to when I oversee you turned Fae." Penn scowled. "Wait, why am I leaning into the fourth wheel thing?" He turned and stalked after Elspeth. "There is nothing going on between me and them!" They disappeared into the stable.

"Is Penn really going to watch us without his head being removed from his body?"

I let out a breath. "They would be the only two on the planet who would be allowed. And even then, I still might kill them if I were at my full strength. But you are going to bring me to the brink of death, so it is likely I won't raise a finger." Lifting her chin with my hands, I stared into the marrow of her soul. "No one, however, will touch you except me."

She opened her mouth to speak, but stopped as she caught sight of something over my shoulder. "Switch!"

I dropped my hands instantly, but realized she was talking to the horse—the horse she was now running to with her black bob bouncing around her ears. The mare pressed into her hands. A smile beamed across her face.

I had never been jealous of a *horse* before.

"You found them," she squealed.

"Of course we found them." Penn rolled his eyes. "It wasn't hard."

"How much coin did you spend?" I asked, eyebrow arched.

"Don't ask." Elspeth folded her arms over her chest. "But assuming Iobhar didn't give our reserves to everyone inside the kingdom, we'll have plenty to make up for it once we're back in the royal court."

I sighed as Max nuzzled Switch's face. Whatever the cost, seeing this moment of joy was worth it. Plus, as Blade nudged me, my heart swelled. It was a bit of a homecoming. Every being I cared for in one place. At Alpin's court, no less, where I took Max to be my wife.

Where I gave her the choice to become my queen.

I swallowed. "You did not meet me with this much enthusiasm."

Max tossed a quick glance at me, her blue eyes blazing. "I like her."

"As do I." I crossed to her and held out my hand to steady her. Bracing herself against me, Max swung her leg up and around Switch. The rest of us mounted our own. "Shall we?"

We started the long trek back to the royal court.

❧ ✄ ☙

The hours bled on. Normally, there would be bickering. Either Penn or Elspeth would tell me how to approach the oncoming escapades, or Max would make a seething remark. But quiet filled the air around us, adding to the tension.

Max still hadn't told me everything that happened with my brother. Penn was still faintly inside my head. Elspeth held her anger about being the only one not telepathically communicating.

I could fix that last one, but Max would stab her in the process.

Though it would be entertaining.

Once we made it past a small outcropping of trees and over what used to be a riverbed, we caught sight of the first spires of a large hoswisp nest. My ears pricked, straining for any sound. Sending out a wave of magic, I sensed nothing alive inside the nest.

"It's empty," I announced.

Elspeth's hands loosened on her reins, and Penn let out a sigh.

I glanced over at Max as the strings between us pulled taut. Fingers trembled around the reins. Her face paled and skin prickled with goosebumps. Her pupils dilated as she took in the structures.

She had lost Anya to a swarm recently, even if it felt like a lifetime ago. Pain cut through Max's core. Almost as thick as the helplessness she felt thereafter. Never having time to mourn, but always pushing forward.

A fighter.

But right now, she needed to be something else. The friend who lost too much. The woman who had been through hell and back. My wife.

I whistled, calling Switch in close. My hands grasped the reins firmly as Blade danced underneath me. I picked Max up, yanked her unceremoniously from the saddle, and brought her into my lap.

Most of the time, Max was larger than life, carving out space as if her body craved it. But now, she curled against my chest. Fingers found my shoulders, holding firm. "I don't—"

"Shh," I said, quieting her.

Her thoughts roiled, like a hurricane. They whipped around, threatening to tear her apart from the inside out. "I still *feel* him."

I stilled. Jaw clenched. I pulled her into me, wanting to break everything left on this vile, wretched planet. My heart raced, but I forced myself to listen, to be present and let her say what she needed to.

"The way his magic curled into me."

"Are you able to show me now?" I pressed my lips against her forehead, whispering the words across her skin. "Let me see. Let me know."

A tear fell down her cheek, but her mind bloomed. So wide, Penn stiffened. I dove inside, picking apart everything he said. The words as they spewed vile poison from his lips. He never touched her, but he didn't have to. He took away her choice. My brother had stripped her down and made her feel like she was next to nothing. Worthless, save for her place as a pawn against me. She showed me her attempt at escape; the sword falling from her fingers. Their late night talks.

Her plan to convince him she was on his side until it became too much for her. Her secondary plan was to wear out as much magic as she could, so I would fare better in the fight.

But in the end, it was her. She had saved herself.

"You are so much more than a weapon," I told her.

"I know." The croak came out of her throat as she slammed her eyes shut, shaking her head against my chest. She buried herself in me.

Penn met my gaze from his saddle. His lips pressed into a thin line. *She needs to be healthy for the transition, else—*

I know.

Power corrupts when the soul isn't ready for it.

I sucked in a breath, letting the gentle rock of Blade's footsteps lull Max. Everyone had been right to push this off. I had been too eager, too glad to have her back in my life, that I refused to see the pain she carried. It was boundless.

"What do you need?"

"This." She inhaled, and her shoulders relaxed a fraction of an inch. "You."

"Are you… smelling me?"

Color rose to her cheeks, but she buried her nose further in my chest. "You smell good. Like ginger and heat."

"Take as much as you need." I kept my hands firm around her.

"What about my horse?"

A twitch of a smile. "*Your* horse?"

She nodded into my chest, an argument brewing just below the surface. "My horse."

I loved hearing her possession, the confidence in which she declared it. Max wanted to move on, forward. But there would always be moments to heal in between. This was one of those. "Switch will always follow Blade."

"You named your horses Switch and Blade?"

"Names have meaning. My horses love each other."

"What about Penn's and Elspeth's?"

"Penn named his Mary, because she's a mare, and he severely lacks creativity."

"I heard that," he retorted.

"And mine is named Magaisht."

"Did you just sneeze?" Max raised her head and arched a glance over her shoulder.

"It stands for males are garbage and I should hate them." Elspeth shrugged. "Though, one could argue it's really my *taste* in males that is horrendous, but that's hearsay."

"It's not hearsay if we are hearing the confession from your own lips," Penn added.

Elspeth sniped another remark back, but I turned my attention to Max. Her blue eyes blazed as she gazed up at me.

"How are you feeling?"

"Better." She swallowed, throat working. "Sometimes, it feels like I'm being cleaved in two. A part of me is here, wanting to finish what we started. The other is stuck in the past. Watching her die or helpless as my body does whatever he tells it to."

"It wasn't your body betraying you." I had to stop myself from cracking a tooth. "That was Leveret. So do not for one moment put the blame on yourself."

"But I should have been able to save Anya." Sorrow buried itself deep.

I clutched her against me. "If you need to cry, little fox, do so. You and she had the ultimate goal in the end, to save Marcy. And if I recall the events correctly, you did save her. Both of you."

"And then Marcy threw me away."

I hummed. "Do you believe everyone reacts the same as you?"

"What do you mean?"

"You and Marcy were both in pain—direly so. And perhaps, out of your anguish, you both said some things that you did not entirely feel?"

Max sighed and ran her nose along my tunic, inhaling again. "Perhaps."

"Besides, you have me."

A small chuckle escaped her throat. She sank her teeth into the fabric of my tunic, catching a small sliver of skin. If she tore me apart, I would happily die under her hands.

"I do," she agreed.

"You would also think that since I am your husband, you'd be more excited to say those words."

"Husband." Her eyes rolled, and she gazed up at me once more. "If you were to ask me to marry you right now, I wouldn't find it as repulsive as I once did."

"Your compliments astound me."

"I would still probably try to stab you at the altar."

"Ah, but you are assuming I would dislike the notion." I shifted her weight, so I had one of my hands free to caress the side of her face. She leaned into my touch. The turmoil she felt earlier had settled, turning back to calm. "Do you want to go back onto Switch?"

"Can I ride with you for a bit?"

"Any time you—"

"Don't you dare finish that sentence, Devoss Balgair," Penn's voice cut sharply across the wilds.

"Wow, my full name, Penn?" I shifted Max in the seat so she was in front of me. Handing her the reins, I ran my fingers over her arms.

"Yes, because I would appreciate five minutes of peace from the two of you. I only have a few drops of Faerie wine left, and you both are *horrible*."

I chuckled, nuzzling into Max's neck.

"Doesn't he realize he picked the worst person to blood bond with if he wanted any kind of quiet?"

"You called me a person again." My lips brushed her skin, and I reveled at the way goosebumps prickled across her flesh.

"Fuck off, Voss."

"Yeah, fuck off, Voss," Penn echoed.

Max burst out in laughter, and hearing it was music to my soul. I couldn't help the tightness at which I held her, firm against me, soothing all my inner demons to sleep.

Twenty-One

SCARLET

His hold grounded me. Kept my tether close to the earth. I needed it after everything I had been through. I hadn't realized how much I needed comfort until I had seen those spires. My heart had threatened to stop in my chest. Everything inside me had screamed to run, hide, kill, fight. The warring emotions had left me paralyzed.

And that inability to act had brought everything back with Leveret. Voss had been there, holding me until I calmed, and even after. His presence stretched inside me, taking up space I desired to give him.

Once he set me back on Switch, guilt and worry needled me once again. Guilt because I had spent so much of my time imagining his demise. And because joining his cause—siding with the Fae—that was turning against everything I used to be.

Becoming someone new.

It felt wrong to stray from my path.

But the fear of staying the same was also thick.

If I led him down the path that would end with his demise… I refused to think about it. I no longer wanted his death, but what if the prophecy was true? What if we had stumbled into something bigger than ourselves, and there was no way out but the inevitable end?

We stopped to make camp after twilight. Penn, Elspeth, and Voss kept themselves busy by readying the grounds. I was lost in my own thoughts, chewing on my lip as I considered everything that happened over the last two weeks.

My life felt forever changed.

"All right. You're coming with me." Elspeth snatched my hand and dragged me away from the warmth of the fire. Her eyes lit up as she cast some Faerie lights around us. When we were out of earshot and the fire was nothing more than a speck, she stopped and stared at me. "Spill it."

"Spill what?"

"I'm not privy to what the guys are. They can sense your mood, and I sure as hell can figure it out by the thickness of the silence. What is going on in your head?" Her finger pointed at the middle of my brow.

I swallowed, looking away from her. Elspeth always had an intensity about her, and when she put her hands on her hips, she might as well have ripped the confession from my lips.

She never needed to use magic.

"I wish I could kill him all over again. I keep seeing his face. Sometimes when I look at Voss, I still see Leveret. But I—" I cut myself off. "I'm trying to forget it. Move on, but…"

"There's no moving on from this." Elspeth waved her hand, and the earth shifted underneath us, creating two mounds. "Take a seat, Scarlet. It's time you heard a bit about me."

I arched an eyebrow but did as she asked.

"Huh. It is strange not having you sass back." Elspeth gave me a knowing glance. She crossed her legs in front of her and leaned back.

"Not listening was getting me into more trouble than it was worth," I admitted. Plus, I was safe here. There was no reason to continue fighting with my allies.

She nodded. "Smart. I've learned not to trust myself with males for a similar reason. They have to pass through Voss and Penn before I see anyone new. I have notoriously bad taste."

"How bad?"

"Well, Treborne, for one. And this guy named Evander, who has his head shoved so far up Lady Burke's ass that he'll do whatever she asks, even choosing her over me. He's... not a good person." Elspeth frowned. "Now, the thing is, I've dated other males— casually. But the relationships always end the same. I realize how horrible of a being they are only *after* I've fallen for them. Which leaves me heartbroken and devastated. It's easier to swear them off completely, right?"

I kept eying her.

"Right," she agreed with herself, tucking her auburn locks behind her ears. "My point is, in my heart, I knew they were the wrong choice. There was always something ugly, a prickling in the back of my neck. I could never be myself around them. Instead, I tried to be who they expected me to be." She pointed a finger at me. "And I see you doing that now, likely because of the trauma of Leveret, but you aren't you. You are being someone who fades into the background. And you, Scarlet, do not fade."

"What if I want to?" Glancing back toward the fire, I didn't want to look at her after the admission. "I'm sick of being some kind of savior. I was never supposed to make it this long." I never was supposed to live with the guilt clawing up my chest every day. It threatened to burst through and consume me whole.

I had killed innocents.

I had gotten myself trapped.

I hadn't been fast enough to save Anya.

What good was I? And if I was bringing Voss to the same fate, how could I possibly live with myself after that?

"Do you want to? Because if that's what you want, then so be it. I'll give you the space to figure this out. But if you are collapsing in on yourself because of a toxic male? Fuck that."

"Eloquent," I said.

"I'm serious."

"I'm worried the wrong decisions got me here. If I continue that trend, then where will it lead us? I'm trying to save everyone, but how will I choose if it comes down to sacrifice?"

"Why worry about something that hasn't happened yet?" Elspeth leaned forward and tapped my knee. "The late King Balgair worried the one who opened the portal would be the end of him. Instead of accepting his fate, he did everything he could to prevent his own end. That fear? That's what turned the Fae into the monsters you've met. We fed off his fear like poison, and it turned plenty of us sour."

"So, I should... what? Let the future happen?"

She shrugged. "Worrying about the future and trying to control it differ from *pursuing* a future. You should focus on your intentions, what you can control. It's the same with magic for us. We have to intend for something to happen, and it does, but it needs to be positive intent. If your intention is to avoid death, like the late King Balgair, it will eventually find you. You have to intend to have a life worth living, finding peace. *That's* where the power has always been."

My jaw worked as a chill flooded my limbs. It was easy to say these words, to mull them over in my head, but it was something else to live them. Especially with a looming war ahead of us.

But I supposed my intention had always been to survive. I had done that much so far.

"If you are serious about turning Fae, you need to go into it with the intention of saving Voss, the Fae, and humanity. You intend for your magic to do good, to be the uniting factor. Don't go into it fearing the worst. Does that make sense?"

"How does this relate to you having terrible taste in men?"

"Well, I choose the wrong males because I don't actually want to be settled down. I'm inviting failure because I *fear* success. Having my heart torn out because I realize the male was an asshole is one thing. Destroying my soul because a good male didn't return my affections? That's another thing entirely. The Mother has a funny way of giving us our intentions back to us."

"How does that make any sense?" I asked.

"Self-fulfilling prophecy. It doesn't have to make sense." I opened my mouth to say something in argument of this, but she held up her hand. She continued, "My story serves as a warning not to fulfill your own prophecy."

"Yes, but we're talking about a *literal* prophecy."

"And if I recall, you doubted such a thing existed."

"That was before I broke the curse and was able to be controlled." I let out a long breath.

"Voss tried to protect you from that, you know?"

"I know." I glanced down at the bracelet. When I had found out we were married, it had infuriated me. But in the end, our marriage had saved me more than once. Leveret had been the only contending factor neither of us saw coming. "I'm not letting that asshole win." I shook my head, glancing up at Elspeth. Her skin glowed blue under the Faerie lights. "I know Leveret wanted to drive a wedge between Voss and me. He tried through our conversations, and when that didn't work, through his control. He had hoped for something like this, to ruin Voss's life after he was gone. But… they are so different. But here's my real fear." I looked down at my hands, not wanting to face her as I admitted this. "What happens if I ascend, and I get a flashback? What if I think I'm *there* instead of *here?*"

"Then Penn and I will help you navigate it. We're here for you— *both* of you. While we may have known Voss for most of our lives, you are a part of our group now. We're family, Scarlet. And we don't want anything bad to happen to either of you."

I started at the use of the word family. After the portal opened, I had one other family—Marcy, Anya, Quinn, and Paul—before he was killed. And with Anya gone now, that history felt lifetimes away.

Besides, what I had with them was fleeting—only existing for those quiet, stolen moments in between my killings. We waited on bated breath for the day we would be caught. Fear encapsulated our interactions, as we prayed no one would stumble upon our secrets.

Whereas Voss had claimed me—permanently by marrying me. He had chosen me and rode across the desolate landscape to save me. He wanted to make me his queen. There was nothing quiet or secretive about his feelings.

"Is that what we are?" I had to ask, because the intensity of what I shared with Voss was nothing compared to the agreeable banter I had with Penn and Elspeth.

"Perhaps right now it is born from circumstance, but if we play our cards right, we'll have a long future together. Longer still if you ascend to Queen."

"You don't think it's strange?"

She raised an eyebrow.

"Cumina and Morna wanted me to become Blood Queen. And I can't help but think they had some underlying reason."

Elspeth laughed. The sound caressed me like the glow of the moon. "While the sisters would have enjoyed watching the line die out, I believe they are in this for chaos. The more chaotic they can make the world, the more they thrive. If they knew there was a chance you and Voss would both survive, I doubt they would have asked you to ascend."

"What if I don't like it?"

"Being Fae?" Her eyes swirled as she nodded. "I could see why you'd ask that. Having power can corrupt, true. Voss has struggled since getting the magic of the royal line, but mostly because you are his anchor."

"What?"

"His anchor. The thing to keep him steady, so he doesn't lose himself to the power. Did he not tell you any of this?"

I shrugged, feeling heat rocket to my cheeks.

"It likely didn't occur to him to mention it." Elspeth sighed. "When you ascend, you'll need one too. You need someone to keep you accountable, make you stay yourself."

"Who is that for you?"

Elspeth pointed to herself. "I'm my own anchor, but that comes from being a healer. It's selfless magic. But, in my worst moments, Penn and I cover for each other in lieu of having a partner. Voss will likely be yours."

"Likely?" I choked out a laugh. "If Voss isn't mine, he will burn whoever it is until it finally becomes him."

"You aren't wrong." She gave me a smile, one reaching her eyes. "How are you feeling now?"

I let out a breath and ruffled my hair. My fingers snagged on a few tangled ends. "Still overwhelmed, but grateful." Glancing toward the fire, I watched as Voss clapped Penn on the back. I could only make out their silhouettes but felt a deep appreciation across our connection. It appeared that stopping for the night was good for all of us. "He is my anchor, even without magic. It's strange to say that, because Leveret still haunts me, but Voss isn't him. And he makes me feel like hope is obtainable."

"I'm glad. So many of us become ghosts to our past, and I believe there's someone out there for each of us who makes us feel solid, grounded."

I smiled. "Just not someone you choose for yourself, though. Right?"

She barked out a laugh. "No, I don't trust my own tastes. Who knows, maybe when this is all over, I can throw a giant ball, and you can choose my date." Elspeth winked at me.

"You do know that Voss is the only long-term relationship I've had... and it hasn't even been a month yet."

"Yeah." She stood up on her exhale. "But I see it. The way you both move around each other, you're in it for the long run. And if I'm totally honest, Voss is one of the good ones."

"So you've said." But I knew. I gazed at them, and Voss turned in our direction. I couldn't make out his face, but I felt his eyes on me. He *was* one of the good ones—at least, good for me. He didn't shy away from my violence, my anger, or my fears. Voss embraced all that I was. "Thanks, Elspeth." I smiled as we walked back over to the fire.

Twenty-Two

VOSS

The firelight danced along her skin, and a smirk played unbidden across my lips. She eyed me, a long glance that roamed over the length of my body. I held out my hand, and she took it. I pulled her into my arms, tucking her against my side.

My lips brushed against the shell of her ear. "What did you two talk about?"

"Intention."

I narrowed my gaze, and she taunted me inside her head. Dared me to force her to open. I wouldn't. Not this time, at least. "Well, what do you intend?"

"To eat, right now." Max tossed me a smile. "And perhaps murder you later." The joke left her lips but marred a spot on her soul the moment the words hit the air.

Penn must have felt the shift too, because he glanced at us. His turquoise eyes bounced back and forth, but settled on the stew he heated by the fire.

She fought back a yawn, and I pressed a kiss to her forehead. Weariness overtook her body, weaved into her bones, and wrapped through her soul. There was still another day of riding ahead of us, and we weren't sure what we would encounter. I wished we had more time. If she had been Fae, she would have been able to pull from her magic to keep herself afloat.

But she was still human. Powerful and strong in her own right, but nothing compared to the Fae. She could dip into the royal power through our blood bond, but that drained both of us. We'd have to rest for longer after we got the royal court sorted.

If we had time.

Time plagued me now. There was never enough. I longed for the day where we would have enough of it to settle down and find peace. To have our fears destroyed and finally be living in a space that allowed equality. It was something to work toward, but none of it would come easy.

Even if we won the war, nothing would change overnight.

"You need to sleep," I whispered into her ear. My cheek grazed hers.

Goosebumps prickled on her skin as my fingers trailed along her spine.

"I need to eat too. And you aren't helping." She squirmed under my touch but did nothing to escape.

I pulled her close, bringing her hips against mine. Her eyes widened as she glanced over at our companions.

You told me it would be impolite to do things next to them in the barn. And yet...

Her cheeks flushed.

Penn frowned as steam rose off the pot. "I think dinner is ready." He stood and stretched, his eyes landing hard on Max. "And you *really* need to learn how to shut yourself down. The only reason Voss isn't completely inside your head is by his choice, not yours."

Max swallowed. "Well, maybe if you hadn't been hiding things from me, I would have learned how to do this forever ago."

I flinched, but her fingers dug into my side. She was only saying it to argue with Penn, because there was no anger or barbs inside her words.

"That brings up a good point." I forced the conversation in a new direction as Penn opened his mouth to argue with her. "Perhaps we could better prepare you for the magic of ascending to Queen, so once you have it, you understand how to wield it."

Her gaze shifted back onto me. The blue was so deep, it swept me away. A part of me still couldn't believe she was back in my arms. *Mine.*

"Caveman." She rolled her eyes and slapped my chest. I wrapped my fingers through hers, keeping her pressed against my beating heart. I gazed into her thoughts to understand the meaning of the word.

"Do you want me to throw you over my shoulder?"

"Can we eat first?" Penn asked. His voice hitched with desperation.

Max let out a laugh. It coiled around me; chimes struck into my soul. "Yes, Penn, we can eat. Thank you."

Penn's gaze narrowed. "Did she just—"

"Yup," Elspeth said.

He took a cautious step back from the pot. "I feel like she's lulling me into a sense of complacency so she can slit my throat while I sleep."

Max's grin widened.

Penn frowned. "Why?! Why must you torment me so?!"

"It's too easy," she said, pulling me along with her to grab food.

"Besides, Voss seems to get a kick out of it every time I threaten you."

My best friend sighed. "Voss also likes when you threaten him."

"Yeah, but that's become less appealing to me."

Hearing her admit it made a feral part of me spring to life. "Say it again," I growled in her ear, careful not to put any magic into it.

"Say what?"

"That you want me alive."

"I said no such thing." She yanked herself away, but when she looked over her shoulder, sparkles erupted in her irises. I would have her on her knees again before long. "Fae King."

"Fae Slayer."

She smirked. And the string that bound us together preened in her chest. She grabbed a bowl, filled it, and passed it to me. I stared at the stew as she served herself. This woman, once full of venom and hatred toward all Fae, had given me the gift of a chance. Not just once, but twice. She had forgiven me.

Perhaps it was me who should be on my knees for her.

"Of course it should be," she answered me out loud. "But I like the other way too." Her lower lip went into her mouth, and she chewed on it. Tension coiled around us.

"You read my thoughts. Again."

"Yes."

The smile grew wider on my lips. "Well, then perhaps you can be taught after all."

Penn groaned.

"That wasn't an innuendo." My eyes trailed over her body. "Yet."

"I know, but I can feel it. And frankly, I am disgusted and horny at the same time, and I hate it."

I chuckled.

He threw a stale piece of bread at me, and it thudded against my chest. "When this is over, I am going to find some nice man to—"

Max prickled.

Penn's glare cut through Max's rising emotions. "Have you learned nothing about me yet? Consensually, Scarlet. I have no interest in whatever power play is happening between the two of you. I'm not... like that."

"It's an old habit." Max shook her head. "I'm sorry."

"An apology... Okay, now I am absolutely certain she's going to kill me tonight."

"I will attend your funeral. What would you like me to eulogize for you?" Elspeth smiled sweetly as she passed a bowl to Penn and took one for herself.

"Tell everyone that meeting Voss was the worst thing to ever happen to me."

"If I recall, you once called me the best thing to ever happen to you."

Penn's eyebrows lowered. "You can simultaneously be the best and worst thing."

"Ouch. That hurt more than the bread."

His eyes flared to life, drenching my body with water.

Max yelped and jumped away from me.

Water cascaded down my skin, covering my clothes and hair. My magic welled around me as I glared at Penn. My soup bowl had overflowed with the deluge, and I was no longer playing around. I took one step toward him when Max giggled.

The sound stopped me in my tracks, and I turned my glare to her.

"You think this is funny?"

"Hilarious."

I glanced at her bowl. It was almost empty. Fuck it. I did exactly what she had in mind about the caveman. I prowled toward her. She dropped the bowl. It sank into the deadened dirt. Lifting her up, I flung her over my shoulder.

"I'll be back."

"Hey!" she yelped.

I smacked her ass as I carried her behind an outcropping of rocks.

"Put me down!"

"As you wish." I dumped her unceremoniously out of my hands, and as she was about the collapse, I grabbed her neck, bringing her lips to mine.

She moaned against me, gasped, and opened her lips to allow me inside. I licked into her mouth, savoring the taste of her. The viciousness of a full moon in an empty night sky, the endless way she consumed me.

Fuck.

Her legs wrapped around my hips, and I thrust against her, bowing her back so her shoulders grazed the rocks. She sucked in a breath, pulling away from me; long enough for me to witness the dazed look in her eyes.

Fucking perfect.

The hem of her shirt was up and over her head, dropping to the ground without another word. I slammed my lips against hers, growling when I realized she wasn't wearing a bra. My fingers found her nipples and toyed with them, bringing them both to sensitive peaks as she let out another moan against me.

I was hard, and I wanted so desperately to be inside her. There was a strong part of her that was grossed out by her body right now, but there was another part, too. One that I hoped won out, but she still had all the power here.

"What's your safe word?"

She nipped my jaw. "Why? Are you concerned I'm going to use it?

I growled.

Scarlet rolled her blue eyes. Her eyelids lowered, and she gazed at me from beneath her lashes. She was being a brat, and I enjoyed every second.

My hand curled around her neck. "Your safe word."

"Switch. But as I said—"

I crushed my lips to hers. Her moan made her part for me, and I explored her mouth with my tongue. I grabbed a dagger from my belt. With precision, I cut the seam of her pants open. She tried to pull away from me to protest, but I grabbed onto the nape of her neck with my other hand and kept her against me.

Stop destroying my clothes.

I'll buy you new ones.

My little fox scoffed but thrust her tongue into my mouth. I groaned at the taste of her. Dropping the dagger, I reached inside to her panties. I rolled my fingers over her, and her thighs tightened around me.

Voss, I still have my—

I don't care. If you don't say the word, I'm taking you. I moved her panties aside and used magic to undo my own trousers as I pushed against her. My tongue finally won in the battle against hers as I notched myself at her entrance. I gave her a moment. *If you want me to stop—*

Don't stop.

Good girl.

I thrust inside her, sheathing myself all the way to the hilt. Fuck, it was like a homecoming. Feeling her clench around me. This is how I wanted to live and wanted to die, consumed by her. I loved the way she grasped me. Nails dug into my shoulders as if her life depended on cutting into me for survival.

"Voss." My name tumbled out of her mouth on the edge of a

breath. One of my hands supported her ass, moving her in rhythm with me, while the other one settled on the back of her head. Our foreheads pressed together. A sheen of sweat broke out across her skin as we moved as one, breathed the same air. She panted as I shifted deeper, and her hips settled against mine.

She clenched around me, and I switched my grip to her neck, placing my thumb right over her windpipe. Her eyes went glassy, blissed out as I pressed my lips to hers again. This time, I explored her as every muscle in her body clamped around mine.

Fuck, how I missed this. Missed her.

A silent scream ran through her, cut off by her lack of air. Her walls held me tight, and I lost myself to her, chasing my pleasure. We cascaded over the edge. I clung to her as her body went boneless in my arms. My eyes shut, basking in the aftermath.

Twenty-Three

SCARLET

Voss stayed with me. Our bodies pressed close together. His shirt was still on, pants half undone, and my clothes were… ruined. Again. He started to step back, but my legs tightened around him, holding him against me.

"Stay."

"I'm not going anywhere." His lips brushed my forehead. I sank into the feeling of safety he provided. We had this moment, and maybe every moment after this one would be a ghoulish nightmare, but not now.

Not here.

Not with him.

"Are you ready?"

I nodded against him, and he swept his lips along mine. The kiss was long, deep, and lingered even as he pulled out of me. He left tingles behind as he knelt and smiled up at me.

"I continue to get you messy, little fox."

Leaning against the rocky outcropping, I narrowed my gaze on him. "Something I am sure pleases you to no end."

The pesky smirk was back, giving him the relaxed, overconfident look that drove me wild. His fingers moved along my skin. Magic swept against me. I sucked in a breath but watched as every trace of our sex disappeared. Voss's hands whisked across me. Stitches in my clothes threaded back together, and he left everything clean. He grabbed my shirt and dusted it off. As he rose from his position, his fingers trailed along my midsection.

"How are you feeling?" The gingery scent of him surrounded me, making my nostrils flare. His gaze was genuine and caring, so unlike the hardened way he took me. The way we came together was perfection.

I bit my lower lip and wondered how it was possible to still desire him after having an incredible orgasm.

Voss's smile widened, becoming the knowing one that made me want to stab him. His liquid, dark eyes traveled my body, landing on my breasts as he held out the shirt for me. "Need more, little fox?"

"Not right now. But… maybe soon?" I kissed him, hard and deeply. What existed between us was more than simple longing. I wanted to dive into his soul and be surrounded by him. Curl up in his being and hide there until the war toppled the world, and we could start anew.

His mouth sought mine, pulling me desperately towards an edge I had already fallen off.

"As soon as you get some rest," he murmured as he pulled away from me. He gestured to the shirt, and I rolled my eyes, but lifted my arms up, because there was no talking him out of this caretaker thing he did. "I can feel your exhaustion. We need to sleep."

As the tunic settled around my waist, I knew he was right. Heaviness weighed my eyelids, but relief coursed through me. Being near him ignited me, as my body was drawn to his. His wick to my flame. But I was dead on my feet, and it was the first time in several days that I allowed myself to feel tired, vulnerable.

"Come, little fox." With smug satisfaction, Voss scooped me up in his arms. A protest rose in my throat, but his mind surrounded mine. *Hush.*

A command?

Not a magical one. No.

As I settled against his chest, I realized the feeling I had upon first seeing him after my time with Leveret had disappeared. There had been an underlying suspicion, a fear that he wouldn't be who he claimed. The twins had been identical save for the scar, but the possessive way Voss looked at me, the depths of his desire, the fires that burned inside his soul—none of that matched his brother.

Being with him had settled me.

Finally.

"Max?"

"Mm?"

"I can hear your thoughts. I am trying to give you privacy, but…"

But with me broadcasting my fears, it was hard for him to shut me out—not that he really wanted to. Truthfully, I wanted him to hear my thoughts. All of them.

"I think you are ready," he finished.

"Ready?" I curled my fingers into his tunic. I couldn't possibly be ready for anything except sleep.

"To become my queen. That resolve you felt? That's the centering you need for it to be successful."

"Without killing you."

He nodded.

I blinked at him. "But not in the wilds. That would be too dangerous. When we get back to court, once it's safer."

His arms tightened around me, and I could sense what he felt too. Worry lingered. Safety was a concern, one he didn't take lightly after allowing me to go on my own for so long. Regret painfully scratched at his insides, staking a claim on him.

I stretched, pressed my lips to his, and sunk my teeth into his lower lip. Biting hard until he moaned, then I released him with a pop. "I'm the only one who gets to gut you. Not your feelings."

He chuckled. "Is that so?"

"Yup."

As we approached the firelight of the campfire, Voss placed me down. His grip on me was steady as I found my footing. So unlike the disregarded way he handled me earlier. The more time I spent with him, the more both sides of his personality appealed to me—the male who took charge and demanded the world, and the male who steadied me and made sure I was okay.

"You two are quieter now." Penn's eyes glittered as the red sparks of the campfire caught hold of them. He let out a breath. "That means it's slowly fading, but also, maybe you finally had enough of each other?" Penn's voice ebbed with hope.

I glanced Voss up and down. A smirk played across his lips.

"Yeah, I'm good. For now." I gave him a wink.

Penn breathed out a sigh. "But I heard you, Voss. And I think you're right. Elspeth and I spoke about it before you came back."

A shudder went through me. It was strange being connected inadvertently to two Fae, not just one.

"Whatever his brother did to you, please keep in mind that not every Fae is like that. I personally hate the Fae who go into interactions with humans without giving them a safe word or a way out. But the royal magic is volatile, and I worried it would make you do something you would regret, act without inhibitions."

"You mean kill Voss." I wanted to speak plainly, no more beating around it. We all feared the same thing—me included. If the power overcame me, there was a chance I could lose him. Forever.

"More than that. Voss has practically burned down several rooms since inheriting the royal magic, and he's had control his whole life. Before meeting you, he had never slept with a human."

Voss settled down on a bedroll, not putting any emotion into his expression. I knew they were speaking the truth, but I had only seen *this* side of him—the possessive and wild side, the part of him that wanted to conquer me, the emotional upheaval he felt by falling for me. While I knew he could be gentle too, it was all wrapped up together.

To become the king of Fae, he had to keep that in check. He had to hide himself, become stoic and unmoving even as the ocean waves crashed against him. That indifference was wrong. It wasn't him, but a facade he crafted to make other people believe he didn't care.

"It's why you sent me away."

Voss let out a breath. "Yes, little fox. Not only could you be used against me, but the Fae would have seen the cracks in my armor. In order to make the royal court fall in line, I needed to be the male they expected me to be. The assassin. The killer."

I swallowed. "And how much of your reputation did you destroy rescuing me?"

His eyes flickered to mine. They were endless pits of darkness, but the firelight ignited them the same as his magic. "Honestly? Probably all of it. But I would lead myself to ruin for eternity if it meant keeping you safe."

"Which was why we were so hard on *you*." Elspeth wrapped her blanket tighter around her shoulders. "Because we knew how far Voss would go to ensure your safety."

"But not how far I would go for his." I shook my head. "Fuck, Voss, I'm sorry."

"No sorrier than I am for getting you wrapped up in my schemes in the first place. If I had known—"

"Don't do that." I sank next to him. "If you had known, everything would have been different. There's no use picking it apart now. We're both safe, and we're in this together." I nudged my shoulder against his. He pressed his lips to my cheek, brushing my skin so carefully I barely felt his warmth.

"It's time we planned for tomorrow. We'll arrive in late afternoon, and we need to take back the royal court as quickly as possible." Voss addressed all of us, but wrapped his arm around my side and pulled me close to him. He idly stroked the skin where my pants and shirt didn't quite meet.

"Now we're talking." Elspeth's birchwood eyes lit up. "The way I see it, we have a few options, pending what we encounter."

For the next hour, we came up with plans and alternative plans, because we didn't know what we would walk into. Depending on who was alive, what side they were on, and what needed to happen next, we came at it from all different angles. It felt like a hunt. It felt good to be in a group doing this again. It pained me to admit how much I missed my friends. There had been a sense of camaraderie in our preparations together, and they steadied me more than Quinn and Marcy knew.

But now I had these three Fae. My allies. And the male who had slowly wormed his way into not only my heart, but down into the marrow of my bones. He slid me a smirk, as if he knew exactly what I was thinking. I blushed and turned back to the conversation, because whatever battle we were walking into tomorrow would come sooner than we knew it.

And I feared few would walk out alive.

Twenty-Four

Voss

The weight of travel landed on me like the dust coating my skin. Elspeth, Penn, and I had switched watches last night, but I claimed the middle shift, knowing it would be the worst interruption of sleep. With the royal magic still tied to Max, I dared not tap into the power more than I had to. Anything could risk our well-being, and now that we were so close to King's Court, I didn't want to put either of us at a disadvantage.

A couple of hours before we reached our final destination, we took a break for food and washing. If I were to convince anyone to come to my aid, I would have to act the part of Fae King. Elspeth would use her glamor to cover anything that couldn't be cleaned.

As we approached the outer walls of the royal court, we slowed. The air was dry, acrid, and stagnant. My nose curled from the surrounding smells. Copper hung in the air, holding a melange of tangy death. Being a Blood Hunter, I picked up the nuances, every flavor of blood that had been spilled in my absence. Fae had battled while we were out, and Fae had died.

Humans too.

All because of my brother.

Because I had left to battle him.

Guilt swelled, but I stamped it down as Max glared at me.

This isn't your fault. Her voice was steady in my head. Her pulse thrummed, convincing me she was alive. She was here, and we had overcome plenty of odds. Whatever was through those gates, I was facing it with her.

As we drew closer to the wall, our horses became increasingly unsteady. Dismembered heads sat on pikes, and blood drenched the stakes that were wedged far into their flesh. Flies buzzed around the remains, picking at the leftovers.

Penn choked back bile. Elspeth covered her mouth and nose with her riding cloak. I refused to let myself look away from the chaos I had created in my wake.

Max's glare grew more heated.

You can stab me later, if you want.

I just might.

I took a breath and told Blade to steady. Charred, drowned, buried, suffocated. Their causes of death were frozen on the expressions of the humans and Fae alike. Each was a torment; one I wouldn't soon forget. No one had been immune to the attempted coup.

"Court Iobhar." Elspeth snorted as she read the message painted with Fae blood across the outer court walls. "At least we're certain of who we are fighting now."

Letting him live had been a mistake. At the time, I hadn't wanted to rule like my father. The late king killed anyone who spoke out against him. In my idealistic vision, Fae and humans could question me. They wouldn't always get their way, of course, but I wanted to accept different opinions. I attempted to create the path for openness within the royal court.

I knew better. No one inside King's Court could be trusted. They were rich, lazy, and held themselves in high regard. Iobhar suffered from the belief that he was better and deserved more. I longed to snuff that sentiment out of the Fae, but it would not come easily.

"This is something we planned for," I stated.

Our horses' hooves kicked up dust from the road as we grew closer to the walls. The quiet was eerie and endless.

Max sucked in a breath after a few more paces, sharp enough to echo as if we were in a canyon. "Is he alive?"

I followed her gaze. Below the "r" in Iobhar's name, a Fae was strung up against the wall. My ears pricked, focusing on any sound from the individual. A soft heartbeat and ragged, almost empty breaths.

"Shit. Elspeth."

She understood instantly. "You and Penn cut him down, and I'll see what I can do. Scarlet, stay back with me." Her eyes focused on the upper towers, watching for any signs of guards.

Max bristled but nodded. She pulled out the throwing knives I had supplied her with. Her blue eyes narrowed, watching the edges of the parapet. Good girl.

Penn and I peeled off and approached the hanging Fae. I cursed under my breath again as I realized it was Lylle. Sliding off Blade's back, I pulled out a sword.

"Lylle?"

A wheeze escaped his chest as his head lolled to the side. Burns stretched across half his face. A jagged, crude knife mark cut into the side of his lip, stretching across the non-burned part of his skin in a sickening smile. Blood soaked his face and matted his red hair to his skin. Both eyes were bruised and swollen shut. His arms were stretched over his head, nails driven through both palms and straight into the wall.

Penn retched beside me.

I scanned the top of the wall but caught no movement. Sliding a glance back at Elspeth and Max, they nodded, keeping vigilant. Despite his protesting stomach, Penn readied his magic, eyes looking upward.

"Get him down, Voss."

As I approached Lylle, my magic curled around the edges of the nails and pulled each out with a sickening squelch. Lylle moaned as his body threatened to collapse onto the ground, but I was ready for him. He fell into my arms.

"Don't," Penn warned as I lowered him to the ground. My power was ready, and I was itching to see if I could heal him like I had Max. "Let Elspeth do it. You don't know if we'll need your magic in there."

A cough bubbled up Lylle's throat, and his breath stuttered in his chest.

I swallowed, but knew Penn was right. "*Sleep, Lylle. Wake when you feel better.*" The compulsion was a small dose of royal magic, barely anything to dip into my reserves. His breathing evened out. At least he wouldn't feel any pain while we dealt with this.

"Let's do the same as we did at Leveret's. We'll stick to the wall until we find a shorter point of entry. Once we're far enough from the gates, Elspeth can heal him." I stood up, grabbing Lylle's shoulders.

With Penn's help, we stretched Lylle across Blade's back. Signaling to the others, we walked along the edge of the wall. I stretched my hearing, hoping to catch a sign of guards.

It's too quiet, Penn whispered in my head.

I nodded.

Something feels wrong, Max added. Her eyes darted between the three of us.

They were right. Something *was* wrong, but I wasn't sure *what.* Frustration bubbled inside me as we reached the lowest point of the battlements.

I stretched out my senses. Nothing. Stiffening, I barked, "Elspeth, heal Lylle as much as you can. Let's get him comfortable. Once he's awake, he can tell us what happened here." It felt like no one was left inside the royal court, which made no sense.

It felt like a trap.

Iobhar was too much of a fool to abandon the court once he took it over. He was too pompous to give it up without a fight. Unless he had abandoned it only to leave traps in his wake, hoping he would take me out upon my return.

Still, there appeared to be nothing left behind. No heartbeats, not even a breath. Whatever had occurred, it hadn't been good. We would proceed with caution. Coming back to an abandoned court terrified me more than one at war. The quiet was threatening, looming over us like a caltula.

Lylle's skin knitted together with painstaking slowness. Sweat beaded along Elspeth's brow as her concentration dove into the fallen Fae's body. The swelling around his eyes abated. I wondered briefly if the mother he had been so protective of was still alive. Had Mikel made it out? There were plenty of unknowns, but I had to focus on our current situation.

We were seemingly alone.

"Elspeth." I held out my hand.

As she latched onto my skin, I sent a pulse of royal power to Lylle. She directed it to where it needed to go. I breathed out as the life threatened to tear out of my veins. It shouldn't have been so easy to run myself ragged, but everything with Max appeared to be something new, something different.

Plus, the other blood bond with Penn and the marriage bond could be interfering. Truly, we were in a land of unknowns. Max curled her fingers through my free hand. The steadiness of her allowed me to send another pulse into the fallen Fae. Max's eyes met mine, her gaze icy and cold. Determination set her brow, and I could feel her wanting to meet the monsters who did this and destroy them.

Her desire to *protect* the Fae threatened to shatter my heart.

Lylle sucked in a breath, jolting upright. His forehead barely missed colliding with Elspeth's chin. "Where—" His hazy eyes darted over us. "Devoss. King. Thank the Mother."

"How are you feeling?" I asked.

He shook his head. "That doesn't matter. Iobhar—"

"I saw his message."

"No, you don't understand. He started the civil war, but the humans came in after it began. Invaded. We have to get away from here." His eyes were frantic, darting among us and refusing to settle.

Max tilted her head to the side. "The humans did this to you?"

Lylle shook his head, and she let out an audible breath. Her panic had swelled, thinking she had replaced one hardship for another. "But they didn't bother to get me down, either."

Max swallowed.

"I believe everyone has since left." My ears pricked, but I heard only silence. "There isn't a single thing moving inside my court."

"They took the king's building."

My eyes narrowed. "Explain."

Lylle shook his head, pressing his eyes shut. "There are soundproof rooms inside. The late king had them designed for torture. I believe the humans are utilizing those spaces to remain scarce. And they have... weapons unlike any I have ever seen."

Shifting my gaze to Max, I glowered. "Why do I have a feeling you know exactly what is going on?"

"Well, as you know, we never talked about their endgame, but I can assume. But I thought you didn't like—"

I will bend you over my knee and spank you right here, right now, in front of an audience if needed.

She shivered, but a ghost of a bratty smile trailed across her lips. My little fox was on my side, but she still had a tumultuous history with the Fae. That wouldn't disappear overnight—especially as she had seen the likes of my brother and what compulsion could do to a person.

But she answered honestly, opening her mind up to me so I could see her thoughts along with her words. "Guns, likely. The original hope was to weaken the Fae by taking out the royal court. But now they know how to use Faerie wine to arm themselves against compulsion. I'm assuming others oversaw munitions, as we never traveled with anything of the sort. I don't know any more specifics, but Quinn would. He had connections."

"Again?" Penn whined. "The last time there were guns involved, I got shot."

Max flinched.

"Which I healed within two minutes, you baby." Elspeth leaned back on her heels but shook her head. "If the humans are armed, we need to be cautious about how we proceed."

Lylle's light eyes widened. "Not just guns, not like what the king ordered us to battle against in the beginning. These weren't like those. These… exploded."

"Huh. That's… new." Max's frown deepened. Her eyes darted to the top of the wall, brow furrowing.

I sighed. "Fantastic. So, they are inside the royal court, with all my father's documents and our history, likely having a long lesson in our weaknesses?"

He swallowed but nodded.

"And the Fae who survived?"

"Iobhar promised to be back. But Voss, it gets worse."

"Worse than explosions?" Penn said on the edge of a breath. His hands curled into fists.

"Morna and Cumina are working with them."

Max stiffened next to me. "What? Why?"

Lylle shook his head. "I'm not sure, but Cumina was protecting some blond human. They turned against the Fae."

Her teeth gritted as she turned toward me, thrust out a finger, and jammed it in the general direction of my father's building. "I told you they were planning something."

"Yeah, but none of this makes sense. What are they planning?" Elspeth glanced at us with a shake of her head. "Why bother going through everything with Scarlet if they wanted to turn against us?"

"To make us weaker." I crossed my arms over my chest. Substantial history spread between me and my step-siblings. I never outright hurt them, but I rarely tried to stop my siblings from treating them worse than lesser. I was guilty as much as my family was when it came to them.

If they had turned against me, it was my fault.

"They've wanted revenge against my family ever since my father ended their mother. I believe this was their opportunity for that. What say you, little fox?"

Max had traveled with them, and while she hadn't gotten much information, perhaps she would understand more than I did. She shook her head. "It feels bigger than that. The way they talked about you… they said you were one of the better ones. So, I don't think it's about you this time. They wanted me to become Blood Queen, and that makes little sense to me. Why have someone else ascend to power? Why not try it themselves?"

"Perhaps it's just Cumina being possessive over her new toy," Lylle added. "She had really nice green eyes."

Max whirled and was on him in a flash, clutching his bloody tunic in her fist. "What did you just say?"

Lylle's birch-colored eyes widened as he glanced at me.

"I suggest you answer my wife unless you want to be healed again."

His throat bobbed. "It seemed to me as if she had…" He let out a breath as Max continued to get into his face with a snarl. "Bonded with the human."

"Fuck!" Max shoved him away and stomped off. Sand stormed around her as her boots kicked it into the air.

I took no time to close the distance between us, wrapping my arms around her and pressing her back into my chest. She raged. Guilt and anguish turmoiled inside her, creating a well of destruction that paved the way straight into her soul. Her shoulders sagged, brow pinched, and angry, hot tears spilled onto my forearms. Even as her feet gave out from under her, even as I supported her weight, I tightened my hold.

"Why?" Her voice croaked out a whimper, not really a question. She knew. And I could feel the regret coiling in her. She had wanted safety for Marcy, for her to stay away from the bloodshed and destruction. A part of her had thought if she kept her locked away, then salvation would greet a part of her soul.

"No one gets out of this unscathed, little fox. It's not how war works."

Her breaths grew steady, evening out in the aching quiet of the desert. "We need to see them." As soon as her feet found purchase, I put her down. She wanted to move, to do something—anything except talk about what just happened.

I would grant her this wish.

For now.

We needed to have a longer discussion, because the pain my brother caused had lanced open everything inside her she tried to bury. Max would need to let it out, and I would be there to catch her when she did.

"If we can talk to them, unite everyone under one rule, then we can fight the oncoming Fae together." She turned to me, standing up straighter. My hands gripped her shoulders, refusing to let her go. She continued, "We can make this better. That's the belief behind the prophecy, right? That you and I could change the world?"

"It could mean a lot of things, that included, yes." Elspeth rose and dusted off her pants. She offered Lylle a hand, and he took it.

The other Fae's clothing was torn, covered in blood. A nasty scar stretched up his cheek now but gone was the gaping wound that almost showed his teeth.

Elspeth frowned at him, scanning his face, but turned back to me. "I advise we proceed cautiously, but Max is right. If we can convince the humans that we're on their side—"

"There's no convincing if we *are* on their side," Max snarled. I dropped my hands from her, allowing her the space to fight this small battle. Energy charged around her, crackling straight into her eyes. I wondered if she knew how easily she tapped into my magic now.

I wondered what it meant for us as exhaustion pulled on me.

Elspeth rolled her eyes. "Really, Scarlet? Drop your righteousness. You know where we stand. Yes, we want freedom for humans. Yes, we want equality. Yes, we're fighting on the right side of this. But *they* don't know that. So yes, we need to convince them."

Max stepped toward her. "I need to convince them, because there is no way in hell they will believe any of you."

"We." I curled my fingers through hers. "Because the Mother would have to strike me down to prevent me from going with you. You have the king's blessing on your side, and hopefully, together, that will be enough for them."

Max sucked in a breath. "If I lose you—"

"You won't."

"But if I do, Voss? You understand that there is no hope for *anyone* after that."

Pride stretched across my skin, because I loved her protective side. She was a force to be reckoned with, and together, we would shape this world anew. Fix what my father had broken. We were the future.

Now, we had to convince the humans of the same.

"You're not losing me, just like I refused to lose you."

A tremor ran through her, something I would meet head on later.

"Let's go, little fox. Destiny awaits."

"Voss?" Penn staggered toward us but halted in his steps.

I paused, locking eyes with him. "If there exists a single moment where I believe us to be in danger, I will let you know. Be ready for anything when I call for you, including running. I might be reckless, but I am prepared to leave if it means our temporary safety." I breathed out, looking once again at my wife. "The question is, if they are not on our side, are you prepared to run from the cause you once believed in?"

Max's jaw set. "If they do not hear us out, then they are nothing like the cause I once believed in."

I pressed my lips to her forehead. "Smart girl."

Twenty-Five

SCARLET

I hated and loved the way his voice caressed my skin. "Smart girl." The words hung around me like honey, dripping from my flesh with a sweetness I never thought I'd experience again once Leveret had taken me into his grasp.

Hand in hand, Voss and I walked into the eerily quiet royal court. Whatever happened next, we were in this together. The three watched us go, and despite Penn's bond with Voss weakening, his unease was tangible.

My heart slammed against my rib cage as I went over what I knew. Quinn was a cornerstone in the revolution. If we dropped his name and mine, perhaps we could meet with him and discuss the next steps.

Assuming they didn't shoot first.

My stomach had bottomed out at the mention of Marcy, or more specifically, at the mention of her *bonding* with Cumina. They knew about Faerie wine now, so I had to assume it had been her choice. A choice without me. One of many, now that our lives were on a divergent path. She had been right, after all. My feelings for her had been born from the hope of a future that could never exist. They were awash with desire for a facade.

It had been hard to unpack, but there was still a part of me that felt desperately protective of her. Made worse by what happened with Leveret. Knowing a Fae could have that much hold on someone iced my insides, and the possibility that Marcy had the same done to her?

But no, I reminded myself. They had Faerie wine.

The streets were bathed in blood. After a few feet inside the court's walls, our footfalls left a trail behind us. Quiet stretched between the buildings, allowing every step to echo in the space. It had been like this once before, right after the first wave of Fae came through. After the guns had been taken away, after the ground drenched in human blood, but before the courts truly took shape from the wilds. There had been a long swatch of silence that spread through the humans, almost like speech would invoke the wrath of the Fae.

Now, I yearned for noise. Something to indicate that we weren't heading straight back to where we started.

"How are you handling this?"

"Fine." Voss's voice was cool, calculated.

While traveling with him, I learned he didn't care for unnecessary deaths. Everything he did was with purpose, but the wake of the battle that happened here was anything but purposeful. It had been mayhem, a slaughter. Partially because of the coup and partially because of the humans who intervened thereafter. And while Voss had usurped the throne, only the king had died in that instance.

A large part of me was grateful Voss hadn't been here. If he had… I swallowed the thought, refusing to allow it to take shape.

We were safe. For the most part.

As we approached the inner courtyard's wall around the two towering buildings and court's center, Voss shifted and pulled us behind a stonewall. He breathed out, and I waited.

"My step-sisters are inside, but I saw a metallic glint in one of the blown out windows."

I hadn't seen anything of the sort, but I had been too busy trying to avoid staring at the bodies. It hadn't bothered me before—blood and death had consumed most of my life. But now… Bullets had ripped through flesh, entrails poured from bodies, and blood soaked into the muddied earth. There had been nothing just about this battle, with too many innocents lost.

King's Court was an ugly reflection of who I used to be—death without thought.

Voss squeezed my hand. "Stay with me."

"Now and always."

His eyes flickered to mine. His brow creased, but he turned his focus back to what lay in front of us. "There are people inside. I can sense them, along with my dear step-sisters."

"Can't we do this the easy way?"

"And what way is that?"

"Put our hands above our heads and ask for a parley?"

"Do you think it will be that easy?"

I glared at him. "Sometimes things are that simple. I know Quinn and Marcy, and we both know Cumina and Morna. We might establish a truce at least until we've had a discussion."

"*Might* isn't something I am willing to bet your life on."

I sighed. "Fine. We'll stay hidden, but I am still doing this my way." Clearing my throat, I yelled, "The Fae Slayer is here with the Fae King. We are requesting a parley to negotiate terms of an alliance."

A snicker sounded from somewhere, along with a few rising jeers.

"Tell Quinn that Scarlet is here to see him," I bellowed the words.

"If you are the Fae Slayer, why not show yourself?"

"And risk getting shot? I didn't survive this long by being an idiot."

"And you told me we should trust them," Voss murmured.

I nudged his shoulder with my own. "We'll be fine. Trust *me.*"

His eyes glittered. "Now and always."

My heart soared. "Tell us how we can have this conversation peacefully. No bloodshed."

"No way we're trusting any Fae or Fae Follower," the man spat. I had never heard his voice before, but then again, I knew nothing about Quinn's network.

"If Quinn is here, tell him—"

"Scarlet?"

"Marcy?" My heart leaped into my throat. She was here, which meant this conversation was possible. "I need a minute to speak with you and Quinn. We'd like to negotiate."

"We?" Her voice dipped with condescension. "You mean the Fae King? The whole reason we're in this mess to begin with?"

"He's not his father, Marcy."

"Thank the Mother for that," Voss grumbled. He ran a hand through his blond hair. "If you refuse to have the conversation, we could chat with my sisters. Surely, you are not so much against the Fae to have two among you?"

Grumbles sounded from the other side. I let out the tension in my shoulders, but my hand instinctively curled around my dagger. What was I doing? This was supposed to be *my* side of the war, and here I was, cowering like the enemy.

"Sure, we'll speak with you, *brother.* But we don't see why anyone else should have to." Morna's voice. Clipped and pointed, popping on every syllable.

"Let me speak with Quinn too," I demanded. I felt like a coward, hiding behind the stones as they pressed against my back. We were calling out these words from a relatively short distance, but I had never felt further away from the revolution. I hated the detachment. After all this time, they should trust me, but who knew what Cumina and Morna had been saying in my absence.

Silence surrounded us. Humidity pressed against my skin. The pause felt endless. Held such weight that the rest of the world could sink into oblivion. Sweat beaded along my skin as I waited. And waited.

Voss squeezed my hand with his, grounding me. He always sensed my whirling thoughts before I did. The edge of the precipice. It lingered, ready to suck me down, drag me to the depths, and leave me less whole than I was before.

I let out a breath.

"Fine," Cumina's voice, with the haunting melody which chilled me straight to my core.

When I had teamed up with them, I knew they needed something from me. Everyone always wanted something from me. Whether Quinn and Marcy would admit it, the revolution needed me to end the king's reign. Voss needed me for the same reason.

But that had changed. He no longer needed me but wanted me. And perhaps the prophecy had something to do with it, but we were tied together. His emotions were genuine toward me. I sensed it every time I drank his blood. Voss had tied us together intentionally, because of the marriage bond. And that was before I had finished killing the king.

He had wanted me even then. No, Voss didn't need me.

Which was exactly why I needed him.

"Scarlet?" Quinn's voice. My shoulders relaxed. "How do I know you aren't being compelled?"

"Don't be a dick." The words wrenched out of me in a growl.

Quinn chuckled. "That's her." There were a few whispering voices. He cleared his throat. We waited all the while. "I am told you both would like a meeting—you and the Fae King?"

"Yes. Obviously, no one should raise arms in that time."

"And how do we know this isn't a trick?"

I sighed. "Quinn, I'm not under any compulsion. I'm the one who told you about Faerie wine, remember?" I neglected to mention how I hadn't been taking any since Leveret's court, but Voss was careful with his magic. Voss wouldn't betray the humans, not now. He wanted an alliance as much as I did.

"I know that, but you could still be choosing him over us." The words tumbled from his mouth and turned my veins to ice.

Anger swelled inside me. "How do I know you aren't choosing *them* over me?" Did our history mean so little to him? It had been years of traveling together.

"Touche." He chuckled. "Well, we might as well get this over with. We'll meet you outside of the inner walls—the four of us."

I looked over at Voss. He nodded. His lips pressed together in a thin line, and his brows furrowed. This was likely the best we could hope for, because my people had been suspicious of Fae their entire lives. It was deserved, of course, what with the tumultuous history between us.

Whatever Morna and Cumina had done to convince them otherwise, I wasn't sure. But maybe we'd finally get some answers.

"Sounds good."

"And Scarlet?"

"Yeah, Quinn?"

"If there's so much as an inkling of magic, we have snipers. They will shoot to kill."

"Sparrowbone bullets?" It had been something we'd been toying with, an idea that bounced around our lair late at night. Seemed impossible at the time, but with all the blood strewn across the city and Lylle's talk about explosives, maybe it was real now.

"Sparrowbone bullets."

I sucked my lower lip into my mouth. We shouldn't have anything to worry about, but if Voss got hit...

He squeezed my hand, giving me a sharp nod.

"Got it," I replied.

We waited a few seconds for whoever else was out there to withdraw. Voss's ears pricked, and as soon as he knew the coast was clear, we ducked back through the streets.

Voss's face was taut as he glanced at the gate from the outside. "I never thought I would feel homesick for this place. It isn't home, but I made it what I could with what I was given." He ran his hand through his hair. It fell in silky blond locks back across his forehead. His black eyes shifted to me. "I'd like to take you to Faerie someday. When this is over."

My heart bloomed. The hope he had when he stated things so plainly was infectious. "I'd like that."

A smile inched up his lips. It differed from the sardonic smirk he wore most of the time. Genuine, one that traced up to his eyes. He dusted off his leathers and straightened as the two females and my old friends turned the corner.

Quinn held a gun. An actual gun. I hadn't seen firearms in so long. The weapons that survived the first war weren't used, out of fear the Fae would turn them against the wielder faster than they could fire. The black metal hung from his fingertips, and he held an air of dominion that I had never sensed from him before.

He was different.

Marcy was dressed in leathers similar to the mismatched outfits the two sisters wore. Dark rustic browns, dusty and creased with wear. She placed her hands on her hips, popping one out as her eyes narrowed on me. The green of her irises felt endless.

"Well, you have us. What is it you propose, Devoss?" Morna stood straight, putting on the air of importance I had witnessed from her several times before.

"Getting right to it? No small talk?" The mask slipped back onto Voss's face. I knew it for what it was now. This was the power he portrayed with other people, the kind he used masterfully to keep others are arm's length. His amused smirk would annoy his enemies, and he did that now with his sisters.

And Cumina fell for it. Her jaw ticked. "No small talk needed when there's nothing *small* to discuss. But sure, you want to play this game? Some weather we're having. The humidity is thick, like my desire to shove my boot all the way up your ass."

"Aw, Cumina. I didn't know you cared so much." Voss placed a hand on his chest. "Fine, then. We want an alliance."

Morna rolled her eyes and smoothed her hand over her hair. "More like you *need* the alliance. Your own court was already in the throes of war when we arrived."

"Which makes it the perfect opportunity to get as many Fae as possible united with the humans on our side. Together, we'd be a formidable force."

"We don't need you." Morna's lips curled.

"Fine. You don't need us." Voss shrugged, but the flare of magic in his eyes and the frustration welling in his chest let me know the truth. He was on the verge of fighting his step-siblings. "Guess we'll walk away without discussing any possibility of a truce? Shame. Could have saved a lot of unwanted death."

"Stop," I growled at the same time as Quinn. His eyes flashed to mine. His lips pressed into a thin line, but he gave a nod for me to continue. "What I want to know is why you two were so hellbent on my becoming Blood Queen. What was in it for you?"

Marcy winced. "You wanted Scarlet to ascend?"

"It would have killed the royal line in the process," Cumina provided.

"Incorrect," Voss said. "It would have made both of us share the royal power. But I have a feeling you knew that." His head tilted to the side. "What was your angle?"

Morna shrugged. "Same angle it's always been."

There was a brief stare down.

"Revenge, Devoss. Or do you not remember how horrible your line has been to anyone who is not inside their inner circle?"

"It's not likely I will forget any of it so soon," he replied.

"Then you understand." Morna's attention turned back to me. "As for you, Fae Slayer, you were a tool. A means to an end. But that's something you should be used to."

Marcy's eyes snapped to the floor.

Quinn gritted his teeth. "If we can explore an ending without bloodshed, we should have the conversation." His fingers tapped the metal in his hand. The gun's handle reflected the sun as he gave a sharp glare at Morna. "Or have you forgotten who is running things now, Fae?" He spat the last word from his lips like an insult.

Cumina held up her hands. "You're right. If our goals truly align, perhaps it is something to consider. So, Voss, once the war is over, who will be in charge?"

There was a pause. Weight settled around us. Because I knew Voss's answer. Both of us. But it was the wrong one, because we'd both be Fae. Even though I had human beginnings, by the time we claimed the throne, we'd still be seen as the enemy.

But it was the right answer because it was the truth.

"I'm going to ascend to Fae but become the human

representative. Voss and I will hold immeasurable power, which means we will change things, revolutionize the Fae who are not stepping up. It will be what we were hoping for, for a world where we can live peacefully as equals."

Marcy scoffed, green eyes narrowing. "Is that what we've been hoping for?"

"Peace?" I snarled back. "Yes."

"No. We want a world where people are in charge. The Fae can take a back seat. This is our world; they are guests. That's the way it should be. You've gone soft."

"And you've become everything I tried to save you from." The words shot out of my mouth without a second thought. Knives wedged between us. We might as well have been on different planets. We had changed, and it made my heart hurt.

"I can see this conversation is getting us nowhere. Come on, Cumina." Marcy whirled around and stormed off, back to the two towering buildings. Cumina blinked at us, her eyes swirling silver pools. She didn't hesitate longer than a moment before trailing after the human I used to know.

"Well?" I turned to Quinn. "Are you going to give up on our history just like that?"

"No, I won't. But right now, our end goals do not align. How about this? If you come up with an army and help us beat the Fae who want us to be subservient, perhaps we can have a conversation afterward. About your king taking a back seat." His eyes flickered to Voss. "Or is that not something you are willing to do?"

Voss's jaw clenched. He had fought hard to get his title and strip the power away from his family. He and I had come a long way, but I could sense his hesitation. It went bone deep. Fear lodged inside him, telling him not to trust anyone else in charge. He had seen how the power could corrupt, and he was terrified of it being in the hands of the wrong people.

He knew he could become a great leader, but he also wondered what the cost would be.

"Perhaps a committee instead? But yes, we're willing to have a conversation." I squeezed Voss's hand. "We cannot turn against each other, not now," I added, because the words felt truthful. We'd need to figure out a way through to the end, but we weren't going to get anywhere with so much fresh blood coating the ground.

I turned to Morna. She had her hands in the pockets of her trousers. "And you? Would you be able to shed your history with the Balgair family if it means working together?"

"There's more history than you know." Her eyes snapped to mine. Golden flecks swirled throughout. "But as I said, Devoss was one of the good ones. If you come with something that will aid our battle, then perhaps we can call it even."

"We're done here?" Quinn asked.

Voss nodded. "For now. We'll see what we can do for aid, but once we're fully bonded, Scarlet and I will be like an army."

"Egotistical as always, Devoss. I would say never change, but I am not your biggest fan." Morna's eyes crinkled at her own joke.

"I know a few Fae who would agree with you." Voss turned his back at the same time as Quinn, and they both strolled away.

I was left with Morna, but felt Voss pause through our bond.

Her gaze was on me. Brows furrowed with scrutiny.

"What?" I asked her.

She let out a breath. "He's in that pretty little head of yours again, isn't he?"

"Of course he is."

"Then I have nothing to say." She sauntered away.

My mouth gaped open, wanting to chase her down and demand answers. A prickle of concern came through my link.

Little fox?

Your step-sister is cryptic.

She can be, yes.

I walked back the way we had come. Voss held out his hand, and I slipped my fingers through his, weaving us together. How had our lives become so tangled? How had things changed so drastically?

"Do you think there is a world where you give up being in control?"

Voss let out a breath, squeezing my fingers in his. "Yes, little fox. I would give up the kingdom, my courts, *everything*, if it meant I got to spend the rest of my time with you. But control?" He pulled me to a stop, eyes blazing. "That's something I will *never* give up when you come apart so nicely for me."

My cheeks blazed. "Don't make me stab you."

"Say the word, and I'll stop."

"Please don't."

"Mm." His fingers dipped under my chin, nudging my face up to his. Lips pressed together with a hunger I felt down into my toes. "You're perfect." His forehead rested on mine. "I would burn my namesake to the ground if it meant us living in peace."

"Such pretty words, Voss."

"Truths, little fox. Truths."

My breath hitched. "Would you let the humans be in charge?"

One of his hands had traveled to the nape of my neck, where he held me steadily against him. It was controlling. Everything he did was consuming, but I wanted it. He gave me a way out; one I knew he would respect.

"The problem I have with that is… I don't think they would be any better than me."

"So, what's the solution?"

"A committee as suggested, but unknown how to execute. There will always be those clambering for power. What we need to figure out is how to stop that from happening."

"And leave the right people in charge."

He nodded. "When I say I will walk away, I mean it, but ideally, I'd like to leave the world a better place before I leave my position of power. Otherwise…" His voice trailed off.

"Otherwise, all the death would have been pointless." I swallowed, because my list was likely longer than his. Voss had been in battles and at war, but I had been hunting and murdering Fae for years. So many had died at my hands. If we ended up worse than we started, then all those lives taken would have been for nothing.

We needed more than a truce; we needed an alliance. The Fae and humans needed to come together like at Alpin's court.

"So, where are we going to find an army?"

"You aren't going to like it." Voss straightened, dropping his hand from my skin. I tingled at his absence. "I barely like the idea."

"Oh?"

"Alpin will lend a hand, but we need a force bigger than that if we're going to convince the humans to fight with us. We need someone so powerful that their strength rivals mine."

"Rivals the royal power?" I crossed my arms and eyed him.

"No, my influence." Voss let out a breath. "We're going to need Lady Burke."

My jaw clenched. "I thought she was one of the—"

"I know. But she's swayed more by money and power than others. I had nothing to offer her last time, and she owes me for her attempted coup."

My heart turned cold. "And you're going to offer her the prospect of being on the committee?"

"I will play it close to my chest, but yes, if it comes down to it. She has influence over the Fae, and if anyone can convince the Fae masses to allow humans into the fold, it would be her. If she ruled *equally* besides other people."

"I don't like it."

"I'm not sure I do either, but it could work."

"And if it doesn't?"

"Well, little fox, if it doesn't, I suppose you will have another Fae to disintegrate with those wretched hands of yours." Voss's smirk was back as he eyed me. "And I would watch you do it with a fucking hard on."

"Crass."

He spanked me. I yelped.

"Come on. We have to inform the others. And I have plans for you," he growled.

A flash of images came across our link, and I nearly tripped over my feet from the force of them. I saw his wicked grin as he pumped his fingers inside me, curling when they hit the perfect spot. How my body melded around his. The pressure of my walls against his cock as I came apart.

Flashes, quick and fast.

Fuck. I wanted Voss so much it hurt. Him and his wicked promises. As his hand wrapped through mine again, another possessive torrent ran through me. I would keep this Fae, no matter what I had to do to secure a life with him. No matter how conniving I had to get. We were the end game now.

VOSS

O nce we were well on the road, I explained the plan to the lot of them. Scarlet had her hands firmly on my hips, as Lylle was given Switch to ride until we reached Lady Burke's court. After that, I would allow him whatever he needed.

Elspeth and Penn immediately disliked my idea, of course. It was why I waited until we were far into the journey with no turning back.

Going to Burke was a calculated risk, especially after her recent betrayal. But it had to pay off. Prior to now, I had nothing to offer her. Burke craved power, and if she were to be offered a space on a governing committee? She would jump at the chance to rule. Any proposal to be in charge, she would take it. Her greed would serve us well now.

Plus, I could always kill her if she opted to betray me, the humans, or any of the Fae on our side. I would revel in watching her still beating heart inside my hands before I crushed it.

And then there was what I learned during my travels, if those Fae were to be believed. While Elspeth and Penn kept watch for threats, I listened—every time we went to a tavern, a bar, any moment we stopped for a meal. After hearing from Mayte, Alpin, and other Fae, whatever happened between her and Finian Raskos seemed to change her. She had turned over a new leaf. Inside her court, things had improved for humans—a step in the right direction, at the very least.

While I wanted to take credit for it because of my warning, there was likely something else at play. As I explained this all to them, Elspeth, Penn, and Lylle pulled up short, forcing me to do the same.

Max let out a breath as I turned Blade around so we could face the others.

"Say what's on your mind," I told them.

"Burke tried to kill you." Elspeth's birchwood eyes narrowed as she scanned me.

By now, she trusted most of my schemes, but I had to admit, some of my dumber ideas ran on pure luck. Things tended to work out, but this was a gamble. And with them at my side, there was no way Burke would get the better of me again.

Plus, neither of them had fought against my decision to separate myself from Max and look at how well that worked out.

And you can't get rid of me now. She pulsed her fingers into my sides, which had crept under my leathers. The growl of her inside my head made me blossom with pride.

"But she didn't kill me, so…" I shrugged.

"So, you want an alliance with her because she didn't kill you?" Penn's voice hitched up an octave. "Voss, will you *listen* to yourself?"

"I want to ally with her because both of us have something the other wants. She has amassed an army of those willing to follow her blindly, and I have a spot saved for her as one of the Fae in charge." Assuming the committee became a reality, and assuming any of us made it out the other side alive. But Burke needn't hear any of that.

"I don't like it," Lylle grumbled, but he had no say in this matter as far as I was concerned.

"You think it would be a good idea to have someone like her in charge?" Elspeth raised an accusatory eyebrow.

My little fox's thoughts probed mine, prodding at the history that stretched between Burke and me.

"If the rumors are true, then yes, Burke is capable of change. Fae will follow her if we can get her on board with this plan. She can convert them, which was why I needed her compliance to begin with. If she's on the head of a council or committee or whatever the humans decide they want to do, we'd have a fighting chance at the future we were hoping for. And if we can get a Lord like Alpin to rule by her side, they would even each other out."

"This plan feels too risky, Voss." Penn ran a hand through his hair. His eyes darted to Max. "You talk sense into him."

Lylle watched the exchange with quiet patience. He looked so much better than when we found him with Elspeth's healing, but a weight had settled on his shoulders that wasn't there before.

Max drummed her fingers on my sides. Her warmth flooded into me. "Do you believe she will do right by humans? That's what we're fighting for, right?"

"I believe if she doesn't, we will immolate her where she stands." I glanced over my shoulder at her. A smoldering wickedness invaded her features, and it made every part of me ignite. I wanted to tackle her off the horse and take her in the middle of the deserted landscape.

The amount of time I wanted to spend inside her.

Penn groaned. "Both of you are impossible. Yes, great, we'll set her on fire if she doesn't play along. But Voss?"

"Hm?" I arched an eyebrow, barely sparing him a glance.

Her blue eyes had captured my soul. She smirked, because she knew it. I was going to make her pay for her cockiness later.

"If Burke ends up trying to kill you again, I will walk away."

That got my attention. My brows lowered as I focused on him. "Please do, because you'd be dealing with an idiot if that's the case. She won't try to kill me for a second time. Burke has powerful magic, but she knows nothing can touch the royal line."

"You still aren't at full power."

"And yet, most people who know that are dead." I slid a look at Lylle, who visually gulped. I had nothing to worry about from him. "Besides, once we find an inn at the Port City, that won't be an issue either."

"Fine, but we're going to be smart about this." Elspeth straightened and tossed her auburn locks behind her shoulder. "We'll sneak in under a glamor, check into the inn, and stay there until you can ascend Scarlet. Once you are both at full power, we'll confront Burke. There's less room for error." Her gaze shifted over to Max. "Are you ready for this?"

She nodded against my shoulder, no hesitation this time. "I'm not sure I like the idea of becoming Fae, but... my friends made it clear there's no going back. We've been on divergent paths for a while. It feels... right." Her eyes danced to me with a wicked blue sparkle. "Plus, annoying this one for the rest of my Fae life sounds incredible."

"Annoying?" I arched a brow. *I will tie you to the bed and tease you until you beg me to fuck you. And once I do, I will go so slowly, it won't get you off. You'll writhe underneath me, panting mindlessly, until I decide you get to come.*

She blinked, the hint of her smile fading from her face. Her throat bobbed as she swallowed.

"I take it by Penn's agony that you two have reached some kind of agreement. We'll be cautious and careful, and once you're at full strength, we'll go to Burke. You're right, Voss. If the news is true, and I'm not saying it is, then we might be dealing with an entirely different Fae, perhaps someone who can be reasoned with. I won't hold my breath, as I do not feel like passing out." Elspeth kicked her horse and trotted down the path.

Penn's eyes were locked on Max. "You need to promise me something."

"What?"

"That you'll bring him back."

Max pressed her eyes shut. Her body stilled, but her fingers dug into my skin. When she looked at Penn again, she nodded solemnly. "I don't want to lose him either."

They stayed in the stare down for a few more moments. Penn nodded and guided his horse after Elspeth.

Lylle let out a breath. "I will find my way once we get to Burke's Court. I do want to help with whatever is to come, but I need to make sure my family is okay first. You understand?"

"Of course," I told him.

His lips flattened as he looked us over. "I hope you can pull this off. We need a fresh start here—one we should have had from the beginning." Nudging Switch in the sides, he started off after the other two, leaving Max and I blissfully alone.

She let out a breath and pressed herself against me. "If I end up killing you, I am going to find some way to bring you back and kill you again for making me go through the loss of you." The terror she had threaded between us, coiled around her soul, and pulsed into mine.

"You won't let that happen."

But the core of it was how she wanted me with her. She couldn't imagine a life without me; she was in this for however long we had together.

I twisted around and cupped her jaw in one hand. Smoothing my thumb over her chin, I said, "You're going to be successful. I'll survive, you'll ascend, and we'll save this world as the Mother intended."

"I want your confidence." Her eyes searched mine with a watery film.

"Mm." Drawing her into me was more natural than breathing. My lips pressed against hers. She parted for me, allowing my tongue to sweep inside her. I loved how quickly she'd fall apart underneath me. I would never get bored of this. But right now, I needed something else from her. Holding her firm against me, I sent my thoughts to her. My confidence in her, the strength in my resolve, and all the memories she had already blessed me with.

Watching her annihilate a Fae with the touch of her fingers. How the ash fell away in the silent, shocked aftermath. Every ounce of blood she spilled in front of me or from me. The death she left in her wake as if she were a vengeful god. The defense she had built in her own mind and how it allowed her to get out from underneath my brother's compulsion. She knew the bridge to bring us back together. She would do it again.

She was clever. She was wicked and vicious, and she was mine.

I tugged on her hair. *You have to understand something, little fox. I will not have you talking about my wife the way you do. She's lived thousands of lives in her short time on this planet, and she's a survivor. She's been through more than most have dreamed of. And if you think yourself not strong again, I will punish you for it.*

She sucked in a breath as I sank my teeth into her lower lip. I couldn't do much else on top of this blasted horse with her sitting behind me, but my point came off well enough as a moan escaped her mouth. A bead of blood welled underneath my teeth. I licked the drop into my mouth and pulled back from her.

"Understood?" With my hand still entwined in her hair, I tilted her head back so she would look at me. Our eyes locked. "Little fox?"

Her eyes had gone glassy and pliant, so I knotted my hand further in her hair. She blinked, her bliss drifting amidst the pain I gave her. "Yes, but my comment still stands."

I smirked. "Good thing I'm still looking forward to the day you try to kill me."

"Voss… are you…" Her eyes narrowed on me as she sensed everything through our bond.

"Yes. I ache for you, and I need you. I want to bury myself inside you until you forget the rest of the world exists. That's never going away, no matter how many times I take you." I released my hold and took the reins back up, encouraging Blade to get us to our next destination faster.

"I have plans." I told her as her hands found my waist again. It was the most natural thing in the world, the Fae Slayer and Fae King riding toward their destiny together. We would survive this. I would accept nothing less.

Now that I had found her, there wasn't a single part of my soul willing to give her up.

Twenty-Seven

SCARLET

Disguising ourselves to pass through the gates into the Port City was easy, but the moment we stepped foot inside, my stomach roiled. The walls gleamed bright white, and the domed roofs reflected the dark color of the sea. The air smelled of sweat and salt water, somehow being stale despite the constant churning of the ocean breeze. We stabled the horses quickly and began walking through the reflective, bright city.

Lylle was uneasy on his feet, and every quick movement had him wincing.

As soon as we arrived on the wider boulevard, a cacophony of noise walled around me, most of it being humans filled with… not horror. But joy?

"What happened?" I asked. Through our conversations, it had seemed like Burke would be hard to convince and convert, but the city appeared to be in reverie.

"The rumors are true," Voss said without missing a beat. He

exuded confidence as he slid a gaze over to Penn and Elspeth. "I told you."

I shook my head, because none of this made sense. It was seemingly a change that happened overnight. While Lady Burke and the Port City had fallen off my radar while hunting the royal family, I gaped at my surroundings. She *had* changed for people to be celebrating like this. I wouldn't have believed it if I hadn't witnessed it myself.

"Excuse me," I interrupted a jubilant man, who had a tankard of ale in his hands.

His cheeks were rosy, his smile wide as he turned toward me. His eyes took us in, but no fear passed through his gaze. "Have you come to join the celebration?"

"Celebration of what?" I pressed.

His grin showed off his teeth. Several were rotted out of his skull, proof of the ill health the humans had suffered in this court before now. "Liberation, my dear. You travelers? Well, stop traveling. Burke has done the right thing. Joined us together. Finally."

"And how did she do that?"

"By being everywhere at once." Coils of a dark, raspy voice beaded along my skin, making everything inside me bristle.

I turned toward the voice and blinked.

"There's no hiding from me inside my court, Devoss Balgair."

The man sucked in a breath and bent at the waist. "Your Highness."

Lady Burke waved a dismissive hand. Her skin was pale, almost matching my own. Her yellow hair reflected the sun like moonlight marigolds, and eyes blazed orange like the last embers of a dying fire. "What brings you here?"

"The rumors are true," Voss stated again.

"Of course they are. I placed them, after all."

"What's the point?"

"The point?" She tilted her head to the side. "I'm not sure what you mean."

"Giving the humans equal status. You refused to do so when I last visited."

The man made the smart move and slowly backed away from the charged conversation.

Voss continued, "If I recall, Lady, I had to force your hand into it. So, what changed?"

Lady Burke took a step toward him, but I blocked her encroachment and placed a hand on her shoulder. Her eyes shifted to me.

"If you dare touch my husband, I will end you." Sparks of magic threatened to flood into me, but I beat it back. Anything I did now would drain Voss.

A hearty laugh burst out of her. "Oh, dear. I see the rumors about you are also true. You married the Slayer? Smart move, Devoss. I must say, I am impressed."

"The Slayer?" A few whispers started among the humans.

I rose to my full height, drawing her attention back to me. "We're allies in this, trying to unite the kingdom."

A flicker of amusement stretched up her lips. "Well, what an interesting turn of events. Seems we're potentially on the same side, Devoss. When were you two planning to meet with me?"

Voss's body pressed against mine, and I could feel his shrug as he placed his hands on my waist. Pulling me close to him in a move of protection and possession. "Tomorrow. After a night's rest."

"Hm." The single syllable came out clipped and pointed. "Then I shall allow it. I don't appreciate your coming unannounced or deceiving my guards, but I understand your need for caution after how our last meeting ended."

"As I recall, Burke, it didn't end well for you."

"No. It did not." She frowned and glanced between us. "You must understand your brothers put me in an interesting position. But that conversation will continue tomorrow. I'll leave you to your rest. And I will post guards outside of whatever inn you choose to stay at. Cannot be too careful these days, my King." The Fae disappeared into nothing.

I blinked. "Where did she—"

"She makes mirages. One of her little party tricks. She creates duplicates who aren't really her. Costs a lot of her magic, but being in multiple places at once has its advantages." Elspeth sighed, turning her attention to Voss. She placed her hands on her hips. "Do you trust her?"

"Of course not." Voss glanced around at the merriment. More eyes were on us than before, but he stood taller as he considered the circumstances. "We'll be on guard, switch shifts tonight, and make sure nothing happens. We'll meet with her in the morning, but did you feel that?" He glanced at Penn, Elspeth, and Lylle. His hands lingered on my waist.

"Feel what?" Penn asked.

"She wasn't lying. There was no bitterness around her. Something changed the very being of her soul." His lips pressed together as his fingers kneaded into my skin. "I'm not sure I like the suddenness of her shift, but it bodes well."

"Sir?" Lylle's voice came out cracked and clipped, barely escaping the confines of his mouth. "I'd like to search for the group that fled yesterday, if that's okay."

"You believe they came here?"

Lylle nodded. "My mother was among them, and they were hoping to arrive here. If you wouldn't mind…"

"Do you feel up for traveling by yourself, Lylle?" Elspeth gave him a long, knowing look. Exhaustion weighed on her features. Spending so much time healing him had wiped her out.

He nodded. "Thanks to you. I'll be careful, but nothing here appears hostile. Perhaps I will have success."

"If you need us for anything, let us know," I said.

Lylle pressed his heels together like a soldier and gave Voss a small salute. "I expect to fight by your side once you come to an agreement with the humans and Lady Burke. I believe in the future you presented. There's no reason to run away from it now, especially after I watched several Fae I liked die." He let out a breath. "I'm glad the elderly escaped with a few guards. Hopefully, it was enough to keep them safe from roaming hoswisps."

Voss nodded. "Stay well. You'll know when we're about to move."

Lylle ran a hand through his hair but grimaced at the amount of blood still crusting it. Blinking away any vulnerability, he turned and disappeared into the throngs of people on the streets. Several folks gave him sidelong glances, as Lylle's clothes and hair still wore the blood of battle. But these people should get used to it. There was a war brewing on the horizon, and as nice as it would be to avoid it, likely no one within the vicinity would.

"We should eat and find lodgings." Elspeth brought my attention back to the present. I found myself nervous about what would happen next but was glad we had a plan to put Voss at his full strength.

And I would be the strongest I had ever been in my entire life; the prospect of that was heady. I needed to remember not to lose myself in the process.

❦ ✄ ❧

After we found two suites and booked them—free of charge, per

Lady Burke, which frankly made my skin crawl—we had a quick lunch at the cafe next door. I had to hand it to Burke—now that the humans were in revelry, this place felt like it could rival Alpin's. Despite that, Voss, Elspeth, and Penn were on edge, which only made my instincts flare.

From what we had gathered, it had been a quick and overnight process for her change of heart. Lady Burke left with a portion of her army and came back softer. No one knew much about the details, other than it had been a fight with Finian Raskos. But these overnight changes rarely stuck. It reminded me of New Year's resolutions—promises made only to be broken a few days, weeks, or months later. In reality, it took time to develop good habits.

And longer still to fall out of bad ones. I should know.

My gaze slid to Voss; so much had changed. While I had lost plenty in my life, it had been a long time since I cared enough to worry about losing something or someone. I wasn't fighting for myself, but for the endgame. The weight of the world had fallen onto our shoulders, and I refused to carry this burden by myself.

But there was the possibility I could kill him within the hour.

It saddens me you are no longer excited by the prospect of murdering me, little fox.

Get out of my head, Voss.

But why? When your thoughts stroke my ego so nicely. He tossed me a smirk from his seat. His hands were focused on his meal, but his eyes had settled fully on me, smoldering with liquid fire.

Penn's brows narrowed. His breath came out in a huff. "You are quieter, but still there. This won't be fun for me when you start to drink from him."

"Why?" I dipped my spoon into the broth.

Turquoise eyes turned to me. Lids narrowed. Brows arched low over his eyes. Penn's lips tilted down in a pout. "Do you really have to ask?"

I shrugged, trying to act as innocent as possible as I sipped from the stew.

"Why does blood turn both of you on so much?"

"Because killing people is fun," Voss answered at the same time as I said, "Being so close to death is an adrenaline rush."

We stared at each other. A blush crept across my cheeks.

"It's *fun*, really?" I asked.

"If it's adrenaline you want, little fox, we can think of other ways to get it."

"Why did I ask?" Penn groaned.

"Because you're secretly a masochist."

"I don't *like* pain."

"And yet, you tend to brim with emotional upheaval." Elspeth tipped her ale at him. "Anyway, here's the plan. Penn will be inside the room. Since he can sense Voss, he can help direct Scarlet how to use magic to bring Voss back from the brink." Elspeth's gaze slid to me. "Does that work for you?"

I shrugged. "Why wouldn't it?"

"No reason. I do know how much you like blood." Elspeth waved a hand. "Anyway, let's forget the inevitable sexual part that will come *after* you bring Voss back to life. Penn can leave at that point."

"And drown myself in ale."

"I trust Penn," I said with certainty. "And if anything goes wrong, you'll be outside?"

Elspeth nodded. "But you have to understand, I am not the one who can bring him back. That will only be you, through the blood bond."

I frowned. "Are any of you still worried about why Morna and Cumina wanted me to take this title so much? Especially now that they are working with the humans?"

Voss shook his head. "My sisters were never malicious. While they might still have something planned, I doubt it is to my detriment. Frankly, I respect the game they are playing. Whatever the outcome is, they are likely to be in a position of power after. They've seen the world at its worst, and they would be an asset in whatever comes next."

I tapped my foot a few times, considering the sincerity behind Voss's words. While he felt that way about his step-siblings, I wasn't sure they shared the same trust or faith in him. Morna had hinted at wanting to tell me what was going on, but only when it would benefit her. If she were siding with the humans and we were now on the same team, I supposed that would have to work for now.

But I knew how resentment could fester, especially when someone never stood up for you in the past.

Ah, but I did.

Oh?

It wasn't enough, of course, so I will take whatever blame they deem fit to give me. I tried to defend them once, but Kefira locked me in a closet during one of Namir's worst attacks. She called me weak because I disliked watching them suffer.

And what did you do to get back at her?

Waited until I met the ultimate weapon and then unleashed you on my wretched family.

"Voss."

"Little fox."

"You did not…" My thoughts got away from me. "How long exactly did you wait?"

"Too long." He stood up and dusted off his trousers, which had nothing on them. "Come, little fox. I will not wait any longer for this. Unless you've changed your mind?" A brow arched with a challenge in it. He gave me space to say no, to tell him I wasn't ready.

And while I wasn't ready to lose him, I didn't think I would. Determination shot through me. I had to do this. It would be for the better of both of our people, finally aligning us together.

I slipped my hand into his and nodded. That pesky smirk spread up his lips.

Elspeth sighed. "Right. Lead the way. I'm giving you instructions before I leave the room." She clapped her hands together.

Voss wasted no time. We exited the cafe and headed straight for the inn. The four of us stumbled into the room.

Elspeth slammed the door shut and stared at me. Her gaze was intense. "Okay. How you heal people? This is a crash course." She took two steps toward me and held her hands out. "Follow my lead."

I pressed my hands against hers.

"When you are touching him, you must clear your head. Let the magic do what it wants to do, which will be to bring him back. All the texts we found said the ascension was easy. You won't know how to control magic at first, but it's all about intention. If you intend to bring him back, you will."

"That's it?"

She nodded. "Voss also claims his healing feels more like… fire. We're not sure how your magic will manifest itself. Perhaps more like Voss's or perhaps more like mine, but regardless, our intention with our healing never changes. We always intend to heal the person."

My fingertips tingled.

"Get it?"

I pulled my hands back and stared at my palms. "As much as I can without magic."

She nodded. "Penn, call me if you need me. I'll be out in the hall."

Penn's face turned serious. His brows came down, looking more like a soldier than I had ever seen him. He nodded at her and pulled a chair up to the side of the bed. "I'll tell you when he is near the end."

I squirmed under his turquoise gaze, shifting back to Voss. "I thought you would never allow me to—" My breath halted in my throat.

Voss had unbuttoned his shirt. He shrugged it off his shoulders, folded it, and placed it neatly at the foot of the bed, always so fucking particular. It surprised me how much I had missed that about him.

"He won't see you naked, little fox." Voss's smirk was back.

My eyes roamed over his body, taking in all of him. We had fucked since being back together, but something about this felt different. He was letting me *kill* him to complete the bond.

A bond that would tie us together forever. Our lives intertwined.

He faced down the possibility that I could slip—I could actually kill him—with bravery and fierceness. I found his faith in me equally admirable and stupid. If we ever did something like this again, it would have to be because we were saving the world.

But wasn't this the first step? With our combined magic, we'd be able to win the war and change our society. We would be the ruling powers everyone needed to restore the faith in the Fae and keep those who needed it in check.

"Worried about a little blood on your clothes?" I tried to quip, but my voice snagged in my throat as he ran a hand through his hair.

His brows lowered. "It's not a little blood. It's a lot of blood. Granted, you should be *drinking* it, not spilling it, but I happen to like this shirt."

"What about the shirts I liked?"

His eyes glowed with the deep, fiery embers of liquid lava. "I liked them better as ashes."

Penn coughed and fiddled with a loose thread on his pants.

"Scarlet."

"Penn."

"You can do this."

I narrowed my gaze at him.

"I can feel what he feels. You're fighting back your fear, worried you might not be able to bring him back."

I wrapped my arms around myself.

Voss pulled me into him. His warmth surrounded me.

I hadn't been like this before Leveret's court. Whenever I had my sights set on a mark, I never let myself get distracted. I dove in headfirst and looked at the end goal. But now... there was so much more at stake. And the fear—it lingered.

Having Penn say it out loud brought to light how much I still fought this feeling.

"I trust you." Voss's voice caressed my skin, swirling around me and entering straight into my soul.

"How can you?"

"I trust you too," Penn said.

I swallowed back a sob and pulled away from Voss. His hands trailed down my arms, fingers catching mine. I continued, "Maybe neither of you should. Maybe I don't deserve it. Because I had thought about killing you."

Voss's gaze turned to liquid fire. It pooled inside me and threatened to burst through my veins. His wry smile stretched across his lips. "You misunderstand, little fox. I don't trust you for no reason. I trust you because I love you." He grabbed the back of my neck and pulled us together. His forehead rested against mine. I exhaled as he inhaled.

It wasn't the first time he said it, but it was reassurance. The strength of his words stretched between us, becoming an infinity. He loved me, but was it enough for me to save him from the brink of death? From the cold grasp of nothing?

Voss brushed his lips against mine, as delicate as a whisper. "And I trust you because I know you feel the same way."

My skin tingled. "What if the only way to save the world is to sacrifice you? What if the prophecy is real and the only way out is by getting rid of you?" The words tumbled from my mouth as he pressed his thumb to my lower lip. The heat of his chest surrounded me, and my body sung for him.

He smelled like ginger and violence. "If that is the only way, how would you save the world?"

I swallowed. "If I had to live without you? I wouldn't."

His lips crushed mine as he pulled me firmly against the weight of him. He opened his mind, flooding me with his emotions. I had tapped into his feelings before, and he had given me glimpses of himself, but this was *everything*. He opened himself with such a ferocity he consumed me. His emotions zipped through me, burrowing into my bones. Desire smoldered. The vacuous emptiness he had filled from the sight and sound of me. An instance of me in his life gave him power, wanting to grow something new. Warmth blossomed in my chest, flooding my veins so fast I threatened to burst.

His love.

He was sharing the intensity of it.

How it devoured him.

I gasped because this was how I felt. Every time he glanced at me. Whenever I witnessed the wretched smirk playing on his lips. The feeling coiled around every interaction. Whenever his dark eyes landed on me. The way his blond locks caught in the breeze and flowed around his ears. Every part of him made want to stab him and fight him and…

Love him.

For the rest of our lives.

There it is, little fox.

I hate you. The empty words did nothing against the heavy truth of our combined emotions.

No, you don't.

I parted my lips, allowing his tongue inside me. It was a capture on his part, a reckoning, pulling me into the whirlwind of Devoss Balgair. My King. My partner.

No, I don't, I agreed.

His fingers trailed down my sides as everything in his brain swirled with mine.

Fuck, Voss. I'm obsessed with you. You destroy me, and I am wondering in what scenario do we both make it out of this alive. Because I can't imagine a world without you in it. I don't want that to be my future, but I fear it's the only one I'll get.

He growled as his hands gripped my hips, so tight my skin might bruise. Everything he wanted to do to me flashed inside my head. Voss had no plans on giving me up—never again.

We'll find a way, he promised.

I hope so, because I kind of want to spend the rest of my life with you. You fucking asshole.

Voss chuckled, running his hands up to my shoulders. "If we were alone, there would be plenty to keep us entertained, but Penn isn't much of a voyeur."

Glancing at Penn, he wore a scowl on his face. "Oh no, don't mind me. I can only see and hear everything right now. No big deal. Just like everything else you have done."

"Can't you block him out now that it's weaker?"

Penn sighed. "No."

I turned my attention back to Voss, eyebrow arched.

Voss shrugged and settled onto the bed. "We've had a lot of

history, and we've been blood bonded before. It's difficult to shut it out when the person is that entwined with your…" Voss frowned.

"You were going to say soul." I crossed my arms and pouted.

"He was, but it's not love, Scarlet. He's like my brother," Penn said.

"Now." Voss's eyes flicked to him. "I won't have you soiling our history by making it seem like it never existed. We had a history, and I won't be ashamed of it. Though—" His eyes darted back to me. "—if you are feeling particularly jealous, maybe stabbing me will help?"

I rolled my eyes. "I was already planning on stabbing you." Placing my hands on my hips, I asked Penn, "Will you promise me something?"

His turquoise gaze took me in.

"I can't kill him, Penn. I don't want to cave into a moment of weakness and decide… well, I don't know. This goes against everything I was trying to do, but I know this is the right path. I *feel* it deep down. But I don't want to become so drunk on him that I do something irrevocably stupid."

"Falling for Voss is the definition of that."

I glared at him.

"Since you respond well to threats of punishment, how is this, little fox? If you kill me, Penn will kill you. And then I will find you in whatever afterlife the Mother deems to give us and teach you a lesson for the rest of eternity."

My core tightened.

"There is something seriously wrong with both of you." Penn shook his head. "But in all seriousness, Scarlet, I will do everything in my power to ensure his safety."

"Minus the stabbing part. I do actually need to stab him." I frowned.

"That's foreplay, little fox." Voss's gaze smoldered. "Even he knows that."

"Stabbing is not foreplay." I sniffed defensively. Except it was. Very much so.

Voss's lips quirked, as if he knew exactly what I was thinking. He likely did. "I got you a present to celebrate."

"But you didn't know when I was going to—"

He stared at me.

I nodded. "You got the present before you asked me, didn't you?"

The twitch of his lips told me everything I needed to know.

"Presumptuous of you."

"Have I been wrong yet?"

"No, but that doesn't mean you will always be right."

"I've been alive for a long time."

I climbed onto the bed. "So, what's the present?"

He reached into his pocket and pulled out a silver sheath. I narrowed my gaze but snatched it out of his hand and pulled the small knife out. Sparrowbone, brand new and unused.

"We only found your dagger for you, but I figured you might want something else to hide in your boot or—"

Closing the gap between us, I kissed him hard. His tongue fought with mine as his hand threaded through my hair, fisting it and bringing me into him. Our mouths met in chaos, fighting for dominance, but I broke first, like always. I gasped, and his tongue explored my mouth. I whimpered under his touch.

Voss dug his fingers into my shoulders. "I meant what I said, little fox. If anyone else watches us, I will kill them." His gaze slid to Penn.

"Even Penn?" I smiled viciously.

"We won't tempt me, because we're not doing anything in front of him. So, I'm afraid everything in your mind must wait."

"Until after I'm Fae?"

"Perhaps. Once we're linked together for the rest of our lives, maybe I'll let you stab him."

Penn scowled.

Voss's fingers untangled from my hair. His hand curled around my neck, gripping me tight. "Think of all the fun I can have with magic—when I can wrap you up in coils of fire without having you burn." He brought my head closer to him, so his breath licked the shell of my ear. "Think of all the new sensations I can give you."

I shuddered against him.

His hands found mine, holding the knife between us.

"Make me bleed, Fae Slayer. You were born for this. Take what you need, then make me whole again." With his hand guiding ours, he pressed the blade against his neck.

I blinked, tears welling unbidden in my eyes. My gaze slid to Penn. His stare was intense between us, but he nodded. Turning back to Voss, I pushed the sparrowbone into his skin. I could do this. They had researched it. I would bring him back. I would save him.

Then we would save the world.

With Voss trying to unite the Fae and the humans under one rule, we would deal with whatever came our way—including the consequences of Morna's plan. If they wanted to stage a coup, we'd be ready. With so much working against us, I had to hope we'd create something new, something better. We were in this together.

We could do this.

I could do this.

As the knife pierced his skin, Voss grabbed onto the nape of my neck. "Every last drop, Max." He brought my lips to him as the blade sank deeper.

I lapped at the wound, and a moan escaped my lips the moment his blood touched my tongue. I arched, pressing against him. And fuck me, he was hard. We were intentionally bringing him to the brink of death, and the asshole had the audacity to be hard underneath me.

He chuckled through our bond, likely hearing every one of my screaming thoughts.

Lazily, I sucked long pulls of blood from his skin, using the knife to keep the cut open. Finally, it sank deep enough down that a rush of his blood burst over my tongue. I pulled the blade out and tossed it aside, latching onto him.

It felt wicked, tasting something so euphoric while his heart began to slow. If someone had told me weeks ago I would have enjoyed drinking Fae blood, I would have stabbed them. Now, I writhed against him, seeking friction, wanting more. I trailed my fingers along his neck, and his skin was already cooling.

Voss's hands roamed over my back, settling on my hips as he let out a breath. *Little fox, have I told you how much you amaze me?*

Voss…

Everything you overcame. What you did to survive. How incredible you are. You have every reason to still be my enemy, and you've done the biggest thing anyone could ever do—forgiven me.

You make a good point. Maybe I should kill you. I bit down hard as the flow of his blood ebbed. *You betrayed me, let me be captured, and turned the world upside down. Why shouldn't I?*

Because…

My vision burst with images, promises he held for our future. Voss waking me up on lazy mornings in bed, cuddling. Fucking *cuddling.* His lips brushing my sensitive shoulder in the early dawn. The smell of us, satiated and satisfied, coating the sheets. Our home. Our future.

Our… children.

I am not having kids, Voss.

Maybe someday.

Voss.

Maybe?

Maybe we'll start by having you not die today. If you survive this, I'll think about it.

Deal. His magic lazily circled us, caressing my skin. *Sorry, losing control.* His hands stilled on my sides and dropped to the bed. His pulse slowed, becoming thready underneath my fingertips. *Wouldn't with anyone else.*

Voss, come back to me.

His presence drifted from my mind, no longer connecting with me. He was… gone.

But as soon as the thought pierced through my brain, a flood opened inside me. Heat rushed into my veins. An inferno coiled through my body, igniting my bones. Power buzzed. I could stay awake forever. I could run a marathon.

Forget that. I could *burn* it down. Intoxication left my head feeling light as I pulled my lips away from his neck. Everything around me glowed, as if I were the sun and everything was trying to grow toward me. I unfurled my fists in front of me, ignoring my surroundings as I stretched out each knuckle, savoring how easily I could call the earth to me. The power wanted to be with me. The world would cave to my will. As I drifted my fingers through the air, I was stunned at how potent it was. Ripe. The magic soothed me in a way nothing else could. The ground welled under me, pressing against me as a thank you for simply existing.

Everything would be fine.

"Scarlet." Distantly, a voice trilled. But it was nothing compared to the pulse of magic thrumming in my head. It pounded in my ears, wrapping around my senses.

Giddiness washed over me. I could do *anything*.

I was the royal line.

Blood Queen.

I was *everything*.

"Scarlet!"

I turned to the turquoise eyed Fae. A snarl coiled up my lips. *"You'll listen to whatever I say, right?"* The voice wasn't mine but welled from the power flooding my system.

The male nodded with wide eyes. His irises flared to life as he fought me, but my power would win out. It would *always* win. The other Fae were weak, nothing. Pathetic.

"Then you'll sit there like a good boy and shut up until I'm ready to deal with you."

He sank into his seat. And it felt so fucking good to be in charge. Just wait until I tried this out on—

Voss.

No.

Voss…

"Penn?" my voice squeaked out as my heart dropped.

Fuck.

Oh fuck.

What did I need to do to bring him back?

Voss's body was lifeless. Lips pale, skin pulled taut. My heart skipped a multitude of beats. The world tilted sideways. And Penn watched me.

"Help me!" I screamed, not knowing how to use this magic that crawled along my skin.

But whatever my plea was, it had been enough. Penn flinched back into himself.

I pressed my hands against Voss's chest, not knowing how to

bring him back. I should have revived him from the brink, but we were no longer at the edge of death. This was far from it. This was something more.

Now and always, Voss. The thought landed in a hollow place inside my skull. His presence was gone. Panic welled inside me as I focused on my hands, stretching for the magic coiling around me. It ran through me. I remembered how it felt the night I pulled myself into Voss's dinner with the guards and fried the Fae, and this was similar, but I had no idea how to wield it.

"Fuck!" I screamed, slamming my fist down.

Penn caught my wrist before I could punch Voss in the chest. He grabbed the nape of my neck and crushed our foreheads together. Sweat beaded along his brow. "You can do this. Focus. Like Elspeth said. It might be an inferno; it might be cooling. It might be *anything*, but it's your intention that matters."

Elspeth burst the door open and gasped as she took us in.

I pressed my palms against his chest. "Any advice?" I asked her, but I focused on Voss, wanting him to breathe underneath me. Wanting him to move.

"Scarlet, I think—" she started.

"No!" I growled. Snot dribbled down my face as tears stung my eyes. I refused to let this be the end of us. He had *promised*. Pressing my eyes shut, I thought about how it was when he brought me back. It was like he held a part of my soul with him and shoved it back into my body, forced me to be whole again.

Like liquid fire running through my veins.

We had always been combustible—Voss and me. He was fire, and I was the gasoline.

Flames curled around my arms, creeping down to my hands. Elspeth stumbled back from the heat, but Penn stayed with me. His hand held my shoulder, as if afraid letting me go would mean letting him go too. His water magic cooled my skin. I focused on bringing Voss back.

Now and always. I screamed the words at him inside my head.

The sheets darkened, blistering with ash. Sweat pooled along my skin. Everything smoldered against the magic—magic that felt like it was coming from the earth itself. I needed him back alive. The world would burn before I let myself live without him.

And seeing his blank expression? It carved out another part of my soul. I didn't care for a future without him. I refused to let this be the end.

Flames wrapped around him, singing the sheets. Penn kept his water magic steady, coiling where the fire touched. As the magic sang with my soul, the power lifted us off the bed. The blaze leeched into my skin, leaving black trails along my veins before fire rushed into Voss. My head ached, but I *pushed.*

Penn's hand fell to his side, but he kept his concentration steady. "Scarlet, you could kill yourself if you keep this up."

"Shut up, Elspeth," Penn's voice, caked in the same desperation I felt.

"Don't you understand?" I screamed as the flames roared with new life. "Without him, I'm already dead." Smoke encased us, compressing my lungs, and still I pushed. The heat washed over me, and I pressed my lips against his.

I breathed.

His chest expanded.

And fell.

I breathed again.

Flames crackled between us.

His chest expanded.

And expanded.

And Voss's irises swirled with life. He coughed as the magic snapped between us. The power exploded. I shut my eyes as Voss grabbed onto my hips and pulled me against him. I couldn't feel anything other than him and the heat.

The heat.

So intense.

Everything hurt. There was an impact on my chest. My eyes slammed shut.

Little fox. Calm.

Voss.

He buried his head in my hair, pressed me into his chest. The smell of smoky ash surrounded me, but his fiery ginger scent masked it. *It's okay. You did it. I'm alive.*

"Elspeth, heal her," Penn's voice came out in a gasp.

I tried to open my eyes, but I couldn't. Everything ached.

"Shh, little fox. Relax."

I hadn't realized I was whimpering.

"Breathe through it, Scarlet." Elspeth's hands pressed against my back.

Coolness washed over me as Elspeth's magic swept along my body. I breathed out. My lungs ached less and less as her magic worked.

My lids fluttered open. "Why—"

"You burned yourself trying to revive him." Elspeth frowned, looking me over. "I might need to do a few more healing sessions. That was a lot of skin to mend."

"I thought you said I wouldn't burn." I turned to Voss, and my neck popped as I did. Fuck, that hurt. My skin was taut, raw, and painful.

"You wouldn't burn with my magic, but that's because I learned control a long time ago." Voss frowned as his magic washed over the room. The sheets knitted together underneath us, burn marks erasing like they had never been. The smoke shrank to nothing, and every piece of ash disappeared. "You'll need more training. A lot of training. Penn?" He cradled my head close.

"Hmm?"

"What happened?"

I was happy he was asking Penn, because my throat also felt raw. Listening to his heart beat steadily against my ear was the only thing I could bear to do.

"You were dead, Voss."

"Wasn't that the point?"

I swallowed and whispered, "No, you were... dead dead."

"Explain." His eyes went sharp as he took in the other two. I tried to roll off him so I could look at all of them, but his arms coiled around me and kept me steady. "Penn."

"She lost herself to the power and forgot the plan. In those seconds, I saw it... you *died*."

"You lost yourself to Fae magic?" Voss cupped my chin, forcing me to look at him. "Tell me, little fox, how intoxicating was it?"

I shook my head.

"You don't need to be shy, not with me."

I hit him with my fist. "Be serious. I almost lost you."

"You should still be dead," Penn's voice was flat, haunted.

"He's right, Voss. It makes no sense." With a shake of her head, Elspeth stood. "Perhaps this is something for us to unpack later, after you've had a chance to rest. But with all the information we had about Blood Queen, she should not have been able to bring you back from *actual* death."

Voss's lips twitched. "I'm sure we'll find an answer. Or not, because frankly, it still worked."

Penn huffed out a breath. "I'm going to get some ale."

"Same," Elspeth agreed.

The two of them left us.

"I'm sorry I kind of killed you."

Voss laughed. "Haven't I been telling you? I was looking forward to this day." Gently, he rolled us over. "Is your back okay?"

My skin felt tight, itchy, but the pain had ebbed. "I'm fine. When you mentioned looking forward to the day, did you always envision it like this?"

"Mm, no. Not quite. Sometimes, I imagined your dagger slicing through my chest again. Sometimes, I imagined you opening a wound on my arms and drinking the blood that fell from my veins." Voss kissed my neck, my collarbone, my sternum. He had even mended my clothes, but I still felt the heat of his mouth through the material. "Sometimes, I imagined you calling me out in front of hundreds of Fae and demanding a duel."

"How did that end?"

"With your ass in the air and me teaching you a lesson."

"I thought you said—"

"No one gets to see you except me," he growled. He gazed up at me as he hovered over my stomach—over the scar he had healed—eyes liquid black as he took me in. "And I meant every word. But regardless, I knew so long as you were trying to kill me, I would get this opportunity." He lifted the hem of my shirt, rolled it upward, and placed his lips against my abdomen on the edge of my scar.

"And what opportunity is that?"

"To get you underneath me again."

"You're still egotistical, I see."

"Mm." He hooked his fingers under the hem of my pants and panties. "And you should be too. You did bring me back to life."

"Are we going to talk about it?"

"Later." He edged my pants down, just below my hips. His lips traced the lines they made against my skin. Everything about him was hot. Heat between us sizzled, fueling a fire I felt running through my soul.

We were connected.

More than blood bonded.

I could sense everything about him, even the edge of exhaustion he had from fighting off death.

"Don't worry about it, little fox."

"Don't worry about what?"

"Me." His fingers slid farther down, bringing my pants with them.

The hem trailed over my ass. Knuckles brushed my thighs as he took his time, unwrapping me like a present.

Because you are.

Am I ever going to be rid of you?

No. Now and always means just that, little fox. His grin was radiant as his tongue flicked out, trailing a line over my hip, down, down, down. His eyes met mine and a hot, searing desire welled up inside me. He pressed his tongue flat against my clit and licked.

I thrust my fingers into his hair and pulled him against me. His magic finished taking my pants off as his hands grabbed onto my thighs. He growled, parting me with a firm grip.

"I can feel everything from you." His eyes shut as his hot breath traced over my most sensitive skin, made more sensitive from his tongue. "Tell me what you want."

"You already know what I want."

"I want to hear you say it." Voss flicked his tongue out, toying with my nerves. His eyes flashed with magic, threatening something deep and dangerous. There was so much he wanted to explore. How much time did we have before reality crashed back into us?

"Enough." His teeth grazed my skin. I sucked in a breath. He shuddered. "Fuck, little fox. You're feeling *everything*. It's a marvel."

"Teach me how to use it."

"My magic?"

"Our magic."

The smirk appeared on his lips. "So quick to claim it when you didn't want it for so long." He trailed kisses along my thigh. With his hands, he maneuvered me, so my legs draped over his shoulders, fully exposing me to him. "As Elspeth said, it's about intention. Like this." His eyes whirled to life as fire spun from his fingers. It danced along my skin, caressing up my body.

Then my shirt went up in flames, falling away in cinders.

I scowled at him. "Not cool."

"Mm. I like you better this way." He blew out a breath, and a breeze of magic ran along my skin, brushing the ash away.

I huffed.

"Magic will become an extension of yourself. It's going to take a bit to get used to. Whenever you become emotional, it may flare up, but you need to remember it's the intention of it that matters." He switched to my other thigh, trailing kisses up my skin and back toward my core. I squirmed as his flames swirled around me again, claiming me. "If I intend to hold you down with my fire, I will hold you down." Heat licked up my body, featherlight along my skin, guided by him. The flames cupped my breasts as his mouth pressed the lightest of kisses against my nerves.

I hissed in a breath.

The fire danced along my nipples. Brought them to stiff peaks. An angry kiss pierced through his control, flicked me, and drew out another quick, panting breath.

His mouth closed over my sex at that same moment. *Make no mistake, little fox, I didn't lose control. I wanted you to feel it.*

You wanted to burn me?

Lightly. His tongue entered me. My hands twisted in the sheets.

Because you like when I cause you pain.

The flames curved up my skin, tracing my shoulders and arms. His magic coiled around my throat, applying pressure and making me unable to focus.

One of his fingers pressed against my entrance as he gazed up at me. *Watch yourself come undone.*

It wasn't a command, but the effect was the same. He thrust his finger inside me and found the spot that made my body tremble. My vision blacked out, seeing his perspective. His fire engulfed my body, giving him absolute control over me. The way he played me like a puppet and loved to watch me fall apart. The satisfaction he got from the taste of me dancing on his tongue. How much I bucked as he stroked the soft part of me as he made my body fall to pieces. How satisfied he felt when his teeth came into contact with my nerves, making my body pliant underneath him.

He could do anything to me.

And he would.

"But you always have a way out."

I slammed back into my body as stars burst in front of my eyes. I clamped down on his finger as the orgasm stretched through me. It joined the fire on the outside with a burst of energy. The liquidity of my soul felt ready to explode from my skin. Power spread through my limbs, pressing against his magic with my own.

Mine. My soul called to him, and his answered in kind. As the two fires intertwined, smoke coiled around us.

Voss let out a deep, satisfied chuckle. *And that's how magic happens.*

Twenty-Eight

VOSS

She panted as I withdrew my finger. Satisfaction sang in my veins, because not only had she come apart so perfectly, but her magic had fought against mine. Once she figured out how to use it, we'd be a force against our enemies.

But for now, I wouldn't concern myself with that. No, right now, I savored the feel of her using it against me. Her power matched mine, blow for blow, in an epic showdown of who owned who more. I would win, of course, but it would be so satisfying to watch her try.

"You know," she said in between breaths. Her irises rotated with deeper blues, like clouds at twilight moving over the moon. "I can hear you more than ever."

"Is that so?" I prowled up her body, kissing her along the way. Once I reached her breast, I took my time, trailing my tongue along her soft, delicate skin.

"You think you would win a battle against me?"

"Don't think. Know." My tongue caught the edge of her stiff

peak, and she sucked in a deep breath. "There's a difference." I bent over her, bringing her nipple in between my teeth. The cord of tension wrapped tightly inside her; sensitivity increased from the small burn that bit into her skin. She was slowly becoming Fae, transforming as the magic settled into her. She was healing faster than normal too.

How much could we make each other bleed now?

"I'm the *Fae Slayer,* Voss. I killed Fae for a living. I would definitely win."

"Mm, but yet, I'm still here." I switched to her other breast, nipping playfully at her and enjoying the thrill rushing through her body. I loved sensing everything about her. We wore each other like a second skin. I no longer needed to be consumed by her, because we had absorbed each other.

Truly, it was perfection. My wife, my Queen. For the rest of our lives, we'd be intertwined.

"But I did kill your entire family."

"Yes. About that." I rested my chin on her sternum and gazed at her. "I don't think I properly thanked you."

"Most people do not thank someone else for killing their family."

"You called me a person again." I grabbed onto her neck, feeling her pulse race underneath my thumb. My other hand ran along her skin, grinning as goosebumps welled in my wake.

"I did not."

"Mm."

"How do I—" Her eyes welled as my waist grew hot.

"If you even think about it—" I stopped talking as embers trailed along the hem of my pants. My mouth gaped open as a sly smile stretched on her lips. If that's how we were playing it... I kicked out of my breeches before she could finish her destruction. "What am I to do with you?"

"Teach me a lesson?" Her teeth sank into her lower lip. Pupils blown wide as a cocky smile spread up her cheeks.

I squeezed my fingers against her throat, cutting off her air supply. "You don't breathe until you learn how to use air magic to satiate your lungs." As she tried to suck in a breath, I ran my cock along her dripping entrance.

Her feet kicked against me, but I sent a burst of energy around them, pinning her to the bed. She was exactly where she should be, underneath me.

"Figure it out, little fox."

Voss. A breathless plea of hers in my mind, but it wasn't her safe word. She wanted to do this, down to the core of her. She learned best under pressure, and her trust sang through our bond. From the time that she was ten, her life had been tossed into the deep end. For Max, it had always been sink or swim. Who was I to change her preferred learning method now?

Especially when it made things so interesting.

Blackness crept over her vision, and I had to blink to clear my own instead of going inside her head. "Come on, little fox. Use your magic to breathe."

Her eyes whirled. Such a dazzling sight that I would never tire of.

I pushed myself into her, just the tip of my cock. Her tightness clung to me, but she parted readily as her body welcomed me. I sent a wave of my pleasure to her. Her eyelids fluttered shut as I pulled out and shifted forward once again.

"Use it, little fox," a small command. Nothing that would linger.

Her eyes snapped open as her lungs expanded with no air ever passing through her throat. She swallowed against my grip, mouth opening in an empty pant as I worked myself inside her.

I relinquished my hold on her. She coughed, but her breathing settled into a gasp as I sank to my hilt.

"Voss." My name escaped her lips on a desperate moan.

"You feel what you do to me? How much I crave this?" I ran my hands along her arms, finding her wrists and circling them as I steadily fucked her. Even without my hand around her throat, she barely maintained her breath. "I've wanted to take you long and slow since you were back in my arms. I hope you are ready for this, because I have no plans to stop anytime soon."

"Voss!" Hearing my name as a scream erupting from her coiled into my soul.

I snapped my hips harder, thrusting faster. Shifting my hold, I wrapped both her wrists in one hand and held them above her head. With my other hand, I picked up her leg and lifted her, pushing deeper. Max's body shook around me as I rocked into her. She gasped and writhed, coming undone in a million pieces as I savored the feeling of her clenching around me. The warmth of her, the pressure as it built inside me. My magic shifted, becoming swollen. Urging me onward. Fueling me.

I stilled, taking a steady breath.

Her eyes fluttered open. "Why did you stop?" Her voice was airy and breathless, wanting to fall apart with me. A red-tinged blush crept over her cheeks. I would never stop loving this.

But that was part of the problem.

I clenched my jaw. Losing control wasn't an option. Not with her. Not right now. "My magic wants to…" How did I say this?

Her lids narrowed. "Are you… hesitating with me?"

Releasing her wrists, I cupped her face, brushing my thumb over her cheek. I kissed her deeply. My tongue twined with hers, and she gasped open for me. Forcing my racing heart to slow, I rested my forehead against hers. Sweat had broken out across her brow.

"My magic wants to breed you." I pressed my eyes shut, forcing everything down.

"Oh."

When I opened my eyes again, hers stared back at me with wide astonishment.

"You really want us to be together forever, don't you?"

"Little fox, if marrying you wasn't an indication and making you Blood Queen did nothing to convince you, then I am afraid I'm not sure how else I tell you I am *obsessed* with you. I will love you to the end of my days, and even then, I will fight the Mother herself if it means getting back to you. Do you understand?"

She nodded, looking beside herself. "But I'm not—"

"I understand. You're not sure about kids. So... that puts us in a conundrum." I eased back an inch and sank into her again. It was slow and agonizing but didn't make my magic flare up.

"We could... Do what we did before? Again?"

I desperately wanted her cunt dripping with my cum. I wanted to paint her with it and watch her squirm as I pushed it back inside her.

"No, I need a lesson in control. And you need a lesson on how to make shields. You can tap into the royal power, put a shield in between us just in case I fail."

Her brows slammed down. "You won't fail."

"You're right. I won't." I nodded in agreement, because a youngling was too big of a responsibility with the weight we carried. "Just needed a minute, even so, I'd like you to practice."

"How does it work?"

As I thrust into her again, soft and slow, I explained how to build a barrier around herself. Keep her intentions clear, make it so she couldn't possibly get pregnant even if I wanted her to.

Which, logically, I did not, but my magic had other thoughts.

She understood how I felt, because I opened myself up to her. There was a small part of her turned on by the idea, but a larger part that didn't desire to bring a child into this world. Of course, I agreed with her right now. With the earth on an atrocious precipice, it was no place for a youngling.

But we would fix the world. Then, someday, she would feel safe enough to settle down with me. Once our mission was complete, the revenge quests finished, we would be able to have a family.

Not now.

I felt the barrier grow inside her, and a sigh of relief ran through me. "See?" I said as I shifted our bodies, lifting her hips off the bed so I could sink farther inside her. She groaned underneath me. I chuckled. "That wasn't so hard."

Satisfied that she had created the barrier correctly, I increased my speed. Thrusting into her, filling her over and over again, as I waited for her to come apart underneath me.

I didn't have to wait long. As her orgasm tore through her with overwhelming pleasure, I tamped down my magic, bottling it deep inside me even with it begging for escape. I allowed the primal part of me to take over instead, snapping my hips hard against her. She let out a breathless whine as I came hard. Her body clenched around me, taking everything I had to give.

"Fuck," she said, breathless.

Now that I had released, my magic swirled around me. "Oh, I'm not done with you yet." I pulled out of her. "I distinctly remember my promise to take you in every way possible when I got you back."

"You have."

"Not all in one go."

Her eyes turned to liquid pools. "Voss."

"That's not your safe word." I paused, allowing her space to say what she needed. She stayed silent, glaring at me instead. "Open your mouth, little fox. I want you to taste us on your tongue."

Her eyes softened as she obeyed me without question. I thrust myself inside her mouth, watching with satisfaction as she swallowed me down.

❧ ✄ ❧

Max had fallen asleep tucked against me where I wanted her to be. If I were to be honest with myself, I would admit how exhausted I felt. But her eyes fluttered shut with peaceful dreams rushing through her mind, and I wanted to stay and watch over her. My protective instincts had flared, made worse by my magic's desire to mate with her.

For now, my insatiable little fox was at peace.

I wished for her to have this all the time. Once we united both fronts and fought back against Eero, Iobhar, and anyone else who joined the coup, we'd move on. I wanted to give her this experience, this pleasure constantly. With everything looming ahead of us, this quiet moment wouldn't last. Still, I wanted her to keep it as long as she could.

I watched her rest as my fingers trailed through her hair. My bone-deep tiredness weighed on me, but I finally had access to the full power of the royal line. Now that we were bound together, it no longer felt like ripping myself in two when I reached for the royal magic.

After brushing my lips against her temple, I slipped out from under the sheets and pulled on my tunic and pants. I found my companions in the far corner of the lobby. They had procured bottled ale, and I wasn't sure where it had come from.

Penn nodded as I approached. "The bond is gone. When you died, it went away."

Letting out a breath, I truly looked at him. His haunted gaze told me all the horrors that went through his brain. I had glimpsed the memories through Max, how Penn coaxed her through my demise. It had not been as smooth as we had hoped.

"I'm sorry," I offered.

Penn snorted. "Words I wanted to hear a long time ago, Voss, but not anymore. This is standard for you. Once we're done with this journey, I'm going to find someone who doesn't risk his life at every turn."

I grinned. "I'll be the first one to support your decision." Placing an arm around his shoulder, I gave him a small hug before plucking the ale from his fingertips. "Now, when does Burke expect us?"

"I spoke with her via scytheseer a bit ago. Just before noon would be best for her, and I think it would benefit us to take the extra time. Scarlet needs to adjust." Elspeth sipped her drink. "We also have no idea what we're walking into."

"I don't trust Burke any more than you do, but I didn't sense any corruption from her when we saw her mirage." I took a long swig of ale before passing it back to Penn.

He shook the bottle, and there was only a small amount of the brew left. Sucking it dry, he tossed the empty onto the table. His hands curled around what looked like a book and yanked on it. Part of the wall came away, and a refrigerator full of brews was on the other side. He took two out and handed one to me.

"Burke doesn't leave much to the imagination, does she?" I clinked my beer against his, and Penn snorted.

"She seems to still get off on the ostentatious side of things, so I am not surprised that those in her court do the same thing." Penn pointed to the books, which the titles spelled out *Take as much as you want. We'll charge your room.*

"Ah."

"How is Scarlet?" Penn asked.

"Sleeping. Calm."

"Good."

"Thank you for what you did."

"It wasn't for either of you, but for me. I suppose even I have a bit of a selfish streak. She didn't want you to die, but I also didn't want to live without my best friend."

"Still, I saw her memories. You kept her calm enough for her to try."

Elspeth leaned her elbows on the table, playing with the rim of her bottle. "That's something I don't understand. How?"

"How is any of it possible?" I shrugged, because she was right. None of it made sense. Our powers combined should not have equated to this.

"It has to do with the prophecy, I bet."

Elspeth let out a breath. "Why do you think that, Penn?"

He shrugged. His eyes darted between us. "If Morna and Cumina are keeping something from us, then they might have part of the prophecy that we thought was lost. Do you know if they were ever privy to your father's archives?"

"Until they took over the royal court? No, I don't believe so. My father was too paranoid to give them access."

"But they could have looked for themselves." Elspeth drummed her fingers on the table. "As much as your father wanted to be omniscient, no one could possibly be. They could have figured out a way into the archives without anyone knowing."

"It's possible, but they seemed to think Max would kill me by ascending."

"Which would make sense if they have the prophecy and not the history books. They wouldn't know how ascending to Blood Queen works." Penn narrowed his eyes at the bottle in his hands, as if it could shed light on the puzzle we found ourselves in. "They must have it."

"It doesn't matter what the prophecy says. We have a plan, and I refuse to deviate from that because of what some poor soul said eons ago."

"Voss is right. We can't bank on the prophecy being correct. Just because you found each other doesn't mean you are the bringers of whatever end might come into play." Elspeth ran her hands through her hair. When her fingers caught on the ends, she tapped into her magic to soothe the locks.

"We should play it safe." Penn's gaze shifted to me and narrowed into a glare. "Which I know will be hard for you, Voss, but Scarlet needs to be ready with her magic before we join the other army."

"We practiced tonight."

Brows lowered. Penn shook his head and stared at his drink. "Of course you did."

I slapped him on the back. "She'll get the hang of it. She brought me back, right?"

"I'm going to equate that to beginner's luck." Penn stared at me, his eyes somber. "You scared me, Voss. Both of us."

"I know."

"Do you really think this will be over once we're able to unite the two sides?"

"I hope so, Penn." As much as I enjoyed the chaos this journey had given me, I also craved the quietness of an artist's gallery—a space to allow my mind to expand and be present in the moment. To truly enjoy the small things life had to offer. I hoped to provide Max with that safety and security, something other than killing once the war was over.

And if that failed, I had a list of Fae who deserved to die, starting with Raskos for daring to allow Scarlet near a Dream Walker. I could keep her busy.

"I'm going to sleep." I downed the rest of the ale and put the empty on the table. "Are you both going to?"

Penn shrugged.

Elspeth took another sip. "Absolutely. I need rest. My hair is in shambles, and my magic keeps slipping. Besides, if Burke is putting on a front, we need to be ready for another battle tomorrow."

I nodded, no longer caring to argue with them. They would always worry about the worst case scenario, but things had a habit of working out for the best. Besides, I had felt the defiance in Iobhar, whereas Burke had none of that. My old guard had something tethered and caged, ready to break through the surface and cause mayhem the moment he had the opportunity. I had sensed it, but my magic had been too new, and I had been too cocky to figure out what it had really meant.

Inside this court? None of those feelings had arisen around us, which shocked me due to what happened the last time I was within these walls. The humans seemed pleased, and the Fae did too. If things could shift so drastically here, then I hoped the kingdom could also be saved.

When I reached our room, Max had curled herself around a pillow. I tossed the thing aside and pulled her into me. Her leg wrapped around my torso, her arm around my chest. Her face nuzzled my shoulder, and she let out a long, contented sigh. Whatever future we were building toward, I would make sure it was one worthy of her.

❧ ✂ ❧

When Max woke in the morning, she gazed at me with half-lidded, sleepy eyes. I kissed her long and hard as the sun streamed in from the windows. Then, I fucked her slowly and savored every inch of her body. Once I was through with her, we had about an hour before our meeting with Burke.

Max was the first one to get out of bed, and she pulled on her clothes, despite my protests. I brushed the hair away from her neck and kept kissing her sensitive skin, enjoying how much I distracted her. Finally, she shoved me back onto the bed and got the shirt over her head. "You are the *worst*."

"I don't recall you using those words an hour ago. I believe the word *best* might have slipped out from underneath your tongue."

"It was a mistake, clearly." But the rosy color on her cheeks and the playful look she gave me said otherwise.

With a sigh, I grabbed my shirt. "We need to make sure we eat before leaving for Burke's. Penn and Elspeth still believe this could be another elaborate trap, and it's best if we're fueled before fighting anyone."

"I understand why they do. She didn't treat you well the last time you visited her, and I don't trust her now either." Max shoved her feet into her boots and laced them up.

After tossing my tunic on, I was fully clothed. Max pretended to be insulted every time I tore the fabric from her skin, but she loved it when I took control and kept my clothes on—almost as much as she enjoyed seeing me naked. With her, everything was a delicate dance of our power, and I was happy to meet her expectations, whatever she needed at the time.

"It's strange," she said as she finished her last lace and stood up. "I feel the same, but different. There's power underneath my skin, simmering. It's practically begging to be used. Is that how you feel? Like you're holding yourself back?"

"A little. It's easier to control once you get used to it, but sometimes the edging is what makes it fun."

"Why do I feel like I'm going to regret hearing those words from your lips?"

"Because I have *plans,* little fox." I stepped up to her, wrapped my arms around her shoulders, and pulled her into me. I breathed her scent, loving the headiness of the darkness she carried with her.

"And every one involves you begging me in the end."

"Terrible." Her voice split with a giggle, even as she shrugged me off. Shaking her head, she wrenched the inn's door open and almost stumbled back when Penn was on the other side.

His hand was halfway up, as if about to knock. "Hi."

"Hi," she said. "Uh, thanks for… not letting me kill him."

"Thanks for not leaving him dead."

Her jaw ticked. "We were going to get some food. You want something?"

"That's what I was coming to see both of you about." Penn's eyes swept over us. He looked better this morning as his gaze met mine. It must have been from the lack of blood bond. "And yes, I slept last night. But—" His eyes landed back on Max. "—I recommend doing something to your hair unless you want the world to know the king royally fucked his queen last night." Spinning on his heels, Penn sauntered down the hallway.

Scarlet looked at me with widened eyes. "Why didn't you say anything?" she hissed.

"Because I like to claim you. How have you not realized this yet?"

She patted down her hair. I waved my hand over her, allowing the tangled edges to loosen around her ears. Her narrowed glare brought joy into my soul.

The four of us ate quickly at the cafe next door, keeping our discussions to a minimum. The jubilant air from the humans' celebration carried over into today, and it put me at ease to know the Port City was turning around. What I didn't understand was *why*, but plenty could happen during such a time of upheaval. I doubted my threats did much, as Lady Burke never acted unless there was something in it for her.

Once we had washed down our morning pastries with water, we were back in the blaring whites of the city. The cobblestoned streets seemed to gleam even brighter, and I wondered how many Fae were using their magic to make the Port City appear wondrous, or if Lady Burke had built it this way. Perhaps a bit of both.

When we arrived at her home, the receptionist outside of Lady Burke's office looked simultaneously bored and overburdened. It was how I imagined doing anything with Lady Burke to be, so it fit with the stark white surroundings.

"I have a meeting—"

My words stopped short as Burke's office door opened. Her orange eyes glanced between the lot of us. She ruffled her bright yellow hair. "I see she's Fae now. Very well, I expected as much, which was why I gave you the morning. Good to see you are still alive, Devoss, as rumors say it could result in an untimely demise." Her gaze slid back to me. "Come in. We'll discuss why you are here." She took a step back and gave a slight bow to the four of us, gesturing widely with her hands.

I eyed her as we walked inside. None of the destruction I had left behind was visible, but why would it be? Burke was nothing if not tidy.

"Sit."

"I'd rather you explain why the change of heart first," I demanded.

Lady Burke crossed to the other side of her desk. She sank with a flourish, which puffed out her over-sized dress. Today, she wore a light blue. It hung off her shoulders, clung to her waist, and flared after that. It was nowhere near as hideous as her usual sense of fashion, but still overly exaggerated for my taste.

"What is there to explain?"

"The last time he was here, my husband was almost killed by the brothers *you* summoned," Max growled. She had her dagger in her hands, spinning it every so often. The bone caught a hint of light from the large picture windows with her movements.

Burke waved her hand, as if it were the lightest accusation anyone had given her. "Yes, and after that occurred, I learned a valuable lesson that could only be taught by one person on the planet. I do hope you get to experience it someday. I think it will give you more than either of you realize."

I narrowed my gaze at her. "That's the only explanation we're getting?"

"That's it. Such a thing cannot be explained, it can only be experienced." She pasted a pleasant smile on her face. "But let's talk about *you*. I owe you an apology, first off. I should not have gone against our king. It was a poor choice, seeing as how luck always accompanies you."

"Skill, more like."

"Luck," she said defiantly, ignoring my words.

I gritted my teeth. Max threaded her fingers through mine, still clutching her dagger in her other hand. I let out a breath. "We are here because we are in need of an army."

"You don't say."

"Oh, come off it, Burke," Elspeth snarled. "You know why we're here, so why don't you come out and say it?"

Burke's eyes spun as she turned toward Elspeth. Both Max and I tensed, ready to intervene at a moment's notice. "I like this one, Devoss. You should have brought her with you the first time. Perhaps things would have gone differently." With a sigh, she focused back on me. "You need an army to unite the humans and Fae together. To fight Eero and Iobhar. It makes sense to come to me to ask for help, because you know I am the best court for the job."

I fought back an eye roll.

"But with that being said, my humans are enjoying their freedom now. I cannot possibly ask them to lay their lives down unless there is something in it for my court. You see, they are willing to do things for the freedom they have, but not without reason."

"Of course. The hidden agenda. Out with it," Max spat.

A coy smile crossed Burke's lips, but it was an act. There was nothing bashful about her, and yet she played the part so well. "I want to be a part of the ruling party. I understand there's the potential for a committee involved, and I want in."

"How did you—"

Lady Burke waved her hand, stopping me again.

But I had enough of her arrogance.

I dropped Max's hand and crossed the room in a flash. My fire curled around me, bursting at the seams as I thrust the Fae into the wall. The wall scorched, leaving long black marks webbing away from her body. The Lady tried to suck in a breath, but it was useless underneath my grasp.

"For now, I am your king, and if you dismiss me one more time, I swear to you, you will not live to see whatever comes next. Do we have an understanding?"

She nodded underneath my touch. Her eyes were wide and wild as she grasped at my fingers, trying uselessly to curl them off her. I didn't let go, because I wanted to prove my point.

But Burke had another idea. She made a mirage of herself, a perfect duplicate next to her. "I understand, Your Majesty. It's difficult to change all at once. Please." Her voice strained, as though being squeezed out of her, which I supposed it was.

I dropped her.

She stumbled onto her feet, her mirage helping to steady her. Rubbing at her raw, red neck, she cut a glare at me. "Honestly, was that necessary?"

"Clearly," I spat.

"Fine. Here's the Mother honest truth." She swallowed. "I realized no one will care if I live or die, because my legacy is built on fear. In fact, people would most likely celebrate my demise. I never thought I could change it, until recently. I saw another possibility, another path. But in order for that to stick, I need a chance to start anew." Her teeth worried her lips. "I want to become invaluable to the Fae and humans. I want to leave behind something good, something people want to remember and revere. Freeing the humans was the first step, but it wasn't enough. Everyone still winces whenever I walk in the room."

As I gave her space, Burke crossed to her chair. She righted it—something I hadn't realized I knocked asunder in my haste—and sat back down. She ran her fingers over her hair, coaxing it back into a pristine, curled pile. "So, you see, Devoss Balgair, we need each other. I need the position to show everyone I have changed."

"But have you changed if you are only doing this for yourself?"

"Change has to start somewhere." Burke glanced at Max, looking her up and down. "Tell me. Fae will be killed by your hand in the next battle, right? But you will be approaching your next kills not with malice but fighting for unity. Your story hasn't changed, Fae Slayer. You are still the harbinger, the monster, but you are no longer seeking revenge. Am I right?"

Max's fists curled at her sides as magic welled around her.

I place a hand on her shoulder. "I would be careful what you say to my wife."

"She is right, though." Max's shoulders slumped.

Someday, we will be done with the killing. Someday, you won't have to do this anymore. I promise, little fox. There will come a time when we can move on from this.

She looked at me with glassy eyes. Shadows marred her expression. *But what if this is who I am? What if I always crave blood, death, and violence?*

Then you can slice me open and stitch me back together again. I will gladly watch you bathe in my blood.

I focused back on Burke. "You've changed, but you haven't."

"Correct."

"But you want to change more."

"Also correct. What you two have and what that wretched male has seemed to find... it's inspiring. A partner. Someone who understands you. I cannot continue to be selfish if I want to find someone for me. But I will aways have self-preservation. I will always be self-centered. That will never change. I have simply allowed myself to see the possibility that there may be a better approach. I can crave power and notoriety without making everyone else suffer because of it." Her eyes spun as some of the redness on her neck flaked away, bringing about newly healed skin. "So, allow me to be self-centered with this. I will amass my Fae army and whatever humans desire to join in this fight for unity, so long as there is a place for me at the table once this ends."

"Fine. It is mutually beneficial, after all. The Fae are swayed by you, though goodness knows why, which means the Fae on the cusp will likely follow your lead."

Lady Burke nodded, humming to herself in thought. "You know, I never really liked Eero."

"And yet, you tried to allow the court to take my head."

"That was Bram and Corvin. Make no mistake, Eero's whole family is a dark stain on our kind. Emille held grudges worse than me, and that is saying something. I was glad when you tore out her heart."

"And yet, it didn't persuade you to join me."

"Alas, King Balgair, it's because you had nothing to offer me at the time. Bram and Corvin did."

"And what was that, I wonder?"

Burke let out a snort. "They offered to marry me. I would have been a queen. But that doesn't matter anymore. It's not like I found either of them attractive, but the prospect of being a queen? That I liked very much."

"And how do we know you won't turn against us?" Penn's quiet voice cut through the room, accusation heavy in his tone. He stepped forward. "You've done it before."

Burke nodded solemnly. She folded her hands in front of her. "I cannot become queen when there is already one on the throne, and I know better than to fight the Slayer. I've heard the rumors. Immolation with a single touch while not being in the same room? Impressive. While I don't fear the three of you, there is a reason she's the one the Fae whisper about in the dark."

Max sneered, and I curled my fingers through hers, fighting back the urge to kill this Fae where she stood.

Burke held up her hands. "I mean it as a sign of respect. No one else terrifies me. You, however, I truly believe have the power to change the world. And I am happy to now be on your side." Burke offered her hand, not to me, but to Max.

Her outstretched arm hung in the air between them. Power crackled underneath my fingers as my wife glared at the other Fae.

"I'm going to offer you a deal," Max said. Magic lashed around her. "You promise to stay loyal to the unity of Fae and humans and to treat both sides equally. You promise to keep the well-being of Fae and humans in the forefront of your decisions and votes in the future. You promise to aid us with your army. You promise not to kill the current King and Queen or any of our allies. You promise all that, and if we win, you will have a space on the committee."

I searched for holes in her deal, wanting to stop it if there were any. Glancing at Penn and Elspeth, they looked as bewildered as I did, but Elspeth subtly nodded. She saw nothing wrong with it, either. If we lost, we had an out. If we won, Burke would have to uphold her end of the bargain. There would be no backstabbing us.

It was a smart move, and pride welled in my chest. My little fox was learning quickly how to navigate this world, and the amount of power whipping around her was enough to send me into a frenzy.

Burke felt it too. With wide eyes, her lips pressed up in the smallest of smiles. There was nothing devious behind it. She stepped forward. "Deal."

Their hands met. Shook. And the world tilted as Max's unbridled magic spun around them, joining the bargain together with the royal power.

"I'm glad we're on the same side."

"I would say the same," Max said as she dropped her hand. "But I know you are doing it for the wrong reasons." She turned on her heels, and her boots scuffed the floor as she walked out of the room.

"You will have my army, Devoss. I hope it's enough."

I nodded. "Same. And Burke?"

"Hm?"

"Your deal is not with me, so if you so much as look at my wife wrong again or breathe another insult in her direction, it will be your heart I crumble to dust beneath my fingers. Do you understand?"

She had the audacity to smile. "I think we're going to be friends once this is over. You'll see. Talk to my secretary on the way out. She will see to it that anything you need is paid for by me. It will be great working with you, your Highness."

Twenty-Nine

SCARLET

I took aim once again at the abandoned hoswisp nest. We were just outside Burke's Court, and we had stopped for some much needed magical target practice. But it was going as well as everything else in my life—a complete and utter disaster.

Voss's body pressed against mine. His fingers trailed down my outstretched arm. "I need you to focus."

"Easy for you to say when you're the one distracting me."

"No one is going to wait for you in battle, and since I don't want to kick your ass, this will have to do." He smacked my butt and pointed to the nest with his other hand. "Make it crumble to the earth." His breath licked the shell of my ear, and truly, it was too much. Having him surrounding me like this, all I wanted to do was whirl around, sink my teeth into him, and make him bleed.

We were beyond exhausted. This practice session was a way to gather our strength. And without my power being at my fingertips, I was a liability.

I sighed and pointed at the long, slender spirals that stretched toward the sky. His hands ran along my arms, a featherlight touch intending to lure my focus. Voss was too good at making me pay attention elsewhere.

"Stop it," I growled.

"I'll stop if you get it right." His lips pressed against the sensitive skin of my neck. "Or if I get you worked up enough to make you come without my entering you. Whichever occurs first."

He would also stop if I said my safe word, but that went unspoken. I *liked* his distractions, but annoyance stretched through me. It shouldn't have been so hard to tap into the power. I felt it in my veins, thrumming through my muscles. The hum, the wealth, the vastness of it hung just beneath the surface.

But I couldn't reach it.

I let out a breath. Intention. It came down to that. The power webbed around my arms, down my legs, and grounded me to the earth. But it never seemed to explode outward. Frustrated, I thrust my elbow back into Voss.

He grunted and flew backward. His mouth opened, agape in shock as he righted himself on his feet. The ground had parted underneath his heels from the impact.

I looked down at my arms. "Apparently, getting annoyed with you and shoving you off me was a good intention." I glanced up, only to see mischief in his eyes.

"If you wanted me to teach you a lesson, little fox, you could have said so." He prowled toward me, a delighted smirk stretching up his face.

I readied my stance. "I never was one for easy learning."

"No, you absolutely make things as difficult as possible." Water spun in his hands, switching to something less deadly for our fight. He shot a jet straight at me.

I pushed my magic into the earth, trying to create a wall between us, but I did little more than making a few pebbles shake before the onslaught of water hit me straight in the face.

Wiping it away, I blinked at Voss. "That was supposed to do something."

"You won't learn this within minutes. It takes years of practice for younglings to get a hold of their magic, longer still to find the edges of what their powers can do. You are trying to master something that takes decades of training."

"Decades we don't have the luxury of." I pouted, staring at my drenched hands. *Dry.* I ordered the magic welling in my system, but nothing happened. *Clean. Dry. Remove water.*

You can't chant at it, little fox. Intend for it to be dry. Try… imagining your arms already being dry.

That makes no sense.

Try it, or I'll punish you.

I narrowed my eyes, but let a smile play across my lips. "Can we do both?"

"If you want."

I sunk my teeth into my lower lip but focused on my arms. I imagined having the small hairs dry in the early fall breeze. Imagined how the sun felt after baking the water off my skin. Tried to see the glitter of dirt that would cover me from the wilds soon enough. I focused on how it felt right after a swim, how my skin grew taut as it dried.

But slowly, the water ebbed off me. Dissolving as droplets dissipated into the air. As the magic welled inside me, I also felt something else. A pull, so bone deep I almost didn't notice it. As I summoned the power, something heavy pushed against the earth. A larger gravity? No. With the water evaporated, I shook my thoughts away. The feeling was gone as quickly as it had come. Perhaps it was just the magic.

"It's not as easy as everyone makes it out to be."

Voss shook his head. "Not until you get used to it. Once it becomes second nature, it's like controlling your own body. You don't think about breathing, you just do. Want to try again?"

I sighed. "Why do I feel like this is going to result in me getting soaked repeatedly?"

"We could try with some fire ropes, but I felt that would be a worse distraction for you."

I glared at him.

A smile curved at the corners of his lips, and it made me want to slice through his clothes and tear them off him. And as soon as I had those thoughts, one of his buttons popped off his shirt.

My eyes widened. "Are you telling me I could practice magic by *undressing* you?"

"Was my burning your ample amount of clothes not enough of an indicator of that?" Voss picked up the button and placed it back on his shirt. His magic welled, threading it back into position, as if I had never done anything. "But as I said, I happen to like my clothes."

"And I liked mine."

"Mm. Well, we know how this goes, little fox. Usually, it ends with you naked underneath me, with nothing on you except my breath against your skin." Water pooled along his arms again, welling over his fingertips as he readied another onslaught.

Determination raced through me, because I had to get this right.

He shot another stream of water at me, but I dodged to the side. This time, I focused on evading as he continued shooting from a distance. My speed was another trait I had to get used to. I hadn't had time to explore it yet, but everything about me had become more since ascending—faster, quicker, quieter, deadlier. Even without magic, I still had my body. And my physical capabilities had gotten me this far.

I twisted away from another attack and pounced on Voss. He caught me easily, hands sliding under my ass as he pulled me into him. My teeth nipped at his jaw as he fisted his hand in my hair and pulled.

"You will never learn if you distract yourself."

"I'm never going to learn, anyway." I pressed my lips against his, seeking comfort, solace, understanding and…

Fire.

It swirled around us, welling with my emotions and threatening to burn our hair. Voss's magic fought against mine—the push and pull we always had, but more intense now. We were on the cusp of death every time we got together, both of us ready to sacrifice everything if it meant getting to claim one more orgasm before we died.

He bit my lower lip. Blood welled out, and he swallowed the drops as if they were his tether to the earth. Breathing hard, he wrenched backward, shoving both of us apart. "Distraction," he growled.

"How does it feel?"

"Like I've taught you some things too well."

I laughed, and he fought back a smile.

"Let's try again, little fox. Two more rounds before we get back on the horses and head to the royal court."

I nodded, reluctantly focusing on the hoswisp spires again. It was by far the most boring way to learn, and perhaps, soon we could try something more interesting.

How interesting, little fox?

Shush. A smile coiled on my face despite my best attempts to hide it.

With my hand pointed directly at the spires, I focused on the power that thrummed inside me. Intention. I imagined the spires bursting, shards splintering into the sky. Thoughts of fire and destruction overtook my mind, which wasn't hard to do, considering everything I had seen. I imagined them *bleeding*, which made no sense, but it was how I had gotten through most of my life. Blood had been the one thing to follow me everywhere. It trailed in my wake; it coaxed life into me. Hell, it made me horny—which I could finally admit, thanks to Voss.

And while the spires didn't explode, they did weep, not with blood, but with water.

"Huh."

"That's something at least." Voss eyed my work. "Though I'm not sure it will help us in a battle."

"We could focus on my knife skills instead." I slid him a glance. Even when I wasn't trying to think about it, the wicked taste of candied ginger danced along my tongue. The memories of his flavor ran through my brain.

"You distract yourself." Though, the amount of preening he did under my thoughts told me he encouraged this version of distraction.

I huffed and turned back to the nest. With a sigh, I grounded my feet again, shifting into a stance that I felt was better for magic. Voss snorted. As I glared at him, he slammed his mouth shut, but gave me a look that inquired what I was going to do about it.

The wealth of power hummed throughout my body, but never seemed to rush into my hands like I wanted. As I scowled at the wretched, hollow nest, a strange feeling washed into me from my feet. It felt like inhaling directly into my skull, a pressure I couldn't put my finger on.

I paused, looking at Voss. No nose bleed, no ache for power. His appearance was casual, watching me with hooded dark eyes.

"You're not feeling weak, are you?"

"Why would I?"

I blinked, because it was a strange thing to describe. There weren't words for this thing in our human language, because I'd never had powers like this before. Perhaps it was normal? "It feels like I'm wrestling magic from somewhere."

Voss shook his head. "That's impossible. I feel fine, still at full strength." The spires in front of us burst into flames, exploded, and pelted us with small bits of mud and debris. His eyes narrowed. "More, in fact." He waved a hand over us, making the mess disappear as if it were nothing.

But I had *felt* it. I opened my mind to Voss, sharing the memory with him.

His eyes widened. "Interesting."

"I don't like when you say that."

"Why?"

"Because it means something new is happening, which we're not accounting for in our plans." I breathed out and rubbed my forehead. None of this made sense. I had ascended. We had beaten the odds, which meant we should be on the path to save the world. We should be the answer to the future, but everything we had learned made this feel poignant.

Were we on the right track? And if we weren't, were we doomed to fail because of it? Perhaps magic wasn't meant to be questioned. Perhaps it just was.

"What's my target?" I asked, wrenching myself from my thoughts. The longer I was alone with them, the more destructive they became.

Never alone, little fox. Voss's presence stroked my soul at the same time as he answered me, "Me. You said yourself, you learn better when there are higher stakes. You have one more chance. Stop my attack or else."

"Or else what?"

"I will withhold sex."

I blanched. "What?!"

"It's the only punishment you'll respond to, as you like it a little too much when I am rough with you." His voice turned to gravel. It ran along my skin, cascading goosebumps in its wake. "Which means I will edge you. I will keep edging you until you are begging me to allow you to come, and even then, I won't allow it. I will use your mouth and your body, but I will not allow you to finish."

I blinked. My brain malfunctioned.

"If you lose, I will tease you until you can't think of anything else. Which, really, little fox, such a distraction is not great for your participation in the war. So, you need to defend yourself."

"And if I succeed?" My voice came out of a dry mouth, breathy in a whisper.

"Then I'll edge you just enough for it to be perfection."

My body shivered. Both were torture, but one was, as he said, *perfect*. I bit my lower lip and nodded, reaching again for the power that hummed around me. As magic sank into my limbs, I allowed it in. It felt like suction, like I was a bottomless dry well trying to refill after a rain storm. But this time, the power was within reach. Perhaps this was how it was to be Blood Queen. Maybe this was normal.

"Okay," I agreed.

The sinful smirk on Voss's face told me everything I needed to know. He wouldn't go easy on me, because he liked the idea of pleasing me so much it brought me pain and suffering. Whenever we finally received a moment of peace, I wondered what my life would look like.

You don't have to wonder. Voss's mind flashed with images, every wicked thing he wanted to do to me. His magic surrounded me. His cock buried in my ass as his magic parted me and—

"You can do that?" I sucked in a breath, not losing the grasp of my power.

In his mind, he was fucking me *with* his magic.

"Of course I can."

"Holy shit."

"Are you ready?" Even as he asked, his first attack shot out of his hands. This time, it was the flames he knew so well.

Maybe it was better than using water, because my instincts flared instantly. Staring down a vicious attack, even though I knew he would deflect it at the last second if needed, my brain shut off and my body took over. Despite never having magic before, as I crossed my arms in front of me, it surged to life, surrounding me with a shield of water that pooled in the air between us. The fire struck it, turning to steam instantly.

I narrowed my eyes. "Really?"

He didn't wait. And I knew it was because no one else would. If we were in a battle, I would receive no mercy.

Voss threw bolts, flames, water, and earth at me. My feet were quick, dodging what I could and shielding what I needed to. Magic flowed into me every time I used it, becoming an available reserve right under my fingertips. As soon as I saw an opportunity, I tried to shoot a bolt of lightning at him.

Sparks fluttered over my fingertips but did nothing other than fizzle out as soon as they hit the air.

Voss licked his lips. "I'm going to enjoy destroying you."

"Fuck."

Another bout of flames drew up around him, three coils twining through the air like snakes. They whipped out all at once. I dodged the first, barely avoided the second with a roll. The third latched onto my ankle, and he was so careful with it. The flames singed my clothes, but not my skin. I shot water magic around my leg, drenching my pants and dousing the flames, but his air magic was underneath the fire.

It twisted around me and wandered underneath my pants. Curled around my legs fast, heading toward my thigh. I sucked in a breath as I slammed my foot down, shaking the ground with a wave of earth magic, but it did nothing to disconnect the coil.

Summoning lightning again, I tried shooting him, but his magic was already there, threading through my fingers like his hand would. As I tried my other arm, he pinned that one too. Voss lifted me up in the air and brought me closer to him.

His magic teased the sensitive skin next to my panties.

I struggled, glaring at him.

"It seems I have won." His arms wrapped around me. His magic kept a hold on me. Being at his complete mercy made my body clench. "But you did well, so maybe I will lower your penance." His voice dipped low, growly and soft along my skin. His tongue flicked the shell of my ear.

The magic slid underneath my panties, and the whimper that escaped my lips was almost inhuman.

He chuckled as his hand gripped the nape of my neck. The other traveled down to my hip, settling underneath the hem of my shirt. "Remind me who you belong to?"

"You," I gasped out.

"Are you trying to be a good girl because I might take pity on you and let you come sooner?"

His magic grazed my nerves. My body convulsed, but Voss's firm hold kept me from moving anywhere.

"It won't work, you know?" His teeth nipped my neck. "Because I'm going to enjoy every moment of making you suffer." His lips trailed along my jaw, down my cheek, then found my mouth. He claimed me with a kiss in a way no one else had before. I opened for him, relishing the taste of his tongue.

I realized I would happily suffer for the rest of eternity underneath Voss.

Not eternity, but the Fae live a very long time.

I was about to ask how long—how old he was, because I still didn't know—but his magic tested my entrance. Light, teasing, just a small taste. And as quickly as he had enveloped me, everything was gone, and he had his hands on my shoulders to steady me. Holding me as I weaved on my feet.

"Really?" I whispered.

"If I don't stand by my punishments, you'll never learn." But the look on his face was as heated as mine was, eyes smoldering with liquid fire, and his thoughts whirled with desire. "Plus, we still have to save the world."

"Or die trying. Voss, you cannot let me die unsatisfied."

He pressed his lips to the top of my head. "I would never dream of it."

A brush of magic ran along the outside of my panties, almost like a ghost of a finger. A part of me wondered if I had imagined it, but the look of pure satisfaction on his face told me I hadn't.

"Tease."

"You haven't seen anything yet." He wrapped his fingers through mine. "Come. We need to get back to the royal court. If there's another battle, the humans will need us."

He was right, of course. We were in the middle of the deserted wilds. Penn and Elspeth had stopped to feed and water the horses at a small outcropping of trees while we had trained. There was plenty of distance between us, in case my magic had gone horribly awry. Anyone could happen upon us, but it was unlikely, since Burke's army would soon be at our backs and his brother's court was on the opposite side of the royal court.

Still, it would do us no good to be caught out in the open by hoswisps, fire pauldrins, or an army.

"All right. Let's go save the world. Or whatever."

VOSS

B y the time we arrived at the royal court, the sun had sunk close to the horizon. Shadows kissed the ground, slowing our progression through the destroyed outer part of the city. In the one day away from the court, the humans had already cleaned up a lot of the bodies. Stains from the blood had sunken into dirt, and the earth had greedily lapped it up.

We left our horses at the hollowed-out stables. Penn had found enough fixings leftover to feed and water them for the night. It took only a modicum of time to brush them down and get them settled. The thatched roof was half-missing from the stalls. If it rained, none of the beasts would be happy, but despite the oppressive humidity, not a single cloud loomed in the sky.

As we made our way toward the towers at the center of the court, we stopped shy of the inner walls. I tilted my head, listening and hearing the heartbeat of someone close. I held out my hands, waiting. If the person meant us harm, we'd likely already be staring down the door of the Mother.

"Devoss." Morna's voice was a sharp staccato. "I see you are back and unharmed. Pity, really." She stepped out of the shadows, seeming to materialize out of nowhere.

I had no qualms with my step-siblings. They had been handed a raw deal, but they held resentment against me. As much as I tried to do right by them, I never had the power to confront the evil they faced until now. It had been a waiting game, something I was patient about.

Patience was necessary. Had been my whole life.

Which also explained Max's abundant energy whipping around her. The amount of teasing I had already done had driven her near the brink. And still, she stewed in her punishment. Half delighted, half mad. She had a way out if she needed it, but she chose this for herself.

"Morna. Since I do not have a crossbow pointed at my heart, I take it you'll allow us passage for further discussions?"

She shrugged. "Something like that. I see she ascended fine." Her golden eyes roamed over my little fox, and I fought back the growl crawling up my throat.

"What is it to you, Morna?" Max wasn't afraid to put sass behind her voice. With her hands curled at her sides, my Fae Slayer held an air of a queen, as she should. Despite everything I had tormented her with on the trip over, she refused to back down.

"As I said, I wanted you to ascend. While, yes, it would have been convenient for Devoss to die, it's fine either way, as it turns out." Her gaze snapped to mine. "We do seem to have a common enemy for the moment. Iobhar and Eero are going to be dangerous for the humans to take on by themselves. Did Lady Burke agree to lend us her army?"

"Only those willing to fight, but yes. She released all the humans recently."

"Only recently, but not after your missives. I wonder what changed for her?" Morna's eyes danced, indicating she knew a lot more than she let on.

What had happened after they were forced to leave Max behind with Leveret? I had been furious at their inability to fight off his compulsion, but that had been unfair. No Fae or human could fight the royal line's magic.

"Alpin also promised to lend as much aid as he could. I'm not sure how many courts will fall behind Eero's bid for the throne, but I imagine several will. The more vicious ones are likely to back him, as they never liked my missives from the start." I played my voice passively, as if none of this bothered me. My family's legacy was nothing but a dark stain on our society, which was why I fought against it. I wanted to change things for the better, and the only way to do that was to let go of our histories and move forward—with the humans united under one rule.

"And how many people will die in the upcoming war, I wonder?" Morna's eyes slid to Max. "Would you avoid it if you could?"

"War?" Max stiffened. "Of course. Only an idiot would say they would fight in a battle to the death."

"But if it were only a handful who had to die?"

"You're being cryptic, Morna, so speak your mind." My voice sunk low.

Magic welled around us, and I slid a glance at Max. She had tapped into her power as a shield but didn't seem to realize it. This was becoming instinctual for her, and she felt wary down to her core with this alliance. She had liked my sisters just fine when she had been set on killing me.

It was Penn who placed his hand on her shoulder.

She pressed her eyes closed and breathed. Something deep had shifted between their friendship when she ascended. I felt it inside her. There was an unbreakable trust now. The magic cooled in the air, no more threatening toward Morna than our conversation.

"I see," Morna said, nodding. "I will do so when the time is right, Voss. But for now, it is late, and we are expecting the army in the early hours of the morning, just before dawn."

"Scouts?"

"Of course. Quinn has checkpoints set up to monitor progress through his network. Not as efficient as scytheseers, but the humans can't seem to summon the animals. Pity, really." Morna let out a breath. "We need to have a longer meeting as to what the battlefront will look like as well. With two additional armies joining us, we need to review the traps the humans created and make sure none of our Fae are lost in the crossfire."

"You've been busy."

"Always have been." She flashed a smile. It curved with the sharpness of her jaw. "You just never noticed it before."

Ah, but I had. My step-siblings tried to make life easier for themselves, shift into a better position. It was out of survival and necessity, and I hoped they wouldn't have to do it for much longer. While I wished to trust them, a large part of me understood who they were, created by circumstance. Any trust I gave them would be wary at best.

"Understood. Well, I'm grateful we're coming to this agreement." I reached my hand out.

Morna looked at it, sweeping her eyes up to mine. "I never understood you, Voss. You weren't like them, but you also weren't..." She stopped. "You wanted them all dead from the beginning, didn't you? It wasn't about power, was it?"

"It's never been about power."

Except where Max was concerned. In bed, that was about power, and she was more than willing to give it to me.

"Fine." Morna shook my hand, quick and solid. "But if I so much as see you turning against any of your words or promises, I will gut you myself."

"Oh, for the love of the Mother, dramatic much?" Elspeth shook her head and rolled her eyes. She marched forward, pushing past Morna. "I am going to my room and getting some sleep."

"About that."

Elspeth turned slowly. She wasn't much of a fighter, but the venom invading her birchwood eyes had me building a wall between her and Morna. "Have you done something to my apartment?"

"I haven't dared touch any of your items. But my sister and her little pet have gotten quite comfortable in there."

Max tensed as a stab of regret shot through her. But there was none of the protectiveness she typically felt toward the other human. There had been some jealousy over their relationship, but I also had my past. It seemed, however, Max had moved on.

"Cumina has been using my apartment," Elspeth's voice was flat, but a thread of anger wove through it. "Well, this will have to be rectified. Immediately." She spun again and stalked off.

"Have you been staying in mine, then?" Penn asked.

"Of course not," Morna snorted. "The guest room at Voss's. I wouldn't *dream* of sleeping in his actual bed. Or yours, Penn. No offense, but you kind of smell." She started after Elspeth, leaving Penn, Max, and me behind.

Penn sniffed his shoulder.

"You smell fine," I said.

"Yeah, and if you didn't, I could easily cover it up with the scent of your blood." Max pulled on my hand, leading me toward the towers. "Look, if we don't intervene, Elspeth might actually hurt Cumina. And this is a battle I don't really want to miss."

Penn snorted. "I'm grateful that was a joke instead of a threat."

Max looked over her shoulder at him. Her blue eyes softened. "Never again."

"What happened while I was out?" I asked.

As we hurried toward the towers, Penn chuckled. "Just two people realizing they could have lost you. You wouldn't understand."

I frowned. "Of course I understand." It would have been like losing either of them. Max was my world, but Penn had been my best friend for most of my life. We had an undeniable history, and at the end of this, I needed them to be safe.

If I lost either...

"Stop that," Max said as we got to the stairs. She whirled on me and poked me in the chest. "We're not thinking about losing Penn. Unless it's because I stab him."

"I thought you said you were past threats!" Penn cried.

"Well, I also happen to stab the people I care for. So, you know, it's no longer a threat. It's more like... a loving stab."

Penn shook his head and held the door open. A few sets of eyes of humans glanced at us as we walked inside, but no one said anything. Judging by how many people lingered inside the lobby, they had made themselves at home.

Morna waited by the elevator.

"She ditched you?" Max asked.

"More like intentionally shut the door in my face," Morna sighed. "I told her because I wanted payback. Those two have been... Well, it's been obnoxious, is what it is. Please don't kill me."

"I understand the obnoxious thing," Penn grumbled.

Max shook her head as her eyes focused on the elevator numbers, watching it descend. "Marcy is her own person. So long as Cumina is respecting that, they can both do whatever the fuck they want."

With the amount of venom lacing her words, maybe she hadn't completely moved on after all.

No, I have, Voss. I am angry with my friend and how quick she was to dismiss me after we both lost someone. Max gazed at me, and I understood instantly. Losing Anya had been a major blow, a tremendous loss, and Max wasn't fully over her death. How could she be? She didn't have time to mourn, not when she was on a mission to end the royal line, and not after being captured by my brother.

When this is over—

You keep saying that.

You are going to get the rest you need to process everything, and I mean everything.

And until then?

I'll keep making you feel good enough, so you won't have time for any pesky feelings.

You'll keep me distracted?

As long as you need me to. I'm at your mercy.

Her lips quirked. *I appreciate that.*

Penn let out a breath. "I am so thankful not to be experiencing whatever that was between the two of you."

The elevator doors slid open, and the four of us slipped inside.

"Why not, Penn? You are missing all the fun." I dropped my voice into a purr.

Morna stabbed the button to bring us upstairs. "You haven't changed much over the years."

"Neither have you." I pulled Max against me, bringing her back to my chest as I leaned against the wall.

"Well, that's changed, I suppose." My step-sister looked us up and down. "You never really were one for public displays."

"He's still not. I'm fairly certain he would kill me if he knew how I saw Scarlet naked for a half a second before he kicked us out of

Treborne's office."

I growled. "Take it back."

Penn held up his hands. "I am the *least* threatening among those in this elevator."

"Excuse you," Morna argued, narrowing her golden gaze on Penn. "I have to believe that a female would take that title over a male."

"Please try to convince me you're not terrifying, Morna." Penn leveled a gaze at her.

Her eyes sparkled. "I will do no such thing."

"Because you are," Scarlet snickered. She traced her fingers along my arms. "And Penn's seen you naked, so if I can't kill him for that, then neither can you."

I hummed next to her ear and savored watching the skin on her neck pebble. "The argument's valid."

"Plus, I think we've all seen Scarlet naked," Morna added.

My arms tightened around Max. *Have you been bad?*

Nudity isn't bad.

I think you might need a reminder of how possessive I can be.

I think you *need a reminder that I had to wash the king's blood off me after you allowed me to… no, forced me to run away.* Her face tilted up toward mine.

I kissed her. *I will make it up to you later. On my knees.*

"See what I've been dealing with?" Penn asked as the elevator dinged.

"Similar to my situation, it seems."

The doors opened, and an onslaught of sound ricocheted throughout the hallway.

"My fucking clothes, Cumina? Really?!" Elspeth's shriek reverberated off the walls.

"She needed to wear something!"

"She could have worn *anyone else's*."

"Uh oh." Penn stepped into the hallway. We were quick on his heels.

Marcy, the woman my little fox held such affection for, stood in the hall. She had her arms folded over her chest and a cross look on her face as she stared at the chaos unfolding in Elspeth's apartment. A flurry of items had already been tossed outside.

"You knew this would piss me off!"

"And I think it's fair payback for that time at Treborne's spring party."

"That party was over *four decades* ago! Get over it!"

"I *liked* that dress. It took me forever to convince Balgair to give me the funds for it."

"And I tried to mend it!"

"You made it worse!"

"I was drunk on Faerie wine. And I said I was sorry!"

"No, you said it just now. Just now. This is the first time in four decades you've even apologized for destroying it."

"Because it was an accident, and I *didn't mean to*."

"The dress?" Morna asked Marcy.

Marcy glanced over at us. "What's the deal with it, anyway? Why are they so heated?" Her eyes scanned our group, and she froze for a beat when she looked at Max. My hand was still reflexively on her hip, claiming her every moment I had. The green-eyed girl glanced back toward the apartment.

Morna sighed. "The late king never gave us much coin to spend on ourselves. We had to scavenge and do odd jobs for everything we ever earned. She had saved up for months to go to the spring party at Treborne's place. He was known for throwing lavish events, ones that Fae would go all out for. I never went myself, never cared to dress up like the rest of them. But Cumina? She wanted to fit in, desperately. She spent all her coin on that dress." Morna calmly explained this while Elspeth and Cumina bickered inside the unit. Shoes flew through the air as they chucked them at each other.

I thought about tossing a barrier between them, but this seemed like something they needed to get out of their system.

"And Elspeth spilled a drink on it. When she tried to clean it for Cumina, she ended up dying the fabric all kinds of other colors. And she tried another time but tore several stitches out."

"Cumina couldn't fix it herself?" Max asked.

"Not after Elspeth's magic was done with it. It looked like rags."

"Usually she's great with fabric."

"Usually she is, but not after a bottle of Faerie wine." Morna uncrossed her arms and held her hands up. She clapped twice, and the strength of it made the sound bounce off the walls with a resounding *whack*. "That's enough."

"She raided my wardrobe," Elspeth snarled. Her reddish brown hair hung loosely around her shoulders, strands flying out of place. Face bright red from exertion.

Cumina's short spiraled black hair in contrast was untouched, perfectly in place. Her silver eyes swirled, but she glanced at her sister. "Only because I needed something to wear, as did Marcy."

"You have armor," Elspeth snarled.

"And you have plenty of clothes to spare," Cumina retorted

"Enough!" Max this time. She shook my hand off and marched between them. Honestly, that was more brave than facing down any of the Fae she had done in the past, because while my healer was gentle most of the time, if you wronged her clothes, all bets were off. "Cumina, Elspeth said she was sorry. And she is, right?"

Elspeth crossed her arms over her chest. Her nostrils flared, but she gave a stiff nod.

"And Cumina, you are sorry for borrowing from her closet

without her permission?"

Cumina opened her mouth. "I am not—"

"Let me be clear." Max took a step toward her, eyes blazing bright blue. "We have plenty of other things to be worried about right now. This is trivial and stupid, and we need to put it behind us." She turned and glared at Elspeth. "Both of you. Now, are you both sorry for letting this impede our planning for an invasion?"

They muttered apologies instantly. Elspeth glanced down at the chaos on the floor. She waved her hand, and a lot of the mess went right back to where it originally belonged. Her gaze caught on Marcy, who stood in the hallway, taking this all in.

"Look, none of those are practical, anyway. Let me get you something good for fighting," Elspeth said.

"She's not fighting," Cumina growled.

"We've been over this." Marcy straightened and crossed the threshold. Her hands went to her hips, and she lifted her chin. "I'm fighting if it comes to it, but I'll be using the bow from a distance. And you'll be with me if anyone breaks through."

They stared at each other for a beat, but Cumina acquiesced first, nodding in agreement with the woman. I was impressed that her stubbornness didn't come more at the forefront, but then again, neither did mine when Max made up her mind.

My step-sister had fallen hard. I hadn't seen her like that since her late partner.

"Then I'm getting you better clothes. If you are going to borrow from me, you at least need to have something that looks good while still being practical." Elspeth blinked, gaze reaching the rest of us in her foyer. "And the lot of you, get out. After I set them up in my *guest* room, I will rest before the meeting. We meet after twilight?"

Morna nodded. "Sounds good to me."

"Thank goodness. Go!" Elspeth waved us away. Penn was quick

to head into his apartment. Marcy and Max gazed at each other for a minute, and Max gave her a single nod before heading out. I followed close behind. Morna was already at the elevator.

"You aren't seriously coming up to my penthouse?" I crossed my arms.

"Just to grab something. Trust me when I say I want to be nowhere near any of this." She flicked her fingers at us.

Max nestled against me, leaning against my chest with hers. Her fingers roamed over my shoulders. "I think you have a promise to fulfill." She whispered the words loud enough for Morna to hear.

She was right. I wouldn't let us face down our possible demise while she was still on the edge.

"How did Penn manage to not kill both of you?" Morna said as we ascended to my floor. "You know what? I don't want to know." And as quickly as she had entered my guest room, she left, leaving Max and I blissfully alone.

I turned toward her. "Shower. Now."

"What if I don't want to?"

My eyes narrowed. I lifted her up over my shoulder and spanked her ass hard. She let out a yelp and a giggle, which was perfect music to my ears, as I hauled her into my bathroom. I made a distinct promise to my wife, and I planned to fulfill it. And I had several hours to do so.

&ð; ✂ ﻌ

"Voss." Her voice came out in a high-pitched whine.

My hand rotated the soap bar, gathering a thick lather. "What?"

My little fox leaned with her back against the cool tile of the shower wall, barely able to stand. I had been cleaning every inch of her. And I wasn't done yet. Placing the soap down, I trailed my fingers underneath the swell of her breasts, up to the stiff peak of her nipples. I massaged the soap around her sensitive nerves, using my fingernails to stimulate her further. She tried to buck, body convulsing, but my water magic pressed her back against the wall.

"What, little fox?"

She was breathless as the water roamed around the curves of her thighs. Her mind blanked out, completely empty, save for the void of need. All this buildup, and most of it was without my touching her. I had been teasing her all day, making every part of her wanting.

Once her pert nipples were perfectly hard, I took down the shower head and washed the soap from her skin. I grazed my mind over hers—her tender skin felt each droplet of water. I didn't need fire to ignite her from the inside out, because this worked just fine.

"Please," she murmured. The word barely escaped her lips.

"Please, what?" I replaced the shower head, picked up the bar of soap, and began the process again. So far, her neck, face, hair, arms, and now breasts were perfectly clean. But I wanted every inch of her to be pristine.

So I could take my time ruining her again.

"Please let me come."

"I don't think you deserve it yet." I dropped the soap and trailed my fingers along her stomach, making sure every inch of her soft skin was covered. I roamed around the edges of the flaming scar, satisfied. Using my magic, I spun her, so her breasts pressed against the tile.

She moaned, and the noise went straight to my aching cock.

Picking up the soap once more, I ran the bar along her back, savoring every time my touch was so light that her ass clenched. Working another lather, I focused on the smooth skin of her ass, running my fingers down her center. Her body tightened as I worked the soap around her tightest hole.

A glorious whimper escaped her lips. "Voss."

"I know, little fox. I know." I sank just the tip of my finger into her and pulled out immediately, giving her a light smack on the ass.

Her body shivered. "Please."

"Not yet." Water magic ran along her skin, removing the soapsuds from her. My magic grazed her hole, and she sucked in a breath as I pushed it into her, teasing her. Her mouth made incoherent noises, more begging coming from trembling lips, but I had no desire to stop now. I was just getting started.

Using the soap, I washed off my cock, making the ache stronger, but my slow torture of her was going to be worse in a moment. I planned for it. Once I was clean, I stepped up behind her, pushing my magic into her entrance, making her nice and wet for me.

"Voss," she squirmed against the invasion. "What are you doing to me?" Her breath choked in her throat.

"Shh. Do you trust me?"

"Yes."

"Then let me do this for you." I ran my erection over her, using my magic to create more lube between us. This was about control, coaxing and slow. I wasn't going to fuck her. No. That would give her too much pleasure. This was all about the buildup, the tease. The relief she'd feel at the end… that was worth the wait.

I pushed into her ass, just an inch. She groaned, tried to arch against me, but my magic kept her stagnant. Summoning the soap into my hands, I worked another thick lather. This time, I allowed her a small amount of space away from the wall. My hands trailed over her hips as I continued to enter her, slowly.

Max took advantage of having space and thrust back against me as much as she could. I stilled her with a firm grip. My magic shifted around her, getting a tight hold on her, and I released my hands from her. She mentally squirmed but did nothing to fight me as I continued to penetrate her.

"Voss, fuck." Her voice quivered around the last syllable. My name came out like a vicious song.

Making another quick lather with the soap, I rounded her hips, dipping toward her thighs. Her muscles twitched every time my touch shifted along her skin. I ran the suds over her mound. Fingers parted her. I trailed soap around every inch of her nerves. Her breath quickened as I parted her folds, running my palm along her skin as I thrust farther into her from behind. She groaned.

"Voss, please."

"You know what I'm going to do?" I pulled out and thrust slowly back inside her, almost halfway. She was so worked up from my teasing touches that she completely relaxed against me, allowing me to do whatever I wanted to her. I loved seeing her like this, compliant and malleable. "I'm going to sink all the way into your ass, and then I'm going to sit there as I use my magic to clean the rest of you."

"Voss." My name was becoming a prayer on her lips.

Good, she should learn to worship me. As I pushed inside her, I clenched my jaw. She was still so tight, squeezing my cock every time I moved. With every push, she breathed out, accepting more and more of me. My palm cupped her front as I rocked into her. She wanted to rub against me with every fiber of her being, but still, my magic kept her immobile. With one last thrust, I bottomed out inside her.

"You feel how full you are?" I gave her a flash of how she felt around my dick, clenching and pulsing against me. Feeling every part of her open to me in response. She needed so much more than I was giving her for her release, but not yet. I promised her edging, and I was ready to deliver. "You're going to stay this way." My cock twitched inside her as she let out another whimpering moan. "I'm going to finish cleaning you with my cock inside you, and you're going to accept that no amount of begging will get you out of your punishment."

"Please." The word was like a liquid lubricant on my soul. She was so pretty when she begged. "Voss, I need—"

I didn't let her get the other word out, because my water magic coursed along her skin, washing all the parts of her I had gotten soapy. She jolted, her muscles tightening involuntarily at every caress of magic. Max ached to fall apart. She wanted me to give her the friction she needed.

"Take a breath for me."

"Voss." She exhaled.

"A breath, little fox."

With a half-lidded, wild gaze in her eyes, she sucked in a breath, and I pushed my magic inside her cunt.

Thirty-One

SCARLET

The warning he gave me hadn't been enough. My brain short-circuited. Everything was so intense, and I was certain tears streamed down my face, but who could know with the water around us. Voss parted me and placed his magic inside me, filling my pussy like he had filled my ass. The breath hadn't prepared me. I wanted to move, wanted to scream, wanted to lament the day I met him, but in truth, everything felt too good to do any of that.

The only thing I could do was to relax and allow him to take me.

His magic spooled into me, filling me. It pressed against my nerves inside, gently stroking, but not enough to do more than make me wetter. I *needed* him. Needed more. I sucked in a few breaths, desperately in need of air.

"Voss." His name became a mantra, a chant, a craving. My body had turned against me, becoming consumed by everything he offered. It no longer listened to me. But I knew with one word, even if I thought the word, he'd release me.

I wanted this. Needed it. Every moment with him felt stolen, precious, and if this was our last night...

I'm not doing enough to distract you. His teeth sank into the skin on my neck, and everything inside me clenched as blood pooled out of me. His magic swirled inside me, expanding. Fuck, it felt like too much, but it wasn't enough either, because he wasn't *moving*.

"This is a punishment, little fox. Remember that."

"Yes." The word fell from my lips as an ache, a demand, a hope. He pressed his lips to mine, capturing my words, my tears, everything left unsaid between us.

Utilizing his powers, the bar of soap traced along my thighs, twisting in a figure eight around my skin. The bar drifted lower as his magic pushed impossibly far into me until he was pressed against every fiber. I had never been so fucking full before. I wanted to push against him, grind down, and take my pleasure where I could, but he held me steady.

"You feel how hard you make me? Even without moving. Just being inside you." His cock twitched again, and every time he did, it was like my nerves fried my brain. I was nothing but a primal need.

"Please," the whimper didn't sound like anything. I couldn't think of the words to beg properly for what I needed. He knew, of course, because Voss was inside every part of me, including my head.

The bar of soap reached the back of my knees. Tension trickled throughout my body as the threat of an orgasm loomed. From my fucking knees being touched.

"What is happening to me?" The words squeezed from my lungs as the orgasm continued to whirl around my body, just out of reach for the relief I needed.

"You're Fae now, remember?"

The soap traced along my skin on my right leg, over my calf, around my ankle, toward my feet. My body tingled in its wake, wanting to fall off the edge and come apart.

"All of this feels more intense than you imagined, doesn't it?" Voss pulled back only an inch and pressed himself deep inside me again.

I groaned, and the sound came out like an animal. There was nothing human left inside me. I had those thoughts even as the soap traced around my other leg.

Voss buried his nose in my neck. His breath was hot against my skin. "I love controlling you like this. I love how you've never allowed anyone else to see this side of you because you're mine."

"Yours," I agreed. "Please, Voss."

"I love hearing you say it." He pulled slowly out of me, and I greedily tried to bring him back into me. His magic swelled, grasping me tight.

The cool tile pressed against my breasts. Everything was sensitive. I might as well have been on fire as his magic swept over me in a wave, gathering all the soap and rinsing it from my body. I could feel *everything*. Each droplet as it ran down my thighs, the water as it parted over my shoulders and found every groove between my skin and the tile, the way the water parted around my nipples, not grazing the sensitive parts that I needed to finally lose myself. I sucked in a breath, unable to keep myself steady for much longer. The myriad of emotions and sensations swelled, and I forgot how to breathe.

My magic brimmed inside me, coming from a place so deep it welled like a second soul. A survival tactic. I pressed my magic against my clit, aiming to give myself the relief Voss refused me, but he pushed mine back down.

"Little fox, if you keep that up, your punishment is going to be a lot longer."

"Please." My voice shook—no, not just my voice. My body. My legs. My arms. Sweat beaded along my brow. I wondered how long Voss could keep this up. Would he spend the rest of his life buried inside me if he could?

"Yes, I would." He released his magical hold from my arms, only to thread his fingers through mine. He brought both of my hands up above my head. His cock moved inside me with the slowest undulation.

My orgasm welled but ceased as soon as he had me back under his grasp. He stopped moving. I couldn't breathe.

"I think you've had enough. What do you think?"

"Please." It was more of a wheeze than a whine. My lungs collapsed. I floated outside of my body, waiting for a moment to spin back to earth.

"Here's what's going to happen. I'm going to use your ass, and I'm going to come. You are not."

I whimpered.

"If you get close, I will stop."

"Voss."

"You can say 'blade' if the pain of not being able to come is agonizing, and then I will allow you to if needed. Otherwise, you'll come at my command."

"Voss."

"Do you understand the rules, my Queen?"

"Yes."

"Do you want to use either of your words?"

I focused on the cool tile pressing against my cheek. No, I didn't. As much as I was on the precipice of blacking out, I wanted this—no, needed this. "No."

"Good girl." He wrapped my wrists in one of his hands. "Once I'm done with your ass, I'll clean myself, and you'll take my cock in your mouth. And once I'm done with that, you know what happens, little fox?"

"I get to come?"

"Around my cock, buried in your cunt."

My body shuddered. Involuntarily at this point.

"Keep in mind your words."

"Uh huh." It was more of a grunt than anything.

With his other hand, he grabbed hold of my hips, and he wasted no more time. He thrust into me from behind, filling me so completely as his magic still held firm inside me, a tease against my nerves as he fucked me. My vision blacked out, and as much as I wanted to let go, as much as my body threatened to lose control, I fought it, holding out because he asked it of me.

Voss's voice coaxed me, soothed me, praising me for taking him so well, for allowing him this. I lost track of time. Nothing made sense anymore, except the feeling of him inside me, taking me for everything he could. Everything lost meaning as the sensations grew around me, creating a fire from the inside out. I panted against the tiled wall, unable to still a single muscle on my body as I trembled around him.

With several forceful, deep thrusts, he came.

My body clenched around him, wanting release, but he whispered for me to hold it. "You can take it." So, I did.

His magic slowly released me, removing the pressure from my pussy and around my legs. I sank to my knees, almost without a thought. He kept a gentle hold on me, guiding me down. Water pelted my face, but I floated somewhere outside myself.

"You still with me?"

I nodded. Glancing up at him as he ran the soap along his length.

His satisfied smile was back, and I had done that to him. At least, my body had. "You're doing perfectly. How do you feel?"

335

Words no longer existed, so I opened my mind to him. At least, I thought I did.

Perfection. His voice purred throughout my body as he cupped my chin. It was with a delicate touch. Precise and with care. Voss leaned over and pressed a kiss to my lips. "You are everything." His breath mingled with mine as he gripped the sides of my face. Freshly cleaned, he notched himself at my lips.

He took my mouth in the same manner he had in the dungeon. Fast. With force. So much that I gagged. His magic made lazy circles along my nerves. I could barely focus on keeping my jaw open for him. He had promised to drive me to the edge, and he had, and then he had taken me *further.* Voss's mind unfurled, and I felt his unrelenting desire to do this to me every night. Once we were safe. The sheer wonder and satisfaction roiling through him was enough to make me preen under the stars threatening my vision.

When he came for the second time, I swallowed down everything.

"Incredible," he whispered as he shut off the water. With ease, he lifted me and carried us back to the bed—both still soaking wet. The tender way he placed me down held reverence, almost like worship.

"Because I do." He placed his hands on my thighs, coaxing me open for me. He dropped to his knees.

"Voss, I won't be able to—" I felt his magic inside me, coiling around me. I sucked in a breath.

"You can still speak, yes?"

"Yes." I shuddered, because his magic had numbed my body—wrapping me up and refusing to let me drop over the edge. Somehow, he had managed this, all to keep me grounded.

"Do you want to use your words?"

I shook my head.

He lowered his, breathing against my skin. His tongue roamed around my nerves, and he flattened it against my entrance. My body wanted to let go, to unfurl underneath his first touches, but his magic kept me under pressure. Even as I tried to lose myself.

My thoughts disappeared. The feeling was too much. Everything was too sensitive. I reached for words to speak as Voss backed off, already sensing it.

"Little fox?"

"I need—" The word wouldn't come.

But he knew. "Okay." He climbed on top of me, lined up, and thrust inside me with one quick movement of his hips. His magic's hold released at the same time, and holy—

The universe collapsed on itself. My vision darkened. I forgot how to breathe. My synapses shorted out. I grasped onto him, barely holding any sense of reality. Fingers clawed at nothing and everything. The sky opened and swallowed me. I was pretty sure I had died and gone to the hellfires, and Voss was there, still fucking me even though I had already disappeared from this plain of existence. Everything shattered.

"Come back to me," he said, voice soothing the ache that stretched taut across my skin.

"Now and always," I replied as my eyes fluttered open. I hadn't remembered closing them. Breathing came easier. My limbs were heavy. It felt like I had run a marathon. Whatever that had been, I had never experienced anything like it. And Voss had known exactly when I was at the breaking point. He sensed it, and he pushed me over the edge, giving me exactly what I needed to spin out into the ether and come back whole.

Voss's lips pressed against mine as he pushed my hair back from my face. "Are you okay?"

I nodded. "Yes, Voss. I'm fine."

"No snarky come back?"

"Not this time." I sank my teeth into his lower lip.

He was still hard inside me. "Do you think you can give me one more?"

I laughed but hitched my legs around his hips. "Only if you can make me."

His smirk appeared, overconfident as always. He kissed me again, deepening it. And this time, when he thrust inside me, it was deep and slow, languid and savoring.

Love. It was love. No longer a push, a pull, or a play for dominance. No, it was just Voss, showing me how much he cared with long, powerful strokes inside me. And that made me come quicker than before. He followed me shortly after, and I basked in this feeling.

A feeling I wasn't ready to lose.

A feeling I refused to lose.

"We have to win this," I whispered, running my fingers through his hair from where he lay with his head on my chest.

"We will," he promised.

I hoped this was one we could both keep.

Thirty-Two

SCARLET

The meeting with the human leaders—Quinn, Marcy, and two other people I had never met—as well as Morna, Cumina, and the four of us was going as well as expected. That was to say, it was a shit show. Every so often, I had to stamp down the power inside me. It desired a fight, called for it. While I didn't want to battle with those at the table, their standoffish attitudes made my magic ache to quell them.

I understood their distrust. I had started this journey the same as them, only seeing the darkest side of the Fae. Because I constantly looked for the worst Fae at bars, clubs, and taverns, I found them. When one seeks evil, one will find it. But now, these humans were hypocrites. They had accepted Morna and Cumina without question, but us?

Voss, Elspeth, Penn, and I had dressed in leathers, which likely wasn't helping. We looked more like an assassination squad than representatives from the royal line. However, Voss had made a good point. If our enemies attacked tonight, we needed to be prepared.

After five minutes of introductions around the table, Voss explained his plan. Then, everyone bickered. Voss watched the volley back and forth casually with amusement, but I contained no such lightness. He placed a hand on my thigh, discreetly out of eyesight. His magic pulsed into me, keeping me grounded. I felt like burning the table, the room, the building. We were arguing when we should have been planning for the battle ahead.

Blood stains and ash marks peppered the carpet, but otherwise, it was the same ballroom we had dined in before I killed the king. It felt the same as in Leveret's court. I hated how that place was seared into my memory, the vision of it appeared behind my eyelids every time I blinked. So, I began the meeting feeling off balance by being in the room. And the asinine words spewing from one of the man's lips—Francis—fueled my rage further still. From the moment he introduced himself, I knew I would hate him.

The other one seemed fine enough—Kilroy, which didn't sound like the name he had been born with, but neither was mine. A scar etched diagonally across his face, and his muscular arms crossed in front of his body. A permanent scowl kept residence on his mouth. Men like Kilroy were easy—they craved battle, and we wanted to give it to him—against the enemy.

Francis, however, was distrusting. He had light eyes, a dark beard, and no hair on the rest of his head. His skin was ruddy, worn from the wilds. Every time one of us said something, he argued against it—even when we agreed with him, he seemed to switch sides.

Which meant he wanted to create chaos and nothing more.

This was who Quinn deemed worthy of our future?

"Furthermore," Francis said, making his long-winded speech even longer. "We cannot trust any system you create, because anything you come up with will be inherently corrupt."

"It's a bit like putting the cart before the horse, don't you think?" I curled my fingers around Voss's, biting my nails into his skin.

Voss liked it, and the thoughts whirling through his head gave me confidence to continue.

"You want us to plan for the aftermath of a war that hasn't happened yet, for a battle we might very well lose? What we should focus on is how to *win*. Any further negotiations should occur after the war. We can discuss everything until both sides are equally satisfied."

"And we're supposed to trust that?" Francis asked, leaning forward while steepling his fingers. While he likely intended to appear menacing, I had killed the entire royal line of Fae, and there was no way this man would get the better of me in a verbal altercation.

"Yes, for the time being."

"Scarlet's right." Quinn cleared his throat. His hazel eyes met mine, and he nodded. "We need to focus on the war front. I like the ideas thus far, but we can iron everything out if we survive this."

"I liked you better when you were a name on a screen," Francis spat.

"Likewise." Quinn breathed out and pinched his nose. "Look, I wanted us to meet so we could learn how to fight together. I know reinforcements are coming from the Fae side, both Burke's and Alpin's court, but do we have a word on their arrival time?"

Voss smirked. "Burke's will likely join us before this meeting's finished. Alpin started gathering those willing to join us shortly after we left." He frowned. "I will send another scytheseer, because it does seem strange his reinforcements aren't here yet."

"Fine, do that. Now for our traps. The inner courtyard is full of them, which means most of the fighting will happen outside the walls. We'll have a place to fall back to, should we lose ground. We'll mark the areas for our side to avoid, but it must be something innocuous. We cannot have the enemy figuring out our signals."

"Leave that to me." Elspeth wiggled her fingers. "When I am not drunk on Faerie wine, it's kind of my thing."

"I'll help." Cumina shot her a look. There was a pause, but neither started up.

Finally, we were getting somewhere. The rest of the evening went by without a hitch. Whenever Francis interjected, however, the room stilled for a beat. I took solace in knowing that I wasn't the only one who was furious with him for his negativity.

As we were wrapping up, Francis stretched his arms over his head. "Well, it was nice getting to know you. Hopefully, some will still be alive tomorrow, and we can put the right ones in charge." He crossed the room and slammed the door shut behind him without further preamble.

I let out a breath. "Is that asshole always like that?"

"Unfortunately, yes." It was Marcy who answered. She spun a lock of blond hair around her finger. It was still strange seeing her here, in the thick of the planning. "He's a dick, but he also had the most amount of weapons stockpiled."

"I'm keeping him in line," Quinn added.

"Not well," Kilroy barked out a laugh. "For what it's worth, I believe we have a chance to change the world. With any luck, we'll be better than ever before." He grinned, and his front tooth was chipped straight in half. "Folks, have a goodnight. Try to sleep. I'll have my crew ready with our explosives when the battle begins." He left the room, and Morna slipped out right behind him.

Elspeth put her feet on the table and leaned back. "Do you think we'll be able to create some kind of governing body with those two involved?"

Quinn shrugged. "They have to be involved. Collectively, we are leading the humans. The four representatives of our future were in this room."

"And if one of them happens to get hurt accidentally tomorrow?" Elspeth pouted.

"Elspeth," Voss warned.

"What? It would be an unfortunate turn of events, but surely, there is someone who is *not* Francis."

"I don't like him either, but we can't go around killing people," Voss said.

I stifled a laugh, and Voss's fingers dug into my thigh.

Elspeth stood up. "I never said I didn't like him. And I have horrible taste, which means he's horrible." She tossed her locks behind her shoulder. "Maybe I can make him feel better if I make something for his…" While performing a distracted monologue, she walked out of the room.

Quinn blinked after her. "She's not serious, is she? Francis is like… fifty."

"And Elspeth is older than him."

Quinn sighed. "Why do you all look twenty-one?"

Penn drummed his fingers on the table. "I look at least twenty-seven. Voss?"

"Definitely twenty-seven."

I snorted.

"Too young for me," Quinn said.

"How old are you, Quinn?" Penn asked.

"Thirty-four."

"Too young for me," Penn stated. They stared at each other for a beat.

Marcy and Cumina stood. They were holding each other's gaze. A conversation happened between them, and oddly, none of the jealousy I expected to feel reared up. Cumina seemed smitten, which was saying something, because neither of the sisters had been particularly soft while I was traveling with them. But here she was, gazing at Marcy like the moon rose and set with her.

"We're going to sleep as well. Might want to get settled before Elspeth has any ideas." Cumina wrapped her arm around Marcy's shoulder.

When they crossed by my chair, Marcy paused. "I miss her every day." Her green eyes blazed with the admission.

I nodded. "Me too."

"I was thinking we could do a memorial after?"

"I'd like that."

Marcy squeezed my shoulder. The briefest of touches, but it felt like having my friend back. The two of them ducked out of the room, which left me, Voss, Penn, and Quinn behind.

Turning back to my friend, I said, "You're a natural leader, you know?"

Quinn ran his hand over the back of his hair. "I'm not so sure."

"You are," Penn said. His turquoise gaze barely strayed from Quinn's. "And you do it without pushing anyone's buttons. If we make it out of this, I'm fairly certain you'll be the reason the committee doesn't tear each other's throats out."

"What about me?"

Penn slid a glance at Voss. "You'll be the reason someone challenges another person to a duel to the death."

I laughed again. Voss's thoughts surged, focused on how he was going to punish me later.

Bring it, I teased.

"And you're not much better. You'll be the reason humans kill Fae again," Penn said.

I glared at him and put my hands on my hips. "I am Fae."

"Exactly."

Quinn laughed. "Don't look so disheartened, Scarlet. This was the plan all along, remember? You're the brawn, I'm the brains."

"I would be upset with you calling me stupid, but you complimented my ability to kill people. So…" I glanced at Voss. "What do you think? Should I be insulted to the point of his demise?"

"Not yet, but teetering."

"Oh, good. They've moved on to threatening you." Penn clapped Quinn on the shoulder. It was a playful move, but his hand lingered. "You'll get used to it after a while."

"Should I be scared?"

"Terrified, but it means they like you."

"We're sitting *right* here." I glanced between the two of them, then back at Voss.

Oh, I see it too, little fox.

"Is there any way we can get some food before the impending end of the world?" I asked, putting a little lilt into my voice.

Quinn eyed me suspiciously. "Chef Mikel stayed. Said it was the best pantry he's ever had access to, and he was damned if a few humans were going to chase him out of his kitchen."

"I knew it," Voss said triumphantly. He grabbed hold of my waist. "You two coming?" We were already halfway out of the room when the others answered.

"Sure," Penn said.

"Did you know he threatened to gut me with a spoon if anyone stepped foot inside his kitchen, pantry, or gardens uninvited?" Quinn added.

We walked outside, and the stillness in the air was enough to make my hair stand on end. So quiet. Too quiet. I had spent most of my life knowing this kind of silence was dangerous, the calm before the storm. Voss thrust out his senses, and I felt it as he scoured the earth for anything out of the ordinary.

"I think we have time for a little food."

And we did. As we ate, we received word that Lady Burke's soldiers, as well as the Lady herself, had reached our borders. They set up along the perimeter, with the other Fae from the royal court who had come back to fight. We still hadn't received word from Alpin's court, which was surprising, though he could have been held up along the way, having a much longer route to reach us.

But the moment everything seemed organized, and the meal settled in our stomachs, the warning bells sounded.

Thirty-Three

VOSS

A t the first sound of sirens, I stiffened. Despite knowing this was coming, despite understanding we'd be facing the enemy soon, I wasn't ready. Correction, I wasn't ready for her to be in danger. I had made the mistake before, placing her in a foreign court without my assistance, and that wouldn't happen this time.

We had to make it through this.

She had to make it through this.

Max caught my eye, and our fingers threaded together. Fitted so perfectly, it was a wonder we hadn't known each other our entire lives. Her moonlit blue gaze swept over my tense body language, and she gave me a curious smile.

"Worried, Voss?"

My jaw ticked. *Only for you.*

I can handle myself.

I know you can, little fox, but I pray to the Mother for anyone who lays so

347

much as a single finger on you, because my magic will not allow it without tearing them to shreds.

Quinn let out a breath. "The pause was too good to be true. I imagine this is Iobhar, back to finish what he started."

"Likely with Eero," Penn added.

"I'm going to enjoy ripping them limb from limb." I stood from the table, dragging Max with me. Quinn looked me up and down. I arched a brow. "What? You doubt my ability to?"

"No, just… I never thought I would fight on the same side as the Fae, let alone the Fae King. For what it's worth, you are ten times better than your late father."

"Only ten times? Ouch."

Quinn snickered. "Whatever happens next, I will do my best to unite us under one force. It would take something short of a miracle to make that happen on our end, though. Humans felt slighted for too long, and while there are good courts out there, there weren't enough to make up for those who were horrific."

I nodded. "Understood. I do hope we can put it past us once we've proved a willingness to change. We do have plenty amends to make."

With a nod, Quinn slid his gaze to Max. "I believe *you* already have. You gave this one something else to live for. Please don't fuck that up."

Max sucked in a breath. "Quinn—"

"Don't deny it. You spent your life expecting to die as soon as you killed the king. For once, I don't see that venom inside you. I hope it stays. I hope you get your happily ever after. If anyone deserves it, Scarlet, it's you. Now, if you'll excuse me, I have to prepare my team for war." Quinn ducked out of the threshold into the empty twilight sky.

Faerie lights and a few electric lamps were strewn about the courtyard, but several winked out as generators powered down. Since they were attacking earlier than expected, it meant we could use the cover of darkness to our advantage. Not sure how much of an upper hand it would give us, but if they were traveling with their own lights, they would be like hoswisps in an open field, giving us targets to hit long before they reached the court walls.

"Penn?"

"Hm?" My companion had lost himself gazing after the figure trailing away from us. "What?"

"You good with this?"

"When have I ever shied away from venturing into a battle with you?"

"Frequently, actually."

Penn puffed out his chest, and I stifled a chuckle. Max, however, did not. She barked out a laugh, so thick with humor it made me want to wrap my hands around her nape and pull her in for a brutal and claiming kiss. If that laughter was cut short from this world, I wouldn't let anyone survive this.

No one.

Turquoise eyes cast downward, shaking his head. "You two are the absolute worst. And whatever plans we have for the kingdom next, neither of you will be a part of them."

"You're going to stage a coup against me?"

"If I have to." His gaze snapped up, but mirth ran thickly through them. Crinkles appeared at the edge of his eyes, and a slight curve held up his lips. "But I hope my coup will be friendlier than the battle we're about the face."

"Iobhar was the one who almost incited the riot the first time I saved you, yes?" Max asked. Her arms crossed over her chest.

"He was in the room when you eviscerated the other Fae, yes. To be honest, I'm surprised he would have tried to take over the royal court after he bore witness to what Scarlet could do," Penn admitted.

"He has a death wish."

"More than a death wish," Max said. "I'm going to turn him into fertilizer. And I'm going to make sure all of his atoms are still conscious when the worms devour the pieces of him I leave behind." She pulled her sparrowbone dagger from her belt and stalked out of the room. Another mission for her, another goal, another plot of revenge.

At some point, we would break the cycle. We would reach the end of the people and Fae left alive who had wronged her, and she would be free to move on. But today was not that day. And while she tore them asunder, leaving nothing but bloodied bodies behind her, I would watch with the reverence she deserved.

"You're in love with that."

"She's perfect, Penn. Absolute perfection."

His eyes twinkled as he leaned against the door frame. "You're sticking by her for the battle?"

"Of course."

He nodded. "I'll find Elspeth. She and I will be close in case you need us. The four of us are stronger together, but I know how volatile your magic can get, especially if Scarlet is hurt. We'll maintain a healthy distance."

"I appreciate that." I held out my hand.

He grasped mine, and he pulled me in and clapped me on the shoulder. "If you die during this battle, I will bring you back, and I'll break your ribs. You understand me?"

I laughed. "I don't plan on dying tonight."

"Good." Penn pulled back. "But my promise stands. Broken ribs, Voss. And you know those are by far the worst to heal from." He strolled back toward the towers, likely to find Elspeth before the battle reached our gates. I watched him go, fighting back the annoying concern that rose inside me.

Now was not the time for doubts. Now was not the time for anything but steadiness, a steeled heart, and focus. Catching up to my little fox took barely any time. We ascended to the parapet, and her eyes sharpened on the horizon as we waited.

"They are about two miles out," a messenger updated us. She gave me a salute. "Iobhar, the traitor guards, and Eero's Court. Several others joined their forces from the royal courts."

"Are any of Leveret's court among them?" I asked. Technically my court now, but none of the Fae knew it to be so.

She shook her head. "None, Sir. None from Averett's either. Still no updates from Alpin."

"Thank you for the news."

She nodded and carried on down the parapet, updating the next set of Fae who had readied to fight. The plan was to put us at the forefront, whereas the humans would take a defensive stance. While they might not be able to be compelled any more, the firearms wouldn't do much against a typhoon of magic.

A breeze kicked up. The sky lost the final hues of twilight as dark clouds rolled in. The humidity had heightened, giving the air a damp smell. My magic could feel the water coursing through every molecule. It was the first signal of the change in weather.

Max glanced up at the sky and let out a breath. "Of course, now a thunderstorm rolls in." She leaned against the wall and glanced at me. "I had been hoping for one of these all summer, something to breathe life into the land, but the weather chooses now."

"The Mother delivers."

She snorted. "Seems like the wrong time."

"Perhaps it is the right time. Think of it, mud and water can be used in battle, especially with the royal power. Our magic was made for this. Plus, there's less of a risk of you accidentally lighting someone on our side on fire if the skies open up."

"I haven't accidentally lit anyone on fire yet."

"No, but what if I get injured?" I captured her hand in mine, pulling her into me. I leaned carelessly against the parapet wall, with her hips pressing into mine. "Will you light the Fae on fire that causes me harm?"

"If a Fae so much as cuts a single hair on your head, I am sending them to the hellfires where they belong."

"With magic or your dagger?"

Her teeth sank into her lower lip as a flush rose on her cheeks. "Depends. Which would make you want to take me in the middle of battle?"

"Mm. Either. Both. I'd take you right now if the other guards weren't looking at us." I cupped her jaw. "Because we both know I'm never allowing anyone else to watch you come apart with pleasure." Her lips hung inches from mine. "When this is over—"

"Voss, look." Her eyes narrowed as her gaze fell on the horizon.

The landscape was mostly flat, with rolling hills and small peaks, but there was virtually no ground cover, especially surrounding the Royal Court. When the fire pauldrins came over, they had left an ample amount of destruction in their wake. With no trees in our line of sight, as soon as the incoming army crested the hill, we could make out the Faerie lights surrounding them, the torches held in hands. They glowed like the rising sun, which was perfect for us. With most of the lights removed from the parapet, we had the advantage here. They were a beacon approaching.

"Hold steady," I announced, letting my voice swirl around my fellow Fae on the walls.

"King Balgair."

My jaw clenched, and my fingers reflexively tugged Max into me. "Lady Burke."

She held up her hands. "I plan to stay out of the way, let my duplicates do their job and add to our side. If you need messages sent throughout parties quickly and efficiently, I am here to serve."

I narrowed my eyes. "Why do I find that hard to believe?"

The Lady shrugged. "It's not my fault if you cannot accept assistance or do not want it."

Loosening a breath, I allowed myself to relax. "You're insufferable."

"Noted. It's been a problem most of my life." Her arms crossed over her chest. She wore another ridiculous get up. Camouflage pants that might have blended with the thick jungles of what Faerie used to be. They flared away from her hips with vast amounts of fabric with deep pockets on both legs. Her blouse was more frilly than practical. Still, she leaned against the parapet wall. Magic swirled around her as duplicates pooled out among our people. Her orange eyes fixed on the incoming enemy, and her lips flattened. "You know, what happens today determines our history forever."

"No pressure," Max scoffed.

Lady Burke looked at her, standing up straight again. "Lots of pressure. And it should be that way. Frankly, we've been at odds too long for it to be any other way."

"I was joking."

"Oh. Oh. A joke. Yes. Quaint." Burke's face contorted.

"What are you doing?" I asked, head tilted to the side as I considered her expression.

A grimace crossed her features. "Smiling? I believe they call it that. Right?"

"You should stick with the sinister ones; it suits you better." Max looked back at the horizon. "It's okay, you know, to be who you are. I found people who liked me for who I am."

Burke sighed. "I tried that. Seems no one likes a power hungry, narcissistic, egotist, but it also could be because they were jealous."

Max laughed. "See? You can joke without making your face look like… whatever that was earlier."

"Yes, that was a joke, wasn't it?" The Lady sent off three duplicates running into the night. "I will let you know what I figure out once they meet the enemy lines."

As the shadows of her beings slipped into the darkness, we waited in amicable silence. Finally figuring out how to navigate conversations with Burke had not been one of my goals, but I was grateful for her being on our side. While I was confident I could send out royal magic now that Max and I had bonded, a part of me still hesitated to tap into it. If I ran out in the middle of the battle, well, that would be the worst-case scenario.

Burke's eyes swirled, glowing in the darkness of the parapet. "They've amassed about five hundred Fae and some humans. Most of them consist of the royal courts who felt it was unfair to be left without a powerful Lord or Lady. Which is ironic, as several of the new Lords and Ladies are among them."

"How are you getting this information?"

She turned. "Obviously, my duplicates have talked with the enemy."

I sighed. "And I am supposed to trust that you aren't spoiling our tactics?"

"Why would I bother telling you this if I were trying to ruin things for you?" Burke placed her hands on her hips. "Oh. Uh, well…" Her body shook. "Unfortunately, one of them got suspicious and drove a knife through one of my duplicates. I am not as charming as I think I am. At least, that's what he said. His name is Verl, but it won't be for long."

"Burke, please don't—"

She held up her hands. "Don't worry, Devoss. I am waiting until they get within reach. My other two duplicates have left the fray, but I will wait for Verl to be alone. And I will kill him." Her eyes narrowed at the slowly approaching army. "They are idiots for not trying to sneak in, or not to wait until the morning. Truly, so many amateur mistakes. If it were me, I would do a much better job of attempting to overthrow you."

"Would you now?"

"Of course. I would go in with the illusion of an army, because didn't you know?" Burke thrust her hand out and two more of her appeared, but they quickly changed appearance, no longer looking like her, but resembling other Fae. "I am my own army."

"How many Fae are actually with you tonight, Burke?"

"Enough." She huffed out a breath. "Really, you shouldn't question me so much, Devoss. It's hurtful." Spinning on her heels, her platform boots slammed against the stones as she marched away. She paused in the doorway of one of the guard towers. "They are estimating twenty minutes to their arrival."

Which meant there were fifteen minutes before the first of the traps went off.

"Thanks, Burke."

"Never again, Devoss, so don't make the mistake of allowing a coup twice." She ducked into the guard tower, along with her two non-clones.

"She's unnerving." Max's fingers tightened around her dagger.

I cupped her chin. "Some Fae may say the same thing about you."

Her lips quirked. "Yes, but it makes sense to me. I've killed a lot of Fae. For her, it's the way she carries herself."

Brushing my thumb along her lower lip. "Max."

"Voss."

"I love you."

She softened. Her grip on the dagger no longer bleached her

355

knuckles white, and the tension in her jaw bled out of existence. "We have to win this, Voss. I refuse to let you go."

I kissed her as we waited for war, like the anticipation of a sunrise before a new dawn.

☙ ✄ ❧

The first explosion tore through the night air with a concussive boom. Max and I straightened, readying our stances as the army crossed into our territory. Her head snapped up, staring toward the fire shooting into the sky.

"Are you okay?"

Her unease whirled around us. An unsettled feeling crept through our bond, but she shut down her emotions and schooled her features—determination pulsed through her. "I'm fine. It was startling to see it so close. They know we're here now."

We watched as the enemy shot off more Faerie lights. They spread into the surrounding wilds, swooping low to the ground.

"As they draw close, imagine plunging them into darkness."

Her lips pressed flat, but she nodded. The memory of the caltula flashed through her mind.

The perfect comparison. We need them to be at a disadvantage. A full blackout.

Max hip checked me as her smile widened. Idly, her fingers twirled her sparrowbone dagger. While the small weapon wouldn't help her much from this vantage point, it was a comfort. It steadied her heart. Giving her waist one last squeeze, I released my hold on her and focused on the incoming lights.

"Practice," I demanded.

"Now? Practice now?"

"Pressure, right?" I crossed my arms over my chest.

She widened her stance. Several Faerie lights came toward us, tossed upward by the approaching massive crowd. Her brows lowered, her empty hand thrust out, and her thoughts whirled. They ranged from imagining the lights snuffed out by the caltula to thinking about the sky opening and swallowing them whole.

Even so, the lights glowed as the army grew closer.

"Feel the magic inside you." I moved behind her, pressing my hands on either side of the parapet and caging her in. "It should come from the ground. It wants to be used, wants to be called on." Leaning toward her ear, I whispered, "You feel it?"

She nodded.

"Now, push the magic toward the lights. Remove them from the sky. Make them wink out. Slice their metaphorical throats."

Max whipped her hand to the side—not a necessary move for magic, but it worked. Three of the oncoming lights disappeared out of existence. Four others shot toward the approaching army. The orbs grew three times their original size, heightened by the power she thrust into them. Each bolt slammed into the approaching horde, exploding on impact. Shouts rose, fires erupted, numerous Faerie lights rained out of existence from the sky.

My jaw hung open.

"You don't have to look so surprised." A shyness crept over her as she leaned into me. "I'm only doing what we need to do." There was a wistfulness in her voice.

I long for the day where I can give you something more than this.

You already have.

The next wave of magic was retaliation, and it occurred fast. Fireballs rose from the offensive line, flying straight toward us. I welled a water wall in the middle of the field. The flames smashed into them, sizzling before they had the chance to make it near the parapet.

The royal magic created a levity in my bones—one I hadn't

experienced for a while. Power rushed through me. I squeezed Max's shoulders one last time, placing a chaste kiss on her neck. I took a single moment to enjoy the bumps that rose from my touch.

"Are you ready for this?"

"Born ready, wasn't I? Seeing as how there was a whole prophecy about me."

"There was." I threw out another attack, if only to slow them down. The terrain below became more uneven, leaving larger cracks and divots between the royal court and them. Several horses whinnied, and I suppressed a gleeful grin as several mounted Fae were thrown to the ground. The horses took off, scattering into the night. "If it makes you feel better, little fox, the prophecy existed before I was born, and if we're to believe it was talking about us, then we're both destined for this."

She let out a sigh as she tossed another Faerie light back at the crowd. I could kiss her. "I hope it's something good, Voss."

"Me, too."

The army drew closer still, and we no longer had the luxury of talking. The voices below us became distinct. Several orders rose as our attackers volleyed for their next launch.

"Devoss? Shall I tell everyone to turn on the Faerie lights?"

"Yes."

Burke nodded and ducked back into the tower. All at once, the Fae on our side lit their lights, casting an eerie glow on the army below. Hundreds of illuminated orbs, set up ahead of time and prepared for this moment.

"Now!" Quinn's voice bellowed. He used some device to project his voice. It echoed throughout the parapet, clear as day.

The humans opened fire. The gunshots ricocheted off the stone wall, causing a cacophony of noise around us. I threw up a magical block between Max, myself, and the rest of the sounds. I glanced at her. Her face blanched white.

"Little fox." I turned her toward me, cupping her jaw. "If you need to go—"

Her hands flew on top of mine. "No. We're in this together. I'm not leaving you now. Not again."

I nodded. "Is it easier?"

"The barrier helped, yes. Reminds me of what Finian does at his club."

My spine stiffened. "Thanks for reminding me. When we make it out of this, he deserves a visit. The bastard put you in Nightmare's path—"

"I'm fine, Voss." She turned toward the fighting. Her eyes homed in on the blood that coated the ground. Her throat bobbed as she swallowed.

Several earth Fae from the enemy side stepped forward, building ramps up to the parapet.

"Ready?" I yelled, forcing my voice to echo over the crowd.

The water Fae used their magic to slick the paths down with mud. As the rushing army tried to ascend, their feet clambered for purchase. The humans took advantage, giving them a chance to reload and create another barrage of gunfire. Bodies fell, slamming back down into the earth. While I relished punishing the Fae who deserved it, this was senseless. As more Fae fell to the onslaught of attacks, their side retreated, creating temporary barriers. Someone was directing the show, but not with enough foresight to prevent mass casualties.

As soon as the barriers dropped, I pushed my power forward, eliminating more Faerie lights.

Max squinted into the crowd. "What are they—"

"Aim for the Fae casting right now!" I called out.

Magic hung heavy in the air as several enemy Fae blanketed their power over the group. Much like I had done when we had traveled over the walls of Leveret's court, they were lifting the Fae. As soon as the group was levitating, several air Fae were struck down. Their magic severed, and their pod fell back to the earth. This distraction, however, had given them time to rebuild their ramps. They kept coming. As our enemies got hurt, healers had gone into the fray and fixed them. Any battles between Fae were uphill, but the sparrowbone bullets had left more than a few dead already.

"Ready, little fox?" I asked as several Fae crested the walls.

She nodded, licked her lips, and held her dagger out in front of her. What had I done to deserve a woman who so fearlessly faced down an army with nothing but her untrained magic and a dagger? I wanted to devour her.

As the first groups cleared the parapet, wails echoed off the stone surfaces. Swords clashed, and bursts of fire lit up the stone. Several Fae dropped, slamming into the earth below with sickening sounds.

"Humans, fall back!" Quinn's voice blared as several scurried out of the parapet. Against magic, none of them had a chance at close range, regardless of their firearms. Quinn hustled by us and gave a stiff nod before disappearing down the tower.

Unknown to our enemy was the clever idea Elspeth came up with. Our Fae were glamored with a tag that lit up underneath a black light—something the humans had set up at the choke point before their next wave of explosives. The humans would guard that point— and any non-marked Fae would be killed on sight.

With the humans out of the way, the Fae left wasted no time unleashing chaos. As the enemy scaled the wall, power swirled around us. The wind whipped, and Max clenched her dagger, readying for the next fight.

A Fae shot a bolt at her. She dodged with her newfound speed and jammed her dagger into the attacker's stomach. She twisted and flayed them open alive.

With no time to enjoy the blood she spilled, I whirled fire around me. As Fae clambered for purchase on the wall, I struck anyone who dared get close. A water Fae snuffed the flames on their tunic out, the smoldering material flaking away from their body. He met my gaze with purple, dilated irises.

"Imagine if I'm the one who takes down the hated king," he sneered. A smile crept up the corner of his mouth.

"Imagine," I said, adding a bit of whimsy to my voice.

Latching onto my fire magic, I slammed an ember down his throat. His eyes burst open as he grabbed his stomach, scratching himself from the outside, but it was too late for him.

"Imagine being burned from the inside out." I snapped my fingers, and my magic tore through him in an explosion. His body burst apart, piece by piece, and became nothing more than ashes on the wind.

Max grunted as a Fae grabbed her from behind.

I growled and stalked toward them, but she beat me to it. Her foot slammed backward into the Fae's knee, splintering it in half. As the Fae buckled to the ground, she slashed upward, making a clean gash across the Fae's throat. She breathed hard as blood dripped off her nose. Her eyes flickered to the ground below. So many more were coming. Those who were already on the walls grappled with the Fae on our side. Powers swelled. Gusts of wind knocked several Fae to the ground below.

The fight was similar to when we first came over—unnecessary and destructive—but this time, it was Fae fighting their brethren. We had a choice then, and we had a choice now. We were choosing wrong.

Farther down the parapet, several Fae from our side fell. Magic bubbled over their skin. Screams rang out on both sides as explosions sailed into the night. One section of the wall crumbled to dust as earth Fae razed the stone. As soon as the pathway opened, a flood of the enemy crossed through the broken walls.

"Fae, fall back!" My voice echoed across the parapet.

Several Fae used their air magic to get to safety. Earth Fae constructed temporary bridges over to the internal walls. As soon as our side cleared, they demolished the passes behind them. I tossed a wave of fire, preventing any others from crossing. Scarlet and I held the parapet as more Fae rushed inside from the ground level.

Lightning simmered in the atmosphere.

Burke rushed from the tower. "In good news, Alpin's troops have arrived. They have bolstered the defense of the inner courtyard. In bad news, this is Eero's magic." She gestured to the thickening air. Storm clouds rolled above us. "He was always a fan of the dramatic." She duplicated herself in rapid succession and rushed to the stairs of the parapet. Every time one of her clones met an incoming Fae, she charged them, toppling both over the side.

With the influx of Fae, we had no way of holding the fight here. Several bodies lay at our feet, but dozens more of the enemy were coming in. Every time we took down one, it seemed another two would take their place.

I slammed another wave down a constructed ramp, tossing several Fae off to the earth below. "Max, we have to—" I sucked in a breath.

Eero had reached the top of the parapet, and right behind him was the scoundrel Iobhar. They had clambered in between us, separating my little fox from me yet again. Magic crackled through the air. Eero's pink eyes were trained on me, whereas Iobhar's were locked onto Max.

"We're doing this now?" I let out a breath. If we cut off the head of the snake, our side would have an easier time. While I knew killing them wouldn't instantly end the war, it would give us a small upper hand. One I would be happy to take.

"Devoss Balgair," Eero sneered, standing up straighter. He had a stick-straight nose, plush lips, and angular cheekbones. His ears were close to his face, clipped to resemble human ears. He wore leathers with his family seal on it. "It will be my pleasure to end your life."

"You can certainly try." Flames coiled around my forearms. *You okay fighting Iobhar?*

You mean the one responsible for causing the chaos that knocked you out all those days ago? Of course. A smile flickered across her lips. "You must be Iobhar. I should have known from the sour look on your face. Has anyone told you to smile more? It'd make you cuter." Max's voice lilted over the firefights.

A growl curled from his lips, and he charged at her.

I had no time to watch them, as Eero thrust a bolt of lightning straight from the sky. Leaping out of the way, I snarled as a few strands of my hair singed off. I thrust a whirlwind of fire at him. He summoned rain, drenching the storm I created with his own from the sky. The clouds loosened, and a deluge of water streamed around us.

"Cute," I told him, chancing a glance at Max.

She grunted as Iobhar came at her with a short sword. Their weapons clashed mid-air. She pulsed her magic through her stance and pushed him backward, giving her space to parry his next attack.

"You should be focused on yourself." Eero smirked as the lightning struck at my heels. The concussive force threw me forward, but my magic swelled around me, helping me back to my feet. Eero barely gave me a chance to think as another attack came. Then another.

Max breathed heavily through our link as some kind of pain

welled inside her. An anguished noise sounded as she grappled with the other Fae.

I threw a shield in between the two of them, giving Max enough time to ready for another attack. In that moment, Eero swept a high wind out, aiming for my ankles.

I shot back an electric charge. The current sizzled on the rain, and while Eero had enough time to duck out of the way, I hadn't been aiming for him. The bolt slammed into Iobhar's leg, and a howl reached my ears.

I don't need your help, Voss.

But I'm giving it, anyway.

Eero thrust his hand forward, sending another wave of water toward me. I tired of this game. Shoving out my hands, I wrapped my magic around the male at the same moment he unleashed another attack. Mine curled around him, slamming him to the stone floor of the parapet, wrapped up in bindings. His attack glanced off my cheek. Blood oozed from the wound. I touched my fingers to my face, annoyed by how deep it felt. While my face knitted back together, I let out a curse.

Eero's pink eyes met mine, a cruel smile on his lips. "You never wanted to be like him, but maybe that will serve as a reminder of who the better twin was." His words cut into me.

I prowled toward him, forgetting everything else. "Tell me how you really feel, Eero. Please." I pushed compulsion into my words, wanting to hear the vileness tumble from his lips to justify everything I was going to do to him.

Max sucked in a breath as blood burst from a wound on her arm. A shock ran to my core. With magic, I gagged Eero's mouth before he could listen to my compulsion. His voice became desperate, muffled underneath my magic, as he tried to obey my command. My eyes focused on Max.

Specifically, at the power rising off her.

She screamed and thrust out, magic whirling around her as she did. She moved so fast toward Iobhar, there was little he could do to defend himself. Her fist smashed into his nose, and red ran from his nostrils into his mouth. Her dagger sliced along his skin. With nothing more than her hands, she latched onto his sword and crumbled it away into ash. Her attacks forced him backward.

With one final move, she plunged her dagger into his stomach. She pushed upward, twisting as she went.

Iobhar grinned, and the blood leaked wickedly between his teeth. Eero tried to summon his magic again, but I slammed my boot into his head. Iobhar latched onto Max's wrists. Her dagger was still deep inside him, and he pulled her closer. She kicked out, trying to free herself and her weapon from his iron grip.

It was no use.

She tipped over the edge of the parapet.

Thirty-Four

SCARLET

Iobhar tilted backward, my dagger still caught in his stomach. He latched onto my hands. "I go down. You go too." He sneered with bloodied teeth. His eyes whirled as his magic wrapped around me, holding us together.

I kicked hard, trying to dislodge him. This Fae had tried to hurt Voss, had come so close to killing him. This Fae was the whole reason we were in this mess. He started the coup. He questioned too many of Voss's actions, leaving room for others to rise against him.

And now he was going to be the reason I died.

Gravity took over, launching him off the parapet, and because of his grip on me, I fell, too. There were so many bodies underneath us. So much death, so much—

White flooded my vision.

My mother was on her knees.

My father begged.

The screams curdled around me.

The way my brother stayed so silent and still, until he couldn't any longer.

Seeing Voss lifeless on the bed.

Dead.

Gone.

Forever.

Because of me.

Rage swelled inside me. "Fuck you, asshole." I didn't know how much time I had left before we hit the ground, but I sure as shit refused to die now. Magic flooded into me, like the earth mourned for my loss. The power stormed through me. It came out as an inferno, catching fire to Iobhar's hands, his mouth, his eyes. His mouth opened in a silent scream as the skin dripped off his bones. It was a flash.

Over before I knew it.

And I hovered in mid-air.

A firm grip on my dagger.

With nothing holding me up, except… me.

I pushed my way back to the parapet, landing next to Voss and brushing my fingers along his skin that was healing. Underneath my touch, it knitted back together, no scar in sight. No marks. Him. Whole. He eyed me with astonishment and awe. He was safe.

He was here.

And I was…

I was…

My heart pounded in my chest, making it hard to see. The air was thick. No matter how much I breathed into my lungs, none of it made a difference. My family. Losing Voss. The idea of it split something inside me. Thousands of thoughts whirled through my head, each more horrifying than the last. I couldn't make it stop.

"Breathe, little fox." Voss's hands were on my shoulders, but he was thousands of miles away.

I grabbed onto him, but the moment I did, he slipped through my fingers. Becoming nothing but ash. Voss had always been mine and watching someone else cut him open... his blood spilling...

Something was wrong with me. This war was going to make me lose everything and everyone I cared about. Ourselves, each other.

Like Anya. With blackened veins.

Like my parents.

Like all the Fae I killed before.

We were doomed to live this.

Doomed to die like this.

Little fox, breathe. Voss put a small amount of compulsion into his words, but my fingers dug into his skin. I couldn't breathe. Not now. Not when the air was so thin.

"Penn!" Voss's voice bellowed, the only thing letting me know I was still, somehow, alive.

I didn't feel alive.

Maybe I never felt alive.

"Voss?" My voice was a squeak. It might not have been mine.

His arms wrapped around me, but how could I feel anything when I wasn't here?

"What's wrong with her? We came as quick as we could," Elspeth's voice.

"Lady Burke told us something went wrong on the parapet," Penn gasped. Winded.

More murmurs around me. A kiss on my forehead. My legs no longer touched the earth. Blood. Copper. Endlessness of death. Decay and rot around us. What if everything I ever touched was doomed to become this?

I opened the door.

I did this.

I ruined us.

Everything was my fault.

I hated it.

Hated me.

How could Voss ever look at me like he wanted me after everything I had done?

"Scarlet, listen to me." A hand on the nape of my neck, soothing strokes. Grounding me. "You're okay. Voss is okay. You're safe."

"Focus on your breathing," Elspeth's instructions.

My breath. I sucked one in, pulled it into my lungs and fought against it as it tried to sputter out of me. The blood, the battle, the war. The magic, the coercion. The helplessness I had felt, like when Leveret went into my brain and—

"Scarlet!" Forceful this time. Turquoise eyes stared into mine as Penn pulled me upright.

"Voss is okay?" My voice choked on the words, hoping against hope.

"Can't you feel him?" His eyes softened, turning to liquid pools I had tormented so often.

"Yes," I gasped.

"He's fine. You're not," Elspeth said.

They were both on the floor—with me. We were in the lobby underneath Voss's penthouse, far away from the throes of battle. "What the hell happened?" I leaned back on my palms, feeling the cool tile press against me. My heart beat rapid-fire, and I felt light-headed.

"You had a panic attack." A frown pulled at Elspeth's mouth. "Any idea what triggered it?"

Everything. Nothing. Over a decade of trauma, most likely. But the war itself—the battle. Death had never bothered me before now. Hell, blood had turned me on. But seeing it blossom from Voss's cheek, watching several Fae fall from the parapet, the stench of it. It was no longer sweet, like it had been all my life. Leveret's power over me had turned something sour. I no longer wanted this. The endless cycle of death.

My eyes watered. "How the hell am I supposed to fight out there with this… this… whatever this is?" I felt useless.

Penn and Elspeth exchanged a glance. Tight-lipped expressions which told me all I needed to know.

"I am not sitting this one out." My throat threatened to close. We had fought so long and hard for this. I had almost lost Voss for this. There was something we were missing—a way to fix this.

Penn grabbed my hand. "You don't have to sit the whole thing out, but we can't have you losing yourself in the field either. If you lose control of your magic, everything we've fought for to date will be lost."

"I should be able to stop it, though." The words cracked inside my throat.

Little fox. Voss's voice. *You can come back out when you are ready, but you need to be steady.* He grunted through our link, and my anxiety spiked again. *I am fine. I heal fast.*

My nostrils flared. He shouldn't be fighting without me.

"Do you really think you are the only one responsible for this?"

I swallowed. "I opened the door, Penn."

"And without you, the Fae would still be over there, suffering. Without the late King Balgair, there never would have been a Fae door curse. Without his parents being complete assholes to him, perhaps he would have never gotten paranoid. How far back do you want to go?"

I blinked. Because what could I say to that? He was right. If we went farther back, there was always more room to place blame. "But it's my responsibility to fix it. And this isn't fixing anything."

Elspeth let out a sigh. "It was your responsibility to keep Voss and yourself safe. That was it. And you've done that plenty of times. The world was headed for this, eventually. If you hadn't opened the door, someone in Faerie would have found another way through. Trust me. A lot of us were looking to escape."

"But if we don't win, then there was no purpose to all of it." Even if we won, there might not be a purpose to the death and destruction. Humans didn't trust the Fae. While a lot of the Fae wanted to be on equal standing, there was clearly enough opposition to that to make this an uphill, lifelong battle. And I was supposed to be their queen, their leader.

But in truth? I was a monster.

A broken one.

"Well," Elspeth said while standing up, "you can stay here and recover, or you can find a reason to keep going. Whichever it is, Scarlet, figure it out soon. I'm going to head back to the battlefield. There are likely Fae and people who need healing. You're welcome to join me. I'm sure the royal magic would do wonders on the wounded."

She left without a backward glance.

I didn't blame her.

Penn snatched my sparrowbone dagger from the floor and offered me the handle. "Are you going to join us again?"

Magic welled around me, and again, I got the sick, twisted feeling inside me—it didn't belong. I could join them on the field. Flashes of the battle came to me through Voss's mind. He was holding his own, but too many Fae were falling under his spells. Charred flesh hit my nostrils, and I dampened my senses.

"Voss needs you," I said, ignoring the outstretched handle.

My fingers itched to coil around my dagger. Maybe if I just used that and no magic... maybe if I stuck to what I was good at. I knew killing this way. It was familiar.

But I didn't want it to be that way. Not anymore.

"Voss needs us," Penn corrected. He stared down at the dagger. "You know, you were once unconquerable, and I believe you can be again. If you want the fighting to stop, make it stop. You and Voss have the power. I know you do." His irises flashed brightly as he laid the dagger next to me. "Even if you don't believe in yourself, know that I believe in both of you." He stood and turned around.

My mouth gaped open. Someone had stabbed Penn in the shoulder, as the tunic on his back was sticky with blood. "Penn," my voice dipped low. "Who stabbed you?"

He blinked and glanced over his shoulder. "Not you, I'm afraid." His eyes slid down to the dagger. "But don't worry. Quinn ended up shooting the Fae responsible." He strode from the room.

I sucked in a breath, trying to steady my racing heart. All our lives were in danger out there, and seeing his blood made it all that more apparent. I might be safe for the moment, and I couldn't accidentally kill anyone with my magic while in this emotional state. But... I needed to be out there.

A wash of the nightmare came over me again. It should have been quiet tonight, with nothing but the distant bleats of hoswisps. Instead, there were screams, crackling fires, explosions, and magic swelling around us. It echoed in the lobby, despite the door to the outside being closed.

Little fox?

Voss?

Do I need to come get you?

No, I'm okay.

Are you sure?

Stop checking in on me. I curled my fingers around my sparrowbone dagger. *Where was your father's library?*

Why?

Because I'm done with this. There has to be answers in there. We are part of some stupid fucking prophecy, and I want to know why. If I'm some kind of chosen one, I should be able to fix it.

There she is. I could feel his grin spreading across his face as he focused on me, having a moment in between the battle to address me. He was safe. *Welcome back. What are you going to do now?*

Figure out how to take out their army all at once or find a more permanent solution to our problem.

I like it. Stay safe.

Bring me back if I don't?

Now and always. His response fueled me with confidence. I could do this.

After Voss showed me where it was, I headed to the library. I cringed upon exiting the building, hearing gunshots in the distance. The constant barrage of pops and bangs was unyielding. Still, I continued. There had to be some record of the prophecy, and Voss had given me his memories—where he had already looked, where was left possibly unturned.

Ever since the Fae door had opened, I had allowed other people to guide me. I had believed what was right in front of me and, for the most part, never questioned anything. While I had been lucky, I had also been oblivious. But no more. If I wanted to save the world, I had to figure out what we were overlooking. I had to become the solution.

After all, if the prophecy were true, perhaps we were only waiting on a catalyst for the transformation—something to save everyone.

When I reached the archives, I found the library in more disarray than when Voss had last been in here. It made sense, seeing as how Quinn's group had taken over the tower. When I saw the hole in the wall, I smiled, knowing why Voss had made the gash in the first place.

His frustration at being separated from me had been a slow, searing rage underneath his skin.

I climbed through the burned out hole and stared at the massive volumes left in the room. There were several missing from Voss's memory—where he had dropped everything to come to my rescue as soon as he realized what Leveret could do by being his twin.

Pressing my eyes closed, I reached out with my magic. It was a pulse along my skin, thickening into the air and weighing on me. Something deep inside told me none of it should feel this way. "Guide me, please." I didn't have to speak the words, but something about that centered me.

When I opened my eyes, the room glittered with the dust left behind. I approached the shelf and pressed my fingers along the wood. Tingles rushed up my arms. Everything was smooth and cold, but something in the room had a hum to it, a life of its own.

Reaching for a shelf, I went to pull it out, but noticed all the screws were already loose. Gently, I pried the board off. Underneath it was a stone encasement—one that matched the red jasper hanging around my wrist. I stared at the box for longer than a moment, then I removed the lid.

Inside, there was a nestle of blankets, and an indentation where something had been previously.

"I would ask if you were looking for this, but it's pretty clear you are."

I whirled toward the entrance of the room, magic flaring around me on instinct.

"Whoa." Morna held up her hands. "Listen, I'm here to give this to you, but I've taken the liberty of highlighting the good parts." She held a green book in her hand. Leather bound with silver foiling on the surface. I chanced a glance at the cover.

Etched into the surface in foil was a perfect little fox. The hair on my neck rose, because whatever that book was, it carried the power I had sensed earlier. It would change everything.

"And you didn't give this to me before because?"

"Because Voss is in your head. He's always in your head. But he has to focus on the battle, so you can read it and make up your own mind as to what happens next."

"What happens next?"

"Yup," Morna's outstretched offering hung between us.

Gingerly, I took the book in my hands, staring at it like it was a fire pauldrin ready to attack. "Care to give me a preview?"

"Oh, the Balgair line fucked us. That's the preview. And you're not going to like the ending." Morna crossed her arms over her chest. "But I also believe you're going to do what's right."

I flipped open to the first section she highlighted.

The conversation Leveret and I never finished rushed back to me. He had theories as to why Faerie was dying, but he never confided what those theories were. Now, there was proof. The royal line was tied to everything. They were the reason for the failures. They were the reason for Faerie's death.

They were tied to all of it.

I flipped to the end and sucked in a breath.

"Remember, don't kill the messenger."

"No," I said, glaring down at the book. "There has to be another way."

"There isn't."

"But I'll be—"

"It's a sacrifice you'd have to make, yes." Morna leaned against the threshold. "So, what will it be, Fae Slayer? Are you going to fulfill the prophecy?"

Prophecy was a misnomer, because no. This wasn't the future.

This was the past catching up to us. This was me suffering the consequences of a self-righteous male who existed centuries before I was born. This was my life being dictated to me because of decisions the selfish and greedy people wrought onto the world.

"I'm not fulfilling anything. I'm *stopping* it."

Morna's grin widened. "Glad to hear it."

Thirty-Five

VOSS

Penn's words echoed in my head. "We'll make sure she's okay." Before he and Elspeth got Max out of here. Seeing her in so much emotional anguish made a small part of me turn to ash. I had been ready to dive off the parapet to save her, fall to my demise if it meant wrapping her in my arms one last time. Keeping her safe.

But now she was uninjured. She had defended herself, even if she lost herself soon thereafter. Time. Time would heal, and at least with Penn and Elspeth taking care of her, we would have it. I opened my mind to her, allowing a conversation to run along with her whenever she needed me, but her fierce independence kept me from muddling too much in her thoughts.

I snarled as I stared at Eero.

Our armies had abandoned us, leaving us to fight on the parapet. The other Fae on Eero's side were happy to give me a wide berth, knowing exactly how quickly I could cut them down. But Eero had thought his wretched band of merry Fae could kill us. Eero was the last of his family—and there was something final about killing all the descendants of a line. Unfortunately for him, no one would save him from me.

"I would ask you to explain yourself, but I don't care." I squeezed my magic along his skin, enjoying the way his veins bulged. The gag was thick in his mouth, no longer allowing conversation. It mattered not. I would get my point across, regardless.

Anyone who dared to harm my little fox was doomed to die in the worst kind of pain.

Iobhar had been lucky—she had killed him.

Eero had no such favors left.

"You know, I always wondered what it would be like to extract someone's bones one by one." I leaned over him, crouching.

The war carried on around me, the screams, the smells, the taste of bodies, blood, rot, and ash coating the air. My little fox was safe, so I had time to play. Magic whirled into my veins, flooding my body.

Rotating Eero through his constraints, I forced the Fae to sit up, thrusting his arm in front of him. I pressed my fingertip against his outstretched arm, sliding down to his hand, then his knuckle. I found what I was looking for, and I pulled. He screamed, but it was muffled by the gag I had forced down his throat.

Bone ripped out from the skin of his finger, popping free from the knuckle. Sinew and blood dripped from the gnarled, empty skin, coiled veins dangling. I gripped his bone in my fingers, staring at the shapes of the joints.

"You know, Eero, your cousin once tried to touch what was mine."

I tossed away the useless bones and stared at the male. A light pink color to his eyes, ones that ran rampant with fear. His blood smelled delectable in a way that only vengeance could. A useless finger hung limp at the end of his hand, bleeding thoroughly. His eyes rolled back in his head.

"Now, that won't do. You'll pass out before I've had any fun." Fire welled inside me, and I cauterized the wound. As the smell of burnt flesh hit me, so did the wash of Eero's screams. I should have taken more time with Emille. I forgot how much fun it could be to be so truly rotten.

My family had been the ones who got off on ruining the lives of the innocent. They loved their power trips and standing above everyone else. I had never been such a way. But, when someone had wronged me or a person I loved, and I had the ability to do something about it? Well, I was my father's son, after all. And while I had fallen very far from the tree, whenever revenge came to mind, I was capable of everything my step-siblings feared.

Eero's brow caked with sweat.

"You want to say something?"

His eyelids fluttered shut.

I used water magic to force him awake, icing him to the bone. "Tell me what you want to say, Eero. Let me hear it." Unwrapping the gag from his mouth, I waited patiently, watching as he coughed and sputtered, unable to catch his breath.

"Monster." The word curled out of his mouth, as if popped from a simmering pan.

"Ah, there's probably so much more you want to say to me, isn't there? See, the thing is, I didn't get raised by monsters only to become a really nice guy, Eero." I paced in front of him, using this moment to check in on Max. Her determination had shot through her, striving off the worst of her emotions. Which allowed me plenty of time to focus on the male in front of me.

"You see, I wanted to be the hero everyone needed. I desired to make a better world for the Fae and humans. All of us, really. But you know what happens when everyone keeps fucking with the hero?" I knelt back down again, and without preamble, I wrenched his ulna out from inside his arm.

His scream echoed off the wall, soothing a part of my soul I didn't care to think about right now.

"They become the villain. And that's the role I'll play for you tonight, Eero. You fancied yourself the hero." I held his bone aloft, watching as blood dripped down his sagging skin. "And now you'll get to watch yourself fall apart. Like they all do, in the end." I licked my lips, tossing the bone over the parapet.

"Now. How many bones do you think I can extract from you before you die? Let's try for a baker's dozen, shall we?" I ignored his whimpering gasps, the spittle falling from his lips, and continued my experiment.

Unfortunately, Eero's heart stopped beating when I reached eight.

Perhaps I tore out his spine too early.

Cleaning myself off, I raced to the fallback point. Any Fae or humans in the need of healing along the way, I stitched back together. There were too many dead in the field already, and we didn't need anyone else to join them. Too much chaos had occurred tonight, and I still hoped this would bring about a new beginning.

When my father created the curse of the Fae door and closed us off from the human world, we had been on the cusp of a civil war. Turmoil ran in rivulets through the Fae. Divided between those who sided with my father and those who wanted to destroy him for the chaos he created.

That had been the turning point for our kind. The rift grew worse when we came here, with those who wanted the humans as servants and those who didn't.

I recognized my role in this. My missives had made the divide worse. My optimism had gotten the better of me, or perhaps a bit of naivety. My little fox changed the world because she was prepared to do whatever it took to make it through to the other side.

And now, I realized, I was too.

A few humans screamed as a fireball rushed straight toward them. I tossed up a water shield just in time. Steam surrounded them, burning their skin, but it was nothing compared to what it could have been. I tossed the attacking Fae backward, and they slammed into a shop, splintering the walls apart. Groans came from inside the structure.

"You able to take it from here?" I pressed a palm to the one with the worst of the burns.

She nodded as her skin mended. "Thank you." Her fingers curled around the firearm. "Never thought I'd say that to the Fae." A small laugh escaped her lips as she brushed past me to confront the fallen Fae.

Little fox? I brushed my thoughts along hers.

Trepidation ran through her skin. *Voss.*

What happened?

I know how to fix everything. At least, I think I do. Do you trust me?

Yes. You don't have to ask. What is it?

There was a long pause, long enough that I took the time to lift another enemy Fae into the air and launch him hundreds of feet past the outer wall. He flew into the nighttime sky.

She opened her mind to me.

Fuck.

Voss?

Yes, little fox.

I'm coming down now.

Okay.

You have to.

I know. I swallowed. *But for once, I find myself not wanting to.*

She chuckled, but the sound was empty and hollow, matching both of our moods. *Well, it might be our last, so we should give them all a show.*

You know how I feel about giving any of them a show of you. I set another Fae on fire, as if to prove my point. As the firelight and shadows danced along my skin, I let out a long breath. *I will inform Lady Burke to gather everyone near the dais.*

Thanks, Voss.

You shouldn't thank me for giving you exactly what you don't need.

It's not about me. And it's not about you.

I know.

We're going to fix it.

Yes, little fox. We are.

And there was no way out, except by putting faith in the Mother that this would work. Everyone always said I got lucky. Maybe it had finally run out.

"Burke?"

A duplicate of her seemed to form out of thin air.

"I have a message for the Fae on *both* sides. Might as well tell the humans, too. A temporary ceasefire while we figure out who gets to rule us, once and for all."

Her lips flattened into a thin line. "I take it you have something more up your sleeve, because that's not what I agreed to, Devoss."

"You'll have to put some trust in me, like I did you."

She frowned but nodded. "Where should we meet?"

"The courtyard with the dais. If anyone so much as breaks the ceasefire, they will be immolated on site. They know I can do it too." I stalked toward the courtyard with a sense of foreboding chasing at my heels.

SCARLET

B y the time I reached the courtyard, voices had risen among the crowd, but the sound of screaming and the scent of death had lessened. For now, it seemed like our plan had worked. A temporary truce. One so everyone could bear witness to what happened next, one to figure out the future.

One where I had to end the royal line.

And there was only one way to do that.

If we did this with enough flare, maybe it would leave a lasting peace. Something that stretched eons away from us. I had to hope. It was the only thing I had left. Hope. A fickle thing that had never done me well in the past.

Voss stood at the dais, hands folded behind his back, rocking on his heels. His blond hair floated in the breeze. His head was held high, chin up, looking very much like the king he was. The king this world needed. One willing to do whatever it took.

They had no idea how lucky they were.

I swallowed, halting at the entrance.

The other Fae and humans grunted and grumbled, but whatever Voss had said to Lady Burke had gotten the message across. I didn't know how she had done it—ceased the fighting with nothing but words. She would be an asset to whatever future our world had, now that she was on the right side of history.

I took him in—everything Devoss Balgair was. The power emanating from him; the danger coiling in his veins. He was possessive, egotistical, and a bit needy. But he was also sensitive, understanding, and hadn't let his power go to his head. He still had idealistic views for the world, and perhaps that was our downfall—both of us wanted what was best.

And this was the only route out of this. He knew it. I knew it.

My heart still stuttered at what we were about to do.

This was for the future. This was for the children who needed a stable environment. This was for the humans who lived subserviently for years. This was for the Fae who wanted equality. This was for the unborn younglings. This was for a future where things could be brighter.

Searching through the crowd, I found the dark brown hair and turquoise eyes of Penn. He was the only one I could trust. He had to understand. I thrust the book at him. "Read it. Please recognize what this means, Penn. There's no time to explain."

He opened his mouth, but I placed my finger on his lips. He glared at me. I glared back, but those were the only seconds I could spare.

I cleared my throat, digging into the earth as I pulled magic from it yet again. "Devoss Balgair." I took a few steps forward, the crowd parting around me. "I represent the side of the humans, the human sympathizers, the ones who want the royal line dead and buried. I, Scarlet the Fae Slayer, challenge you to a duel to the death. With no outside interference. If I win, I will take claim of the earth back for the humans. They will become the ruling body, and all Fae must fall in line. If you win, the Fae continue to lead."

Several cries erupted from the crowd.

"Do you accept my deal?" Magic welled inside my veins. It stretched toward him, singing something so pleasing I wanted to collapse into a puddle then and there. A deal. One where we would battle to the death.

This was very dramatic.

Voss thought so too, because the corner of his lips quirked upward. "Scarlet the Fae Slayer is offering me a deal. What do you think, my brethren, should I take it?"

"You'll probably lose on purpose!"

"Yeah, you hate the Fae!"

"Well, I do hate how much death has amounted today." He slid me a glance, irises churning their fiery red. "And if the Fae Slayer is offering a way out, then perhaps we should take it. No more deaths today, except one of ours."

You need to make this look good.

Isn't that what I'm doing, little fox?

"What do you think?" His voice echoed over the crowd.

Murmurs raced among those around us. It was Burke who spoke up first, in the hundreds of voices of her duplicates. "I say let them. I'm tired of fighting, and this will settle things once and for all."

"And you would bow to the humans if she wins?"

"Do you have such little faith in our king?" Burke pointed to me. "She has been Fae for a short time and barely understands her power. She almost died at the hands of that weakling guard, Iobhar."

If she doesn't shut up, I might kill her, Voss growled.

You would have to beat me to it.

The Fae, however, grumbled their acceptance of her insulting speech.

I let out a breath.

"Then so be it. I accept your deal, Scarlet the Fae Slayer."

The magic settled around us, locking us into place. This would be it. The battle to the end. A show for the masses. A way to close the door on this forever.

Don't hold back, little fox.

Neither should you, Voss.

I sprinted toward the dais, sparrowbone in hand. My first attack intentionally went wide, and he tossed up a fire shield in between us. Reeling back from the heat, I used my speed to cut to the side, thrusting the blade forward. Another shield, this one so hard, my arm vibrated from the force of the clash.

"That all you got?" he mocked.

I sneered. If we were in the bedroom, he would have thrust me against a wall already and shoved himself inside me, impaling me as a punishment for my brashness.

If you keep thinking like that, little fox, I might have to.

Shut up, we're fighting.

You're the one who thought it first.

Except he slammed the image of us wrapped together, my face pressed against his dining room table, as he fucked me from behind.

I rolled and thrust out a small amount of air magic. He chuckled at the barest whisper of air, but it gave me space. That's what I needed. I took the opportunity to attack next, bringing my dagger across his palm.

Blood blossomed out, and he sucked in a breath. Eyes narrowing.

I really, really want to teach you a lesson right now, little fox.

So do it. Take all that anger and rage and make this real.

He swallowed. His fire coiled around me, squeezing every part of my body, not enough to create pain, but to make a point. He turned toward our audience. "You see? Easy. And you Fae doubted me."

Several jeers sounded from the crowd, ranging from kill her, let her go, and the word "die" echoed on repeat. The Fae sure still didn't like me, but I couldn't blame them after I had spent so long murdering their kind.

Remorse, little fox?

Not as much as I will have at the end of this.

A pang of guilt shot through me, and an agonizing wave of hurt threaded into his veins. He glanced at me again as he used water magic to put his own fires out. The Fae sucked in a breath, because he made it seem like the power came from me.

I was still learning how to use my magic, but Elspeth, Penn, and Voss always said it was intention.

You better learn fast, little fox.

I know. I leaped forward, thrusting my dagger toward him.

He parried with a shield. I flew backward with a sweep of his air magic, but I landed on my feet, skidding to a stop. My head snapped up, and I rushed him again. We swapped attacks like this for who knew how long. Bruises coated my skin, blood bubbled from the wounds I had inflicted. We weren't healing quickly anymore.

Which meant the show had gone on for long enough, or I hoped it had. If this wasn't believable, then no one would give credence to what I was about to do.

I smiled and straightened, bringing the sparrowbone dagger up to my own neck.

Everyone went still and silent.

"This was a fool's deal in the end, wasn't it?" I asked. "Because when one of us dies, both of us die. That's what it is to be Blood Queen, to be linked together. Forever." The sparrowbone nicked my skin. "For the sake of the human race, I'm finishing what I started. I'm ending the royal line *forever*." I dragged the dagger across my skin, hissing from the pain.

His magic wrapped around me, stalling my progress.

Our eyes met. Everything in him held me taut. His fear, his sorrow, his endless wish that this could go another way. We had searched for a way out, a way to end this, but this was the only thing left to be done.

And it was with these intentions that I had to move forward. I had to stop this. Magic welled in my body, filling me directly from the earth. Magic that shouldn't have been mine for the taking, because it never belonged to me.

As I stared at his liquid fire eyes, I said the one word I never thought I would say to him, "Switch."

His eyes softened, and my heart shattered.

VOSS

"Switch." Her safe word shook me to my core. She had never used it before, but now... Now.

My magic had wrapped around her hand like a vise, because I wasn't ready for this. This wouldn't work. It was a surety that ran through me on repeat as I watched the dagger cut through the first layers on her throat.

It was why my magic had coiled around her, stopped her. An instinct to protect her, because I knew she wouldn't protect herself.

We breathed. I stared into her eyes, and I felt her determination, her solace, her steadfastness, something I lacked as I saw the blood trickling onto her neck.

"Voss, *switch.*"

Her hand shook around the dagger. The onlooking crowd gasped, noises of murmuring stretching up around us. She fought against my magic as she fought against me in every other aspect of our lives. It made sense now. Everything clambered together in my mind, and all of it made sense.

But I couldn't let her end this, end us, potentially tearing us apart until the Mother deemed us worthy of coming back together, without saying something first.

Little fox.

Voss, please.

Give me a moment. My eyes begged her, and the sharpness in her features softened, but her grip held firm. The resolve overtaking her told me everything I needed to know. This was happening. And I steeled myself for what would happen next. *I love you, and I'm sorry I accidentally compelled you that one time. I never wanted you to be tied to me forever.*

Voss, shut up. I would happily choose to be tied together forever.

But the kind of magic I used—

Brought me back from death.

I didn't mean—

I don't care. I love you, Voss, but we have to do this. We have to try.

She had thought it. Plain as day, no longer hiding her feelings. Love. The only thing worth fighting for… and in this case, worth dying for.

And if we fail? My thoughts sounded too hollow.

Then at least we've failed together.

I nodded, because that would have to be enough. *Intention, little fox.*

I know.

Come back to me. My thoughts were thick, heavy. Watching the woman I fell in love with—the woman I would sacrifice anything to keep safe—hold a dagger to her neck had opened something inside me. She never planned to see the dawn of a new day of man, and I had given her hope. She had given me the same.

And now, I had to cling to that.

Now and always, her thoughts came back to me as breathy whispers. Tears welled in her eyes as her own resolve cracked. If I didn't let her go now, she'd never be able to do it. This was our last chance.

Save the world.

End the royal line.

For good.

Voss.

Yes, little fox?

It's time.

I love you, Max.

I love you, too.

My magic loosened around her, and she drove the dagger into her neck. Tangy blood bubbled into my mouth. I coughed, falling to my knees as she twisted the blade. She stared down at me, an apology running through her very soul.

Come back to me. The words became a mantra, echoing throughout my dying body. The hole she ripped inside herself echoed inside me. Our blood linking us together, her ascension making us become one.

If she died, I died.

If I died, she died.

If we both died, the royal magic would too. That's what it meant to be Blood Queen. That was her sacrifice to make.

Now and always. Her knees slammed against the dais as red raced down her chest, covering her clothes. It was a nightmare witnessing this.

As more blood flooded my mouth, I crawled toward her. I choked, unable to catch a breath as my throat had been filleted from the inside out. Our link. Our bond. All of it. Agony flooded my system.

Noises faded into the background. Just a steady pulse in my ears, slowing as more of our lifeblood cascaded onto the stones. A fitting end to the life cycle we had begun when we had killed the king together.

I reached for her, fingers barely grazing hers. Her eyes blinked. Tired. So tired. Both of us drained. Her fingers twitched against mine.

Love you.

Always, little fox. Always.

I threw out the last magic I had, everything I could grab, into the intention she had when she started this whole mess in the first place.

End the royal line.

End the royal line.

My breath stopped.

End the royal line.

Then my heart.

End the...

Then...

Thirty-Eight

PENN

What. The. Fuck.

My fingers curled around the book in my hands, because why the hell was I put in charge to deal with this aftermath? I needed them to wake up immediately and explain themselves. Except…

Blood covered the cobblestones. The scene was eerily similar to when the king tried to hang Scarlet, but she and Voss ended up standing over his corpse. Except now it was me.

And the hundreds of people and Fae waiting to see what would happen.

No one had expected that.

I hadn't expected that.

And as I stared at their bodies, a strange sort of annoyance swelled inside me. Because of fucking course they would both leave this to me. After all the shit they put me through, of *course* this is how it would end. It was absurd, and absolutely poetically *them*.

In the quiet of them collapsing, the world softened. And I felt it. A shift, a deep rattle inside my bones—the royal power had ceased to exist. The absence of it sank into my skin, threatening to hollow out my insides. Because I recognized it instantly for what it was.

A sacrifice.

The sacrifice.

The book Scarlet had pressed into my hands moments before the fight made sense now. Her eyes had been pale blue, glassy. "Read it. Please recognize what this means, Penn. There's no time to explain."

And then she charged toward Voss and challenged him to a duel with the same heedless care she did everything else.

The worn pages of the book felt like they cut into my soul as I held it. I hoped she had been right, but there was a chance she was wrong. And of course, she had to tactlessly shove it at me before fighting to her death. Her scrawl was on the last page of the small notebook, and the recklessness of the two fools made me want to scream.

But I couldn't let this moment go to waste, because it was a pinnacle, a moment where all the Fae were listening, waiting, watching.

And despite our king and queen's ability to make rash decisions, being best friends with Voss had never given me such a luxury. What I wanted to do more than fix everything was figure out a way to wake them up and kick their asses again, because *why me*? Why did I have to watch them become motionless? Why did I have to watch their blood being spilt?

Why was I always the witness?

I sucked in a breath.

Calm washed over the Fae as they tried to parse the feeling in their magic. The royal power was dead, gone. And what welled in us now? It was our *true* power. It settled across our skins, and it was *easier.* I wondered if this was how Voss felt with the power of the royal line. Controlling his powers and his compulsion so easily.

Which only made his siblings worse if that were true.

I stared at the book for another moment as confused mutters rose from the crowd. Once locked in battle, but now left in the wake of two deaths no one saw coming. I traced the etching on the cover. A little fox.

A little fucking fox.

I fought down hysterical laughter.

The humans reached once again for their arms, but I had seen enough death today. We all had. And now the Fae were changed. Free.

"Stop!" I reached into the well of power I never had before. My voice echoed throughout the court, reverberating off the walls with ease. The royal power had gone, seeped back into the world where it belonged.

Which meant we had access to the *same* power now—for small moments when we needed to call on it. For protection and peace. The Mother had gifted this to us to save us from the monsters, not for us to become them. It was an ebb and flow. We gained the power and let it seep back into the land when we were done.

All of this was inside the book.

And the book described the original curse. Not a prophecy, but a *curse.*

I flashed a glance at Elspeth, and she nodded. Tears brimmed in her eyes, because there wasn't a Fae among us who didn't feel the change in our powers. Even the traitors.

I nodded to the bodies. Cumina and Morna knew what I needed instantly—of course they did. They were probably the reason behind this. With Marcy and Elspeth's help, they dragged the bodies out of the line of fire, if it were to start again. Regardless of Voss and

Scarlet, the world had to move on.

I had to try.

For too long, I had stood in Voss's shadow. I had traveled with him through all the careless, idiotic ideas he ever had—the latest one being possibly his last. Now, however, I was no longer his sidekick. I had to become a leader in this new world.

There was no royal line to walk beside.

I gritted my teeth. "To my Fae brethren, you felt that. You know what happened, and I have proof." I stepped up to the front of the dais. Searching the crowd, I called out, "I would like Quinn to join me."

"So you can kill him, you bastard? Not a chance!" Francis's voice. I was going to have to do something about that man. Not kill him but teach him how we had to be in this together. *With* him, not against him.

A few humans screamed their agreement in unison.

"Please understand me." I held up my hands. "This is so one of you can witness what the Fae have just experienced. The Fae Slayer—one of your own who killed so many of ours—handed this book to me before she... did that." I grimaced, not wanting to put power behind the words. There was hope. Hope. A precious, fleeting thing. My heart ached. "She made a sacrifice so we could have a chance at peace. Do you refuse her that? The woman who freed you from the curse of the Fae door?"

Quinn hobbled out of the crowd. Blood dripped off his nose from a sizable gash in his forehead. My fists curled around the binding of the book. His light hazel eyes met mine. His square jaw lifted as he walked through the crowd. He spoke reassurances to those he passed, but several tried to hold him back, wary of this proposed alliance.

The person who should be scared was the one who did that to

his face.

His brows were deep, long furrows. "What did you find, Penn?" It took him another moment to reach me. The crowd shifted on their feet, waiting on bated breath.

"Penn, what the fuck just happened?" One of the new Lords called out—from Averett's Court. Their joining us had been a pleasant surprise—the reinforcements we needed to level the playing field. They showed up with Alpin's court.

I held up the book. "This is from the royal archives. It holds the prophecy in full."

Not a prophecy, but they would learn that soon enough.

A few Fae sucked in breaths.

"Since the humans don't understand what that means for our magic and didn't feel the shift how we did, I am inviting them to read this and join us in knowledge."

"But the royal magic can't be—"

"Gone!" another screamed.

"It can't be!"

Whispers grew into a roar. Disbelief, horror, and shock. But more than that, several Fae were healing their wounds—not only theirs but healing the people around them too. Did they notice how easy it was to tap into this now that we were no longer separated from the Mother? Did they sense it?

We took, but then returned. And as quickly as they healed, the power rushed back into the earth, as if thanking us for being a part of it.

Instead of dying like Faerie had.

Quinn lurched up the last step, and I reached out instinctively, steadying his shoulders. He gave me a small, weary smile. Blood smeared his teeth. I hadn't expected such a lanky man to fight so hard on the battlefield. He had spearheaded the revolution, and if we had any hope of uniting everyone today, we needed to come together.

While Francis might have been against the idea of a committee, Quinn understood the necessity for it. And now, with the Fae powers being forever changed, I believed such a feat was possible.

Quinn and I, for better or worse, needed each other now.

"You good?" I whispered.

He gave me a solemn nod and got his feet underneath him. "Couldn't have met me down there instead?"

"I don't think you would believe it if you didn't see it from here." I nodded to the crowd. "The Fae are healing themselves, and without realizing it, their magic is healing the humans."

He glanced up, and as he did so, a flood of power rushed into my veins. The gash above his head stitched back together. He winced, touched his forehead, and stood straighter. "Everyone?"

"Everyone left alive."

We couldn't bring people back from the dead.

Except two had. Multiple times.

"What do we care what a human has to say about this?" a Fae objected in the crowd.

"Shut up!" my voice boomed once more. "None of you listen, and it has been our downfall. Faerie died for this. Our inability to change killed our homeland. We came *here* because *we* ruined our world. Not the other way around. We will not continue on our dark path. This world must survive, and we have to do it in peace. So, unless you want me to order the Fae around you to kill you, *listen*. If not to me, then listen to your magic."

I shoved the book at Quinn, opening it to the first relevant page. "Read, please."

"I don't—" He frowned, perplexed as his voice echoed over the court. I amplified it for him. "Oh. Okay. Uh… *Whereas she was the reflection of the full moon, he glowed like the midday sun. The world does not exist without both pulling against the other. After the blood trail and the untruths brought into light, she will ascend. Together, they would become the next rulers of the world, the likes of which had never been seen before. Through her anguish, she will make the ultimate sacrifice, ending the reign of magical terror and creating a hope that will blossom into brighter tomorrows. And he will love her, despite his inevitable end. Love will save the world."* Quinn wrinkled his nose. "How the fuck is *that* love?"

I laughed. It choked and died in my throat, but it was a laugh regardless of how fucked up this day had gone. "Obviously, you've never burned so desperately for someone else that you wanted to kill them."

Quinn's eyes roamed over me as I narrowed mine on his.

"So, what, the Fae are uniting on one side?"

I nodded. "The royal magic is gone." I turned back to the Fae and held up the book. "This is a good thing. Centuries ago, before most of us were born, the royal line created a curse on Faerie. They wanted to harness the magic of the Mother for themselves, so they siphoned it from our home. They created a curse, and the prophecy was the way to break it." Whispers erupted again, but I waited with a steady gaze until they settled once more. "Their magic killed Faerie. They are the reason we had to leave. They are the reason we're here. But this world also has magic." I pointed to Quinn. "These people have magic. There's power all around us. You can feel it now that the royal line is gone, but it's not like it was before. This is different. We can get back what we lost. We can rebuild this world. Together." I shifted my gaze to Quinn. "Hopefully, if you'll have us."

The crowd muttered.

"Where do we start?" Quinn asked.

"What?" someone in the crowd yelled. "Just like that?"

I ignored the human. It was likely one of Francis's allies. "We form a committee. Four humans, four Fae." A few people shouted. Fae shot expletives around. I didn't want to be dealing with this right now.

Quinn nodded. "In the event of a tie, we will have an elected ninth person or Fae. Popular vote only. We will vote every two years. Maximum term of twenty years."

Twenty years was a blink for us Fae, but a portion of a lifetime for humans. That felt fair.

"Agreed?" Quinn held out his hand.

"Agreed."

"Who appoints the first officials?" someone yelled, a Fae from the ethereal sound.

"We do." Lady Burke rose from the crowd, seemingly out of nowhere. "Well, we appoint and if there are strong objections, then we don't elect them."

I swallowed. She had stayed oddly quiet during the fighting. Of course, her mirages had been in the swell of battle, but she had kept herself hidden. I would have too, if I had her power.

"I'm assuming there are no objections from the Fae if both Penn and I take seats?" Her orange gaze met mine. She was clever, I would give her that. She was securing my place, which was precarious, by also securing her own.

The Fae stayed silent.

"No objections heard. You can continue, Committee member, Penn."

"Francis?" Quinn called out. "I'm assuming you will not go along with this if you aren't involved."

"Damn straight."

"Kilroy?"

"Only if you are serving too, Quinn."

Quinn nodded. "Of course."

"Marcy too!" someone yelled, a woman.

"Yeah, we need a woman."

The four had returned from carrying Voss and Scarlet away, and I assumed this was what made them decide on her. Her eyes widened, but she shrugged as she met our gazes.

"Alpin?" I called out. "You up for this?"

He sighed. A low sound that echoed throughout the space. "If I must." A few Fae cheered.

"Cumina, too." Surprisingly, this came from the Fae who had ascended to the Lord of Eero's court during the battle—Baihl. How he had survived the onslaught, I wasn't sure. "I trust her to watch out for those of us who were on the outs at one point. I imagine there will be consequences upcoming, and she's... well, she'll be as fair as possible." Several Fae's voices rose in agreement.

I glanced over at her and Elspeth. I had imagined Elspeth would join me on the committee, but she held up her hands, as if dusting off the power and claiming she didn't want it. Bull shit. But maybe this way, she could run to be the fifth Fae serving. Fine. So be it.

"Cumina, do you accept?"

Cumina glanced at Marcy, exchanging a long look similar to what Voss and Scarlet would give each other when their conversation went on deep inside their brains.

"Yes," she said finally.

"Any objections?"

A few mutters arose, but no one called out.

"Elections will be held in two months. Anyone caught tampering with votes will be punished. Lords and Ladies, please add human advisers to your teams immediately." A few more objections, but mostly, no one made much of a fuss.

We were all still reeling from the power washing over us.

"Come." Burke held her arms out wide and made several

duplicates of herself. "I will discuss the needs of your courts with each of you. Please find me, so we can best address this during our first committee meeting in a few hours."

Hours. I felt like I needed days to get over what had just happened.

"So," Quinn said next to me. "Is she going to be a problem?"

"Only as much as Francis will be."

"Fair." Quinn's hand grasped my shoulder. "I'm looking forward to working with you, Penn. You seem to have a good head on you. I'm sorry about your friend."

I frowned. "Come with me."

"What?"

"Elspeth?"

"Hmm?" She stepped toward us.

The others had dispersed into the crowd, discussing the next steps with humans and Fae alike. Thank goodness, because we had other things to attend to.

"I'll tell you when we're—" I nodded in the general direction. Exhaustion crept into my bones as we weaved through the crowd. We burst out onto the street and headed toward the tower with Voss's penthouse. I knew full well it wouldn't be his anymore, but I refused to think about a problem that would occur tomorrow. There was too much to think about today.

And I had someone's ass to kick.

Two asses to kick.

With any luck.

I stabbed the button for his penthouse and turned toward Quinn. "Read the last page."

His eyes roamed over the scrawl. Scarlet's scratchy handwriting. *If this fails, I'm sorry. But we have to try. It's all about intention, right?*

"What the hell does that mean?" Quinn asked, giving the

notebook back to me.

"It means our fearless leaders are still alive and well, if this went to plan. She intended to kill the magic—the royal magic, which she did. But I wonder if she killed herself in the process." I stared at the numbers on the elevator as they climbed and climbed. Too slow.

"It worked," Elspeth said.

"Worked because they are alive? Or worked because we're finally at peace?" I shot her a glance.

"Peace. But they weren't… cold when I was carrying them."

"Dead bodies don't cool that quickly," Quinn said. "But I still don't understand what the intention part means."

"Magic is about intention. If she injured herself intending to hurt the royal magic, then Mother's magic should also save her once she freed it," Elspeth explained.

"That makes no sense," Quinn said.

"Welcome to my world." The doors slid open, and I marched through the penthouse. Both were on Voss's bed. Paler than they had been a few hours ago, but a light flush was across their cheeks. "Wake up, you idiots." I tossed the book onto the nightstand and crossed my arms. "You have explaining to do for your reckless behavior."

Thirty-Nine

VOSS

My body ached. My head throbbed. Every part of me felt like it had been turned inside out. My pain was so acute, I could do little more than groan. The last thing I remembered was my little fox dying in front of me from the knife wound in her neck. Had it worked? Were we with the Mother, or had we gone somewhere else?

If I were still alive, I didn't want to exist in a world where she wasn't among the living.

And there was a chance that could have happened.

"Wake up, you idiots." Something thudded. "You have some explaining to do for your reckless behavior." Penn's voice dripped with vehemence. I had never heard him so furious before.

"Max." The word choked from my lips, barely escaping my dry mouth.

"She's right here, and you sound pathetic." Elspeth's harsh words had never settled me so deeply.

I ripped my eyelids open, watching as blurry shapes took hold in the world around me. We were in my apartment. The sun was rising, casting an early morning glow across the space. How long had we been out? Everything felt dry and gritty.

Like I had died and come back. Again.

"You killed the royal magic." Penn scowled, frowning at me. He nodded to my side.

I rotated my neck. It cracked and popped, like my healing had slowed. My magic was… my own again. Normal. Every bruise from the fight had caught up to me, each slash from her dagger—I felt all of it. But despite my broken body, relief flooded me when my eyes caught on her.

Elspeth sighed and knelt next to me. "For the record, I don't think you deserve this after everything you put us through." Her hands pressed against my chest. Immediately, the bone-chilling pain subsided, and warmth flooded my limbs.

"She made it?" I rolled onto my side, placing a hand on her stomach.

"Barely." Elspeth's nose wrinkled. "Your magic started healing you, but it took Morna, Cumina, and me to heal her back to this." She gestured to her.

I brushed the blood-stained hair from her face.

Max's skin was ghostly pale. Lips almost as blue as her eyes. But there was a bit of warmth to her. Pulling her into me felt like the most natural thing in the world. I reached for the royal magic instinctively, wanting to bring her back to me.

I let out a breath, knowing I would have to wait.

"Did you know the plan going in?"

"Of course I did." Pressing my lips to her forehead, I felt the moment she warmed. Perhaps from my body being so close to hers, or perhaps as a gift from the Mother herself. "I hated it, but she shared everything." I shook my head. "Sorry, Penn. There hadn't been time."

"She gave me the book. I didn't truly grasp what it would mean until I saw you both… lying there. Alive and dead at the same time, somewhere in between."

I thought about the compulsion I used on her, and I had to wonder if it had tied us together. Had that brought us back? If our souls were magically interlocked, then that would explain plenty.

"What's it like without the royal magic? What's going on out there?"

"Well, you and the Fae Slayer are dead for good, so you're no longer king."

"Great, I don't want it."

Penn stared at me.

"Okay, I *liked* the power, but it was going to my head a bit."

"There's the honest truth." He ruffled his hair. "We set up the committee, as suggested before. It's going to take some getting used to, but I think we have a decent mix on it. I might end up strangling Francis."

Quinn chuckled.

Penn slid him a look. "For now, it's peaceful, but that only works if you two stay dead, if you understand what I mean."

"Disappearing. Got it." I pressed my lips to Max's forehead. "Once we're rested, that is."

"I don't need to be in your head to hear your thoughts, Voss. You want to fuck her."

"Of course I do, Penn. We survived *death.*"

"Fuck," Max groaned. Eyelids fluttered open. "Ouch, Voss."

"Sorry," I murmured into her neck, so thankful to have her scent hit my nostrils. I had wrapped myself around her too tightly.

We could have failed. We almost did. If it hadn't been for my friends, we would have. Or she would have.

Max shook her head. "Being human sucks." Her eyes met mine. "I can't hear you anymore."

"We'll have to bond again. Seems to be a thing whenever one of us almost dies."

Her eyes drooped shut. "It feels like I got run over by a truck." She wiggled underneath me. "Everything hurts."

"Yeah, yeah, I'll try." Elspeth crossed to her side of the bed.

The deep etched pain eased slightly across Max's brow, but it looked like some of the ache remained. At least the bruises from our fight were mostly gone.

"How did you figure it out, anyway?" Elspeth asked.

"Morna gave me the book."

Elspeth snorted. "That's what she wanted all along. You couldn't kill the royal magic unless you were Blood Queen."

"The prophecy was more of an… instruction manual. Only someone with the royal magic could kill the royal line. I had to ascend to destroy it." Max waved her hand in the direction of the book. "It was another curse, created by one of the stupid male Balgairs from a long line of paranoid men." Max glared at me. "Are you paranoid, too?"

"Only when it comes to your safety."

"I will accept that answer, seeing as how I get myself into a lot of trouble."

"Too much." I helped her sit up, propping pillows behind her.

She gave me a grateful look. "Did it work, though?"

"Exactly how you were hoping." Penn scratched the back of his head. "How did you get out of that deal, though?"

Max snorted. "We used the same trick Voss did with his step-sisters. My name isn't Scarlet."

Penn shook his head. "Should have seen that one coming."

"But none of this makes sense." Quinn sank onto one of Voss's sitting chairs. "How can you kill magic?"

I squeezed Max's hand, encouraging her to tell the story, everything she unveiled to me before we made our decision to do it together.

"Balgair," she said, reaching for the book. Her fingers ran over the emblem on the cover. "It means fox, doesn't it?" Her eyes searched mine.

I nodded.

"You've been calling me little fox not as endearment, but as a possession." Her brows fell over her eyes, but she could claim annoyance all she wanted. I wasn't going to stop.

And no, it wasn't just because of the name Balgair. It was the same reason my twin called her little rabbit. But again, my little fox jumped to conclusions quickly. Maybe someday I would correct her, while I was deep inside her, after I spanked her raw for daring to make me watch her die for a second time.

"Did you expect something less?" I asked.

She shook her head, lips quirking. Her eyes sparkled. "That's the Balgair curse. The royal line didn't exist until *his* family created it. Way, way back." She looked at Quinn. "And it wasn't a prophecy, it was how to break the curse." She cleared her throat, turning to what the Fae believed was a prophecy. "*She will make the ultimate sacrifice, ending the reign of magical terror...* That's what I focused on. My intention was to end the royal magic. And it was a sacrifice to give up a long life with you, a future I believed in. You were the first one to make me feel like happiness could be caught."

Had we been alone in the room, I would have pinned her wrists above her head and taken her, fucking her until she couldn't breathe.

"And the *creating hope* part, I had to make it into a scene, because in order to bring hope, the end of the royal magic had to be witnessed. And… well, your inevitable end was just that. The end of the royal line, the end of the royal magic."

"And love saved the world." Elspeth rolled her eyes. "It's a bit cliche, don't you think?"

"Did you not finish the book?" Max tilted her head to the side. She must have realized at the same time as I did that none of them read the last part. She turned the page. "*Not traditional love. A passion so deep, the only way to keep it is to strip its power once and for all. For a love so intense only changes the world once.* So, yeah, I needed to be the one to end the royal magic. You kept saying it was about intention."

"So, she used the royal magic to destroy the royal magic," I summarized.

Max's existence had been wrapped up in so many curses. The Fae door, the royal line. Her existence reaffirmed how much she belonged to me.

"I'm just glad you were able to heal me enough so we could both survive." A blush crept over Max's cheeks.

"Your plan made sense to me. Sparrowbone is toxic for Fae, not humans. By using it on yourself, you could be healed as a human." My fingers squeezed around hers. "It was a good plan." Except for the part about her being human again, I thought bitterly. I still had access to my typical magic—fire, as well as what felt warm… almost like healing magic.

But with Max being human again, she wouldn't live longer than a short lifespan. It wasn't long enough. I didn't care if we had several decades left, because all the time in the world wouldn't be enough. I had tied her life to mine once before, and I would do so again willingly.

"We need to find an eternal gem." I hopped out of bed and crossed the room to my dresser, pulling out a fresh shirt. "We need to go to Faerie, track one down, and—"

"You can't leave this apartment, Voss. Not now." Penn's voice halted me in my steps. He had never commanded me before, but if I didn't know any better, it was as if he had tried to compel me.

I pivoted. "Excuse me?"

He crossed his arms over his chest. "Everyone thinks you're dead, and it needs to stay that way. At least for now."

"We can come up with some story. I was the king after all—"

"But not anymore, and the committee is just forming. If the Fae see you, if they think you survived, that will undo everything we just accomplished."

I frowned, glancing at Max. Every second that ticked by felt like one too many. "I'm not staying here forever. I'm not dead, and I refuse to live like a ghost haunting my own penthouse."

"Not forever," Elspeth said.

"Just until the committee is functioning. A week or two, maybe three. But then you two are free to disappear into the night, gallivant across the land. Maybe make a rumor or two about how the Fae Slayer is still alive and well and killing any Fae who deserve it." Penn shrugged.

"Besides, going to Faerie is a death sentence for a human, Voss. We'll help you like we've always done, but you don't need to oversee this anymore. You're free to do whatever. Just... don't be stupid about it."

I straightened. "When have I ever been..." I held up my hand as both of them opened their mouths. "You're right. Faerie is dangerous. But I happen to know someone else who needs a little visit and might have information on the eternal gems." I slid my gaze over to Max. "You up for paying an old friend a visit? We owe him our gratitude."

"Is it the friend I'm thinking it is?"

I didn't need to read her mind to know we were on the same

page.

"Fine. After we've been hidden for however long the new world needs, we'll take off. Besides, we could make hiding fun." Max ran her hand through her hair, but grimaced as her fingers got caught in the sticky, bloody locks. "Maybe after a shower, too? Or several."

I crossed the room to the bed and hooked my fingers under her chin, forcing her to look at me. "How exactly will we make hiding *fun*?"

"Uh," her eyes slid over to the three of them. "I'm sure we can find ways to pass the time."

"For fuck's sake, Voss, can't you wait until we're done with our conversation?" Penn pleaded.

"Bring food back in two hours, and I'll be happy to finish whatever discussions then." I glanced over at the three of them. "And thank you. I'm glad it worked, but if it hadn't, it's nice to know the world would have been a better place either way."

Elspeth rolled her eyes and started toward the door. "Whatever, Voss. We'll see you later."

Quinn clapped Penn on the back. "I think I need you to explain how this magic stuff works some more."

Penn's jaw opened as Quinn slipped out of the room.

"Go for it," Max said.

"What?"

"For Quinn."

Penn's brows shot low over his eyes.

"You both have this quiet intensity about you. I think you'll be good for each other."

"Scarlet?"

"Yeah?"

"If I *ever* ask you for dating advice, please kill me." Penn strode from the room and shut the door behind him.

"What did I say?"

I turned her face back toward me. "I have a lot of aggression to work out."

"So do I."

"And I have control issues."

"Happy to help." Her voice dropped lower, becoming a breathy whisper.

"And I hated watching you die."

"Then punish me."

My lips curled into a smile. "Shower first." I scooped her into my arms and strolled into the bathroom. I twisted the water on but didn't wait for it to get warm before walking underneath it. As soon as Max shivered against me, I used my magic to warm us both.

"Neat trick."

"I'm full of them." I hooked my fingers underneath her shirt and peeled it off her. Next was her bra, then her trousers and panties. I nipped the skin of her neck. "Now, what am I going to do with you? Your plan was reckless. You could have killed us both."

She beamed. "But it worked."

"No, I think you were a naughty little fox, and I think you need a punishment that fits the crime."

"Yeah?"

"Yeah." I rolled my thumb over her nipple. "I'm going to fuck you until you stop breathing. And after I come inside you, I'm going to push my fingers into you again and again, making you come until you beg me to stop."

"Voss?"

I moved her head under the stream of water, beginning to work out the tangles in her hair and the mess of the battle. She unbuttoned my shirt and peeled the wet clothes off me.

"I want to be bonded with you again. Make me yours."

I circled my hand around her wrist. "You've always been mine, little fox. You've been mine since I first saw you, but I'm willing to remind you in case you've forgotten." I crushed my lips against hers, and I couldn't wait to watch her fall apart.

SCARLET

We were in the stables outside of the royal court—or the capital, as everyone was calling it now. Nothing royal about it without royals. We had spent two weeks held up in his apartment together, curled around each other, fucking, and growing closer still. On the nights when darkness threatened to close in around me, Voss held me. Because of our blood bond, he knew exactly what I needed when I needed it—space, comfort, sex. He had become everything I never risked dreaming of.

But now, Voss had me bent over a barrel, making good on his promise to teach me another lesson in the long line of lessons.

"Say it," he growled as he buried himself inside me. "Say why, little fox."

My ass was bright red. Everything stung as he slammed into me, but it felt good. I belonged to Voss in a way I belonged to no one else. And he held me with such care most days. But not tonight.

Tonight, he couldn't wait to tell me the reason he truly called me

414

little fox. But we had been playing a guessing game, and every wrong answer had been another smack on my ass.

I had gotten a lot of wrong answers.

"Because… of your…" I grunted.

He spanked me again.

I clamped around his cock as he thrust, coming so hard I saw stars. He groaned but kept the quick snap of his hips moving at the same speed. "Why, little fox?"

"Because of your name!"

"Which name?" He threaded his hand through my hair and pulled.

My back bowed. I latched onto the barrel with my hands, using any leverage I had to keep myself from falling. Though, I didn't need to worry—Voss would never let me fall unless he so chose to. "Because of Devoss?"

"Correct." He leaned over me, pressing his chest against my back. "I've been claiming you since the moment I saw you, not because of the Balgair name, but because of *mine*." His teeth closed over my ear. "I would have claimed you sooner, had I known where you were. And I will continue to claim you for as long as you allow it."

"Yes," was the only word I could edge out of my breath. We were destined from the start, but this felt different. We had the possibility of tomorrows, and we wouldn't let that go to waste. "I love you," I whispered.

He groaned against me. *It feels better when you say it without a knife involved.*

"Who says a knife isn't involved?" I kicked backward. Voss stumbled away from me and narrowed his gaze. I brought out the sparrowbone knife, the one he had gifted me, and held it in between us.

"Oh, you want to play?" He pressed himself into the blade and bit my lower lip. Hard enough to make me bleed. His tongue roamed over my skin, but he stepped back with the familiar smirk on his face. "Let's play." Voss wrenched the weapon out of my hands. He twirled it in his fingers, a delicious glint in his eyes. He pulled up his trousers, tucked himself away. "You have ten seconds to get your clothes on."

As he counted down, I jerked my trousers back up and tossed on the shirt. I was fairly certain the latter was inside out.

"What now?"

"Get on Switch. I'll give you a head start. Then Blade and I will take off after you. If I catch you, you're going to wish you still had the barrel to hang onto." He cupped my chin in his hands and grinned. "Run, little fox, run."

I kissed him, lingering for a moment, before I sprinted for Switch's stall. I wanted him to chase me. And this time, he did.

VOSS

Escaping the capital, the royal line, and politics gave me a sense of freedom I had never had before. We became two anonymous faces in the crowds, but whispers still rose wherever we traveled. I used a bit of glamor to make us not immediately recognizable, but Penn and Quinn wanted the rumors.

If people and Fae believed our spirits lived on, we became a cautionary tale, a warning, a haunting. The story had evolved quickly. *Be kind to each other, else the spirits of the Fae King and the Fae Slayer will get you.* We would rise from the grave and take justice.

Of course, the rumors were founded. There had been just two bodies—one Fae, one human, both of whom had spoken out against the alliance adamantly. They had tried to bring the world back to its chaotic state. The committee had voted, those two had been sacrificed. We had obliged.

Save for the committee, we were dead to the rest of the world. It had started with just Penn, Quinn, and Elspeth, of course. But once Cumina figured it out, she tired of keeping secrets and told my other step-sister and the committee. It was easier that way. We were trained assassins, after all. A blood hunter and a Fae Slayer, ready to track down any who threatened the peace we had found.

After those kills, the rumors spread like a fire pauldrin's flames. It was beautiful.

Two weeks inside the penthouse, two weeks of traveling, and another week of fucking, and I had decided I liked Max's smile more than watching her come. Her smile became easier, more uplifted than before. It was something she needed—healing.

Our aim now was my court, as I was still a Lord after all. Despite my absence, no one had risen to power in my wake. Max and I conceded we could take care of a small part of the world—let the rumors linger and recluse ourselves. We planned to make it a home—one to replace what she lost long ago.

But we had one place to stop along the way. Unfinished business that needed attending to.

We had been traveling for a while. I glanced at Max. Her clothes were rumpled, hair deliciously messy, and a fine layer of dirt coated her face. We'd have to find a shower, but not before we got a bit dirtier. I planned to have us rest at the Sparrowhawk, once everything was settled.

"Are you ready?"

She spun the sparrowbone dagger in her hands, toying with the edge of the blade expertly with her fingers. "Checking in on me again, Voss?"

"Now and always, little fox."

A blush crept across her cheeks. I fucking loved this girl, and I loved pushing her buttons. I thrust my magic out and knocked the door inward. It slammed against the other wall, revealing the darkened bar of Ceilidh.

A woman nearly jumped out of her skin as she yelped with surprise.

"We're here to see Finian Raskos and Nightmare." Because rumor had it, Nightmare had never left.

The woman blinked, tugging on her ponytail. She had brown hair that reached down to her shoulders and honey-hued eyes. "I thought you two were… dead." Her voice trembled over the last word as her eyes darted between us. "What do you want with my husbands?"

Max balked. "Husbands?!" I sensed her shock alongside my own.

The woman crossed her arms over her chest and sniffed. "Yes, we got married just over a month ago."

"You married a Dream Walker?" I growled the words, still in disbelief.

"If you're going to be like that, I'm not getting them for you."

Fire magic crept around my wrists. "I suggest you do."

"Voss," Finian Raskos's voice rang out from his office. He adjusted his trousers and walked into the room with wary eyes on me. "What brings you here?"

"You should know."

Raskos let out a breath. "Revenge, fire, and brimstone?"

"Something like that." My flames pulsed against my skin, wanting to ignite something. "I believe you owe my wife an apology."

"As you owe mine—threatening Jules like that." Finian's eyes churned with bright green.

I shook off my flames, knowing full well he had placed a shield between us. If I were to try to torch either of them now, it would blow back into our faces. With her being human, I couldn't risk it.

"You gave that sicko free range to do whatever he wanted to

me." Max stepped forward, pointing her dagger toward him. "You knew what I was stepping into, and you didn't give me any warning about who or what he was."

I winced as the Dream Walker himself walked out of the shadows and placed his arms around both the woman and Raskos.

"I think the issue you have is with me and less with Finian." Nightmare's silver hair caught the light, and he winked at Max.

She tried to stab him, but it glanced off Finian's defenses. Growling, she spat, "You're both cowards, hiding behind defensive shields. You should face us like men."

"What about like a lady?"

Faster than a blink, the woman rushed through the shield, stepping up to Max. She shrank the distance between them faster than I could track. I stumbled forward, hitting my face on the shield that Finian placed around me. I was stuck in a box while the woman approached my wife.

"Bastard. Drop it!" I whirled on him, fire looming in my eyes.

"I'm not letting you hurt my wife," the Lord growled.

The woman placed her hands on either side of Max's face, bringing their lips close together. Her eyes glowed a rich yellow as she stared into Max's eyes. Max's blue eyes went soft along the edges.

Little fox? But there was no read on her right now.

"What the fuck, Finian, is she *feeding*?" My mouth hung open in disbelief. I had thought Night was the last surviving Dream Walker, but now... Panic swelled inside me. One I was stupid enough to try to fight, but two?

"Yes, Jules is a Dream Walker."

Finian was a fucking dead Fae.

Night crossed his arms over his chest, watching the woman with admiration in his silver eyes. "But she doesn't feed like I do."

With clenched fists, I pivoted toward them, readying my magic once more. If I had to, I would burn this club down. "How the fuck is that supposed to make me feel better?! Release her *right now*." Flames licked around my skin, causing smoke to fill the air. Wisps hit the sides of the box Finian had trapped me in. The air grew thick.

"She feeds off joy, not fear. Whatever Scarlet is experiencing right now, it's nothing like what Night does." Raskos tilted his head to the side. "Perhaps rumors of your demise were exaggerated, but have you heard the rumors about Ceilidh? We started treating Fae and humans for their mental ailments. Night allows them to confront their fears for those who need exposure therapy, and Jules provides closure. We have a wait list for clients, and your girl is getting a free service."

"A free service she *never asked for*," I spat the words through my teeth, fighting back a cough as the plumes whirled in front of my face.

"Perhaps you need some closure, too?" Night suggested, arching a silver brow.

"I want nothing from you." I turned my gaze back to my little fox, but her jaw had slackened. The tension in her brow had disappeared. Her eyes brimmed with tears.

Jules pulled back her hands. "Better?"

Max sank her teeth into her lower lip, gazing at the woman with some kind of awe. Her eyes went back to me. "Voss! For the love of the Mother, please stop immolating yourself."

I cut the magic off immediately, because as of late, it seemed like I couldn't say no to her.

"If I drop the shield, Voss, are we going to have issues?" Raskos crossed his arms over his chest.

I looked at Max. She shook her head.

Setting my jaw, I said, "Let me go to her."

The magic dropped. I crossed the two feet, wrapped my arms

around Max, and pulled her into me.

Her fingernails dug into my back.

"I think we should give them space," Jules said.

"It's my club," Raskos whined.

"And it's my therapy session. Back. Both of you." She let out a shriek as Night grabbed her and threw her over his shoulder. They crossed over to the bar area, giving us a wide berth.

"Are you okay?" I stopped watching the other three, focused only on Max.

"Yeah, I mean… I don't think I've felt better." Max pulled away, and her blue watery eyes searched mine. "I know it wasn't real, and I know they are dead, but Jules gave me the opportunity to say goodbye."

I frowned. "What?"

"I've only had nightmares since this all started. That was the first… pleasant dream I've had of my family." A tear trailed down her cheek, and I caught it on my thumb. "I know they are dead, but… hearing them say they are proud of me, of the things I've done… Hearing them tell me it's okay. My brother gave me forgiveness."

"But—"

She shook her head. "I know it's not real, Voss, but I *needed* that. I needed to say goodbye." Her fingers clutched the front of my tunic. "But I never want to say goodbye to you, not like that. We have to find an eternal gem."

"Night," Raskos's voice cut across the space.

Max jumped as Nightmare had closed the gap between us. I bristled, ready for a fight.

Night held up his hands. "An eternal gem?" His gaze flicked to Jules and Raskos.

"No," Raskos said, putting his hands on his hips.

421

"We kind of owe them," Night said.

"We already gave them something," Raskos growled.

Night rolled his eyes. "Finian, they are dead in the eyes of every Fae and human. Who is going to believe them?"

"Believe what?" I stepped in front of Max. She clung to her dagger behind me, but I wouldn't let either of them get close to her again.

"Night," Raskos warned.

"I have access to eternal gems."

"I hate you sometimes," Raskos grumbled.

"No, you don't." Night sent him a familiar glance.

"So, the rumors about Dream Walkers were true?" I hedged. Paying them a visit to teach them a lesson had been half of my plan. The other was to get information on the gems. I had never needed one before now. "You did hide them?"

Raskos shook his head but dropped his hands to his sides. It hadn't been that long since I had last seen this Lord, but everything about him had changed, almost like a lifetime had passed. The way they exchanged looks with each other was so familiar, so full of *love*. Which was strange, seeing as how Night had tormented Raskos's court for centuries.

Then again, I had seen stranger things happen.

Jules stepped forward, and it was quick. One moment, she was near the bar, the next she was in front of us. She held out her wrist. "It's a contingency plan, in case my Dream Walker side fails to extend my lifespan."

I gaped at the stone, practically glowing with iridescence under the spotlights. "You married her with a fucking gem?"

Raskos shrugged. "Night knows where they are in Faerie."

"To answer your earlier question, Voss, the Dream Walkers stole them back from the Fae and hid them before the curse of the Fae door. We were hoping to use our knowledge of their location to save us in case of a war, but we all know how that went." Night wrapped his arm over Jules's shoulder. "I cannot let you use this one, as it's meant for my wife. But if you give me two days, I can acquire another back from Faerie. I feel as though… I owe you." His silver eyes landed on Max.

Jules clapped her hands together. "Then we can walk you through the ceremony together." The woman beamed, grin wide.

I was still reeling from the fact that she was also a Dream Walker.

Max's eyes were glossy. She nibbled her lower lip, and a pulse of fear shot through her. "I don't really want to be Fae again. I thought we'd have time to talk this out, but—"

"You wouldn't be Fae," Raskos chuckled. "It ties your lifespan to Voss's, and he has a few hundred years left in him."

I glared at Raskos. "You're decades older than me."

He shrugged, unapologetic.

"So… what, I'd just stop aging?" Max glanced between us.

"Technically, you'd be as old as I am."

"Which is… how old, exactly?"

I smirked, enjoying the fact that she still didn't know.

Truthfully, neither did I. Time ceased to matter after the first hundred years went by. I lost count—as had every Fae I knew, though most of us refused to admit it. We remembered who was older and younger, and I imagined now that humans were involved in our lives, the passage of time would have meaning again.

"Two days, and it will be yours. I'll show you how to use it, and you can decide when to use it. Whether it's with us or on your own."

Max hooked her fingers through mine. "It sounds like a plan. But what are we going to do in the meantime?"

"We'll stay at the Sparrowhawk." My eyes settled on Finian's. "You know I'm alive, but no one else can know. You understand?"

He laughed. "Trust me, I don't need the wrath of the ex-Fae King or the Fae Slayer to come down on my club. I was originally dreading this day, but I'm pleasantly surprised to still have my head attached to my neck." He held out his hand.

I took it with my free one.

"And if you need anything at all while you are in town, another session or anything, I am here."

"I like her," Max said, pointedly looking at the two males. "And I've decided that if either of you two mess things up with her, I will kill you."

Night chuckled, but Finian blanched.

"You don't need to threaten my husbands." Jules crossed her arms over her chest. "I can take care of myself."

The two of them sized each other up and burst into laughter at the same time.

"What is happening right now?" I asked Finian.

"I think our wives just became friends?" He let out a breath. "If you two want to stay in the guest room instead..."

Jules clapped her hands together. "Yes! Please stay. I have this amazing bottle of wine—" Without waiting for agreement, Jules tossed her arm over Max's shoulder, and the two of them strolled toward Finian's apartment entrance.

I snarled at the two males. "This does not mean we are friends."

"Absolutely agree with you," Raskos said at the same time as Night said, "Oh, but we will be." They exchanged a glance. Raskos shook his head, and Night's eyes flashed blue.

"You two bicker more than Max and I."

"And yet, it's more fun that way. But Finian knows his place." Night's voice dipped into the land of something promised and unspoken, much like I would do with Max. "We'll get along fine, Voss, you'll see."

424

"Not sure how much I trust two Dream Walkers, but…" I gazed at the two women, paused at the threshold of the door that exited this part of the club. They were chatting idly, but Max's eyes drifted to me. Somehow, there was a lightness back in them that I only ever witnessed when I was buried inside her. "That seemed to help her."

Finian nodded. "We've helped many people. Could even help you."

I lowered my brows.

"Not that you need any help," he amended.

"Good save."

"Voss, are you coming?" Max glanced over at me. "I want to shower, and… maybe some other things."

"On that note…" Night pressed his lips to Raskos's quickly. He shadow walked to Jules and kissed her too. His fingers thrust into her hair, and it was more like a devouring than anything else. "I'll see you both in two days tops." He disappeared from the club.

Finian ran his fingers over the bridge of his nose. "Please be respectful inside my house."

"I'll be as respectful as she allows me to be." I breezed by him.

Jules led us up to their apartment and showed us the guest room. I was instantly grateful for the shower, more so when Max pressed against me with the water cascading over our skin. A sly smile curled up her lips.

"Do you want to recreate the night we met?"

"Dagger and all?"

"It's more fun if I get to stab you again." Her fingers trailed along my scar. I hadn't let Elspeth heal it all the way, because I knew if I never saw Max again, she had already left a mark on my heart.

I captured her hand in mine and bit one of her fingertips. "Vicious little fox."

"You love it."

"I love you." Pleasure coursed through me as a blush spread across her cheeks.

She breathed out, contented. "I love you, too."

And because it would never do for my back to be pressed against the wall, I switched our positions, wrapped her legs around my hips, and showed her how much I adored every inch of her. For now and always.

Don't miss **Mister Nightmare**, a Blood Hunted Novel.

Nightmare - the creator of his namesake.
Raskos - a Lord with too much to lose.
Jules - seeking happiness in the apocalypse.

The three are an unlikely group, what with Lord Raskos and Nightmare being century-long enemies. But as fate would have it, the two are solely focused on Raskos's hired bartender, Jules.

She's determined not to get involved with her boss, but when she meets the mysterious silver-eyed Nightmare, her safety is in question. Raskos offers her shelter, and who is she to refuse? She finds herself thrust in between the history of the two—her boss and the creator of nightmares.

Worse? She wants both of them for vastly different reasons.

As tensions mount, there's one thing that could bring them together and it's the same thing threatening to tear them apart—the possibility of losing Raskos's club and court.

Mister Nightmare is a why choose in between novel. While it is not required to enjoy the main series, there is a tie in with the third book.

Suggested Reading Order:

Blood Hunted
Blood Trail
Mister Nightmare
Blood Queen

Acknowledgments

Wow, readers, what a journey. I need to sit in this for a moment, because the end of my first trilogy… It's unreal. But *you*. You have been there, reading this story, coming to this end with me. My emotions are all over the place, and I'm sure yours are too. We're at the happy for now, but life as a writer is never done. There are always more stories to tell.

I'd like to thank my partner for this completely unreal ride. I am a different person today than the person who started writing this series, and he's been a stable pillar in my life. You're lovely. Thank you for being you.

My parents and sister, who have been gracious in their support. My sister especially who yelled at me more than once to give her the last book. I operate better under pressure, and I appreciate that she gently nudged (demanded) the sequels.

To Amber D. Lewis. I am so happy to have found you in this chaotic world of writing. For us to have stumbled upon each other only to realize we share a similar brain… honestly, it's been fantastic.

Thank you for the early feedback. Blood Queen is a better story because of you.

To Jacqueline, Marialuisa, and Victoria, thank you for being part of my beta reading team. Seeing your feedback gives me more strength than you realize. You also made this a better piece, and I am so grateful to be able to bounce ideas off you.

To my ARC readers who took a chance on this book, thank you for being part of the team. Thank you for reading the series.

And to the person who made it to the end of this page… thank you for being so *good*.

Subscribe to the publisher's newsletter on https://www.spacefoxbooks.com for regular updates, apply to become an early reader, or apply to become a Cadet Fox and join the street team!

Follow the publisher on Instagram, TikTok, or Facebook @spacefoxbooks

Thank you for reading.

About the Author

Ariel Rae was raised in a small New Hampshire town, but left it behind to attend Emerson College in Boston. After graduating with a degree in Writing, Literature, and Publishing, she moved to southern California.

Working as a barista, she somehow turned her life into a cliché and met her husband while serving him coffee. They fell in love, got married, adopted a bunch of cats, moved to the rainy side of Oregon, and eventually moved back to New England.

When she's not writing, she plays video games, drinks tea, reads way too much (though, she wonders if there is such a thing as too much reading), and snowboards.

She also writes YA literature under R. A. Desilets.

Find her online @arielraeauthor

Other Work

Remember to sign up to the newsletters to be kept up to date with the latest releases: https://www.spacefoxbooks.com/newsletter

Carter Ortese is Trouble by R. A. Desilets
YA Contemporary Romance

Everyone knows Carter Ortese is trouble, so it's a shock when band geek Emma asks him out as a dare. When he says yes, she refuses to back down. But no one knows why she asks him on a second date. Or a third.

A contemporary young adult romance you don't want to miss.

Break Free by R. A. Desilets
YA Time Loop with Mental Health

What happens when your best friend is stuck in a time loop and you reset day after day?

On Tuesday, Leida skips school with her best friend, Ozzie. Today will be a perfect day at the local amusement park.

But as Ozzie repeats Tuesday over and over again, Leida has to cope with Ozzie's erratic behavior. Can Leida help Ozzie break free, or are they doomed to live the same day forever?

Start Small by R. A. Desilets
YA Contemporary with Found Family

My bucket list was meant to stay buried—a wish list from a dying girl. But when my best friend Harper finds it after our senior year, she wants a do-over with our friend group. It's our last summer to say goodbye. We've graduated, and there's nothing left to lose.

From holding our breaths to shooting off fireworks to climbing a mountain, we complete the items. Maybe before the end, I'll tell Owen how I feel. But since he's flirting with another girl and pretending I don't exist, it might already be too late.

Other Young Adult titles by R. A. Desilets
Girl Nevermore
In a Blue Moon (Blue Moon #1)
Hipstopia (The Uprising #1)
The Collapse (The Uprising #2)
My Summer Vacation by Terrance Wade
The End Diary

Free Short Stories with Young Adult Newsletter Sign Up
Zero
The Body in the Basement
Blame it on the Rain

www.ingramcontent.com/pod-product-compliance
Lightning Source LLC
Chambersburg PA
CBHW060215030726
47499CB00004B/1064